THE
BACKWARDS
KNIGHT

Matthew Siadak

SWORD & SPIRAL PRESS

Book Design and Illustrations by Laura Siadak (https://www.fallenlights.net)

First edition 2025

Hardcover ISBN: 978-1-964375-02-1

Paperback ISBN: 978-1-964375-03-8

Ebook ISBN: 978-1-964375-04-5

Author's Website: backwardsknight.com

To my wife, who is the other side of my story.
To my goat, who will carry our tales ever onward.
To Erica, my sage in the darkness.
To you, who brings my dream to life.

Contents

Content Notice · VIII

Prologue · 1

1. Turn About · 6

2. To Camp · 15

3. Gaulf · 20

4. The Next Day · 26

5. Preparing For The Festival · 33

6. The Campfire · 41

7. The Festival · 46

8. What A Tale · 58

9. The Cell · 63

10. The Castle · 72

11. The Trial · 85

12. A Lull · 92

13. The Escape · 97

14. Burn It All · 104

15. Where To Go? · 107

16. Here Again   113

17. The Meeting   123

18. The Village   128

19. Back In Town   136

20. She Comes   142

21. That Night   154

22. Chaos Ensues   157

23. All Hell Breaks Loose   164

24. The Elf   170

25. After The Fight   175

26. The Quiet River   182

27. The River Rages   187

28. Waking   192

29. To The East   202

30. Falling   208

31. The Next Town   220

32. Into The Trees   225

33. The Mountain Falls   233

34. Camp   239

35. The Watch   251

36. A Familiar Face   254

37. The End   261

38. The Ruins   267

39. The Hunt Is On277

40. The Old One286

About the Author297

Acknowledgements298

Also By300

CONTENT NOTICE

Alcohol use
Swearing
Death
Blood and gore
Body horror
Violence
Maiming

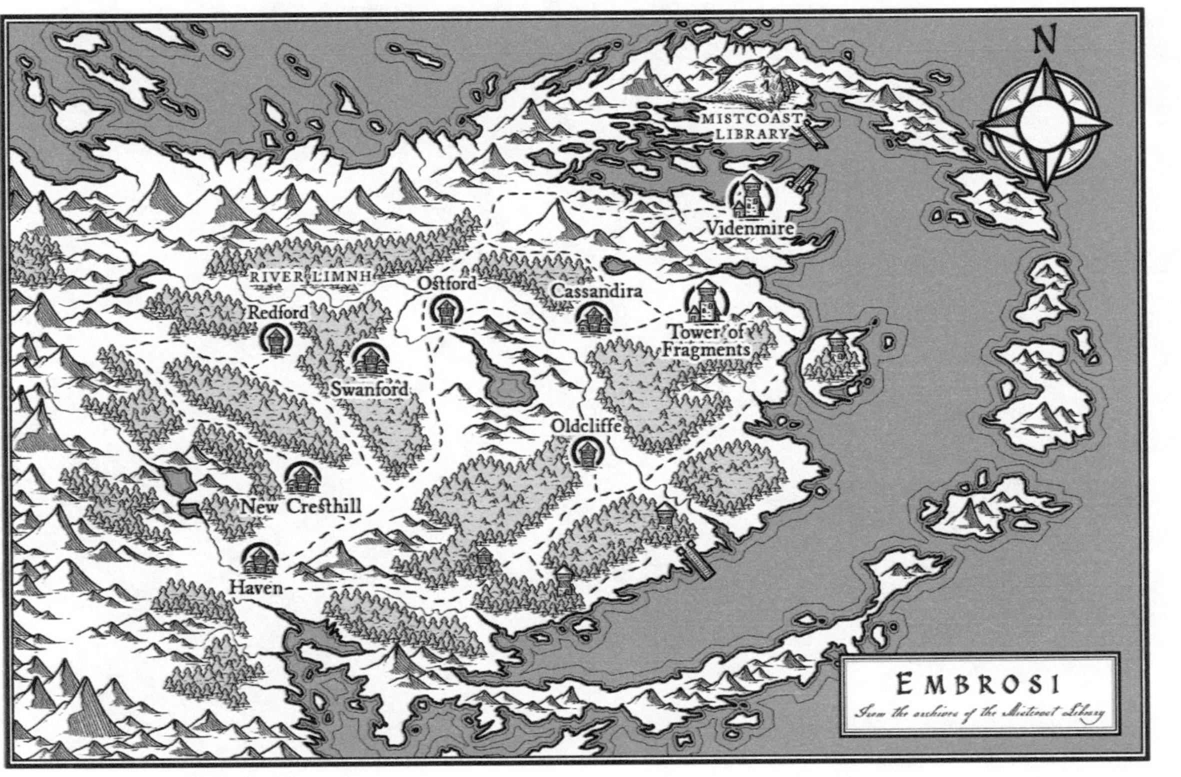

N
MISTCOAST LIBRARY
Videnmire
RIVER LIMNH
Ostford
Cassandira
Tower of Fragments
Redford
Swanford
Oldcliffe
New Cresthill
Haven
EMBROSI
From the archives of the Mistcoast Library

PROLOGUE

S ER GREGORIS PACED IN front of the dais in the throne room. The tapestries hanging on the wall were a mockery of everything for which he had struggled. Turning on his heel, he forced the images woven into them to the back of his mind. His footsteps echoed in the cavernous room, the churning in his stomach intensifying with each footfall.

Confronting the Queen of Embrosi would terrify any who dared demand an audience at this hour. But he would not be so easily deterred. Despite Thaddeus' earlier warnings. If the queen detected a whiff of hesitation, he would surely fail in his purpose. After all, he could not wield magic.

Ser Gregoris paused briefly to spit at the empty room, then resumed his pacing. As he came about, his gaze fell upon the ornate throne perched atop the dais. It was a menacing thing, looming as a predator over its prey. Branches without roots consumed the stone chair so that it seemed as if the two were one. Ser Gregoris strode to the perimeter, hoping that distance would settle his stomach.

This only brought him closer to the tapestries. Each one bore a marking, and each one had haunted his every waking moment for many years. Even now Ser Gregoris' mind recoiled from the thought of magic and its symbols, though he wanted little more than to control it. His mind traced the poem Thaddeus once taught him, a beginner's rote to understand the nature of magic.

The Spiral of Magic itself, marking one's flesh to bind.
The Hand, to Grasp and to Hold, to shape and mold.
The Door to Open the way from where dreams are made.
The Wheel to Move that which stands in the way.

The Quill to Mark upon the fabric of reality.
The Scythe to Harvest your intentions.
The Lightning Bolt to Rend the darkness and Light the unknown.
And The Sword to Banish it all and cut to the bone.

The words were simple enough. Understanding their meaning and casting, less so. Watching others unlock the secrets to wondrous feats, working spells with such ease that it seemed unpracticed had only served to enrage him. Why did magic elude him so?

Unable to stop his mind as it raced, Ser Gregoris remembered the sensation of magic brushing over his flesh like a lover's touch when he witnessed someone call upon the symbols, bending magic to their will. It was not unlike standing exposed in the midst of a raging storm, wholly addictive and exhilarating. How he wished he could move a mountain with Spiral and Wheel, or even pick up a pebble with The Hand, or find his way in the dark with Lightning Bolt. Any hope he had to put his mark on the world itself with The Quill, to see *beyond* and through The Door, was denied him in every attempt.

Now, magic was anathema. Filth invading the world. Something not meant for the hands of mere mortals. He sniffed at the symbols, and a musical laugh erupted behind him.

Ser Gregoris shuddered as Queen Alizandra murmured something nondescript. But he knew the shapes forming on her tongue: The Spiral, Lightning Bolt, Quill. Magic soon flooded the room, winding around him with an odd warmth and *wrongness*. Goosebumps swept across his skin as the torches on either side of the throne flared to life, casting him in shadow.

When he turned, he was met with the sight of her wild brown-and-bronze hair and the fluidity of her gait as she moved to the platform to sit upon her throne. She was silent as she placed a crown built from brambles and branches on her head, regarding him with that penetrating golden gaze while a smirk played on her lips.

"Long have you lived, and may you live longer yet." Ser Gregoris dropped to one knee, lowering his head, offering the elven queen the same greeting Thaddeus often used.

"May your Tree grow eternal," came Queen Alizandra's flat reply. Ser Gregoris felt like little more than a candle before the sun, the first destined to burn out long before the latter. He worked his jaw, rankled as ever by her indifference. The noise, probably louder than his whining armor, echoed as he placed a gauntleted hand over his heart. When he stood, his hand drifted instinctually to the hilt of his sword.

"Have you decided to listen to reason?" Ser Gregoris asked. That Queen Alizandra had permitted him an audience bolstered what remaining hope he had that he would not wage this war alone, but it was difficult to hide his disapproval of the golden-eyed monarch.

"I've come to tell you for the last time to cease this tirade, Nichor. Go home to Arxila. End this folly and accept there is nothing wrong with magic. Rather, you—" she started, but a growl from Ser Gregoris made her pause.

Ser Gregoris drew himself up to his full height as he spoke. "I know you do not believe the truth I lay at your feet, that there is hardly friendship between us enough to foster the sort of trust required of my request. Nevertheless, it is too late to stop what I have begun, and if you stand in my way, well, the war will bleed your lands. Embrosi will know my might, and the passion of those who follow me. Allow me passage once more, join me in my hunt of the rogue mage. Or fight me."

"Do you speak for all of Arxila in this matter?" Queen Alizandra sneered and shook her head.

"I need not. I am a man going to war, and I do not stand alone. I ask once more that you join me in pursuing this foul mage." Ser Gregoris' words slipped through clenched teeth, every passing moment tugging at what remained of his composure.

"Will you not even speak his name?" Queen Alizandra asked, her question charging the air between them.

"I ask that you join me in hunting Thaddeus Maji." His own voice sounded distant to his ears. Cold.

"Thaddeus." She tapped her fingers against the bramble-and-vine arm of her throne. "The one you called brother not so very long ago? You two were inseparable when you first came to my lands. How often have you followed him on his journeys?" While her line of questioning continued, the queen seemed to expect no answer, and Ser Gregoris surmised her aim was merely to goad him. "And what has driven this chasm between the two of you? What drives you against your own brother by bond? Against magic?"

Ser Gregoris opened his mouth, then closed it, thinking before giving his answer. "Magic is not for mortal knowledge or convenience. I can *feel* something twisted lurking, waiting inside of it. Tampering with these forces is an offense to the natural order." With that, Queen Alizandra straightened in her throne, a knowing gleam in her eyes.

"And with what authority do you declare this?" Queen Alizandra asked.

"I am but a man who sees the threat magic poses. Who seeks to end it before it can fester. I felt it," Ser Gregoris said, struggling to forget how often Thaddeus bade him to stop entertaining such nonsense. That it was his envy which drove his fear of magic, nothing more. But Ser Gregoris was right. He knew it. And now he had to stop it.

"How very perceptive of you. There *is* more to magic, yes. Even if you are mostly wrong, part of what you say rings true." Queen Alizandra hummed in thought, her gaze fixing Ser Gregoris where he stood. It was the only hint of emotion amidst the stone of her expression. The sheer weight of her judgment pressed against Ser Gregoris, but he refused to break beneath the weight of it. Not again, not anymore.

"I ask that we ally ourselves to strike down not only those who would use magic, but I would have you and your people denounce it. Add your strength to mine own and help me drive magic from your lands. The kingdom of Arxila will have no choice but to follow where Embrosi and her queen lead." Everything came down to this moment with the queen, and he worried he had already failed.

But the small, almost imperceptible, nod of her head said otherwise. "I can help you, knight. But know that there will be a price." A grin crawled across Queen Alizandra's face, a vision he would not quickly forget. "You must be willing to sacrifice that which you hold most dear. Can you do that, Ser Gregoris? Can you be the martyr for your own cause?"

Ser Gregoris nodded, holding his fist over his heart once more, the clank of armor echoing in the room. "Whatever the cost must be to banish magic from this world, so be it."

"The price to pay will be written in the magic itself. My aid extends only so far as sharing this knowledge."

"The question that remains is whether you will uphold your own end of the bargain." Ser Gregoris did shift then, unable to help himself.

As much as he had hoped for this moment, he never dreamed that he might have it within his grasp. "Can you forswear magic yourself, and take it from your people?"

"A petty price to pay when one considers the greater picture, yes?" the queen remarked, that glint sharpening in her golden eyes.

"Then let us destroy Thaddeus and the magic he holds dear. Let us give this world a fresh start, free of filth and perversion." Ser Gregoris hesitated, then asked, "I must know what has changed your mind? You and your people have clung to magic since time's dawning."

Queen Alizandra's fingers slid along the length of the throne's thick arms. "I have my own reasons. Doing away with magic will put right so many wrongs. Is that not aligned with your cause, Nichor, even if it means we must use magic in the ending of it?"

"Do not call me that," he snapped. "If I must succumb to magic to achieve my purpose, to save the world from itself, then I shall."

"What would you have me call you instead?" Queen Alizandra's tone raised in pitch, not unlike the way a mother reprimands her child. Ser Gregoris swallowed his rising temper.

"You and Thaddeus Maji gave me a title some time hence, and that, henceforth, is how I shall be known. I am The Paladin, and I will see that these lands are protected. More than that, all of Osivesi will be safeguarded from the depravity and corruption of magic. Of those who have turned to worshiping it. I will eradicate magic and those who would wield it," Ser Gregoris said firmly.

"As you say then, *Paladin*. At all costs. A price you are willing to pay, sight unseen. If you falter, if you *doubt*, then all you do and fight for is for nothing. Say it, and say it now: on your sword, on The Sword, you will do what needs be done." Queen Alizandra rose from her throne and came to stand at the edge of the dais.

Ser Gregoris craned his neck to glance up at her. "I swear it on my sword, on my life. I will see this through."

"Good. Thaddeus Maji has already crossed these lands and is presently on the way to The Tower of Fragments for his yearly pilgrimage. And he is not alone. We have long nights and days ahead of us." That sinister grin never left her face. "Let the hunt begin."

Chapter 1

TURN ABOUT

ORN SPLASHED HIS FACE with murky water, the spiraling mark of magic flaring painfully on his arm. His bounty lurked nearby. Orn bit down on the inside of his cheek to squelch the sensation the mark incited. His efforts for nothing, and he spat the brackish water out of his mouth, glancing behind him to where his foot was caught in a rope. *His* rope. Knotted with his slip knot and reinforcing leather so that whoever it caught would be held tight. He knew it was his rope, as sure as he knew this wasn't where he had left it.

"What do you think you are doing, ser?" Though the words were quiet, they weren't timid. Spoken carefully, as to not draw attention. Orn glimpsed a mud-caked face with vivid blue eyes staring at him from the bushes.

"No sers here, friend." Orn grunted, working to free his foot from the snare. The muck coating the rope botched his attempts.

"No friends here. Ser." The bush rustled, and Orn paused, waiting for an attack from whomever lurked in the darkness.

"Not yet." When the noises faltered, Orn resumed picking at the knot and leather, loosening the length of it enough that he could wriggle his foot out. Once that was done, he scrubbed a hand over his face to scrape away what mud remained. Then, with a violent shake of his hand, he sent globs of mud flying in all directions.

"You aren't like them," the hidden man remarked.

Orn pondered that for a few moments as he studied the stubborn knot in front of him. "You are right. I guess we can agree for the present that I am no ser and we are not friends. One of those we can fix.

Maybe." Orn undid the knot fully, dropping to the ground gracelessly. *Shame. It was a good snare.*

"Friends don't chase friends through the woods." The man's statement stopped Orn short.

"I would have to agree that this is hardly the usual behavior between friends. For what it's worth, I'm sorry. If you hadn't run, I would not have given chase nor had reason to set up these traps. But I have not come to capture you for some dark purpose. I only want to talk, I swear." Orn raised a hand in what he hoped to be a placating gesture.

"If you hadn't clanked around like *they* do, I wouldn't have run." There was a certain level of cheekiness in his tone, and Orn could not help but smile. The longer he kept the figure in the bushes talking, the warmer their attitude. That was a good sign. Or so he hoped.

"You have a point, but no, I'm not going to *clank* after you. I'm only here to ask a few questions of you, that's all. If it helps, I have some bread to share."

No answer. Orn sighed. He was nearly ready to surrender in his efforts until the autumnal bushes parted and a figure emerged. A few branches clung to the stranger's clothes, and Orn bit back a chuckle at the man's flailing endeavor to dislodge himself. He thought to lend a hand but dared not. It risked sending the stranger into a panic. The last thing Orn needed. Instead, he busied himself with searching through his pack to retrieve the last heel of bread and some cheese.

"Here," Orn said, extending the paltry offering. As he neared, Orn could make out what appeared to be a young man barely out of childhood wearing a ratty cloak, the hood framing his face. Whatever his age, the startling blue eyes he boasted spoke volumes of what he had endured. They darted every which way, as if expecting danger in every shadow.

"Thank you." Orn could practically hear the stranger's stomach growl. With surprising quickness, the young man strode forward, yanking the bread and cheese out of Orn's grip, scurrying backward before he could react. Orn grumbled inwardly, then rummaged through his pack in pursuit of any scraps he might find. A strip of dried meat that had surely seen better days was the only thing left. It would have to do. He chewed on a piece thoughtfully while he waited.

Patience was key. That Orn knew, and this hunt already surpassed his wildest expectations. Orn stood and the young man shuddered. "Peace. I'm going to collect my rope, since neither of us need it. Okay?" When the younger man nodded, Orn returned to the tree, albeit with slow, exaggerated movements. This was decidedly *not* where he had left this trap, but neither could he fault the placement. Hidden near a large tree, and with the snare in a puddle? He would have to remember that one. "Clever kid," Orn muttered. He made quick work of unlooping the rope from the branches above then shook it dry before tying it into a tight bundle. "You led me on a merry chase. Right into my own trap, which you moved. I'm impressed."

The stranger said nothing but continued eating.

"Do you have a name?" Orn asked. When no answer came, he added, "My name is Orn Corraidhin." His gaze roamed the forest surrounding them. "I suggest we get ourselves as far away from the road as we are able, in case anyone else decides to come along. How does that sound?" That merely earned him a wary nod.

"I didn't mean to get so near the road. I keep getting turned around," the young man said, his cloak rustling as he shifted in the dirt. For a moment, Orn could not help but feel it too, something skulking around in the woods. Orn drew in a deep breath, steadying himself while his nails dug into the meat of his palm.

"We'll need to recover my horse from where I left her. Then we can continue to my camp. If you're not keen on walking, I am sure I can convince Delilah to let you rest in her saddle. I have a bit more food there, and some water."

"I-I don't think so." The young man withdrew to the bushes.

"I know you have no reason to trust me but please hear me. You are out here alone, and I only want to help. If anyone else is chasing you, I'll deal with them. On my honor." Orn leaned forward, his hand outstretched.

The young man remained quiet, narrowing his eyes at Orn.

"Come on out of the bush and let us get moving. Sooner we reach camp, sooner we can eat. How's that sound?"

"That sounds good," the stranger replied shakily, his lips struggling to form a smile.

Orn returned the gesture, placing his trust in the effect of his actions. He had shared his bread and cheese and the promise of more, so perhaps he would not find a blade planted in his back at some point in the night.

The two of them headed along the road, and Orn kept watch for danger as they went. "Do you know why they are chasing you?" Orn pressed gently. He had an inkling as to why already, what with the writ burning a hole in the pocket of his trousers, but the reward wasn't his primary objective. "You can talk to me. I am not going to pass undue judgment on you, whatever you may have done. I want to help."

Silence.

This far into the forest the road was little more than ruts in the mud, the greenery creeping alongside in a bid to reclaim the paths. He cursed himself for having tied his horse up when he found the trail, but that would have made traipsing about damn near impossible. And had Delilah hit the snare things might have played out in an entirely different manner.

Orn fidgeted in the dark, futilely picking clods of dried mud from his beard. The young man by his side did the same, plucking at leaves tangled in his sandy hair. Orn wanted nothing more than a drink of water, or better yet, some bitter beer. Anything to wash the taste of dirt out of his mouth. He glanced behind him and saw the young man following, maintaining his distance just outside of the tree line. Orn could hardly blame him for that.

Daylight had long bled into night, but it was far from quiet. A nightingale's song echoed through the trees in chorus with the crickets. It was peaceful, a rare thing of late. And that peace was broken when came a familiar noise Orn could not mistake. The young man froze behind him. The clanking repeated in the distance, this time much closer.

"Listen—" Orn started, the stranger flinching when the sound did not cease.

"They said they would hang me," the young man stammered while Orn centered himself in front of him and took hold of his shoulder.

"No one will hang you, understand? Not while I'm here." Orn took a deep breath, inviting the boy to do the same.

"You don't have a sword."

"I had hoped I wouldn't need one today," Orn countered, stepping off of the road and gesturing for the boy to follow him. "How many were they, the men who are after you?"

"Two, I reckon, se—Orn." The stranger finally using his name was promising. "They're after me for what they think I did. Which, I did, but not like they think."

"What did you do?" Orn asked, though he knew the answer.

"I hurt someone." Shying away, the youth raised a hand to his own arm. Under Orn's scrutiny, the boy began babbling. "Magic. They came for me, for my magic." At that, something twisted inside of Orn.

"I figured as much. We'll need to talk about all that, and soon. I am here to help you. I want to hear your story. Unfortunately, that will have to wait. Give me your cloak." Another series of clanks put a little fire into the young man. He tugged the old cloak off and gave it to Orn. "Go hide in the forest. Don't come out until I whistle. Or scream. If it's the latter, run and do not stop."

In short order, Orn was left alone on the road holding onto the threadbare scrap of fabric that stank of a firepit. Several yards away, two men in heavy armor emerged from the brush, poking at the overgrowth with their swords.

"Ho there, friends. Looking for someone?" Orn called, making sure he was loud enough to catch their attention. Though he could not see their faces, he felt their eyes on him. The two armored knights stalked toward him. Orn's fingers twitched at his side.

"Where did he get off to?" the taller of the two knights barked as he pointed the tip of his sword at the cloak in Orn's hands. The other knight tittered nervously inside his helmet, his own sword limp in a loose grip.

"Sorry, sers, but who might you mean?" Orn waved the cloak playfully.

"Do not think to play games with us," the tall knight warned.

Orn answered haughtily, "I wouldn't dream of it. I hardly know you, nor what sort of frivolities that you might find fun. We'd spend half the night figuring out what rules we want to go by, who gets to go first, whether we're going to bet with real money, if I'm going to have to stab you for being a dirty cheat, whether your friend here—"

"Where's the mage, ser?" the tall knight asked through clenched teeth, stepping forward menacingly.

"I don't know, sers. I found this cloak in the road, on my honor," Orn replied, suppressing the edge to his tone. This was not the time to enrage a couple of trained knights.

"He's wanted for crimes against The Paladin," the shorter knight said, and Orn could almost sense the wicked grin masked by his helm. "He's a mage. A murderer."

"Must be a handsome reward for his capture then." Orn produced the writ from his pocket, much to the chagrin of the knights.

The tall knight grumbled and turned to his companion, the two whispering to each other and casting glances at Orn every few seconds. Perhaps they would not consider him worth the hassle, but Orn doubted that. They were hunting the same quarry, and knights were famously unwilling to miss a chance to hang a suspected mage. It mattered not. Whatever they meant to do, Orn had a plan. He only prayed the cloak was studier than it looked.

Orn rushed the tall knight on the left, seeking to loosen the grip on his blade. He tossed the cloak over the knight's head and wrapped it behind his neck, knotting it hastily.

"What the—" the knight shouted, flailing as he dropped his weapon to claw at the cloak covering his face.

The second knight's reflexes proved better than those of his companion. He brought his sword to bear, taking a swipe at Orn, who dodged it, shoving a heavy boot into the knight's plate. He was sent sprawling backward, and struggled to rise to his feet. Orn surmised that the knight was new to his position, unused to armored combat. An advantage he would exploit.

"Try rolling over. I hear that might help." Orn otherwise ignored the prone knight's shouts for help, instead striding over to him to relieve him of his blade. A sharp cry pierced the night air when he pinned the knight's wrist under his boot and pried the sword from his trembling grasp. It was unlikely he fractured a bone, but the knight wouldn't have use of that hand for what remained of this encounter, and that was good enough for Orn.

"I will run you through, you bastard!" The tall knight charged, having freed himself from the cloak. Orn barely had time to bring the pilfered sword to bear to deflect the powerful blow of his opponent's weapon. In short order, steel met steel, the force of it driving Orn backward.

"A bastard I may be, but at least I'm not slow on my feet," Orn mocked as the tall knight forced him into a retreat blow by blow toward his wailing companion in the dirt. "And you don't hear me disparaging your parents here, do you? Your mother's damn near a treasure, spreading herself for so much cheer."

"Why won't you fight back?" the tall knight barked, his movements becoming more chaotic as his fury grew.

"I'd really rather not," Orn answered, blocking each blow as they became frenzied. Once his heel tapped against the leg of the knight still squirming on the ground, Orn turned and leaped, then the tall knight tumbled over his companion after overextending his reach. "You see, I've been paying attention."

Before the tall knight could shove himself off the ground, Orn dug his fingers into the eye-slits of the helmet and yanked, eliciting a surprised shriek.

"Sorry, sers. Today's just not your day." Orn thought to enjoy the scene, but he couldn't risk the escape his ruse had afforded him. The tall knight tried to reply, but his words were lost in a gurgle when Orn forced the blade through his neck. Blood spilled from his mouth and filled his helmet, pouring from the dented holes.

Orn rolled the tall knight off his companion, who labored with renewed fervor. He managed to get to his knees, but he would never stand again. Orn pushed the sword through the knight's armpit until the point of the blade encountered the metal of breastplate. Swaying, the knight glanced at Orn, an indecipherable expression on his face, then collapsed to the dirt and moved no more.

Expelling a breath he had not realized he'd been holding as he studied the two bodies, he wiped at the blood on his armor and his face, which served only to mix with the lingering mud. Were he to be spotted in this state, he'd be questioned, and he was not so skilled at crafting excuses on the spot.

When his breath caught up to him, and he was certain that neither of the knights yet lived, he drew the sword out of the knight's armpit, wincing as it stuck. *Probably caught on a rib.* Gathering his strength, he jerked as hard as he was able, and the blade slid free with a terrible *spluck*. Even coated in the knight's viscera, it was plain how very poorly maintained the weapon was, and Orn sighed at his misfortune. He drove its point into the ground and patted the knight down, searching for anything of value. There was little to find other than a mostly empty coin purse.

The armor was no different, worse than his own, though there was something worth salvaging. He stripped off his gloves then tossed them on the first corpse, taking the fine leather pair for himself. They were a bit snug, so he hooked them to his belt. Orn checked the boots too, but those were too small by far. With great effort, he dragged the body into the bushes before returning to the tall knight. He checked the gloves.

"These'll do just fine, ser. Thank you." Orn grinned, slipping his hands into the new gloves. He could hardly help but sigh with contentment at the feel of the supple leather. Granted they were a little sweatier than he cared for, but he could get past that. Orn compared the size of the knight's feet with his own, hoping that they would match. He was stalled in his task when he heard a rustling in the bushes lining the road.

"If that's you, kid, just come on out. There're some boots and gloves available, if you need 'em. Too small for me." Orn held out the gloves to the young man as he clambered out of the bush.

"My cloak?" the youth asked after accepting the gloves. His gaze followed Orn's gesture to where the cloak had been thrown and he quickly retrieved it.

"There's the boots." Orn pointed, working his new ones free of the corpse. With that done, he slid them on his feet and wiggled his toes for good measure, smiling as he did so. "At least we won't leave empty-handed." He flexed his hands in the gloves then nudged the body with his boot. "Still work to do, though."

"What do you mean?" The young man approached, and the sudden nearness made Orn's heart leap straight into his throat.

"We're not going to leave them out here on the road where anyone can stumble across their bodies. We'll find somewhere to stash these two, then we need to put distance between us and this place. For as long as the two of us are together, our problems are one and the same."

The young man didn't seem convinced, already hiding in his cloak's hood, his blue eyes staring at him from the shadows.

Orn wanted to ask the questions burning a hole in his stomach, but with how very skittish this new friend was, he swallowed them. *Not yet.* "Do you fancy swinging a sword about?"

He held the blades in front of him for the boy to see. They were quite similar in design, and Orn worried keeping them would arouse suspicion, but the stranger needed a weapon. And it might just be the tactic to get the kid to trust him.

"No? Fair enough." Orn slid the swords back into their scabbards on the corpses before he turned to look at the young man, who had not made to help him. It wasn't surprising, in light of his recent experiences. "Give me a few minutes to take care of these two, and then we can be on our way." He hooked fingers into the neck of the tall knight's breastplate and pulled the corpse with him into the underbrush. Before he could argue, the young man was there beside him, helping to drag the body into the tree line and deeper yet.

When they were far enough into the woods that the ground started to slope downward, Orn turned them about so they could grasp hands and feet alike. With a few hearty swings, they heaved the body down the hill. Shortly after, the other knight followed his companion into the dark ditch.

"Should we say a word?" Orn asked. The look on the kid's face was answer enough. "Let's go collect my horse. Once we get settled, we can talk about this magic business."

Chapter 2

TO CAMP

T HEIR PATH DOWN THE road found them in relative silence, apart from the plodding hoofbeats of Orn's horse.

"Go ahead and have a seat. That stump is comfortable enough," Orn said to the stranger when they arrived at camp. The young man took Orn's advice, studying the little home Orn had made for himself amidst a small copse of trees that provided a decent shelter from the outside world. Orn set about brushing and feeding his horse, clucking at her soothingly. "Did you miss me, Delilah?" Every so often, the horse seemed to glance at the newcomer, who relaxed in the quiet. "Don't mind our new companion. We'll soon be friends." Delilah said nothing in reply, and when he was finished, he strode over to the young man. "Ready to share that name of yours, son?" For a moment, he was certain the stranger would refuse again. After being chased through the forest by no less than three men in armor, Orn figured he, too, would have kept his mouth shut.

Well, he might have. *Maybe.*

If he knew how.

He found himself smirking at that thought, of how many times he had talked himself into trouble. This time, though, he had done it with purpose. "Maybe later—"

"Gaulf." A simple answer, and in that single word Orn could tell that the peace between them was indeed tenuous.

"Nice to meet you, Gaulf." Orn itched to extend his hand. That would hardly do here. Instead, in the anxious need to fidget, he scratched at his left arm absentmindedly, drawing his hand away sharply as if he had touched something hot. "Like I said, I'm just looking for some answers—" He cut himself off before he said that word again. *Friend.* "And the way I see it, you might be able to help me."

"What? How could I even begin to help you?" Gaulf laughed, an incredulous expression plastered on his face.

"First, I'd like to hear your story," Orn said flatly.

"But, why?"

"Well, truth be told, I need your help. And you clearly need mine. See, there's a price on your head, but I think you already know that."

"Can I really trust you?" Gaulf asked, a noticeable tremor in his voice.

"Risking my neck for you like I did back there wasn't sufficient?" Orn shook his head, a smile playing at his lips. "For what it's worth, I think you can. Not saying you should, but if I wanted you dead, if I wanted the coin, we wouldn't be talking." Gaulf hugged himself on the stump, but he was listening. Orn took it as a sign to continue. "When did the dreams start?" A gamble, one he hoped would yield results.

Orn could hardly count how many times he'd had this conversation. Of trying and failing repeatedly to get at the heart of what was causing this explosion of magic in Embrosi. Why it was marking people seemingly at random.

"How did you know about them?" Gaulf asked, a threat building behind the question.

"You aren't the first I've come across, but the first this far north. I tend to stray far from Haven, but the number of marked people is increasing."

"Haven? Where The Paladin rules?" Gaulf's face twisted in disapproval.

"One and the same. Outlawed magic, put a price on the heads of those who end up marked." Orn started to scratch at his arm again, but stopped himself, letting it drop to his side, which caused a slight *clank* that made the young man tense briefly.

Gaulf paused as if to consider something, then asked, "Where are they? The others? Are you marked too?"

Orn met Gaulf's gaze. "They've been dealt with. Either by The Paladin and his knights, or me. The ones I usually run across are much further—" Orn snapped his mouth shut and grimaced.

"They're what?" Gaulf brimmed with a dark curiosity and leaned on his stump toward Orn.

"Too far gone. Listening to whatever they hear, falling headfirst into the dreams. There's little left but a gibbering mess." Gaulf's face appeared to age by years in that instant, conflicting emotions shaping his features.

"What did you—"

Orn held up a hand. "We can discuss the others later. Right now, my main concern lies with you."

"But what does any of it mean? Why the mark? Why me?" Gaulf asked, suddenly frantic.

"That's what I'm trying to—" Orn noticed Gaulf had become rigid as stone, and he worried he was losing the boy. "Rest assured that I am here to help, in whatever manner I can." Was he losing his chance? Had he pushed too hard? What Gaulf had endured would make any man fearful, never mind his fate if he were caught by The Paladin's knights.

Instead, Gaulf sighed. Not that he was calm, but he looked decidedly less ready to bolt. The young man rose from the stump and kneeled in front of the firepit, arranging fallen sticks and small branches to light.

Orn distracted himself by upending his waterskin over his face, washing away the stubborn mud and blood. He swished the water around over his tongue then spat. "There's more," Orn said as he motioned. Before Orn could offer him a dagger and some flint, Gaulf had his hands cradled outward. "What do you think you're doing?" Orn said with a growl.

But it was too late.

Orn hissed at the snap of energy in the air, at something slamming home in the depths of his stomach. He felt an ache spurred by the sight before him, terrified by something strange awakening inside of his body. Again. Sweat and grime mired the young man's brow, his blue eyes catching the light when fire pooled in the palms of his hands then spread outward to coax embers to life. The smell of smoke quickly filled the campsite. Orn choked back a cry, turning his head away from the fire and how it drew him in.

Orn's breath caught in his chest as he tried to swallow the lump of bile that rose in his throat when he felt the mark on his arm twitch, his hands throbbing with the need to *try*. Attempts to suppress the urge—clenching his jaw, biting his tongue—failed, so Orn counted to five. Five breaths in and released in turn.

"Don't do that," Orn said, a bit harsher than he intended.

"Magic? Do you hate it too?" Gaulf shied away.

"No. They claim magic users are foul and twisted, a danger to the world. Causing sickness in crops and livestock, turning people into abominations, bringing shadows to life." He shook his head, warmth roiling through him. "But what I see is innocents being marked, then the madness taking hold."

"Are *you* marked?" Gaulf asked, his eyes searching. He was still kneeling in front of the fire. For a moment, Orn saw himself in Gaulf, or the self that might have been. Destined for a life of farming, dancing at the autumnal festivals, growing old with someone. Until being marked took that all away. When Orn did not answer, Gaulf pressed, "Did you feel that? The words, do you hear them? Do you see *her* too?"

"Let's not get too far ahead of ourselves." Orn drew a shuddering breath, forcing himself to calm as he strode toward Gaulf. As if he were not ready to retch right then and there with the way his body buzzed like a hive of bees. Angry bees. On fire. He sat on the abandoned stump.

"What questions did you have?" Gaulf looked at him with an intensity that stripped him bare.

"I want to know about the mark. I want to know where it came from, what you have seen, done, all of it. More than that, I want to know why. Why you, why this is happening. And that's what I mean to find out."

Gaulf shook his head. "I'm at a loss to explain what's happening to me. The dreams. The voices. The fire."

Orn hummed thoughtfully, chewing on Gaulf's words.

"Sheriff Caspar tried to help, but then he turned on me like the others. The Paladin outlawed all magic... I-I didn't ask for this."

"I believe you. It's been the common thread. Something did this to you, and I aim to find out what. Before it happens again." Orn offered a gentle smile. "The Paladin has spread fear of magic, and that has made it a difficult task to figure out the cause. Anyone marked is either on the run, whether from The Paladin or their friends and family or the dreams have overtaken them," Orn said. "Not all of them have been as talkative as you, and it's something I mean to take advantage of."

"How many have there been?"

Orn scrubbed a hand over his face, feeling the conversation slip out of his grasp.

"Do you hang them?" Gaulf persisted.

"No. Wouldn't wish a death like that on anyone." Orn shook his head. He looked away, toward his horse, where his sword was still wrapped up in his bedroll. Probably for the best, but he itched to feel the hilt in his fingers.

"That's good." A pause, before Gaulf continued, wringing his hands. "I didn't want to hang." Orn could see the words written on his face, the ones that wanted to spill forth. Something kept them burbling just beneath the surface.

"It's time to tell me your story, Gaulf."

Chapter 3

GAULF

GAULF PERCHED PRECARIOUSLY AT the verge of a strange stream. It hadn't been here yesterday, winding beneath the sun shining high above now that the storms passed. Rain and thunder enough to shake the earth itself. The young farmhand's mind wandered, but whatever he had been dreaming of quickly faded as the water rippled, drawing his attention. The water's motion, the shimmering light that danced upon the mirrored surface, beckoned him toward the edge. Something moved out there and he found he could hardly tear his gaze away. Cold mud squelched beneath his foot as he dared take another step.

Gaulf's breaths burned in his chest as he tried to hold himself still, but the frenetic run he and his friends had taken through the forest left him struggling for air. He tried to ration his breathing so as to not startle the trickle of light that flitted about the water.

He heard shouts from his friends in the distance.

"Gaulf! By The Scythe, where are you? It's almost time to go. The *elves* will get you!" Gunter shouted, his voice colored by laughter. Calls of Gaulf's name followed from each of his friends: Jannie, Chindler, and Adit.

Not quite adults but well past childhood, they were shooed out from underfoot as everyone prepared for the festival, which meant escaping the confines of Redford to the woods beyond so that they might explore to their hearts' content before night fell. At that time of the year, darkness descended early. Not that they paid any mind to the concerns the coming season brought with it. How could they, with the excitement of the harvest festival outshining the looming change of seasons?

"Gaulf! Where are you?" His head turned at the sound of his name, but the light flickered out of the corner of his eye. The very air brimmed with their contagious excitement, and Gaulf opened his mouth to answer his friends. Before he could, though, the light danced further away from him. Gaulf stared at it, moving unlike anything he had ever seen. The longer he gazed upon the light the further and further the calls of his friends seemed.

"No, please don't go!" Gaulf shouted and gave chase. He felt a burbling giggle escape him, and his quarry seemed to share his elation. At first, he thought it was a firefly, but that was quickly discarded in light of the way it moved. His mind reeled.

Maybe it was some sort of ancient treasure that he could give to Jannie at the festival dance beneath the full light of the moon. And so, he moved further into the water, the ground suddenly slippery beneath his feet. Whatever he chased wanted to play with him in return, leading him further along the stream. It turned sharply away from the farmland and raced toward the trees. With the sun so high overhead, Gaulf saw the blossoming shadows created by the trees but barely even paused in his mad dash. One moment he pushed through warm water without resistance, and the next the water grew cold and pushed back against him.

The light danced further ahead, pausing when he did, remaining just out of reach. No matter how Gaulf tried, he could not close the distance between him and the shining orb. He realized he was running ragged in water that was rapidly rising. And, in following the stream, he was that much deeper into the heart of the forest.

Where the sunlight had been bountiful, what managed to filter through now was strangled before it could reach the ground below. Gaulf stopped as the stream emptied into a small lake lurking underneath the trees, where the sun was barely more than a memory. His teeth chattered, and yet he could not turn back. Not when he was this close.

"Gaulf! Gaulf, where are you?" He heard his friends shout.

There was no creek, no stream, no flowing water that carried him here. There were just the trees, which had closed in as if to swallow him whole. The sound of the leaves rustling seemed to tickle the back of his mind. Gaulf strained to hear, and just as the woods came into focus, he realized the breeze carried the glimmer along with it.

Gaulf took a step forward, and then another. The water rose to meet his torso. He cried with glee, leaning over with an outstretched hand. The water churned, suddenly warm and inviting again, despite shadows curling around the strange space. Here, autumn had come and gone already.

The forest around him burst to life. One of the larger trees creaked loud enough he thought it an animal's angry snarl. The light danced toward the middle of the lake. "Oh, no you don't," Gaulf muttered under his breath, forcing away any distracting thoughts of the harvest, quickly replacing them with a burning curiosity for this darting, daring light. Step after step, he moved forward until he felt the ground slope dangerously.

Even so, he could not stop.

One foot forward onto nothing, but Gaulf kept pace, floundering when the water came rushing upward to wrap him in its cold embrace. He struggled, but there was little he could do in the surprise of the moment, and the water swallowed him, dragging him down into its depths. Fighting against it, his body shivered in anticipation of a cold shock that never came. As he ceased in his efforts to escape, he felt himself drifting along a soft current, and there in the dark waters, he saw that sparkle beckoning him onward.

Gaulf kicked his feet in the fight to orient himself. When that proved futile, he instead forced himself to swim after the glimmer. Any glimpse of the surface was gone. Nor was there a bottom, or if there were, it was shrouded in the same darkness that surrounded him at every turn. The lake was no longer as small as it had seemed. Panic struck Gaulf's heart, and he understood that he was indeed lost.

Further into the darkness he went, straining to hold onto what little breath remained. Gaulf's hand stretched ahead of him, searching the dark waters. No longer did that flicker of light dart away, but waited for him. In that moment, Gaulf seized the opportunity, grabbing the light and drawing it to him.

In one hand he felt the trickling tickle of whatever the light was flutter against his skin, but he dared not let go. His free hand retrieved the golden lock of hair wrapped in a deep blue ribbon from his shirt pocket. Here, in the dark, he was alone. His mind wandered to Jannie, to when she had gifted him the keepsake. How long had it been? Regret filled him, cursing himself for the words left unspoken between them. Even though she had shot him that knowing, radiant look that weakened his knees, he wished he had said something. Anything. He wanted to return to her, to tell her how much he loved her.

More than that, he wanted to breathe again. His lungs screamed for air he could not provide. His body spasmed, and he watched while air fled and burbled toward what he believed to be the surface.

The light called to him, a nearly imperceptible shockwave that echoed his name through the water. He squeezed the light as hard as the water around him pressed in from every side. Then something inside of him let go, and everything changed.

Whatever darkness Gaulf thought he had been in was but a fraction of the absolute lack of light he abruptly found himself in. The depths around him faded, and his mind scrambled for purchase, finding only what little light remained curled in his fist. Any warmth to the water was leached away, replaced with a sickly, stark chill that wormed through his very bones.

He wanted to scream, to howl against the cold's burning touch, but he could not. Gaulf swam in the direction he supposed to be the surface, but his stomach reeled and he was certain he was suspended upside-down. Turning about, he kicked in the opposite direction before shifting again. Wrong. He twisted, flailing in his search for the surface. Gaulf kicked for his life and held onto that light, to the promise of warmth in his fingers.

Before Gaulf knew it, heat trickled in, and he saw that his chest glowed with the light in his hand, held tightly against his heart. The sensation was a pain countering the ache of the chill, and the two battled for his life. Ripped apart by the burning sensation in his hand, smothered by the chill surrounding him, Gaulf kicked on. Tendrils of darkness threaded with a blue light slithered out of the depths, twirling around his legs. He saw himself reflected in the break of the surface. He reached for the other Gaulf while the other stretched toward him, but their fingers never met.

However, the tendril held him firmly. So close to the surface, Gaulf sobbed, releasing what little air lingered in his lungs. Then he was yanked down into the dark.

Gaulf welcomed the vision of Jannie dancing through his mind, as she would have undoubtedly done at the festival. In her finest dress, and with a crown of flowers in her hair, she called to him. Even in the water he could hear the music, could feel the thrum of his heart in his chest, could imagine what would come next as he took her hand. The dancing, the laughter, before they ducked away into the forest. He'd bring her here, to this lake, and show her the clearing he had found. The burning light in his hand.

Something flared in his palm, matched by the fire in his chest, and he kicked again. Whatever held him stretched, then snapped loud enough to vibrate the water. Gaulf kicked until he broke through the surface and found himself free.

Sucking in a lungful of air that burned for how fresh it was, Gaulf retched with a violent cough, a desperate need for *more*. He gasped, fighting to stay afloat, and kicked toward the edge of the lake. His muscles ached, but he clutched his prize tightly. The chill receded, the trees seemed to part to let in sunlight, and Gaulf crawled to a patch of muck.

"What are you?" he whispered after collapsing. He could only smile as he closed his eyes, drew in yet another breath of air, and clung to his prize. Safe from the water, Gaulf dared. He unfurled his fingers to get a good look at what lay in his palm. A small flicker of flame that swayed, the heat of it withering the grass he lay in, however there was not a mark on him. But his heart moved to its rhythm.

He leaned toward the little ball of flame. In answer, it grew brighter, and he shut his eyes against the lancing pain that seared afterimages into his mind. He saw Jannie once more, in her dress, moving to and fro. This time, shadows loomed in the corners of the image, as if she cast them out with her own light. The bonfires roared to life, as if he were the kindling.

Gaulf soon realized the light was gone, and that his hand was empty. For a moment he felt alone, adrift. His eyelids grew heavy, exhaustion threatening to pull him under. Before he gave in, the light flared to life.

Not in his hand, but somewhere *inside of* him, a burst of radiance in the clearing as he rolled over onto his back.

Chapter 4

THE NEXT DAY

"THERE YOU ARE." A sweet voice woke him, and he observed light filtering through the trees above, framing the prettiest face he had ever seen. Jannie's hair was practically aglow, and the smile that split his face appeared to be answer enough for her. She took his hand and dragged him to his feet.

Gaulf made to scrub at his eyes, before realizing the strange light was missing. Panicked, he searched the ground around him, his gaze combing the clearing then returning to his barren palm. What had he lost? The lake was restored to itself, the serene and murky depths undisturbed. Fragments of the previous night trickled in—chasing after a light, nearly drowning in darkness.

"You scared me, scared us all half to death." Her features were contorted by concern as she sought out any possible injury.

"I'm sorry, I—"

"Don't you dare ever do anything like that again, you hear? Running off and taking a nap in this place. Not alone, anyhow." Jannie glared at him, but it was not long before that severe expression cracked, an eager grin forming beneath.

"W-What?" Gaulf stammered, his head still muddied.

"Yes," she whispered, standing on her tiptoes, close enough to speak right into his ear. With her so near, and his mind fogged from sleep, Gaulf was not sure what she meant. His heart raced for an altogether different reason.

"What?" Gaulf blinked away the lingering clouds of slumber.

"I said *yes*," she replied, and led him out of the little clearing.

"I know, but what for? What was the question?" Gaulf scratched at the back of his head. With Jannie this close to him he could hardly speak or make sense of things. Had he been talking while dreaming? There was a flush to his face that he tried to ignore when he felt the warmth of her against him after she brushed his arm, but he failed in his efforts. Had she noticed?

"Because you waited too long to ask, so I figured it was time I just said it. Yes, I will go to the harvest dance with you," Jannie sang, and he was certain he had strayed into another dream.

Gaulf splintered, trying to remember more than meager bits and pieces of the day and night before while also feeling steeped in this exhilaration of Jannie having agreed to attend the harvest festival at his side. The two warred within him, but the former fizzled away when Jannie squeezed his hand. He could not stop smiling. Neither could she, it seemed, and happiness took root in him. Their stroll through the forest was quick, only stopping so that Jannie could plant a peck on his cheek.

But the hold of the strange light and the dark of the forest was stronger than he thought.

"Where is your mind disappearing to, Gaulf?" Jannie's voice plucked him from where his mind spiraled, from grasping at the burgeoning sensation inside of him. A heat suffused him, begging for release.

"I'm just trying to keep up with you." Gaulf offered Jannie a small smile when faced with her scrutiny. She could be as intimidating as his parents at times. Gaulf grappled for some explanation that would satisfy her, but how could he possibly describe the events of yesterday? He wasn't even sure himself what had happened.

"Jaaaaaaaannie!" Nearing the edge of the village, they heard Jannie's mother calling. She rolled her eyes playfully and leaned up to place another kiss on his cheek.

"Two more nights, Gaulf. The festival this year will be the best one ever," she said with a giggle, then sprinted toward the village. "Coming, Mother!" She paused for a moment to look over her shoulder at Gaulf. Her hair was caught in the wind, and the view brought an even bigger smile to his face.

Gaulf meandered through the fields and then the village proper without a care in the world, waving to people as he passed the town hall and the mayor's house. Some of the buildings sat empty, their wood rotted and thatching in disrepair. The people he had known his entire life scurried about, preparing for the festival. Those working their stalls waved back at him and called out their greetings.

"Your parents were looking for you, Gaulf! You best hurry home!" Del shouted from the stoop of his general store where he worked mending the sign. A storm had rolled through not a week ago, and it had taken a beating in the heavy winds. There had been no real major damage to the village, but little pieces here and there for the community to come together and bond over while fixing.

"Yes, sir!" Gaulf felt bad that he had been out all night with nary a warning to his parents, and he hurried home to their smaller farm on the other side of the village. Even so, he vibrated with elation at the thought of escorting Jannie to the festival, and he had not even had to ask! Beyond that, there remained the echo of what had happened, a pit of burning worry in the depths of his stomach that he kept shoving down anytime it tried to surface. *A flash of light, a tide of shadows.* No. One problem at a time.

The sight of the house he lived in with his parents and his sisters gave him pause. Gaulf examined the fields, sparser than they were the year before. The goats stared him down, as if he might be tricked into feeding them. He crept toward the house, hoping he could convince his parents that he had been asleep in his room. He knew which boards to avoid on the porch and in the house, but as soon as he opened the door it was already too late.

"There you are! Do you know how much your mother fretted through the night when you didn't come home?" his father barked, arms crossed over his chest. Gaulf shied away from the stern ice-blue eyes of the taller man.

"I'm sorry, Da, but I got—" Gaulf drove a hand through his sandy-brown hair, and his father matched the motion as both sighed almost in unison. He saw himself in his father, beyond the shared traits of their hair and eyes.

"All of your friends returned without you, Gaulf. They said they could not find where you had gone off to. We were going to organize a search this morning." The worry was clear in his father's tone, even if his da would not admit it. Angun tried to maintain a stoic, but loving, demeanor.

The people of Redford often offered their help with his family farm, for it had seen better days, but Angun would hardly accept it. Gaulf heard the whispers of the other adults when they thought his attention elsewhere: that the land had turned, that Angun tilled barren soil. It was left to his wife, Cortney, to accept on the family's behalf. He hated to think he added to their troubles.

"I'm sorry, Da. It will not happen again. I found a lovely spot in the woods. I took a nap and lost track of time." Gaulf shuffled his feet. He hated lying, but he didn't know how to put the truth into words that would make sense.

"Go apologize to your mother, boy. She spent half the night worrying."

"Yes, Da," Gaulf said, and headed straight for the kitchen where he found his mother. She was decorating some of her cakes—a favorite of the locals—for the festival. Her black hair was streaked not just with silver, but also flour. The kitchen was a scene of organized chaos, with his younger sisters helping to orchestrate things. His mother was ordering Ola and Elga about and when she spotted him, relief relaxed her features as her hazel eyes filled with tears. Without a word she came to him and started checking him over for various wounds that she had likely imagined. From behind her, his sisters peered at him with their own blue eyes, their black hair practically white with how much flour coated them.

"I'm fine, Ma," Gaulf finally said after a few minutes of letting her satisfy herself that he was indeed fine. Once the words were out of his mouth, she took the towel off of her shoulder and started hammering him with it. Flour sprayed into the air, and his sisters ended up joining in until he was coated in the fine white powder too.

"Don't you ever, *ever* do that again. You hear me, Gaulf?" his mother yelled before pulling him into a fierce hug. "Now, go get cleaned up and come straight back. I have a list of supplies that we're going to need to make the next batch of cakes." She shooed him out of the kitchen and returned to overseeing his younger sisters. Gaulf made his way through the house, collecting clean clothes as he went. Feeling worse than he had mere moments ago, he made quick work of cleaning himself up.

When he slipped into the kitchen again, his mother tossed him a pouch of coins and a list for the shop, ordering him out of the house after Gaulf tried to steal one of the cakes fresh from the oven. He stopped to check on his father, but Angun was nowhere to be found.

Without further delay, Gaulf headed back up the path toward the village proper, waving again to people as he went. Quickly his thoughts turned to Jannie and the coming festival, so he hardly noticed when a foot came out of nowhere, sending him sprawling into a puddle. The shock of the cold water was enough to end his reverie. Arthur and his band of cronies stood over him, braying like mules, and when he tried to find his feet again Arthur's larger friend Sige shoved him right back into the muck.

"Come on, you've had your fun," Gaulf said, wincing even as he tried to laugh it off.

"You are right, and if you do not wish us to have any more fun," Arthur said, seething when he leaned down into Gaulf's face, "you are going to stay away from Jannie."

"Too late, Arthur. She's already agreed to attend the festival with me, so you had best go ask your second choice. I hear you are more than passingly familiar with your father's favorite horse." Gaulf knew it wasn't wise to rile the mayor's son, but he lobbed the insult at Arthur anyway. The boy loved throwing his father's weight around. Gaulf also knew what would come next, and as Sige hauled him off his feet Gaulf found himself ready. There was a fire in him this day, and he could only think of Jannie. As Sige held him aloft, Gaulf used his feet to push off the bully, catching Sige by surprise, who stumbled backward over his own large feet. Somewhere in their tumble together, the larger boy ended up beneath Gaulf.

Gaulf threw punches he knew he would have suffered on any other day. A beating he had fallen prey to more times than he could count. Hitting Sige was not unlike punching a rock, and the shock on the larger boy's face was worth it. Arthur squealed in outrage and shouted incomprehensibly. It took a few moments, but eventually the other boys sprang into action, yanking Gaulf off Sige. They landed blows of their own before they tossed him aside and scampered away, likely to tell Arthur's father.

Gaulf spit after the lot of them, then took stock of his injuries. There would be retribution for his insolence, but so be it. With the festival coming, there was no reason to be in poor spirits, even after a beating like that.

But as much as he wanted to forget what had happened, the memory of the lake in the forest and the strange light lingered deep within. None of it made sense, and that scared him. Surely it could not have been a dream, could it? Swallowing hard, Gaulf stood and dusted himself off.

Del was still working on the sign as Gaulf approached his store. "Back already?"

"Ma needs supplies for the cakes, so she sent me." Gaulf retrieved the list from his pocket, smoothing the wrinkles from the paper.

"Here, let me," Del offered, taking his list. Gaulf followed him into the small store and rifled through the shelves while he waited. His hand idly traced over some of the goods, some from familiar villages, some not. He knew the names of several farmers over in Swanford, had heard his parents talk of them in hushed tones. Del cleared his throat behind him. "That'll be five silver and six copper, Gaulf." Gaulf gave his coins over to the shopkeeper, who jingled the satchel in his hand. Then, he shook the coins out onto the counter and started to count.

"What's wrong?" Gaulf glanced at the coins on the counter. "That's what she usually sends me with... There's not enough, is there?"

"No, not with the taxes going up again. Between this and the roads being what they are, I had no choice," Del replied, not doing much to keep the edge from his tone. His face softened as he noticed Gaulf step back. "Look, I know your ma, and that she's good for it. You can square up with me—maybe help around the shop after the festival?" He was already sweeping the coins up and into the purse again, his anger all but forgotten.

"Oh, yes, sir. I can do that. Thank you, sir." Maybe now he could find a way to help his parents save their farm. The year had not been kind to his family, and he couldn't bear to hear again the whispers of his parents in the dark of night when they thought he and his sisters were sleeping, talking of their worries and wondering what the future held.

Gaulf, with his head full of promise, lifted the box of supplies and headed out of the store toward home. And though Del's concern over the rise in taxes worried beneath his skin's surface like a weevil through grain stores, by the time he arrived home, Gaulf managed to shove every trouble to the side and could only think again about Jannie and the upcoming festival.

Chapter 5

PREPARING FOR THE FESTIVAL

GAULF NUDGED THE DOOR open, carrying the supplies from the shop. Hope that he might drop them and escape unnoticed, maybe crawl into his bed for a proper nap, was dashed the moment he entered the house.

"Put the supplies in the kitchen for your mother. Then come straight back. I need your help out in the field today." Angun hardly wasted time in general, but this day he seemed especially driven. Gaulf suspected a forthcoming lecture.

"But, Da—"

"No. We have a long day ahead of us to get everything right for the festival," Angun instructed. Gaulf did not reply. He knew it was wise not to when his father was in a mood like this, even though his friends had made plans for shenanigans, some sort of caper that would be the talk of the town. How Gaulf wanted to be part of that, if only to see how it would make Jannie laugh. That thought, at least, was enough to bolster his spirits as he trudged toward the kitchen.

The memory of her laughter never failed to provoke a tremble in his heart. He remembered all too well the first time he had heard it. But no, that wasn't quite right either, was it? It was the first time he had noticed her as a woman, rather than simply a girl he had known his entire life, at the harvest festival a few years prior. One glance that had threatened to stop his lungs from drawing in air, that threatened the world as he knew it.

His mother was nowhere to be seen, so he placed the box of supplies on the floor and began unpacking it. *"Everything to its place,"* as his ma would often say. Gaulf hummed to himself while he worked, leaving out what he knew his mother would need immediately for baking. The kitchen was still in its usual state of ordered chaos, and once Gaulf finished with the supplies he set to cleaning.

When he was done, he surveyed the results and spied the pile of cakes.

"Don't mind if I do," Gaulf whispered to himself as he snatched one of the small delicacies from the platter, devouring it in one bite. A dizzyingly sensational taste of cinnamon and sugar, of apples and maple, exploded in his mouth. He quickly realized that the platter's pyramid of confections was now oddly shaped, and he wiped his hands on his trousers and rearranged the stack of desserts so that his theft was not obvious. His mother would notice it eventually—she was keen like that—but it would give him time to get out of the house before he provoked her ire.

Gaulf took the empty wooden box and headed out of the back of the house to join his father in the fields, pausing only to check on the animals. There were fewer there now, as one of the cows was recently sold to cover the previous year's taxes. Gaulf hated that his family was being bled dry like the rest of the village, and no one could do anything, say anything. He and his friends once talked of staging some sort of—what? Rebellion against the tax collector? Sending him away before he could ever reach their tiny corner of the world? What would that do, but bring down an army's worth of trouble upon their heads?

"Come on, boy! We have work to do," Angun called from the fields. Gaulf followed the sound of his father's voice, hardly noticing the small curl of smoke following him, though it vanished into the breeze.

Angun was quick to direct Gaulf to where help was most needed, and it took most of the day to harvest what their dwindling farmland yielded. Gaulf was left with an ache in his muscles, for the workload had increased without farmhands, who long ago deserted Redford to search for more profitable prospects elsewhere. He remembered well his father pleading with them to remain until the fields were healthy again, but none would listen.

They had taxes to pay too.

Angun stood staring at the cart where the pair piled what crops they could harvest. He watched as his father's shoulders slumped at the sight, the yield scarcely worth the effort of gathering it. There had to be something Gaulf could do. Maybe his friends were right, and they could incite some sort of change, or at the very least, run the tax collectors out of the village.

"Go on, son. The work here is done," Angun said flatly, patting Gaulf on the shoulder.

"Da, are you sure?" Gaulf asked, only now realizing how tightly his fists were clenched.

"I can handle the rest here. Go have fun with your friends." Angun smiled, but it did not rise to meet his eyes. How long had it been since Gaulf heard his father's laughter?

"Yes, Da, but you call for me if you need anything." Gaulf straightened his spine, wanting to appear as sturdy as his father—a man meant to last, to endure.

"Run along now." His father strode to the cart and tightened the harness for the mule, his focus seemingly fixed on tasks rather than the gravity of their circumstances.

Gaulf took off at a sprint, wondering whether he were merely trying to catch up with his friends or to leave behind the image of his father's face when he saw the state of their crops. It was perhaps a bit of both, for in the company of his friends he might fare better in forgetting his worries for a time. He headed for the nearby forest, watching the sun sink toward the horizon. There was a shortcut to the clearing that circled the village, and the greater the distance he put between himself and his home, the lesser the weight of his earthly cares, as if space made all the difference.

Gaulf heard Jannie's laughter long before he spotted her in the clearing with his friends, finding their place amongst the half-buried stones. She had the power to lift the weight from his chest, to wipe away the burden of his woes. Following that musical sound through the dense foliage, he pushed bothersome branches aside, pausing near the edge of the clearing to listen. They were talking about the festival, as expected, but he caught his name being bandied about more than once as they wondered where he was at this hour.

"I wish he were here," Jannie said wistfully, and Gaulf stood in reply. As much as he wanted to cross through the bush and declare his presence, a different sort of idea formed in his mind. Gaulf crashed through the brush and barreled into the clearing with a loud roar. He felt bad for the look of fright on Jannie's face, but the scrambling of Gunter, Adit, and Chindler made it worthwhile. Gunter grabbed one of the nearby branches they were using to start a fire, but he snuck behind Jannie, the momentary bravado dispersed. "Gaulf! You scared me!" Jannie smacked his arm, but he suspected she wasn't truly upset with him, which was confirmed when she smiled. "About time you arrived, because these three are having a heck of a time lighting the fire."

"Well, if Adit hadn't forgotten the tinders," Gunter said with a scowl. His expression was rarely anything other than severe, as if he were always mad at something.

"I did my job. I brought some logs," Chindler offered, shrugging. He ducked behind Adit when Gunter glared at him. Not that hiding from their larger friend did much good, being a foot taller than Adit. The two were as different as night and day, and not only in height. Chindler's hair was lighter than Jannie's, whereas Adit's hair was a raven color that rivaled that blackness of night.

"I was going to get them, but then I saw Arthur skulking about with Sige." Adit grimaced at the sound of those names, and Gaulf knew exactly what that look entailed. All of them did, with the way Arthur had grown more cocksure over the last few years. Ever since his father became mayor, Arthur had become insufferable.

"Maybe one of us," Jannie said, looking pointedly at Adit as she drew her shawl tighter around her shoulders, "should head back to town and find some."

A shiver raced through his skin from a strange chill. Gaulf closed his eyes, listening to a whirling inside of him, and somehow, the world fell away, replaced by a wintry bluster. His skin was chapped raw against the wind, and Gaulf dared open his eyes against the gusts. His mind tilted. Briefly, he stared at hands that seemed not quite his own. The image of his friends faded, melting into a haze of smoke and fire. He kneeled in the small clearing next to the pile of wood. *Cold. So cold.* His teeth chattering, Gaulf squeezed his eyes shut once more.

Remember.

Something guided his fingers, moved his mouth. Warmth. He needed to be warm. Shapes squiggled in his mind's eye. A spiral of blue, a quill scratching frantically against paper, a door opening. Everything pouring from the whispering inside of him. Gaulf knew what he needed to do. His palms conjured fire, and Jannie's face twisted in confused fear at the scene, driving that part of him back into the dark.

Gaulf blinked. "I might be able to help," he said before understanding the words leaving his mouth were indeed his. Four sets of eyes observed him closely, and Gaulf felt heat rise in his body.

They had found the clearing two summers prior and claimed it for themselves. The firepit was their first addition, and the hammock came shortly thereafter. They talked at length about building a cabin, but the group thought it would make their secret space too visible.

Gaulf reached into the crisscrossed stack of kindling and grabbed two to rub together. He had seen his father do this many times but had never been able to get it right. Patience and Gaulf weren't exactly on good terms. However, with Jannie watching him, anything felt possible.

The world came to a standstill as Gaulf concentrated on that divot he drilled into the wood. His breath caught in his throat, suddenly remembering the lapping waters of the murky lake and of how he struggled to find the elusive surface.

That moment stretched like an eternity caught between his hands. Whispered words escaped his lips, accompanied by fingers discovering remnants of something ancient, forgotten. *Spiral, door, quill.*

Gaulf bathed in that golden light, that odd thing that sunk inside his body, letting it lead him. There came a flare, a flame between his palms, and within the wood he felt it: the spark. He smelled the smoke, and his heart ached in his chest as flames licked at the kindling, though he couldn't understand its cause.

"Careful, Gaulf!" Adit was leaning over, hissing through clenched teeth. Gunter tugged him away from the fire, clucking his tongue.

"You'll kill the fire with your hot wind, is what you'll do. Let him work," Gunter snapped, but the words lacked a sharp edge.

The heat that beckoned Gaulf captured his gaze, and he blew at it to draw out its strength. He could feel the warmth of it spread from branch to branch as it intensified, snaking up along his hand and arm. Awash in a shifting orange light that danced within his eyes, he closed the distance between himself and the flame.

"You'll get a face full of cinder," Jannie warned, that sweet face of hers not unlike the flicker of the flames, a beacon that called him like a siren's song. She hugged his arm, gently moving him away from the fire to sit beside her. But Gaulf couldn't tear his gaze from the flame.

The five friends engaged in excited conversation about the harvest festival. It signaled an end to the year and a promise of bounty to last the winter. Gaulf could hardly follow the discussion, his thoughts flitting between his family's struggle and that dancing flame in front of him, as well as Jannie's soft scent that seemed to permeate the very air while she huddled against him.

"—and that's what we should do. Next time the tax collectors come, we give them a box of milk and blood. Milked and bled us dry, they have," Adit said, keeping his voice low so as not to draw attention to themselves.

"What good would that do?" Chindler asked, rubbing his hands together near the fire.

"Change has to start somewhere," Gunter added. It was the same discussion they'd had for some years now while watching their village suffer.

"Arthur's father has to confront them at some point," Jannie said, nestling against Gaulf when he wrapped an arm around her. It was right, the way they fit together.

"What if we just burn it all down?" Gaulf said, only realizing the weight of his words after they were out of his mouth. "What?"

"Gaulf?" Jannie asked, horrified.

"Y-Yes?" Gaulf said, not certain why Jannie was upset. "I mean, no taxes to collect if there's nothing left... No...not a good idea, but I'm not the brains here, am I?"

"You certainly are not," Adit said, biting back a chuckle. "I say we lay in wait for the next tax collector, and we invite them in with open arms."

"That's hardly lying in wait, Adit," Chindler teased, and Adit returned the favor with a rude gesture.

"So maybe not lay in wait, but we set a trap. Invite them in, and say we have a festival going on at the time. We get them comfortable, and drunk, and *we* take *them* for all they are worth. All of the taxes, and send them on their way empty-handed." Adit's hands were animated as he spoke, mimicking each action. His pale green eyes flitted from friend to friend, as if waiting for approval.

"I think that would be worse than refusing to pay," Gunter said. "Might get a good message across, though, especially if we can use it to trade before they lop all of our heads off for being treasonous gits."

"Always the shining light of hope, Gunter." Adit shook his head, the humor drained from his tone. "We have to do something."

"Might at least make someone stop and listen. Enough is enough," Gunter said, ignoring Adit's outburst.

"Let's get back to the matter at hand, and what we want to do to lighten up the festival," Chindler interjected, driving a hand through his white hair, pushing it out of his face. "Something to make our parents smile again."

Gaulf didn't hear them. The fire had drawn him in with its dance in the ring of stones, blackening the wood then bursting forth in a riot of red and orange. Every flame seemed like a word written in a language he could hardly begin to understand, and yet, he could *feel* them.

"What was that?" Gaulf lifted his head, surprising his friends.

"What's eating you? You have not been yourself all day, Gaulf," Jannie said, pulling away to study him. She caught his chin with a gentle touch and made him meet her gaze.

"I found something, Jannie," Gaulf whispered, unsure of what her reaction might be to his revelation.

"What do you mean?" she asked.

"Yesterday, when I disappeared?" Gaulf said.

"Go on," she said, hanging on his every word.

"I found a strange light, and it flew from me. I chased it, and I could not stop myself." He paused, thinking of how to describe what had happened that night. "I found myself in a lake, struggling to reach the surface, when the light went *inside* of me."

"Gaulf," Jannie started, her back straightening, putting inches between herself and him.

"Ever since then—I do not know how to explain it—but I have felt something growing, burning within me," he whispered. Gaulf gripped his arm, then quickly withdrew, fussing at his shirt sleeves. How could he explain it? That something extraordinary happened, and to him of all people? Jannie yelped and Gaulf saw a golden ball of swirling fire within the palm of his hand. He stared at it, that light he had chased through the forest and now was part of him.

"Is that—" Jannie started to ask, but the words died on her lips.

"Gaulf?" Gunter said, clambering over to them. He stood there slack-jawed and wide-eyed. Gaulf's fingers closed around the ball of light, suppressing the urge to let it explode. "What have you done?"

"I haven't done a thing," Gaulf said defensively. Jannie grabbed his wrist to keep him from retreating further.

"What's going on? What is it? What does he have?" Chindler and Adit scrambled to get closer, and it was hard to tell which one said what. Gunter put out an arm to block their path. "What did he catch? Is it a toad?"

Gunter sidled closer, brandishing a thick branch like a blade. "You know what that is, right?" His eyes, normally mahogany brown, shone black. "Jannie, back up."

"Gunter, put that stick down before you hurt someone." She did not leave Gaulf's side and kept a firm grip on his wrist.

"He's using *magic*, Jannie," Gunter hissed, bringing himself to his full height, his stance threatening. Gaulf heard that word, and it was as if someone had walked right over his grave. Then the world went sideways.

Chapter 6

THE CAMPFIRE

"Guys, it's me," Gaulf said warily, hardly able to form the words for the shiver threading through his spine. The gravity of the situation finally clicked, and he could feel the blood drain from his face as he stared at the golden light that pulsed through his fingers.

"Magic has been outlawed since before we were born, Gaulf," Gunter countered.

"Why do you have to be such a downer, Gunter?" Adit chimed in, ignoring Chindler's attempts to quiet him.

"I listen to my parents, you addled nitwit. That's where your parents got your name, right? Shortened it to Adit?" Gunter snapped.

"Really, Gunter. It's Gaulf. It's not like the elves—" Chindler clamped a hand over Adit's mouth.

"Where was I? Right. I listen to my father. You know? The sheriff? *'The law is the law, son. We bring mages before the mayor for proper handling. We send word for help. May The Paladin save us.'* " Even as Gunter mimicked his father almost perfectly, doubt crept in his tone.

"This is Gaulf we're talking about here. You can see he's no terror, no threat to our way of life. No foul fiend lobbing spells and magic about." Jannie blocked Gunter's path to Gaulf.

"We hang with him if we do not turn him in, Jannie," Gunter warned through clenched teeth. "I've heard my da talk about problems in other villages, that there's a plague of magic upon the land."

"That's a pack of lies and you know it, Gunter. Even if that were the case, *look at him*." Jannie slid her hand over Gaulf's shoulder reassuringly. The light within his fingers had faded, but he saw a threaded blue light, an afterimage that stained his hand. He stood, if only to be that much closer to her.

"It's me, Gunter," Gaulf finally said, opening his empty palms to his friend. "I don't know what's going on any more than you do, but it's *me*." At that, Gunter lowered the makeshift club, letting it dangle at his side, but Gaulf sensed the threat was far from over.

"Can you do it again?" Chindler asked, Adit and him pushing past Gunter to stand in front of Gaulf and Jannie. "What else can you do?"

"I don't know," Gaulf replied, watching Gunter. "But maybe we can use this to protect our village. Please, Gunter, we're in this together. Friends, right?"

"Tell us how this happened," Gunter said, and Gaulf heard more than saw the makeshift club hit the ground as his friend joined them. They huddled there together, the dwindling fire in the pit forgotten as Gaulf recounted his mad dash through the woods. And as he talked, the feelings of being lost and trapped, his hands started to form a light again, this one large enough to fit in both hands. Gunter hissed at the sight, and Adit elbowed him.

The light was confirmation of something they had only heard stories about. *Magic.* Gaulf worked with the raw emotions inside of him, and anytime he looked at Jannie the light was that much brighter. The smile she gave him, the hope he saw kindled in all of their faces, filled that hole in his chest to the point he thought he'd explode.

Gunter returned to the pit, stacking the firewood amidst the smoldering embers.

"Can you step back?" Gaulf asked, wincing at the flare of suspicion on his friend's face. With hardly any room to breathe, with *magic* still tingling in his fingers, he needed space. There was a storm brewing inside of him.

"It's not natural," Gunter whispered, putting distance between himself and the firepit. Between him and Gaulf. He shook his head and took a seat next to Jannie, Chindler and Adit following suit.

"No one's saying that it is natural," Jannie said. The sting of Gunter's words was fierce, and Gaulf did not want to make matters worse by flinging his own barbs. "We all know the stories."

"This is not going to end well," Gunter said flatly. "Hunters come and they deal with these magic-wielders, but not soon enough. I overheard one of my da's meetings, and well, sometimes The Paladin sends *the elf...*"

Gaulf stomach dropped. The one who was usually the rock of their group was afraid? That was unsettling enough. But he was also afraid of Gaulf? He could hardly comprehend that, though that seemed more of a recurring pattern lately. Gaulf's eyes were drawn to the fire again, the logs burning brightly, illuminating the faces of his friends in an eerie glow.

"That's not me, Gunter. I would never hurt anyone," Gaulf pleaded.

"Tell that to Sige," Adit said, immediately regretting his words after Jannie glared at him. "What? My ma saw Gaulf lay him low. Heard her telling my da over dinner."

"No doubt she's spreading it all through the village too," Chindler added.

"That's not helping, and anyway, Sige deserved what happened," she said with a huff, crossing her arms over her chest.

"If my da finds out, he'll have to send word to The Paladin," Gunter said, an internal war evident on his face. "We'll have more problems than increased taxes if he hears." Gunter looked anywhere but at Gaulf as he fidgeted with some of the large stones buried in the ground.

"Then we do not tell anyone," Chindler offered, leaning his elbows on his knees. "This stays here, with the five of us." He rubbed his hands together closer to the fire before settling his gaze on Gaulf. "At least now we have an advantage over the tax collectors."

"I'm not going to hurt anyone, Chind," Gaulf barked. "Not even them."

"That's just it, you hardly have to. If we know when they are coming, we meet them out on the road. Right?" Chindler said. Gaulf fell silent with the rest of his friends. They knew when Chindler got started, there was no stopping him. "See, when they are arriving, we go for a hike, or that's what we tell our parents. But we'll go into the forest and then cut off the path that follows the road. Skulk about until we see the tax collectors. If we have time, we can get a bunch of kindling out in the road." Chindler's hands flailed about as he spoke. "And that's when Gaulf sets it all ablaze. We can have Gunter—"

"No, no, no. I want no part of this," Gunter interjected.

"It has to be you. You're the only one large enough to be an imposing figure striding by the flames, warning them of the evil of their ways," Chindler continued with hardly a pause, talking over Gunter as he tried to break in again. "Just a bit of fire, right? Enough to scare them away."

"I am not sure I like this idea much either." Gaulf sighed and shook his head. "Too much at risk. I do not want to hurt anyone."

"Again, that's the beauty of it. There's little chance they will even get close enough to get hurt, and we'll make sure Gunter is as safe as can be. Even if we only deter them for a few days, it's something." Chindler sat back with a satisfied smile on his face, but that look did not last long.

"That is all fine and dandy until their elf strings her bow and peppers Gunter with arrows," Adit added, eliciting an exasperated groan from Chindler.

"There's no saying they even send her." Chindler threw his hands in the air. They started to bicker over the details, which promptly brought the discussion to an end. Both of them were right, and wrong, but that was the pair. How many times had their schemes gotten the five of them into trouble?

"We should probably get home. Now that Adit and Gunther both mentioned the elf, I've no hankering to stay out too late," Jannie said, rising from her seat.

"Do we have to?" Gaulf whispered, never wanting the moment to end.

"I can hardly see the stars, and we all have quite a bit of work tomorrow," Jannie answered, pressing her lips to the corner of Gaulf's mouth. His face flushed with an entirely different sort of heat, his mind reeling while the world spun. "All right, boys, let's get the fire out and leave, otherwise not a one of us will be able to enjoy the festival tomorrow if our parents wake up before we get home."

Jannie ordered them about and as tired as they all were, no one argued. They worked together to extinguish the fire, and once the embers were completely cool, smoke lazily drifting upward in small tufts, the five of them departed the clearing. Gaulf and Jannie were still locked together at their hands, following behind their friends. One by one, as they neared their village, Chindler, Adit, and Gunter split off to their own homes. Once they were alone at the small path that led to Jannie's house, the pair stopped. Gaulf's eyelids were heavy, but before he knew it, she was kissing him again.

"You are magical, Gaulf. Never doubt that," she whispered against his mouth and was then gone. He stood there dumbfounded, certain that he had just been struck by lightning for the tingling in his body. She glanced over her shoulder at him before she climbed through her bedroom window. And when he began the walk to his own home, he hardly felt the ground underfoot.

Chapter 7

THE FESTIVAL

G AULF SWAM THROUGH THE water with hardly a care in the world. The weight of Jannie's kiss still lingered against his mouth, a buoyancy he had never experienced holding him aloft. Before he realized, coiling tendrils of darkness woven with bolts of blue light burned as they wrapped around him, stripping him of the carefree weightlessness and the warmth of Jannie's lips. He struggled against them but that only drew the creeping sensation further along the length of his body. The water soon turned stagnant, the light then dimmed.

On the surface of the water, Gaulf spied his reflection, the panic and fear written across his face. The sight spurred him to fight. The tendrils' grip on him loosened, and he kicked hard one last time, bursting through the mirrored surface before spewing water from his lungs.

When had he last felt the warmth of the light?

His heart ceased its hammering in his chest, and his head surfaced from within the blankets of his bed while he uncoiled the sheets from his legs. Gaulf fought to remember the dream, trying desperately to hold on to the sharp edges, but part of him wanted to cast it all away and let it slip into oblivion. What remained was an overwhelming sense of foreboding.

Gaulf barely managed to get out of bed. His limbs were heavy and each step across the floor a monumental task. The taste of smoke and ash coated his tongue while the smell of firewood clung to him. Dim light was a lance to his brain, and Gaulf rested his head against the door to his room briefly. Grimacing, Gaulf opened it fully, shielding his eyes as hiccups brewed in his diaphragm.

After some light chores and a quick breakfast, Gaulf helped his mother make the icing for the cakes in the kitchen. He even helped Ola and Elga with wrapping them in wax paper, the dream seemingly forgotten, replaced by the happy tedium of the festival tasks. However, the gnawing sensation in his gut remained firmly fixed in place.

"Ma," Gaulf started, feeling the next words lodge in his throat as his mother looked at him. He swallowed hard before he continued. "Is this enough?" His gaze searched the pitiful stack of cakes, much less than they'd baked together in previous years.

"It will do," his mother replied with a warm smile on her face, but it did not reach her eyes, and so Gaulf resolved to drop the matter. How could he prod at such a raw wound?

He shifted in his chair. "What if we charged a bit more this season?" The dark look that crossed his mother's face spoke volumes.

"I will not demand more from our own people, our friends." She would brook no further argument, that much was clear. But Gaulf opened his mouth to speak anyway, and she squeezed his shoulder tightly. "We'll make do, heartling. We always do." And with that, she moved to get everything bundled for travel. Ola and Elga hurried along behind her, their tittering a sure sign that these burdens had not yet reached them in a real sense.

Gaulf sighed. "Yes, Ma," he said to the empty room, then shuffled out the door to his little home.

Harvest time had come, the festival was already underway, judging by the chaotic noise echoing through the village. The town would come together to celebrate another year. And the rest? They could deal with that tomorrow, right?

Gaulf inhaled deeply, getting a whiff of cinders and ash once more. But there was nothing in the area that indicated a fire. No plume of smoke in the distance. No flames on the wind.

There were streamers hanging from the trees in the colors of fall alongside unlit lanterns framed in ivy wreaths. The sky was sunny and clear, and Gaulf lost himself for the moment, shoving away the worries in favor of enjoying the festival.

"There you are!" Jannie called, the words reaching Gaulf before he saw her. She launched herself at him, and Gaulf caught her clumsily.

"Good morning to you too, Jannie," Gaulf managed to say as she clung to him, her arms wrapped around his throat. "Where to?"

"Hm, any direction, really. Just, not *that* way," she whispered, pointing toward the eastern side of the open square. Gaulf followed her finger and his heart stopped in his chest. Through the milling crowd of people hard at work in preparations for tonight, he saw Arthur staring daggers at the two of them.

There would be a reckoning.

"It's about time Sige sported bruises of his own," Jannie said mockingly. "My hero. Onward!"

Gaulf headed toward the communal area, weaving in and out of clustered tables, chairs, and people. Everyone offered smiles for the pair, and Jannie's lilting laugh echoed through the village. His grip on her hand was tight, wishing that he didn't have to let go. That came to an end, though, when they met with Adit and Chindler.

"Where's Gunter?" Gaulf looked between his two friends as Jannie slid from his back. Adit shrugged his shoulders, which earned him a light shove from Chindler.

"Last I saw, he was helping his gran leave her tribute," Chindler replied.

"I don't know why. The statue's as old as she is, if not older. I'll swing by later and steal the apple before it rots." Adit ducked the next swat before Chindler could land it, but he had no long reprieve to celebrate his escape. He missed Gunter's looming figure and squeaked as he collided with the larger boy.

"I'll tell your parents how your chores really get done if you do that," Gunter warned menacingly, forcing Adit to retreat. When the group of friends tightened the circle around him, Adit's face fell as he realized there was nowhere for him to run.

"Oh, what's the big deal? She's going to leave an apple in front of an old, useless statue. The scythe's going to break off any day. Last statue of the seven will be washed away, probably by the next big storm, mark my word."

"Bite your tongue, Adit! Bite it right off. If his grandmother wanted you to have an apple, she'd give you one. Maybe show her a little more respect than planning to stick your hands where they hardly belong?" Jannie's quip shut him right up, and Gaulf and the rest of them broke into giggles.

Adit groaned. "I still don't see what the point is, is all."

"She leaves tribute to The Harvester and The Scythe, that we all might have a plentiful harvest. Says we'd all do well to mind the old ways. We've fallen too far from the faith, from the seven that guided us," Gunter instructed.

"She also ran through the village in her nightgown last year, yelling her head off about The Paladin," Chindler added, quickly covering his head in preparation for an attack.

Gunter sighed. "Don't remind me."

A few good-natured jabs later, they made their way into the village proper.

Gaulf lost himself in these precious moments with his friends. Even the worries of taxes, of his parents, of fragmented, fiery dreams seemed distant. Almost distant enough to forget entirely.

The friends roamed the festival from table to table, booth to booth, tent to tent. Chindler and Adit competed at the games of chance, and Gunter marked himself down for one of the pie-eating contests. Gaulf hung back when he could as his friends rushed forward, spending their own harvest bounties, his own pockets empty.

As the day progressed, the sun sank low in the sky. The evening bell rang, announcing dinner, the clanging noise drawing everyone's attention. The entire village congregated within the dinner tents or found seating at some of the vacant tables. Everyone chipped in a bit of food here and there, and for a moment, Gaulf felt at peace. Gone were the worries of the day. His parents laughed and smiled those secret smiles at one another, and his friends were nearby. Dinner came and went, and dessert followed. People moved and mingled until the sun set completely, and the fires were soon lit.

Gaulf and Jannie sat side by side with Gunter next to them, Chindler and Adit occupying the other side of the table. The two, often at odds with one another, sat close together. When Jannie noticed she nudged Gaulf, and they shared a knowing glance. Though dinner had consisted of dishes provided by different families throughout the village, and Gaulf ate as much as he could, hunger swelled inside of him.

"May I have this dance?" Jannie whispered against the shell of his ear. Before he could answer, she pulled him up and off of the bench. Gaulf dropped his fork and started to protest but his heart certainly was not in it. Instead, he wiped his face with one of the napkins that he tossed back to the table, blushing when he heard their names in the chatter of the villagers. There was a sea of faces in the crowd, people he had known his entire life, and they were all watching the two moving toward the dance floor.

Before he could engage in the revelry, however, he noticed an unfamiliar face staring at him amidst the crowd of people he had known his entire life. And yet there was a sharpness to the face that was as known to him as the turn of the seasons. Gaulf stumbled as he caught sight of *her* between one space and the next. Between one blink and the next. Then she was gone, vanished utterly among the villagers' faces. He felt torn in two as he was dragged along by the exuberant Jannie in the sweeping steps of the dance. Where had she gone?

"You will have to let me at least ask once, Jannie," Gaulf whispered as they moved further toward the center of the dance floor. The music was jubilant, honoring the tone of the festival. There were several pairs of villagers waltzing alongside them. The energy was frenetic, and Gaulf swore he could taste magic in the air.

"Why should I wait for this shy little farm boy to make up his mind?" she teased, hardly waiting for an answer before she swept him around her, their feet nearly meeting.

How many songs they danced to, he couldn't keep track. The world melted away, leaving only him and Jannie, whose eyes sparkled in the orange glow of the lanterns.

That is, until he saw that face again.

She stood at the edge of the tent near the dance floor, staring at him. Through him.

A scowl was etched into her features. The dress she wore swirled as she turned about, searching, dancing, until her eyes landed again on him. The scowl deepened. She tucked her hair behind her ears, and their fine points made Gaulf's skin run cold. His heart thundered in his chest.

The elf.

The word came to his mind unbidden, a spiral of fear uncoiling in his chest. Local tales said that elves came for children who did not behave. They had mentioned her numerous times, the skulking creature bound to The Paladin.

"Did you see *her?*" Gaulf asked Jannie. Whether she heard him he could not tell, but she offered no reply. With every turn he scanned the crowd for that face. *Her* face. His heart would sputter whenever he thought he spotted her in the shadows before lurching into motion again as the image faded into the night.

Eventually, the music slowed, and the frantic pace and celebration diminished as it stretched into the hours of the early morning. Gaulf realized too late what was going to happen when the tune slowed. Jannie stepped to him, pulling him flush against her. Somehow, she avoided his clumsy, leaden feet, preventing them from stomping on her own. He was only too happy to let go and follow wherever she led him. He never wanted the moment to end, the music to stop, the dance to quell. To see that strange, ethereal face again.

"May I have this dance?" With those words, the world tilted dangerously. Too late Gaulf noticed the crowd had parted, the music had stopped. Trouble had found them. Arthur stood there expectantly, his hand outstretched. She opened her mouth to speak, but Gaulf stepped in front of her and shook his head.

"No." Jannie's simple but firm reply made Arthur furrow his brow.

"I believe she's spoken for, Arthur. For tonight. Tomorrow. And if I haven't missed my mark, for quite some time after that." Gaulf felt Jannie there as a solid presence against his back, bolstering his resolve.

Arthur visibly bristled, his face contorted in anger. "I would hate to remind my father how far behind in payments Angun is." The threat was meant only for him, but he heard Jannie's sharp intake of breath behind him.

"By the harvests, Arthur, do you have to be such an ass?" Jannie demanded, tugging at Gaulf's wrist. Whether she sensed the heat rising in him, the shame and fury mingling together in a way that made bile boil within him, he had no idea. Did she feel the same revulsion?

"You had no problem handling your own fight yesterday, Gaulf. Why hide behind a girl now?" Arthur's words stung, and Gaulf growled in response.

"No more than you hide behind Sige. What happened, Arty? Did your father's horse have a better proposition for the evening? Maybe Sige'll put on a wig for you." The rage he saw building in Arthur's features erased the gnawing emptiness in his stomach.

"I will have a talk with my father. About Angun's debts and how I've seen him stockpiling some money. Skimming from the top, maybe?" Arthur spat. The villagers drew in close around them, watching the exchange with some interest. Gaulf saw little more than fire as he balled his fist tightly.

"Gaulf, he's not worth it," Jannie said, planting a kiss on his cheek and then at the corner of his mouth. Jannie stepped around Gaulf and looked between the two boys. "You two used to be the best of friends. There's a reason we stopped letting you hang around us, Arty." Then Jannie returned her attention to Gaulf. "I love you, silly farm boy. Wait for me." The glint in her eyes was a promise, one that Gaulf was happy he had not missed. He nodded and retreated from them, that gnawing feeling receding momentarily.

"That's right, farm boy. Run off while your betters enjoy a dance," Arthur said dismissively, waving him off before closing the gap between himself and Jannie. The music resumed shortly thereafter, once Arthur leveled a glare toward the stage. His movements were rigid for someone who had only ever danced with a tutor, and he fumbled when he attempted to take Jannie into his arms. It was clear he intended to lead her in a dance, but she was more than prepared for this. The look of surprise on Arthur's face as she refused and twisted about so that she stole the leading steps from him was more than worth it. Jannie did the same to him that she had to Gaulf.

Where Gaulf had been all too happy to let Jannie lead, Arthur wanted none of it. His efforts to wrangle her into following him were for nothing. Jannie outsmarted him at every turn, and anytime he tried to wrest control away he earned kicked shins and flattened toes. What whispers had rippled through the crowd during his dance with Jannie quickly morphed into barely contained laughter. Arthur realized too late his predicament and struggled to escape.

Jannie was having none of that.

Gaulf snickered and left Jannie to save herself in the most spectacular way. The lesson being taught was a long time in the making. "And who better to do it than Jannie?" Gaulf whispered to himself as he departed the dance floor.

He imagined the look on Arthur's face when the laughter swelled and cherished that vision as he searched his pockets to find what coin he had.

"Drat," he muttered after he counted the few coppers he had. Maybe he could work out a deal with one of the people selling their crafts. He doubted he had enough to get Jannie something, but if he agreed to do a few odd jobs surely someone would grant him leniency. He found he was whistling to himself, and he searched for his friends. Their table was empty and Chindler, Adit, and Gunter were nowhere to be seen. Gaulf shrugged and figured they had likely found their own form of entertainment.

Something caught his attention, and he sharply turned his gaze to the bonfire, to the face that stared at him over the flicker of the flames. Gaulf blinked, stopping short of the blaze. The figure was a specter, their visage muddled by the shadows and the haze of the heat. There he saw *her* again, alien and unfamiliar. Something tugged at him, drawing him toward her. His heart lurched in his chest, a cold sweat broke out over his flesh, and when he rounded the bonfire, he collided with the throng of people. By the time he scurried around them, she was gone. Gaulf turned this way and that, trying to see where she had disappeared to, but with so many people milling about, it was hard to tell.

And yet, there remained the notion that he should have seen *something*.

"Did you see where she went?" Gaulf stopped one of the farmers, his hand on their arm.

"Jannie? She's still dragging Arthur all over the dance floor," the farmer said with a laugh.

"No, the other one. The—" Gaulf started and quickly stopped. He tried to figure out how to describe the face he had seen but had no luck. There were no words that seemed to be right, and he could only conjure images and shapes that refused to coalesce into more than a vague sense of knowing in his stomach. Gaulf shook his head. The farmer shrugged and departed from him.

Gaulf found his way back to the tables laden with handmade goods. Nothing caught his eye, nothing was quite right. He could hardly shake that other face out of his mind. There was little left in his head but smoke he tried to hold, to remember, but it was gone in a blink. He walked past the tables and toward the village proper, scanning the crowds for her, finding her nowhere.

He soon arrived near the outskirts of the village and there the darkness felt inviting. The lack of people was enticing, and he was able to catch his breath for the first time that day. He moved off to the edge of the light cast by the torches and lanterns and sidled along the shadowed edge of Redford. The sound diminished, and he was able to breathe a little easier.

He closed his eyes and tried to find solid ground beneath his feet. The earth seemed treacherous at best, and everything wobbled along with it.

"Breathe, Gaulf. Just breathe," he whispered. The music in the village had stopped, he realized. "Hopefully, Arthur has had enough of learning his lesson." Just a few more moments alone to catch his breath and he'd scoot off to find Jannie. He was already starting to smile at the very idea. That thought did not last long, though.

Gaulf's head whipped sideways as a punch landed against his cheek. He let out a strangled cry of surprise and tumbled into the black.

When he opened his eyes and found Sige looming over him, the night sky behind him was devoid of stars. Before Gaulf could raise his hands to defend himself, Sige fell atop him and began pummeling him in retribution. Each blow was a rock slamming into him, and the first few knocked what little breath Gaulf had straight out of him. He saw white, flashes of red, and then pain ceased to have any meaning.

Whether it was for the lashing he had given Sige earlier, or if Arthur had sent him for his attitude about the dance with Jannie, Gaulf had no idea. He felt woozy, like he was once again beneath the waves, struggling to reach that golden light. Everything was sharpened by the pain Sige delivered, and Gaulf finally managed to raise a hand to ward off the next blow. Somehow, he had caught Sige's meaty fist in one hand. A surge of rage within him swelled, and a scream erupted from between his lips that had been building within him all day.

The noise surprised Sige, as did Gaulf's sudden bucking motion that launched the older, larger boy off of him. Everything hurt as he rose to his knees and then to his feet with a fair bit of wobbling. Copper tainted his mouth. Sweat poured off of him, shouts echoed in the distance. Was someone calling his name? He fell atop Sige, his hand returning punch after punch with whatever strength he could muster.

He spat blood laced with words and shapes at the bully. *Spiral. Door. Quill.* The fire came again, unbidden and burning, to his hands.

"Gaulf!" He heard his name, and he looked about. There were fires blazing in the distance, globs of light moving to and fro, but his attention was drawn to the trees not too far away. This close to the edge of the village, the trees seemed like dark sentinels, and he saw *her* there among the shadows.

The face was blank, but he knew her. Something inside of him was being tugged, drawn toward her image among the trees.

"Gaulf! Stop that!" Jannie's panicked voice snapped at the thread of his attention like the shock of cold water.

The boy beneath him was sporting fist-sized burns on his body. Gaulf's hand was glowing, as if he were still holding that golden orb. He shuddered when pain lanced through him. Sige was heaving below him with eyes wide and full of primal fear. His hands were a broken mess of charred flesh, and Gaulf rolled away from the sobbing mass. He found his feet once more and looked at his hands as the shadows receded.

It was only then he noticed that the entire village had gathered to observe the fight, standing some distance away. Abject horror was written on all of their faces, and the weight of those looks tore at his soul. Jannie stood at the forefront, fear in her eyes. But it wasn't fear of him, it was fear *for* him.

Suddenly, Arthur appeared, pushing his way to the front of the crowd. "Magic!" he shrieked, pointing at Gaulf.

"Shut your mouth, Arthur," Jannie hissed. But it was already too late.

Gaulf paled upon seeing the revulsion of all the villagers, ones he'd known his entire life. The only ones who didn't wear that same expression were Jannie, Chindler, Adit, and Gunter, the four of them creating a makeshift barrier between the villagers and Gaulf. But that barrier didn't do much to hide the whispers.

Magic. Abomination. Trouble.

"You all saw it true. The farm boy's been meddling with forces not meant for mortals. He's harmed our beloved Sige," Arthur explained to the villagers. Gaulf tried to say something around the stone that lodged itself in his throat, but no words would come. He saw his parents there among the crowd, staring in shock at him. His sisters were huddled together and crying, but that was far from the worst of it. Gunter was struggling with his own father as the sheriff pushed through the throng of people.

"Gunter, get out of the way," Caspar barked.

"Da, no," Gunter pleaded, joined in his supplication by the others.

"We have to contain the problem, son." Caspar then shouted commands at some of the nearby men, tension rising through the ranks.

"Get moving! My father will hear of this if you do not." Arthur's own wheedling was enough to drive them into action, and they advanced on the group of friends. Arthur fell back, sneering all the while. Two of the farmers saw to Sige, helping him up from the ground and escorting him to the village proper.

"We're going to need bandages and salve," one of the farmers called while steering Sige toward one of the more modest homes. The large bully hardly seemed a threat anymore, but Gaulf still felt a cinder of hatred burning within him still. He snarled, and that only served to make Caspar and his conscripted men bristle.

"Please, Da! This is Gaulf. We've known him since he was born. He is the same person, no matter what you just saw," Gunter begged, but to no avail.

Gaulf's body was drained, his limbs heavy. He wanted nothing more than to fall asleep and not wake for a hundred years. Jannie noticed and caught him before he fell, wrapping his arm over her as she ducked. The rest of it became background noise, the world falling apart around him. He heard and saw everything, but through the filter of the fugue that had descended upon him. Jannie spoke to him, and while the words were not recognizable to him, he knew what they meant. He cherished them, and the way they anchored him to the world when everything threatened to slip away.

"We'll get you out of this," Jannie whispered.

What came next was the descent back into the water and the crushing pressure beneath it. The darkness was gone, and the water was illuminated with that strange, golden light. He was suffused with it and surrounded by it, even as he struggled to breathe. His chest ached with the need to draw in air, and it burned its way through him. Gaulf screwed his eyes shut against the light but that hardly mattered. There was no escaping the pervasive brilliance no matter how he tried to get away from it. He swam and kicked his feet toward a surface he never reached.

Direction ceased to matter. Gaulf resigned himself to floating there, struggling with the need to breathe. To be. His head swirled, the light pricked his skin with heat, and he let out a bubbling scream. What little breath he had contained within his chest exploded in glints and glitter, burbling bubbles of shine that escaped him. In them, in each and every escaping semblance of life, he saw that face.

Her face. Staring at him with unabashed hatred.

Chapter 8

WHAT A TALE

GAULF TRAILED OFF AS his gaze wandered out into the trees and away from the fire. A few moments of silence stretched on before Orn realized that the story had ended, for now.

"Socked him right in the face? Good on you for that, Gaulf." Orn scrambled for something comforting to say, regretting his jovial tone when Gaulf turned his haunted eyes on him. "Never you mind that this Sige character ended up hurt. Doesn't matter that you burned him, because you had the restraint to *stop*. Not everyone can bury the need for revenge." Gaulf started to speak when a pause presented itself, but Orn waved him off. "Listen. I know you regret what you did. I can see it in your eyes."

"I didn't mean to hurt him," Gaulf said quietly.

"That's what matters, in the end. It does beg the question, though, as to *what* exactly happened," Orn prodded carefully, never taking his gaze from the boy's face. Here was a prime opportunity for getting some information. The questions burbled inside of him, begging for release, but he'd likely send Gaulf skittering into the forest if he cornered him with an interrogation. No, he had to temper his excitement.

"I could see it—the fire. Similar to when we were sitting around the campfire and had no way to light it." Gaulf inhaled sharply.

"Go on." Orn leaned forward slowly so his armor would not creak or clank unduly.

"There, in the darkness, I saw someone cold. It was snowing, and they needed to warm up," Gaulf began. Orn waited for the telltale wrenching in his stomach that happened the last time the boy lit the fire. He had not been paying close enough attention at that point to understand what was happening right in front of his face. "I saw the shapes, the symbols the person traced in the air. The words were long and spidery, but lodged in my throat. I drew on that person's need, the need for fire. It just...came to me. Same with Sige. I needed to protect myself, and it happened again. Unbidden. Oh, the smell was horrible!" Gaulf scrubbed his hands over his face, as if that might drive the memory away.

Orn pitied Gaulf. He thought he could hardly imagine burning someone with his bare hands, but glancing down at his own, envisioning a wreath of fire, he knew how wrong he was. If he let go and slipped into the—whatever it was that had drawn the young farmhand into its grasp—it would only be too easy. And yet, somehow, Gaulf had tried to resist it at every turn. That earned him Orn's trust.

"I can't begin to explain what you did. In fact, I was hoping that *you* could explain a bit of it to me." Orn chuckled wryly.

"Me?" Gaulf asked, his voice echoing through the trees. Birds that had been roosting took off, screeching their displeasure at the sudden outburst.

Orn chewed on the next words before letting them tumble from his mouth. "I've been at this for some time now, doing what I can to help, trying to determine what's at the heart of the matter of magic. Why it's infecting people. And from what I've pieced together, those marked...not one of them knew what happened. Just that they crossed paths with, well, *something*. You and your light in the stream, another with a bolt of lightning from a clear sky. One walked through the door to their house and found themselves falling through some abyss until they woke up the next day."

"Why is it happening, do you think?" Gaulf must have moved, for the firelight flickered across Orn's closed eyelids.

"I'm not sure yet. I don't have enough information. But I've heard that before, that these symbols were tied to whatever brings this magic. Leaning into it, though? Not a good idea." Orn shot a look of warning at Gaulf.

"What do I do then?"

"Stick with me. We'll figure this out. Together." Orn hated not knowing, like he was missing one piece of a much larger puzzle that would bring everything into focus. Hated that he couldn't truly save Gaulf, not until he understood why magic was appearing in the world again.

"What about you?" Gaulf asked with caution.

"What do you mean?" Orn did his best to keep the fatigue from his tone.

"Why are you doing this?" Gaulf studied Orn's armored arm as if he knew what lay beneath the steel. Orn defied the urge to scratch at his own mark, keeping his hand perfectly still so as not to betray what he believed Gaulf had already surmised.

They weren't so different.

"Truth be told, I lost someone to this. The mark. Someone I cared about," Orn replied. "A long time ago, a...friend...and I were wandering somewhere we probably shouldn't have been."

"Did you fall into dark waters too?"

"Not quite, no. Not like the story you shared with me, at least. We thought we knew exactly what we were getting into. We were young, foolish, and loved to explore the forests. Imagine our excitement when we stumbled across some ruins submerged—"

"I thought you said there wasn't water?" Gaulf interjected.

"—deep in the earth itself. Patience, kid." Orn quirked an eyebrow, and the chastened look on Gaulf's face made him smile. "I haven't told anyone this story. Never had the opportunity. Bear with me here."

Gaulf nodded, and Orn waited as silence descended around their camp once more. "Jord and I found a hole in the ground, almost a perfect square, with nothing but darkness inside of it. Against our better judgment, we climbed down into the hole. Should've known better, but like I said, we weren't exactly the responsible sort. Especially when we were together."

Orn paused, his last word hanging in the air.

"In that black abyss, the darkness came to life and launched at us. A stream of shadow, coiling at our limbs, tearing us apart. I tried to hold on." Orn grimaced, his heart racing in his chest as he remembered the terror of that moment. It was a drop in a bucket compared to what followed. Orn shook his head.

"There's got to be more to it than that," Gaulf entreated.

"We found and lit a torch. That drove back the thick blackness we found ourselves in. We then moved through a hallway of stone bricks, green moss swallowing the gray, clogging the air, making it hard to breathe. We pressed on, past a few places where the wall had collapsed, the earth forcing its way in. The further we went, the more the exit receded behind us. Until the hallway opened into a wide, circular room. Imagine our surprise when we noticed someone sitting there, plain as day."

"Who was it? What were they doing there?" Gaulf questioned curiously.

"I wanted to wait, to assess any possible danger, but Jord started shouting. Normally, that would've been me, caterwauling without a second thought. But that day? Jord took charge. Anyway, it wasn't a man, not truly. When we investigated, we discovered the body of someone buried underneath the steel. Forgotten. When I reached for the sword, that's when things went south. That's when the true darkness came.

"Jord screamed for help, but it didn't sound like him. Then the shrieks became sobs, then unsettling laughter. Laughter unlike anything I'd heard in my life. Silence came next. I tried to find Jord, tried to find the torch. Instead, I found the sword laying on the ground, so I took it up. Flailed about, as likely to skewer myself than whatever waited in the dark. I hollered and screamed and swung, until I found Jord. Thing is, I was too late. The torch flared to life briefly, and there was a mural on the wall: a vivid spiral, blue and dancing. And then the darkness came again. And again, and again, slamming into me with intense force. Maybe it did move like water against a rock, against a man dumb enough to fight the darkness with an ancient sword. And yet, against all reason, we got out, but we were not whole. Jord was marked," Orn whispered, the twisting coil of fear inside his stomach knotting tightly.

"That sounds horrible." Gaulf shuddered.

"Horrible barely scratches the surface, but it doesn't quite match what you and the others experienced." Orn laughed bitterly, an odd sound to his own ears. "But not entirely different, is it?"

"How do you mean?"

"Well, the marks came in the day or two following a storm. You said it, I said it, that the storms blew through, thunder loud enough to make the earth rumble. I felt the storm recently; kept me up half the night."

"Scared our goats something fierce. I was surprised they did not escape the pens. What happened next?" Gaulf was leaning that much closer, clearly hanging on every word Orn spoke.

"Whatever that mark is, he succumbed to it. The same way near everyone touched by that magic has. Except you." *So far.* Orn dared not say that aloud, but judging by the look on Gaulf's face, there was no need. Silence stretched between the two of them, and Gaulf rubbed at his arms. "It started with the dreams, seeing people not there. He grew violent and..." Orn grimaced when the taste of ashes filled his mouth.

"Did you...do it?" Gaulf asked.

"Are you sure you want the answer?"

"If you want me to trust you. I deserve to know," Gaulf said.

"Then ask the question properly," Orn replied.

"Did you kill Jord? Did you kill the others?" Orn recognized the resolve it took for Gaulf to ask, and he wouldn't disappoint him.

"I did. Before they could kill anyone else. There was no other way, but even so, I regret it." Orn added another log to the fire. "I suppose it's why I'm trying to get to the bottom of it all. No one else is doing a damn thing, so I might as well try myself." Orn's voice faltered, but he continued. "So Jord's death might have some meaning. So all of their deaths might have meaning." Inhaling sharply, he then said, "I wouldn't mind hearing the rest of your story, son. Might yet be something in there that could point us in the right direction."

"Oh, y-yes. Of course. Where was I?" Gaulf stammered.

"You were being hauled off to jail."

Chapter 9

THE CELL

G AULF WOKE SCREAMING. THE world was dim, unfamiliar and foreign. The stench is what he noticed second, making him almost retch as he fought for air. The threadbare blanket he had been wrapped in was soaked with sweat, as was most of his clothing. His brain was slow to process the sight of the wrought-iron bars protruding from the stone floor to the ceiling, but when he rolled to his side over a pile of musty hay, he understood where he was.

The night before returned to him in fragments, and he remembered the way he had burned so brightly, the way Sige's skin had charred so black it was darker than the hue of night. He watched the scene in his mind's eye as if he were outside himself, a ghost flitting around the edges of the memory.

He leaned further back into the pile of hay, struggling to wrap his head around everything that had transpired. Why had magic marked him? He could feel it inside of him, lying in wait like a spider in its web.

"Where is he? Where is my son?" His da's voice, angry in a way Gaulf had never heard before. "Let us in there, Caspar. For Harvest's sake, this is my son!"

"You know the law as well as I do, Angun. We all saw what Gaulf did," Caspar replied loudly enough that Gaulf could hear him clearly, though he scooted closer to the cell bars anyway. "Magic is not to be tolerated but destroyed at first sign."

"You're daft. This is Gaulf! He's no *mage*, Caspar. Please. This is no evil blight upon the land, as The Paladin would have us believe. This is hardly similar to the reports we've received of people gone crazed.

We all know the stories, that the mages overreached, caused the earth to break, and The Paladin saved us with The Rising. But this is Gaulf. *My son.* For the sake of The Scythe, you swaddled him for me once. I know what reports you have received, but this isn't that. It cannot be," Angun pleaded, causing a shudder in Gaulf's chest. He pressed his face against the bars, feeling an immediate spark of heat in his veins. *Magic.* The word was barbed, no longer as wondrous as it had seemed at first.

"My hands are tied," Caspar said flatly.

"There has to be something, anything, that we can do. *Please.* This isn't right!"

"I've already sent word. Don't make this any harder than it has to be." There was something that savored of grief in Caspar's tone, surprising Gaulf. His shock did not last long, however, for he soon heard a loud thud and a cry of pain followed by a scuffle and a growl from Caspar. "That's your one free hit, Angun. I am sorry. But do it again and you'll force my hand. I do not want to make this any worse than it is. You'd hang next to your son."

"For what?" Angun shouted, the sound twisting Gaulf's gut in knots. He wished he could fix all of this, undo the horrible thing he had done.

"For daring to harbor him, for protecting him, for assaulting me. If word gets out, if Arthur has reason to blab, the entire town may follow suit." With that, Gaulf rose to his feet, gripping the bars tightly when silence descended between the two men outside.

Gaulf felt helpless. Caged. Trapped. He rattled the bars time and time again, but the effort was fruitless, as he suspected it would be. Eventually, he curled back up on the hay, the only comfort the thin blanket, and tried to sleep. But each time he closed his eyes, he saw the noose. His impending death. And the possibility that his family might hang next to him, a length of rope for each of them. Or even the entire town.

Gallows as far as the eyes can see. An entirely different sort of harvest.

That was enough to send him back to his feet, and Gaulf paced the cell. Through a little window he watched the sun chart its course across the sky, and only when moonlight replaced it did he hear someone approach. The wooden slab that was the door creaked as it opened, the orange glow from a torch casting eerie shadows against the walls. He shuffled to the corner and screwed his eyes shut. Gaulf did not want to see whoever this was, nor did he wish to be seen. Not like this. Already he felt as if part of him had cracked and fallen away, like ashes in the wind.

"Gaulf, I have some food for you," Caspar said barely above a whisper, as if he were afraid. Slowly, Gaulf drew his eyes open. There was a steaming platter in Caspar's hand, and Gaulf realized how very empty he was.

"Please, just open the door. Let me out." He hated the desperation in his own voice, but he could not help it. Caspar shook his head.

"You know I cannot do that." A part of Gaulf understood this without Caspar having to say it, but hearing it made the grim reality sink further into his chest, settling there like a stone on the riverbed. "Eat, and I will be back come morning." He slid the platter through the tiny horizontal space at the bottom of the bars, then left without another word.

"At least he left the light," Gaulf murmured to himself, staring at the flickering flame in the lantern. Full of oil as it was, he wondered how long it would last. Till morning? Transfixed by the flame, he stared at it as he ate, tasting nothing. It was all dust in his mouth, but he swallowed it anyway.

The fire in the lantern called to him, and he did not listen.

Somewhere in the depths of another engulfing dream, Gaulf touched the surface world enough that he started to pick up the threads of a conversation that was happening around him. The world came in fits and spasms, tearing him away from the comfort of oblivion. Gaulf wanted nothing more than to sink back into sleep. To flee this waking world and the aches and pains it brought him.

"Maybe the kids are right. I mean, this is *Gaulf*. He's hardly a menace," came the familiar voice nearby. His mind reeled as he tried to piece together what part of it was a dream and what actually was happening. He tightened his hands into fists around the cold iron, standing on shaky legs. The stench of sulfur and ash filled his nose, and soot coated his fingers. Yet his flesh remained unmarred.

"The law is the law, Caspar. You would do well to remember that. A mage is the last thing we need here, and we must do something before Gaulf starts turning people inside out. Or conjures up a plague. Maybe that's why our harvests falter." Manfred paused, if only to draw in a deep breath. "How long has The Paladin held strong in our stead? Staving off the depraved mages to the south, reinforcing The Rising that keeps us safe? How long has he protected us from those who would sully the world with magic? Since he ran the elves into the ground, every last one of the pointy-eared bastards."

"Well, not all of them. Manfred—" Who Gaulf took to be Caspar grunted as another voice spoke over him. That one had to be Arthur's father, the mayor.

"All the more reason we need to deal with this problem. As quickly as possible. We do not need *her* sniffing around. It's bad enough we've attracted the attention of The Paladin's knights, with you sending that damn letter. We could've handled this ourselves." As the world came into focus, Gaulf spied the two sitting at the desk across the room.

"I followed the law, Manfred, and reported it…" Caspar said with a sigh.

"If we're lucky, we'll be exiled north, same as those The Paladin sent running. And if we're not lucky? They'll do to us what they did to the elves." The wood of the mayor's chair creaked when he shifted. "And who would we be to question him?"

"That doesn't strike you as odd? That he's been at this for so long? Is he an elf himself, turned on his own kind?" Caspar asked, his voice lowering as though he were revealing some dark secret.

"It is his duty to protect us, and I am not here to question it. What he does—"

"Bleeding us dry is what he does, and for what? I have heard the stories. I understand the law, probably better than you do. Set that aside for a moment and think about what we've been told. That there's a resurgence of magic users. Up until now, that wasn't our problem. Add to that the fact that we're being heavily taxed so The Paladin can keep up his war against those remaining mages seeking to usurp him. Season in and out, there's little to no relief. And for what? To have our own taken away from us, strung up before our very eyes?" Casper said bitterly. "It's just not right."

"You are bordering on heresy, Caspar," Manfred warned.

"And who's going to say a damn thing, Manfred? You? Say one word and I'll string you up myself. If friends cannot talk amongst themselves, who can?" Caspar grumbled. Gaulf overheard a slight shuffling, then another creak followed by the sound of a cork popping. "I'm just saying that maybe there's more to this. I've seen the same reports from the other towns. I thought we might be safe here, further away from Haven."

"Quit your foolish simpering. You saw what we all saw. None of this changes the fact that magic's outlawed. The punishment for it is known, and The Paladin has spoken. Through his knights we might be cleansed of this filth," the mayor said, as if repeating from some memorized sermon.

"This is nothing like what we've been told," Caspar argued.

"Did Gaulf not conjure fire and lay Sige low with it? Does that not sound like the mages causing havoc across the country? Certainly does to me. We're lucky he did not burn the entire village."

"It hardly does—"

"You heard the histories of before The Rising, when The Paladin moved the earth itself to protect us. Mages summoning creatures from the dirt, doorways to nowhere and everywhere, striking down their opponents with bolts of lightning from the sky. Altering the natural order of things on their own whims, often causing only heartache and pain. Greedy, destructive, evil. They would have subjugated us. The Paladin saved us, Caspar. Ignoring this problem will only cause misery for the entire village," the mayor said, fear coloring his words.

Caspar shook his head. "This is going to break his parents' hearts, if it hasn't already. Angun and Cortney are already struggling to make ends meet. Not to mention, poor Ola and Elga were beside themselves when Gaulf was carted off." Gaulf bit back a sob at the thought of his family, of how they must be feeling while he rotted in this cell. He needed to see them, to talk to them.

"I offered to buy his land but he refused," the mayor replied. The chair beneath him groaned again as he adjusted, the thick wood complaining with the movement. "I take pity on them, I do, but the taxes are the taxes. The law is the law. Mages are to be executed once they are found guilty. Gaulf did what he did, and Sige is going to be laid up with burns for at least a week. Who's going to help *his* parents?"

Gaulf heard the sheriff's angry growl as he spoke. "The boy got what was coming to him twice over and you know that as well as I do. The boy's a bully. As for his parents, don't even get me started on them."

"That may be so, but no one, not a single living soul, deserves what happened to Sige. Dare we say otherwise, we invite the foul taint of magic into our village. Into our very lives. Are you sympathizing with a known mage, Caspar?" The intent was clear, and the silence that followed told Gaulf all he needed to know.

He was alone, and there was no one to help him.

"I am just trying to make sense of a horrible situation. He's just a boy," Caspar explained.

"Dilly-dally too much and The Paladin will send his knights to *investigate* matters more thoroughly to make sure all traces of this corruption, this filth, have been wiped out. You've read the missives just as I have. We have to deal with this quickly and decisively. Do the job you were hired for and none of us will have to worry about our *own* families."

Gaulf held his breath, waiting for a reply from the sheriff that never came.

"Be sure that you deal with this problem by tomorrow."

"Gaulf must stand trial first." Caspar paused with a slight scowl on his face as he held up a hand to forestall the mayor's argumentative squeal. "By your own words, Manfred. I will do my job and we will see this through by the law. A trial to sort this out. One way or the other."

"There is but one way that sees us all keep our heads," the mayor said before he turned and brushed past the sheriff, trudging out the door to the cell area and then disappearing into the darkness beyond. Gaulf watched as Caspar's shoulders slumped, and the sheriff stood there in the torchlight in silence for a moment before he, too, headed out the door. Gaulf stretched his hand between the bars, a whimper escaping his lips.

He wept, his face pressed against the now-warm iron bars, as if he could force his way through them and flee from this wretched place. Briefly, he thought to call upon the fire again. Felt the iron grow that much hotter against his hands before his stomach recoiled.

"No, no, no. I will *not*," Gaulf cried even as the urge inside of him swelled. He could see the symbols of The Spiral, The Door, and The Lightning Bolt clear as day. With them, words he knew but hardly understood waited upon his tongue.

He had but to surrender himself. Much as he had done to start the fire for his friends, much as he had done to burn Sige. It was there. Worming through him. Something twisting and writhing, making him want *more*.

"No!" Gaulf screamed into the darkness. With a violent shake of his head, he tore away from the iron bars that had grown red-hot where his face had been. "I will not, I will not!" He scurried away from the cell door, tripping over his own feet and ending up as a pile of limbs on the floor.

It was only when another sob wracked his body and the darkness became too much to bear that he relented. Gaulf did not surrender to the need to *burn,* no. Not quite like the whispers enticed him to. Instead, he coaxed a small fire to life in his palms, letting it drive out the darkness that had coalesced around him, threatening to smother with its distinct lack of light. There, within the glow of the swirling fire, he lost himself. Transfixed by the hypnotic pull of the fire's movements, Gaulf closed his eyes and let the light sweep across his eyelids.

"*Beware...*" came a voice not his own, and Gaulf shuddered when he realized the words had come from his own mouth.

His eyes shot open as he looked around the small cell. He was alone. Had the voice truly been his own? Between the stress of the day and those words echoing in his ears, he felt the sudden heaviness of his limbs.

Closing his eyes, letting the fire in his palms extinguish, he welcomed sleep once more. Every fiber of his being ached, and oblivion embraced him like a lover.

"Who are you?" Gaulf asked, glancing through the bars of his cell. At first, as he looked at the form that stood in the room, he thought it was *her* asking him that question. She stared at him expectantly, hatred in her eyes, her mouth contorted in anger. She then turned about with a swirl of her dress and stalked away, disappearing into the shadows.

Gaulf blinked away the vision.

He shivered and stretched his hands through the bars toward that lamp, drawing in what solace he could. The world outside seemed so distant, and he looked toward the window once more. Clouds gathered in the sky, blotting out whatever light was out there. Was it morning, or was the sun on its way beneath the horizon?

Gaulf pressed his face against the bars again until the metal grew hot not just from his frantic motion, nor the flush of his face trying to squeeze through, but the heat that was building inside of him. One he held tightly in the grip of his hands, but even so it seemed to slip grain by grain through his fingers.

"Who are you?" The words were parroted back at him, and he retreated further into his cell. His own voice was hoarse and came from every nook and cranny from within the cell. Gaulf cowered in a corner and wrapped the torn blanket around his head to blot out the world.

But the voice soon called to him again, and Gaulf tossed the blanket aside and started pacing the length of his cell.

"I swear it has grown smaller, hasn't it?" he wondered aloud. The cell seemed to fluctuate even as he watched, his stomach threatening a storm. "No, if anything, it has grown larger," he answered himself, which hardly came as a surprise. There was no one but himself to talk to. The cell was breaking him down piece by piece, and something else was filling in the cracks. With every moment that passed, Gaulf felt that much more agitated. He tried to count his laps around the small cell, but even that was hard to keep track of in the mindless course of the passing of time.

The days came and went. He'd fall asleep and wake, left adrift in the nebulous and shrinking confines of that cell. Darkness and light played an eternal game of chase outside of the window, and he was helpless to alter their paths. Eventually, in frustration, he threw himself to the ground again as if that might change anything.

Nevertheless, sleep came again. And again. And again. Gaulf turned beneath the onslaught of nothing and everything. She was there, and then she was not. The forms that lingered and lurked became more and more frequent until they refused to leave at all. He heard their voices, a thread that pushed its way into his brain and unsettled him. He could not hide from it, and eventually the lamp flared as he beat his hand against the wrought-iron bars of the cell.

Burning bright, the lamp consumed its oil. In that sudden burst of brilliance, the shadows fled. Even that was temporary, however, for as the lamp's fuel ran low, the entire jail fell into absolute darkness. Gaulf let out a cry in that pervasive lack of light and scrambled against the iron once more. What dim light filtered in through that window filled in the darkness as his eyes adjusted to the change. Gaulf's chest heaved with the need to breathe, spurred on by the need to see.

Then the lamp would go dark. The shadows would return, and Gaulf had nowhere to hide. Not from the darkness, and not from himself. Not from *her*.

Chapter 10

THE CASTLE

Laela's gaze was fixed on the castle from where she stood amidst the throng of people waiting to pass through the gate. Despite having her hood pulled up to cover her face, the people shied away from her. It was hardly new. Laela had heard the whispers her entire life, but paid it no mind. Rather, she fancied parents told their children stories about her and what The Paladin would do to them if they misbehaved. Sallow faces froze in their beseeching cries to get in once they saw who was jostling past them toward the gates.

Thick stone comprised both the walls and the large keep within. There were a few other fortifications surrounding the middle structure and a number of buildings that were hastily constructed over the years to accommodate the influx of villagers flocking to the capital to escape failing farms or answer The Paladin's call for fresh soldiers.

Driving the forests further into the countryside.

Some poor sods had even tried tilling the rocky land around the castle some years ago, not that it had gone well for them.

A memory then struck her.

"The Paladin and his army are coming! We of Embrosi are now all that stand between him and our people," said a familiar voice spreading over the courtyard like smoke on the wind.

"What are we to do?"

"We're cut off from the rest of Osivesi!"

"The earth itself has risen against us, and magic is no more!" These cries and others rose in a burble of panic that spread like wildfire through the gathered elves.

"We stand and we fight, then we take this bastard down," the queen said.

The stench of blood filled her nose, and the remnants of some centuries past threatened to overcome her, but Laela shoved them away with great effort. The rattle of arrows in her quiver became sharper in her hearing, as well as the chatter of the humans squeezed together around her. It was useless to think on events best left behind.

Ignoring the flare of pain, the pang of a feeling she dared not put a name to, Laela straightened her spine, weaving through the crowd until she at last came to the heavy wooden gates set atop a cobbled path.

"There she goes, The Paladin's *elf*," said someone in the faceless throng. Laela paused briefly, long enough to study the rough peasants who sported a week's worth of dust from the roads. There were so many of them, appearing day after day to beseech The Paladin for relief. Taxes were too high, there was not enough food, mages destroyed their homes. It hardly mattered to Laela.

"What do you think you're looking at?" asked one of the peasants, squaring off in front of her. There were more curses and nearly unintelligible words lobbed at her from the press of bodies that found their way into her path. Ignoring them, she took a step forward and kept her attention on the one in the middle. Whatever they saw in her and the dagger she brandished caused them to have second thoughts. The lot of them, except for the leader, had turned tail and ran as she approached, baring her teeth in a grin.

The two met, nearly chest to chest, and it was his turn to run.

Laela was tempted to give chase, but so long as they were out of her way and no other thought to fling more curses at her, there was little need. Under the weight of countless eyes and murmured words, she headed for the castle.

The people in the streets were bundled up against the cold, huddled and shivering in their threadbare clothing. Where there was room there were makeshift firepits, and the smell of smoke set her on edge. She held her breath to calm her racing heart until it burned in her chest and her eyes started to water.

Between that smell and the memories it threatened to summon, as well as the group of peasants who had not yet moved, Laela felt trapped. She wanted to claw her way through to the castle, but at least the stomach-turning scent of burning wood covered the stench of the people. The chill had not yet managed to smother that funk. Maybe this winter would be harder than the last, and it'd solve the problem of people flocking to the city and getting in her way. It'd also keep the other knights busy with the more mundane task of keeping the roads safe around Haven.

The castle's outer wall stood tall, but the towers loomed above it, overshadowing the growing city. Nearer the wall, the houses were crammed together, made of stone and with slanted roofs. Haven would face a housing crisis soon enough.

Past the gates, the sprawl of homes became more organized and the streets just a little cleaner. Not that they were much clearer, but enough that the smell of baking bread was noticeable over other, less enjoyable, odors. There were some shopkeepers out on their stoops, talking animatedly with patrons as Laela passed. They shut their mouths quickly when they spotted her. She slithered out of the way of a knight atop a horse with a grimace, hoping for a hot bath when she arrived at the castle. The knight rode by with barely a passing glance, dressed in gold-and-white armor. Her horse was with Willaime and she regretted leaving it behind. How quickly she might have trampled her way through the gates with it.

"Stop glaring daggers at them, Laela," said Willaime, nearly startling her. He tugged his helmet off, revealing a sweaty shock of salt-and-pepper hair. When had he gotten so old?

Laela shot a glare his way but said nothing. Williame seemed drained, as ready for a respite as she. His eyes, more gray than blue, searched her face. For what, she wasn't sure. How long had they been on the road? The days blurred together lately. She rolled her shoulders, forcing away the itch to find a dagger to hold onto. Willaime would chastise her for that.

"I hate being inside these damned walls." Laela paused and shook her head. "Almost as much as I hate wading through the chaff every time we come home. Why does he let them mob us like this?" She knew the answer. Heard it countless times. Though the hatred she harbored for Haven ran deep, there was nowhere else for her to go. Elves weren't exactly welcomed in Embrosi. "Maybe next time I will just wait outside the gates while you deal with the busy work. There's an inn that boasts a fine stout ale."

Williame sighed. "I don't see why you bother walking."

"To irritate you." It was only partially false. Laela would never admit to enjoying her last few moments of freedom, despite the cost.

"You know how this works. He has proclaimed that we all report to him when we return," Willaime said. "And *all* includes you, Laela."

Laela knew further argument was pointless.

The streets of the city started out wide on the outskirts where the newer buildings were as the city stretched toward the wilds. Winding her way through, they became narrower when they neared the castle proper. A tall, gray wall was marred by patches of moss and vines that stubbornly clung to the stone. The castle was mostly square in shape but imposing in size. Laela had memorized the layout of the structure many years ago, spending much of her childhood exploring the twists of its stairways and the dark of the hidden passages. Her gaze roamed to the solitary tower looming above the others, which she had long ago claimed for herself. The rest of the castle stank of The Paladin and his men, and she preferred her own company to theirs.

Huddled together at the castle's grand entrance were petitioners who gathered for daily supplications. These were more than the rabble from outside the city—they were permanent residents of Haven, and none bothered Laela when she pushed past them in her trek toward the main doors.

"Hopefully we can stay a little longer this time," Willaime said as they made their way toward the castle's inner gate, looking anywhere but at her. She sneered, rolling her eyes. How many jobs had they been on recently? Hardly caring enough to count, and only wanting to find her bed to collapse in, his comment irked her.

"Bite your tongue clean off, jinxing us like that," Laela snapped. "I am going to my room. I'll be along shortly *for the report*."

They strode through the entrance to the castle together, out of the sunlight and into the relative darkness of the structure. As Laela's eyes adjusted, she noticed the mostly barren walls of the hall. The stone was dull, no different from the exterior, though The Paladin's banners provided some color. The elf sniffed as she examined them, her stomach turning at the sight of the red sword in a field of white.

Further along the wall there was some discoloration on a few of the stones, outlines of tapestries that once hung there centuries prior.

Willaime sighed. "Be quick."

Wordlessly, she headed for one of the corridors to the side of the main hall that led to a spiraling staircase belonging to the tower she called home. Whatever that word meant. No one dared come there, which suited her just fine, except for when The Paladin sent a steward to summon her.

Laela marched up the stairs, pausing at one of the thin windows to gaze out over the courtyard to drink in the light. At this height, the people below looked like little more than ants. She could almost imagine herself alone, and she inhaled a deep, steadying breath at the thought.

The tower rooms were sparse by design, containing what Laela needed and little else. There was an assortment of weapons, some in various states of disrepair, and a workbench that had surely seen better days. Laela dropped her rucksack onto her bed and set about unpacking. There was not much—she preferred to travel light. What she bothered to keep were the daggers that she frequently secreted on her person. She then hung her bow on its rack, placing the quiver next to it.

Deciding to be anything but quick, Laela sat on the stool in front of the workbench and sorted through the daggers. She set aside those with edges that hadn't yet begun to lose their bite, keeping those she would need to sharpen. Whetstone in hand, Laela took up the first dagger and lost herself in the rhythmic work, the monotonous scraping noise a balm for the chaos in her mind.

"Good enough," Laela whispered to the empty room after testing the blade against her finger. Her reward was a sudden jab of pain. She licked the drop of blood that beaded on her fingertip and then set the blade aside while she searched the collection. Slowly, methodically, she worked the blades on the whetstone until each one was ready to find flesh to call home. Absently, she wondered if Willaime were already standing in front of The Paladin, both of them lamenting her tardiness. With a sigh, she ensured all of the blades were secreted away.

She then strode over to a small door in her room. Laela stared at the wooden frame, not remembering the last time she dared approach it. But something spurred her on, and without further hesitation she opened the door and ducked inside. It was mostly bare, the walls stained with outlines of bookcases and a desk taken long ago. Along the furthest one was a bas relief chiseled into stone.

Her eyes focused on the scene before her. Grumbling, Laela brushed strands of cobwebs from the surface, revealing her mother's severe face, the word *Embrosi* carved below.

"Mother." Laela remembered the queen's hatred of that word and corrected herself. "Queen Alizandra." Here, in Haven, were too many reminders of her mother, of a time that predated The Paladin. Grief sought to topple her carefully constructed tower to cage both memories and emotions, and she seethed when she felt the crack form in her armor. Ser Gregoris had robbed her of so much, and yet she was trapped in servitude to him.

Ignoring the burning in her chest, she whirled about and left the room, slamming the door.

She sniffed. "No point in dawdling any further." The words were loud against the relative silence. And though generally she preferred it that way, in this moment it seemed hollow.

A mixture of knights, a collection of petitioners, even some servants scurrying about like rats populated the corridors. Laela paid them little mind, chattering mindlessly as they did about some gossip or minor incident, though she felt the heat of their suspicious glares all the same. She knew that many of them watched her in hopes of catching her in some illicit deed or other so that they could bring this revelation to The Paladin and be rid of her.

Their complaints would be summarily dismissed. Ser Gregoris would not permit Laela to escape his grasp, no matter what the rabble whispered about her. At least she had stopped goading them.

"Fucking *elf*. I don't understand why he always dotes on you, giving you the lively hunts." It was a knight, a guard of the palace. His words were angry, the vitriol pouring through the narrow slits of his helm.

Quick like a viper, she was in front of him and had the dagger pressed against his neck.

"Do I need to make an example of you?"

"You would not dare. The Paladin—" The knight squealed as Laela increased the pressure at the blade's tip.

"Would lecture me and send me on my way. And you'd be dead." Laela paused, eying him from head to toe, then smirked. "Run along now." Laela withdrew the dagger just enough for the knight to dart away.

The hallway emptied into the throne room, devoid of the gilded decorations one might usually expect. Her mother's throne, creeping with vines and thorns, was long since gone, and the tables that used to line the hall were shoved against the walls in an effort to discourage feasts and frivolity. In the gaps along the stone stood several knights, their steel helmets no doubt hiding their own glares in the wake of the elf's arrival. Laela was deliberate here, moving with forced grace to still her mind.

Her throat tightened at the sight of Ser Gregoris in his famously resplendent armor. Encased in plate and chain, the suit was the envy of Haven. Whenever he moved the metal clanked angrily, the only emotion that spilled from the ruler these days.

Near him lay a crumpled body, a rasping sob emanating from it.

"Is this it, Laela?" Ser Gregoris asked, turning away from his gathered knights, ignoring the broken man on the floor. It was as if The Paladin did not believe that the peasant were something other than what he initially seemed. He knew the truth. There was no lying to The Paladin, not that she hadn't tried more often than she cared to remember in her childhood. His punishments for deception, perceived or otherwise, always earned her a trip to the dungeons beneath the castle. To be housed next to the mages, to hear their unending screams, the darkness alive with pain.

"This is our most recent acquisition, yes," Laela answered flatly.

The Paladin turned his attention to the trembling form on the floor before him. "How do you plead to these charges?" The prisoner flinched but said nothing, so Laela provided motivation in the form of a swift kick to his gut, which sent him sprawling forward. "Answer," The Paladin spat.

"I haven't done a thing wrong. I swear! This is all just a misunderstanding." More gibbering words followed, and Laela could hardly make sense of them. However, the pleading was hardly new. Each of those marked who were brought to justice begged in a similar fashion.

"A misunderstanding? You were consorting with forces unknown, and that is…what? An accident?"

"Y-Yes, ser! I have done no wrong, you must believe me," cried the man. "You have to believe me."

"Your flesh is marked, and thus, you have damned yourself," The Paladin said, leaning forward to speak in the face of the broken man.

"No, not at all, ser. I found a book, an old one, and it came to life. The writing came off of the page and wrapped itself around me, bade me to listen, to watch. I did not want to see, I did not ask for this. I am no mage. Please, you have to trust me. I know you protect us—" A plated hand gripped the roughspun fabric of his tunic.

"You admit it then, that you are marked by magic. My law is clear: magic is forbidden." The Paladin straightened himself, towering over the man. "You have given yourself to dark forces. Where is your mark?" The man sniffled but obeyed, tugging the collar of his shirt down to bare his shoulder where The Quill sigil was burned into the flesh.

Laela winced at the sound of something breaking, the spray of blood and spittle coating the stone after The Paladin dropped the man, who devolved into a mess of unintelligible babbling, pleading with anyone he thought might listen.

"Empty the room," The Paladin ordered. "I have…more questions." There was a pause, and Laela swore the ground wobbled beneath her feet as the weight of that helmeted gaze centered on her. "And you. You are needed again. Willaime has the paperwork, so do not tarry. The horses have been replaced and saddled. Provisions are set."

"Another one already?" She blinked, surprised. Eager as she was, she had to contain herself in front of Ser Gregoris, lest he yank the opportunity from her. "I cannot even sleep in my own bed for a night?" Whether he saw the furrowing of her brow or the edge to her words, she was not sure, but he let out a snort from somewhere within the steel of his helmet, gesturing to Willaime.

"Go," he said with finality. Laela glanced behind him to the place where her mother's throne once sat and felt rage bubble up inside of her. If only he weren't so armored. It would take but a moment. A quick thrust between his ribs. But it was impossible, she knew.

The Paladin ordered, she followed. There was no alternative.

"We'll be on our way then." Laela exited the throne room with Willaime, rebuking his attempts at conversation. The thick doors did little to bar the screams emanating from within once closed.

Laela turned abruptly toward the servants' stairwell, abandoning Willaime in a huff. The twisting, cramped tunnel of age-darkened stone closed in around her as she descended, providing her with blessed silence as she collected her thoughts. They squirmed through her head, defying any effort to rein them in or push them away entirely. She hated remembering, the pain of it, and grimaced as she forced herself to breathe normally.

She shook her head and cursed aloud, drawing the hood of her cloak over her head when she stepped out of the stairwell and into the castle kitchens. There was no good that could come of thinking on things long past. Besides, there wasn't much time to prepare, certain as she was that Willaime was already waiting for her in the stables.

The scent of fresh bread and cinnamon soothed her irritation. Ignoring the scullery maids and servants who scurried out of her way, Laela grabbed a bag, pilfering a few of the fresh sweet rolls and loaves then ducking back out before the oppressive heat of the oven could provoke a sweat on her brow. The corridor beyond was dimly lit, making the shadows of the castle seem menacing. Laela trailed a finger along the stone, her mind drifting. How often had she wandered through here in her youth?

Outside the castle, the courtyard was full of The Paladin's knights, each busying themselves with some task or other. No one dared to speak to her, each clad in heavy armor that clanked, grating on her nerves. Unbidden memories of how lush and green this place once was resurfaced, a contrast to the barren land trodden to churned earth. She remembered too well the tree she had planted, following the drab wall to the corner where the stump remained, as stubborn as her. Laela kneeled before it, her hand tracing the rings from the center outward, a spiraling touch.

Willaime stood on the other side of the courtyard, waiting.

"Where are they?" Laela asked after she strode over.

"I have not retrieved them yet." Willaime stared at her over his own horse as he spoke. She fell in line with Willaime to cross the courtyard, following him down stone stairs whose walls swallowed the light. At the bottom waited a sturdy door banded with iron. They traveled through this one to another set of stairs leading into the depths of the castle, and Laela felt her stomach lurch with the descent.

When they came finally to a lone door set in the stone, Laela wrinkled her nose at the stench of rot and mildew that permeated the wood. It was the smell of unwashed flesh that had been left to stew in a cell for far too long.

"Must we?" Laela asked.

"We must. The wells have run dry around here," Willaime explained, looking ahead and not at her. They both knew what was coming, and he refused to be apologetic about it. Willaime opened the door, and she followed him down the twists and turns while the malodorous air grew colder with every step. They came to a solid iron door with a knight standing at the ready in front of it. "Ho, Ser Roald. "We're here on business—"

"Let me see your writ," Ser Roald said, holding a gauntleted hand outward, the scrape of metal making Laela's teeth grind together. How any of them could bear to hear that constant noise, she would never understand.

"We are here for Dolan Blyth, Alke Gravese, and Gilbert Morley." Willaime offered the writ, which Roald studied slowly. Even here, The Paladin's protocols were rigidly followed. Laela hated the wait and wondered if the knight thought Willaime might abscond with the prisoners. As if either of them were here for anything but business or had any desire to free these men for any other reason than what was intended. She had asked about that once, and Willaime had just shrugged his shoulders.

"You may proceed," the knight said flatly, drawing forth a rusted key from a pouch that hung at his side and handing it to Willaime, who then opened the door. "Second one on the left." Willaime walked into the dungeons without another word, Laela following close behind.

A row of five cells was carved into the stone on each side, no wider than ten feet and no higher than the same, enclosed by rough iron bars she had witnessed countless faces pressed against. Now, they were mostly empty. Either the feckless halfwits of Haven had gone quiet, or The Paladin had taken more men into service. Laela peered over

Willaime's shoulder at the only occupied cell, the light from a single torch casting an eerie glow upon its inhabitants.

"What do we have here?" asked the largest and dirtiest of the three men. Laela rolled her eyes.

"It's your lucky day, gentlemen." Willaime unrolled the writ and read aloud, "You are hereby offered your freedom, if you but enter into the service of Ser Gregoris—"

"Yeah, yeah, we've heard the spiel. Whatever gets us out of here, right, Dolan? Alke?" The man was grimy, balding, and sneered at the two of them. The way Gilbert's eyes followed her told her all she needed to know. Laela's hand brushed the hilt of her dagger, which earned her a severe warning glance from Willaime. "Come here, Dolan," Gilbert said.

"What?" Dolan, the smaller man, seemed slower on the uptake and only then realized they had visitors. Gilbert dragged the man closer and pointed a meaty finger at Laela. This drew the other one's attention from where he had been huddled in the corner, and he came to join the other two in silence.

"She coming with us?" The leer that spread over Gilbert's face was almost comical to Laela. He would be dead before he tried anything untoward.

"You are hereby offered your freedom if you but enter into the service of Ser Gregoris, The Paladin. Vow to help in hunting down those who have turned to perverse forces not meant for man. Do you so vow?" Willaime secreted the writ away in his own knight's pouch, seemingly unbothered by their lecherous line of questioning.

"Perverse? I think he's got you pegged, Alke," Dolan said with a snicker.

"We need men to hunt down a mage who goes by the name of Gaulf Angunson and has marked himself in service to darker forces. We need to find him before he causes havoc. We have sent three men ahead, but we'll need to assist. Let's go." The three men retreated at the mention of a mage.

"If they are too *afraid* to be of any use, let them rot in the cell, Willaime. We do not need them." *We never do.* She narrowed her eyes at the prisoners in challenge.

"Afraid? Hardly! I'll show any damn fool using magic what for." Gilbert puffed out his chest but deflated easily when Dolan poked his stomach.

"I'll take my chances here." Dolan shook his head.

"Told you they were scared," Laela said loudly, making all three of the men bristle.

"Listen, if it gets me my freedom? Sure, I'll help you hunt some mages." Dolan kept blathering on, but Laela tuned it out. It was not unlike what she'd heard many times before.

"I'll have to think about it. Come see me tomorrow." Gilbert chortled at himself, his large mass shaking as he did so.

"This is your one chance. You come with me now or you will see the gallows come the dawn. So," Willaime sighed, "do you vow?"

"I do," Gilbert said with a huff.

"I guess," Dolan added, shrugging.

"Alke?" Willaime's words drew the silent man's attention, who gave a slow nod in response. "I need to hear you say the words." The man's face was vacant until Gilbert swatted his shoulder.

"Say the words, you dolt, so we can get on with this," Dolan spat.

"I do," Alke drawled.

"Welcome to the service of Ser Gregoris," Willaime said, moving to unlock the door. Laela could not help but shy away from the men, and Willaime remained between her and the three as they filed out of the cell. "Proceed, gentlemen, and we will get you outfitted appropriately. Your service is for good, and you will be aptly rewarded." As they passed the jailer, Willaime returned the key. Laela took up the rear and followed the three men and Willaime up the stairs. The stench of the dungeon stalked the freed men, but that was better than the alternative of being the one to lead them back to the surface.

Laela let Willaime deal with getting the men swords and leather armor, not wanting to be in their presence more than was necessary. In the sweet air of the courtyard, she reviewed the items in her saddlebags, ensuring there were provisions enough for the journey. Willaime was across the grand space, giving the former prisoners a cursory explanation of their new gear.

She peeked up and over her horse, standing on her tiptoes, to stare at the scene. The fools were more apt to run each other through than they were to be of any actual use. Gilbert was hacking away with the sword as if it were a hammer, and Dolan looked like he could hardly hold the length of metal without shaking from its weight. Alke stared at the blade as if it held all of the secrets to life within it, and she trusted him even less for it.

After the weapons were sheathed, Willaime introduced them to their mounts. Older horses, ones that had been through this song and dance more times than they could count. She felt Gilbert's hungry gaze on her every few minutes. This one was going to be trouble. It wasn't an uncommon problem. When the men they would free saw her, they lost what little minds they had. She would have to keep her eyes on Gilbert. Dolan was worth a wary glance or two, but Alke was a different matter entirely. He seemed more likely to run off than to accost her.

Either way, this would be no different than the last few quarries they hunted. Bored already, and wanting to familiarize herself with her fresh mount, Laela climbed into the saddle. She leaned over its neck and whispered soothingly in its face, exchanging a glance with a warm, but alien, eye that watched her knowingly. Did it feel the same apprehension she did? The horse was nudged into motion with pressure from her heels, and she directed it into a few laps around the courtyard, losing herself in the movements.

"We do not have enough time to make this scum ready, Willaime." Laela urged her mount to a stop, enjoying the scene before her. Dolan was being dragged along half out of his saddle, and Gilbert had finally managed to climb onto his horse without spooking the beast. Alke was astride his, apparently dozing off. The men, wearing armor not crafted for them, carrying weapons that had passed through countless hands before theirs, were a sorry sight. It was comical, though Laela understood the implications.

"Are you men ready for this?" Willaime called to the trio as he mounted his own horse. How he kept a straight face through all of this, she would never know. "I will proceed, and you three will follow. Laela will bring up the rear. If you tarry, know that you do so at your own peril." He gestured for them to follow, and she rolled her eyes.

If nothing else, she could lose herself in the hunt to come.

Chapter 11

THE TRIAL

LYING IN HIS CELL, pacing about the small enclosure, trying the locked door—none of it mattered. Gaulf's mind spun as he searched for a way out, a way to the fresh air outside. The stench of himself was hardly the worst part of his imprisonment, but it certainly wasn't helping matters.

"They'll have to see reason, to listen to me." His shadow bobbed its head from side to side, disagreeing with him. In truth, he knew better. Deep down inside, something *broke*—more than just his heart—at the onslaught of loneliness.

That is, until the door leading to the cells jiggled in its frame. Gaulf rushed to the bars, pressing his face between them to smell the sweet, fresh air wafting inside as the door opened. The relief died as quickly as it came when he heard frantic whispering on the other side. Whoever spoke did so with no little command and anger.

"The mayor?" Gaulf's stomach churned as he closed his eyes to blot out the world. Whoever Arthur's father was speaking to was urgent in his tone, pleading. But he still could not place the voice.

The sheriff strolled inside, closing the door behind him. He stole a glance at his hand, and Gaulf followed his gaze, curious about what the sheriff was gripping so tightly.

"I do not want any more of the dark. Please," Gaulf begged, his eyes widening.

"I know. But them's the rules. So say the knights, and, well, maybe if we play by their rules we can make this better," Caspar explained quietly, as though Gaulf were some skittish horse and not a young man. "Put the hood on and I'll take you for a walk. Stretch your legs a bit. How's that sound?"

Gaulf nodded meekly, lowering his head to let the sheriff slide the canvas sack over his face, shutting out the world and filling his nose with the scent of old grain.

Caspar patted his back gently but insistently, the meaning not lost on Gaulf. "I'll guide you." Caspar led Gaulf out through the jail, and he heard a scoff somewhere to his left. "Shut your mouth, Manfred. Now's neither the time nor place for your bluster." There was no reply to Caspar's reprimand, but the hand at Gaulf's back pressed more firmly. Sunlight filtered through the canvas sack, and Gaulf choked on a sob. Any bit of light was a welcome sight after the long darkness of his imprisonment.

Wood gave way to earth, the sound muffled while Gaulf shuffled along. He heard the gossip of the villagers as he passed, their not-so-subtle accusations a sharp prick to his heart.

Gaulf.

Magic.

Evil.

The noises faded when another door opened, and what little light Gaulf had felt warm his body vanished, darkness swallowing him once more after Caspar moved him inside another building. Even here he could breathe easier than in the cell, and Gaulf did what he could to savor it. The burlap began to itch, but a loud, unfamiliar voice distracted him from it well enough.

"There are no gallows erected. Why is this?" Gaulf turned his head toward the voice. The anger in it made him recoil, and Caspar must have sensed that. He took Gaulf by the arm and settled him into a small chair.

"Ser Dilton, come now," said Caspar from behind Gaulf. "He has a right to a trial."

"And yet my question remains unanswered. What if this mage gets free? Steals your skin for his own nefarious deeds?" Gaulf spied a looming presence position itself in front of him, a hazy shape that resembled a monster more than a man.

"Build the gallows! Hang the mage!" Another voice, this one higher in pitch, devolved into laughter following the cries for Gaulf's execution.

"What Ser Wybert says is not wrong. The gallows should have been built already. By the time we arrived, to expedite matters. As this is not the case, I expect construction to start immediately." Gaulf's mouth burned, sweat pooling around his head, and he almost opened his mouth to speak.

"Build the gallows? If there is to be a trial, perhaps we should wait on the outcome of that, should we not?" Caspar said, undeterred. "I realize there has been an influx of these incidents, but Gaulf is not a threat. I've known him his entire life. He deserves to be heard."

"If you understand there has been a rising tide of magic, an apostasy of their mortal souls, then why do you insist on delaying us in our duties? Duties that bind, of and for The Paladin?" Every word from Ser Dilton made Gaulf's stomach clench for the finality they evoked.

"Other than a chance for Gaulf to be given a fair trial according to the law, you mean?" Caspar's reply, gruff and stern, bolstered Gaulf. "Surely while there is cause for concern here, it should not make us abandon our ways. Let clearer heads prevail. Let us find out what *really* happened."

"Are you calling Arthur a liar, Caspar?" Manfred's wheedling voice piped up. "By The Harvester—"

"Watch your mouth with such talk. Invoking that name will find you no succor. Instead, turn your eyes and hearts back to The Paladin." This came from the knight clanking in front of Gaulf.

Silence stretched on, until Gaulf wondered if his ears ceased to work, before the mayor spoke. "You said it yourself when you were getting the boy into the cell, Caspar. He's been marked. What more do you need?" Manfred asked, his voice seemingly traveling about the room. *He's pacing,* Gaulf thought.

"By The Scythe, Manfred, you are a blasted idiot," Caspar muttered.

"Marked?" Dilton asked, driving the room to silence. At the mention of it, an itch burned furiously in Gaulf's arm where the mark lay waiting.

The hand on Gaulf's shoulder disappeared, and he hoped to make a break for it. Any breath he took in the hood became that much more sweltering, and he stood quickly. However, Caspar drove him back into the chair, drawing up Gaulf's sleeve in the process. His stomach twisted, and he could practically feel the air leave the room as each of the knights gasped. Instinctively, Gaulf recoiled, but the chair and the crowding bodies gave him little room to maneuver away.

"Cover it," Ser Dilton said, retreating from Gaulf. "How can you wish to delay any further knowing the mark he bears? The boy needs to be dealt with *now*."

"I simply cannot permit his execution without Gaulf having a chance to speak. To defend himself. It is his right," Caspar replied tersely.

They argued in circles, their voices buzzing irritably and coming no closer to an agreement. The hood, sweaty and damp, stuck to his face, making breathing difficult. What little light filtered through the sack shone like the stars through the rough canvas.

Closing his eyes against it did little good, because it followed him into the recesses of his own mind. A barbed web of light ensnared him, making him look. Making him *see*. Striding toward him, the look on *her* face angry. Her mouth moved but there was no sound, and she ran past him at something vague in the distance.

The chattering around him echoed like thunder—words like *trial* and *hanging at dawn* settling like a malevolent force around him. He paid them little mind, even if they stuck like burrs to the fringes of his brain. Ignoring their blustering, Gaulf ran. For all that he was worth, his breath hammering in his chest, he ran after *her*.

No matter how fast he was, he never caught her. She ran toward the rising sun until she became little more than a silhouette on the horizon.

The coming light obliterated even that.

"*Beware*," Gaulf called after her, his throat raw, his breath coming in jagged bursts. Too late he felt the cold press of steel against his throat and was ripped from the vision. "Where—" A tall, lanky knight in front of him motioned with his hand, the blade firm in his grip.

"You will speak only when spoken to." The knight speaking had to be Ser Dilton, as far as Gaulf could piece together from the deep baritone of his voice. "Do you understand?"

Gaulf only nodded.

"Tell us what happened the night of the festival," Caspar said calmly, though his hand trembled on Gaulf's shoulder.

"Where is she? Where did she go?" The words leaped out of Gaulf's mouth, his mind cracking as the images cycled.

"Don't worry about her, son. We can talk about that later. She's fine, I'm sure," Casper said, and Gaulf swore he could hear the smile in his tone. "Tell us about Sige, about what happened at the festival. What did you do?"

"Know that I will have Ser Wybert run you through here and now should you but give me cause," Ser Dilton added, barely letting the sheriff finish speaking. Gaulf's stomach roiled again, bile storming into his throat. His heart hammered faster than he could fathom.

"Give the boy a moment to breathe, damn you!" Caspar stepped closer to Dilton until Gaulf could make out their vague shapes standing nose to nose.

"Watch yourself," Ser Dilton snapped. "I'd hate to leave more of a mess to clean up in here."

"Listen here—" Caspar started but Gaulf cut him off with a whisper.

"He attacked me." Remembering the night, the feel of the fire in his hands, made his head swim. Gaulf paused, but Ser Dilton made a motion with his hand to continue. "I was trapped beneath him, and then felt something overcome me," Gaulf stammered, relying on momentum to carry him through. "I was unable to catch my breath, unable to get free, and it just poured out of me. I was *so* angry that he hurt me, that he has always hurt us. It made me mad, so I fought back. I think it surprised Sige as much as it did me." He inhaled deeply, shuddering, and fought off the sob building inside of him.

"What happened next?" Ser Dilton leaned down and tore away the canvas sack, revealing an ugly grimace contorting his already harsh features. Gaulf glanced over his shoulder at the sheriff. Caspar's body was tense, as if ready to intervene, until Ser Dilton's companion, Ser Eggar, approached.

"I felt the fire come to my call, like out in the woods," Gaulf whispered. Fear coursed through him, filling him to bursting. He clung to the arms of the chair, having little else to hold onto as the world spun around him.

When a small twist of smoke curled into the air in front of Gaulf's face, when the scent of burning wood overwhelmed his senses, he started to gag. Gaulf tried to *stop*, peeling his fingers from the wood only to discover the chair arms had been charred by his magic. A stark reminder that he could not scrub away.

Everyone, even Caspar, moved away from him, horrified.

Gaulf doubled over as pain tore through him. Into him. Ripping along his nerves, from his fingers to his wrists, and progressing along his toes and up his legs. A wave of agony slammed into him, making him cry out.

That golden light *curdled* and knotted inside of him, then began to claw its way out. Climbing upward like dinner gone wrong.

The thought of the fire surged inside of him.

Saliva welled in his mouth and Gaulf swallowed it, wrapping his arms over the sudden cramps in his stomach as his body convulsed. "Please." No one listened, no one dared move, until one of the knights turned toward him. Stepping out from behind the armored man, Gaulf watched *her* emerge.

The face from the crowd at the festival, the one plaguing him in his cell. The hatred in her eyes, the wicked curl of her lips—both of those worried him less than the dagger in her hand. The blade was pointed at him when she stalked soundlessly forward. He could not drag his eyes away from her, nor the way that she moved like smoke. He could see *through* her when she placed the knife against his neck.

Her shadow lengthened, but her dagger never found purchase. Something wrapped around her feet and wrenched her away, back to the darkness. She screamed.

That primal sound shattered the world.

The knights, Caspar, and the mayor withdrew further from Gaulf, from the smoldering marks on the chair. Gaulf tried to stand, tried to push past them to find her, but Caspar ran forward and shoved him back down, placing himself between the knights' swords and Gaulf.

"Where is she? I have to see her. I have to find her!" Gaulf shrieked, a sudden fervor overtaking him as he tried to *remember*. Something caught in the corner of his mind, a niggling sensation that he could not stop prodding, but never could he work it loose. "I have to... I have to burn, burn it all away. *Beware the—*" Ser Wybert shoved a leather gag into his mouth, binding his words in his throat.

"Seal him away," Ser Dilton commanded from across the room, disgust evident on his face.

"Do you want me to run him through instead?" Ser Eggar asked, his fingertips brushing the hilt of his blade.

"Hang the mage? Stab the mage?" Ser Wybert said, laughter lacing his words.

"We should bring him back. One *this* dangerous, The Paladin should deal with. Those are the orders," Ser Eggar countered.

"Stop. We will deal with this ourselves. We hang him come completion of the gallows. Have them done by tomorrow morning. Let all see what happens to those who dare to use magic." As Ser Dilton made a motion with his hand, the sack fell heavy on Gaulf's head once more. The gag and the hands dragging him out of the chair prevented his attempts to cry for help or struggle free.

Caspar and Manfred whispered somewhere in the room at a distance. Their voices faded to silence as Gaulf strained in his seat, and he was almost glad the sack left him blind to their exchange. Two of the knights dragged him along, and the fight left him.

"Do you understand now why we are here?" Silence, before Dilton continued. "That settles it. We agree there is no more need for a trial?" Another pause, a shuffling from the corner of the office.

"Hang the mage!" Wybert squealed, and Gaulf wept as they took him back to his cell.

Chapter 12

A Lull

O RN WAITED IN SILENCE as Gaulf's voice trailed off, mimicking the doughy knight's tittering almost perfectly.

"I find myself oddly without words," Orn said, his voice hoarse, scrubbing a hand over his face. "I am not even sure where to start."

"Should I keep going?" Gaulf's brows furrowed together.

"If you don't mind taking a slight detour from the story, give yourself a chance to catch a breath, we can pause for a bit," Orn said, needing a bit of a break himself more than anything else. The forest had darkened around them, and not just for time's passing. No, sitting here with Gaulf, practically feeling what the boy felt, old wounds reopened within himself. "I need to ask a few questions first."

Gaulf, silent and looking into the fire, merely nodded in answer.

Orn drew in a deep breath before blowing it back out. "This person you saw. What can you tell me about her?"

Gaulf seemed to diminish before Orn's eyes. "She's scary, with eyes like fire. Her dress moves with the wind, and she burns like the sun." Gaulf winced, his face paling. "In my visions, I see her knife, cutting, pinning me to the ground. She's screaming at me, then she stands and hauls me along. Wait, no." Gaulf shook his head, sweat breaking out on his brow. The fire flared to life, casting long shadows across their camp. "She's gone, but I hear them again. *Hang the mage, hang the mage, hang the mage.*'"

Orn clapped his hands together, pulling the boy out of whatever unseen force had brought him down into the depths, if only to save himself from tumbling into that same pit. His hand ached for the hilt of his sword, and yet he dared not frighten Gaulf by drawing it. "I see. Rest assured that I am not here to hang you. Nor will I let anyone else." Orn stared across the fire to where Gaulf hugged himself. "Are you okay?"

"I think so."

"Maybe a detour wasn't such a great idea. We can get back to your story." Heart racing, Orn fought to calm himself. "Where we left off sounded like you found yourself in even more of a pickle. Back in a cell with nowhere to go. That leaves me guessing at how you got out of it. It'll be quite a story."

Gaulf's lips began to curl into a slight smile that held promise. "Yes, it is. I loved listening to Jannie tell it."

"You are not going to leave me wondering, are you?" Orn quirked an eyebrow, leaning forward a little.

"Jannie came to my rescue. I-I couldn't save myself..." That smile threatened to falter.

"I assume the temptation to use magic was strong?" Orn watched Gaulf's face carefully as he spoke, searching for any sign that would betray the magic's influence in his features.

"Aye. In the darkness, it grew cold, until I saw that man again, on his knees, lighting a fire. I thought to, more than once." Gaulf squeezed his hands together in his lap. "The magic was, well...like a warmth I felt underneath my skin. Like the sun itself burned in my chest." Gaulf sighed. "Even now I can feel it gnawing away inside of me."

"Don't go giving in. You held off in the village, right? You can stay strong, Gaulf," Orn said, though he didn't sound as hopeful as he would have liked.

"I did not give in then. Had I done so, it would have been that much worse for my parents. For the entire village." Gaulf frowned. "I could not bring them more pain than I already had."

"It sets you apart from the others that I have come across, and that alone gives me hope that I can help you." Orn offered a genuine smile, praying that Gaulf would sense in him a true desire for the boy's wellbeing.

"Thank you, Orn."

The knight waved him off. "Don't think on it. Rather, tell me how Jannie rescued you."

"She engineered the plan, beginning to end." The smile on Gaulf's face flickered back to life as he scratched his head. "Pulled everyone together. Had Gunter go steal the keys from the sheriff, but turned out his ma handed over the spare key she kept safe, just in case. Didn't want Mr. Caspar to realize what was afoot, and to give us the biggest lead she could. Chindler and Adit were ready to cause a distraction. Those two were always fighting, so Jannie had them cause a ruckus out in the village square while she went to my house and packed my stuff—what little she could fit in a bag. Even enlisted my sisters," Gaulf wiped his eyes on his sleeve, smiling through the tears, "and got them to let the goat out of the pen. Led my parents on a merry chase." Gaulf paused, deep in thought. "She would usually headbutt the gate open, and it was left to me and my sisters to catch her. That is, until the day we weren't home to do so, which meant he had to. So, he finally set to fixing that piece of shit lock." Gaulf blinked, his cheeks growing red, looking anywhere but at Orn.

"I'm not going to chastise you for cursing. Given all you've been through, you still have better restraint than me," Orn said.

Emboldened, Gaulf pressed on. "The goat, see, she didn't realize the latch was new. Da just sat back and watched as she charged up, stamping and stomping with a plan. Stood up on her hinds and then took off running. BAM!" Gaulf slapped his hands against his thighs, the crack filling the camp. A few birds' startled replies echoed in the wilderness.

Swallowing, Orn gave a look full of mock seriousness at Gaulf. The look cracked, though, revealing the grin beneath.

"Poor goat bounced right back. The latch stuck firm because my da knows how to fix stuff. Well, most things." Gaulf blinked, wiping at his face.

Orn recognized the cliff presenting itself in the young man's mind. "Do you need a break, son?"

"No." Gaulf shook his head, as if clearing away whatever had darkened his mood. "I woke up to Jannie dragging me out of that place. All of them were there: Chindler, Adit, and Gunter. Ready to leave with me. For me."

"It's a great thing to have people who love you, and it's a good thing to protect them, right?" Gaulf shot Orn a quizzical look, and the knight averted his gaze. "You wanted them to come, but you knew they could not. Not without drawing more attention."

"I did not want to cause any of them pain. So, I decided to leave on my own." Gaulf wiped his nose with his sleeve and sniffed.

"I know something about sacrifice. But you have me now." It wasn't much to offer, but it was all Orn could do.

"Jannie...tried. She rode with me a ways, but I realized too late that I could not do this to her. I could not drag her away from home and put my crimes on her head," Gaulf said through shuddering breaths.

"I am sure she understands," Orn replied.

"I hurt her! I *made* her run. I marked her, as sure as I am." Gaulf tore at his hair, then scrubbed at his face, making more of a mess of the grime already there. The fire flared to life again as if a new log had been tossed across the coals, the stench of smoke and fire permeating the air.

Orn groaned as he sat up, a few joints popping at the sudden movement, and he clambered his way around the firepit to the young man. "You marked her?" He tried to keep the incredulity out of his voice, but the way his hammering heart leaped in his chest, Orn figured Gaulf would hear it clearly enough.

"Not like that." And yet, uncertainty sat plain as day in Gaulf's expression.

Orn studied Gaulf where the boy sat and squatted next to him, squeezing his shoulder comfortingly.

Gaulf choked on a sob. "I think I hurt her, but even now, I don't *know.*"

"Whatever you did, whatever you caused, this is not just on *you.* A whole mess of people did you wrong, scaring you something fierce in the process." This close to Gaulf, with the youth not withdrawing and with Orn grabbing his hands and holding them, the older man had to reinforce his view. *He's truly just a boy.*

Gaulf blinked, staring at Orn. Tears kept rolling, leaving lines of clean flesh beneath, and finally the boy nodded as he withdrew from Orn's grasp.

Once he could be certain the moment passed, Orn returned to his side of the fire and groaned loudly when he sat down. Fighting a yawn,

Orn stretched. He set about removing his armor, checking each piece for wear and tear and polishing what scuffs he could.

"What came next? Pass over the rough details if need be, but I want to hear it all. Everything that led you to me."

Gaulf screwed his eyes shut. "It got worse. The voices, the heavy weight on my chest overshadowed by something crawling under my skin. I could take in air but felt like I could hardly catch my breath. I could not stop looking over my shoulder and felt on fire even as I shivered in the cold. I jumped at every crack of a branch, of a squirrel jumping from tree to tree, or the birds taking flight as we escaped. All of it became simply too much," Gaulf recounted.

Chapter 13

THE ESCAPE

GAULF'S VOICE BROKE THE silence, the sound distant to his own ears. "Jannie, we need to pause for a moment." Above and beyond the pair, a distinct lack of noise descended around them as they dredged through the muck of a deer trail leading them through the thick forest and away from Redford. He paused, her hands on his arm to steady him. "I just need a moment." The world swayed, and Jannie with it. Gaulf drew in a deep breath, trying to keep his head from spinning.

Jannie nodded, a weary smile on her face. He worried that each second they lingered only increased their chances of being caught. More than that, he feared for Jannie, though he longed to always have her near, especially after his imprisonment in that dark cell. Jannie was light itself, a warm person to cling to. And so he did.

Closing his eyes and drawing what he hoped was another steadying breath, the world lurched once more. The trees burst to life as mounted riders tore through them, headed right for the pair. Gaulf wrapped his arms around Jannie and squeezed her tightly. The earth moved like water beneath his feet as the stampede approached.

"THERE HE GOES! Give chase, men! He cannot get away!"

Screaming, clanking, and horses close enough Gaulf could see their dark eyes.

And then, nothing.

No pain, no shattered bones, no noose about his neck. Gaulf peeked through one eye, spotting Jannie close by. He sighed in relief.

"Where did they go?" he asked, searching the area for any sign of the knights.

"Who?" Jannie's uncertainty was evident.

"The knights. The ones chasing after us?" Watching Jannie's expression shift, the panicked heat that had risen to Gaulf's cheeks quickly vanished. A shiver tore through him.

"There's no one around, Gaulf. The knights will scour the village before they risk coming out this far." Jannie ran a hand through his hair, smoothing back some of his sweat-dampened strands while scrutinizing him.

"And then what?" Gaulf wanted—*needed*—to run. His fingers twitched, but Jannie grasped his hand and held it firmly.

"We disappear. Travel as far away as we need to." Jannie suppressed a sob, still clutching his hand, as if she knew what was to come.

"I cannot risk you." Gaulf tilted his chin upward to meet the sky after rain began to fall, feeling his resolve harden.

He knew what he had to do.

On any other day, being alone with Jannie would have been all he wanted.

Now, the forest came alive with a thrumming noise in the distance, the wind flitting through the branches and leaves, the language of the world lamenting the scene that played out in Gaulf's mind. More than that, the thrum carried an energy with it that lanced through Gaulf's heart to his arm, then through the mark and back, coursing down to their joined hands.

"Gaulf!" Jannie hissed, wrenching herself away from him.

"Do you hear it, Jannie?" Gaulf whispered, hopeful she could perceive the sound of the forest singing, even if the frantic edge to his voice came as a horrid counterbalance.

"Hear what?" Jannie asked, echoing his own fear. He wished for nothing more than to be able to share it—what lay beneath the whisper of rain sloshing against the ground before it followed well-made paths, free to go wherever it desired.

"There's music to the wind, to the rain," Gaulf answered, and Jannie's laugh brought a smile to his face, even if it barely reached her eyes.

"I can only imagine, after being cooped up for as long as you were," Jannie said gently. "But hush now, lest someone hear us and come investigate. We must go." Every step he took echoed, splashing in the quickly gathering puddles.

A bolt of lightning pierced the black sky, and Gaulf winced when thunder boomed shortly thereafter. Jannie pulled him along through the trees at a reckless speed. Gaulf flinched against the sudden burst of another lightning strike, shielding his eyes against the flash of light and rain to see the waiting horse.

The language of the world around him swelled, compelling Gaulf to listen. "Jannie, it grows louder."

"We're almost free now. See?" Jannie cupped his chin when they came to a stop, drawing his gaze to her.

But Gaulf could not see her.

Gaulf could not hear her. Cries ripped through the shadows around him, followed by visions of everyone he had ever known or loved being bent, broken. Swaying in the wind from frayed nooses in a field of gallows populated only by the dead and scavenger birds. Jannie's face was among them, her eyes open but unseeing, her mouth picked apart by buzzards.

"No, Jannie. I can't... I cannot hurt you." Sobs wracked his body as the power within him intensified. The light came unbidden to his hand once more. He had to. He had to leave her behind. Gaulf wept as his hand burned, and in his panic, he took hold of Jannie's face. Fire crackled in his palm, hungry for release. Her eyes widened when magic poured out of him and into her, pinkening a print of his hand against her pale flesh.

"Gaulf, please!" Jannie shrieked, and Gaulf was unsure whether her plea was for the pain or for him to remain with her. He tried to pull the magic back, hoping to do little more than scare her away, yet something *twisted* inside of the power, and he was powerless against it. "Stop! Please, stop!" Jannie frantically pressed against his grasp. His hand glowed and her face blackened beneath it as tears streamed from her eyes. The power surged, but he fought against it. And himself.

Gaulf averted his gaze from her, from what he had done. "Oh, by The Scythe, I am so sorry. I don't know—I don't know why I... Are you okay, Jannie?" Remorse threatened to overwhelm him, to turn his stomach inside out. He reached for her but Jannie recoiled, her eyes wide. "Please, please. I am so sorry. Please," Gaulf babbled, hardly understanding himself.

"What in the name of The Harvester?" Jannie shook, dazed.

"I-I don't know, but I think I have to go this next part alone, Jannie. It's not safe. Not for you. Run. They will think I hurt you, that you had no part in this. I cannot bear to think that you might be hurt. *Again*. Please." Gaulf retreated from her, unable to blot out the sight of the mark on her face. Rain sizzled against it, mixing with her tears. In a flash of lightning behind Jannie, he saw *her*. Her dress, her angry glare, a dagger pointed right at his heart. Gaulf scrubbed at his eyes to little avail. "I see *her* there, waiting." Gaulf's mind snapped in two, watching her and Jannie, the images almost overlapping one another.

"Do what you must. But you come back to me, farm boy," Jannie sobbed, finally withdrawing from him. *Good.* Silence stretched between them, her words hanging in the muggy air. Jannie stood there before him with his blackened handprint on her face, now alone. Magic curled through his fingers, boring through his chest. All that remained—the ache, the need to find *her*, settled inside of him.

"I *am* sorry. I am so sorry that—" His apology was lost in a sudden boom of thunder. Jannie turned and ran into the downpour. Whether she heard him, he would never be certain. He wanted to call out to her, to find some way to fix this, but there was nothing left inside of him. Not a damn thing but the wrenching of his stomach and the feel of the rain on his skin and the magic slowly winding its way through him.

Whatever threatened to reach a crescendo within Gaulf calmed, and he remained still for a time, inhaling steadying breaths until he thought he might faint or his lungs might explode. Only when the current inside of him subsided did he move. There were shadows amassing in the trees, but he noticed pinpricks of light watching him.

Whispering to him.

The words were a tickle at the back of his throat. *Remember. Beware.*

"Who's there?" Gaulf hissed through clenched teeth.

As if in answer there came a noise from the forest. *Clank.* Another followed, then a third. The rest of the world diminished beneath the scraping of metal on metal. Gaulf held his breath, finding himself next to his horse. In an effort to calm himself, he stroked its thick mane, taking note of its rough texture. He climbed into the saddle without further delay, nudging the horse into motion on a path toward the main road.

Before he reached it, however, he veered off onto another trail. He dared not follow the main road too closely, not when there were knights who were surely aware of his absence by now and hunting him. The whispers continued in the forest, and shapes darted about in the underbrush. They moved quietly, but if Gaulf glanced at them from the corner of his eyes, he could spot them. Hiding beyond the trees they stood, watching him. Their eyes aglow, their forms vague, but Gaulf knew they were there.

Remember.

Beware.

The further along the trails Gaulf went, he realized he did not recognize the paths. Anything familiar was gone. The rain continued its assault, and he hunched over the horse and closed his eyes, hoping to shield himself from the worst of it. Kicking the horse into a gallop seemed a fine idea at first, until he thought about how slick the ground was. No use in escaping if he were to break his neck here. His fingers brushed the satchel at his side. The meager fare Jannie packed for him wouldn't get him far, but Swanford lay a short distance to the east. Perhaps he could find sanctuary there.

That idea was laughable.

Stories told late at night when the parents thought the kids were sleeping returned to him. He remembered his da saying, *"Those people in Swanford still hold some very strange beliefs. We can trade with them, but I don't trust them as far as I can throw a gourd."*

"Halt!"

That single word shook Gaulf free of his thoughts. He only just noticed that somewhere along the way, his horse had found its way to the main road. How long ago, he had no way of knowing for sure. What he *did* know was that his fears had come true: someone barred the path ahead.

An armored man stood in the rain. One of the knights from town. Trouble had found him at last. Reining in the horse while trying to slide out of the saddle, Gaulf's mind raced. He wished Jannie were still with him. She'd know what to do. She always knew what to do.

"Time has come to be judged as the anathema that you are." The muted sound of steel on leather as the knight drew his sword from its scabbard rattled Gaulf to his core. Ser Dilton's voice, unmistakable with its raspy quality, drove a spike of fear through Gaulf's belly. *Nowhere to run. Nowhere to hide.*

Gaulf approached slowly, keeping his empty hands raised high. *"Hang him come dawn."* The words from the bickering knights, the bag over his head, all of it settled like a weight on his shoulders. He gagged on his next breath, as if he were still trapped in that sweaty canvas sack.

Before Gaulf could speak, the knight charged him. Time staggered to a crawl. Gaulf waited to die. Then the rain paused, and something sprang to life inside of him. The world was suddenly cast in dim colors, and he saw someone standing in front of him. More of a hint of a person than anything else, but their movements were clear. Precise.

He watched the figure make gestures, he heard the words, even if they were warbled. Gaulf followed the example, his tongue fumbling over the unfamiliar syllables. Magic coiled inside of him, and in his mind's eye he witnessed once more the smug look on Arthur's face, the pummeling of Sige's fists, his parents struggling to survive. That despair compounded within him until he could do no more than choke on a scream.

That scream was mirrored by the shapeless form he emulated, and Gaulf directed all of his anger into it. Every last shred of pain and hatred. When the world again snapped into focus, Gaulf discovered the sword and its knight still racing toward him.

But Gaulf would have none of it.

What came was a blinding flash of light expelled from Gaulf's raised palms.

He shuddered as a piece of who he had been before magic entered his body departed through his fingertips. The fire unfurled into the sword when he took hold of the blade.

Another flash of flames dispelled the shadows from within the knight's helmet, revealing his stunned expression before all that he was ceased to be entirely. Burned to little more than molten metal and ash.

Its intermission complete, rain fell from the dark clouds above, hissing when droplets encountered the knight-shaped lump on the ground. Gaulf shivered with the drop in temperature, or perhaps it was the shock of what he'd done. His breath hitched when he inhaled, struggling to compose himself. *Murder. I've just committed murder.*

Before his heart could cease hammering against his ribs, before he could calm himself, his attention was drawn to the forest after the silence shattered around him. *Clank.* He fought the urge to retch. *No. Not again. Please.*

Another knight was coming.

Gaulf tried to find his horse, but he was alone in the darkness.

No. Not again.

So, he ran.

Chapter 14
Burn It All

GAULF RAN FOR DAYS. Ignoring the pain in his sides, the whispers beyond the trees, the gnawing feeling in his gut that worsened with every footfall.

And yet, he dared not stop.

Each time he slowed that golden light inside of him flared, filling him with pain as if he burned from the inside out. The complaints of his body threatened to derail him, but fear and regret carried him onward.

The whispers soon coalesced into a clear message: *Burn it all.*

Running became all that he knew, his existence a race toward the rising sun. The shadows morphed into hazy figures, their dark eyes watching Gaulf from the safety of the forest canopy. One formed a person all too familiar: Jannie, pain written across her burned visage, mouthing words he could not hear. Gunter, Chindler, and Adit stood just behind her, barely seen in the prevailing darkness, their shouts garbled.

The sight of his friends made Gaulf unsteady, and he tripped, rolling through the soft grass until momentum brought him no further. Above him was a blanket of spinning stars, within him was chaos. Gaulf wobbled to his feet, tears streaming down his face, and he ran.

Burn it all. Remember. You must remember.

Flashes of blue light erupted as he ran, swallowing those faces in the trees one by one. The spiral mark on his arm throbbed terribly. Gaulf drove his hand into his pocket, wrapping his fingers tightly around the lock of hair Jannie had given him, anchoring what remained of himself to it and to her memory.

Burn it all, from the heart to the head.

"No," Gaulf pleaded.

And so, he ran.

Shapes floated in the air in front of his eyes like specks of dust in a sunbeam, drawing his attention. The Spiral floated there, and others, but before he could focus and understand their shapes to name them, they would vanish then reappear.

The voices followed. The faces in the trees changed, becoming ruined statues, their hands reaching toward him. Gaulf doubled over.

The voices changed their mantra.

Find her, find her, find her.

Trapped. Gaulf felt trapped. The sensation of drowning took hold of him, and for a moment he thought himself back in that deep pool of water where magic first came to him. He had to find *her*. He had to *remember*.

And so, he ran.

A face entered the light. Gaulf could see *her*. The pointed ears, the sharp gaze, the look of disgust on her face. She drew a dagger, then a loud *clank* filled the air.

Like smoke on the wind, she dissipated.

Hands not his own, marked with The Spiral, scrambled against the dirt. A horse lay on its side in front of him, unmoving.

"Come on, we have to move!" came a voice not belonging to Gaulf from between his lips. *Remember.* He watched himself stand and limp away. No. That was *not* him. Details swam in front of his head, and Gaulf raised a hand. "Help," Gaulf sobbed. The horse lay still. Gaulf closed his eyes.

When he opened them again, gone was the horse, the lack of control, the darkness of night. Day had arrived in the space between one heartbeat and the next. Gaulf found himself curled up against a tree, shivering from cold and hunger. Of *need*. He waited and listened.

The whispers and shapes and visions retreated, and he felt the loneliness of the forest creep in around him. The need to run was abandoned with the coming of day. With the aches and pains tearing through Gaulf, he doubted he could run anyway.

So, he walked.

Chapter 15

WHERE TO GO?

THE SILENCE GREW THAT much thicker every moment Orn sat there staring at Gaulf, waiting for what came next. By the time he realized the story was finished, he blinked his eyes then laughed. The sound of it made Gaulf nearly jump out of his skin as it echoed throughout their small camp.

"Hell of a story, son," Orn said.

At that, the hint of a grin ghosted across Gaulf's face. "As I am sure you can figure out, I found myself hanging by my feet. Decided I wanted to see who was hunting me, so I took the trap and laid it elsewhere. I was hardly certain who I would find."

"I guess I am lucky that you opted against burning me where I stood. Or *hung*." Orn cleared his throat, swallowing the lump waiting there.

"Almost did," Gaulf said flatly.

Orn let the comment slide. "As much as I wish it were otherwise, I don't see anything yet in your story that strikes me as unique. Hoped you might help put some pieces together. What I can tell is something is lurking out here, marking people. But for what purpose?" Orn paused, pinching the bridge of his nose.

"What is it?" Gaulf asked.

"Normal people in abnormal circumstances. Set upon by magic. Not the accounts of mages from the south waging wars against The Paladin, calling down lightning and moving the earth. No, just people. Like you. Tell me about the storm again."

"The thunder shook the ground beneath our house."

"Not unlike the quake Jord and I felt," Orn whispered.

"What does it mean?" Gaulf asked.

"It's a pattern. One I hadn't noticed before. A rumbling of the earth, and then someone's marked." Orn furrowed his brows.

"Is it the mages? From the south?" Gaulf's eyes widened.

"I don't reckon so, because I haven't seen any sign of that. They'd have to get through The Paladin and his ilk first. And you're no mage. That said, I feel like I am still missing several pieces of the puzzle."

"Are you still going to help me? Help *us*?" Gaulf pressed, hopeful.

"Yes. I'm going to continue to try to find a damn answer to all of this. How, I have no idea. But I'm too stubborn to give up."

"I see." The way Gaulf replied said more than those two simple words. "Where do we go from here?"

"We continue doing what I've done every day. We try to discover why this is happening." Orn's throat felt scratchy, parched, and he wished for nothing more than a drink. Something to dull his senses and the burn of his arm and the ache of existence. A reminder of something he'd rather forget.

"Thank you." Gaulf's voice broke as he spoke.

"Thank me by staving off whatever this is as best you can. Before you end up—" Orn clamped his mouth shut and took a deep breath before continuing, "—doing something we both regret. If you feel it, you just let me know. We'll figure a way out of this." Not quite a lie, but it soured Orn's mouth all the same. Hope surged in his heart. Maybe he *could* help. "You can have my blanket tonight. I'll scrape something together for breakfast in the morning. And I'll stand watch so you can get some rest."

Gaulf nodded eagerly. He took the bedding and scooted closer to the fire, getting comfortable. Orn watched the young man wrap himself in the bedroll.

With a sigh, Orn found a tree to lean against, drawing his sword into his lap. *Just in case*, he thought to himself. Having it near quieted the mark on his arm. Not that he expected Gaulf to be a problem, as clear-headed as he seemed. But there was still something about the boy, an odd shimmer around his edges, a distant quality Orn could not put his finger on.

Even if it was more than passingly familiar.

When the night fell into a steady silence, he carefully drew the length of his sword from its scabbard. With the naked blade across his lap, he set about cleaning it first, then sharpening. Familiar motions that let him find calm without sleep.

"What is that?" Gaulf's voice broke the silence.

"You hear something?" His own voice sounded like the scraping together of stones. His eyes burned, leaving him to wonder how long he had been staring into the flickering flames of the campfire.

"What do you have there?" The young man pointed from under the blanket.

"My sword?"

Gaulf's heavy, half-lidded eyes passed between Orn's face and the weapon. "Looks like nothing, torn from the darkness and made whole." A yawn stretched the young boy's face, his eyes widening briefly. "More importantly, why do you have it out?"

"A blade needs proper care. Only thing I seem to have control of these days," Orn said, checking the length of steel for any imperfections.

"Still looks like nothing to me," Gaulf replied, a faraway look in his eyes. Orn wasn't sure the boy was even awake.

Orn tightened his fingers around the hilt of the sword, feeling the calm it inspired. "It might not be much to look at, but it does the job well enough. How do you mean it looks like nothing, Gaulf?" Orn hated to press for an answer, but he needed to understand what the boy was thinking.

The boy shivered, biting his lip against the chill in the air. "The blade made of nothing calls to me. From the inside. I can feel it, drawing away a part of me. Make it stop!" Gaulf's voice broke, his features twisting.

Orn set the blade aside and clambered over to Gaulf. "Shush now. No one's going to hurt you." He brushed errant locks of the boy's sandy, sweat-laden hair from his forehead. In an instant, another face replaced Gaulf's in his mind's eye. Orn clenched his jaw, willing the vision away.

Gaulf stopped struggling against himself, against Orn, and relaxed into the bedroll. Orn tucked the blanket around him.

"I don't know what you saw, but I like that name. Nothing is a good name for a weapon like this," Orn murmured. He waited to see if Gaulf would reply, but when none came, Orn quietly retreated to his seat against the tree and slid the blade over his lap, cleaning it once more before sheathing it for the night. "One. Two. Three—" Orn started, before a yawn forced him to pause. His eyelids were heavy. Orn sighed, unable to remember what came next.

Sleep caught him unawares, blanketing his exhaustion with a warmth he could not fight. Orn succumbed totally, even if it did feel like a tidal wave of darkness wrapping around him, yanking him down.

With it, came the dreams.

Shapes in the darkness followed him. Flames waited on the edge of his periphery. He twisted, trying to find purchase in a world turned upside-down. Searching for an avenue of escape, Orn's hand reached for his sword, but true to its new name, nothing was there. Pallid faces glared at him from the shadows.

When Orn had killed them, he stared into their eyes because he could not bring himself to look away. Each one a failure. Their faces were unfamiliar and yet, the rictus of pain, the tears—those he knew. An echo of his first disaster.

"Jord," Orn whispered the name in the dark, the shades surrounding him opening their mouths to scream.

"She comes, She comes! She's coming for you."

Orn barreled forward, nearly shoving one of the shapeless bodies out of his way, though it proved no easier than waking himself up. He knew this was a dream, but that, too, became buried beneath rising panic. The skin on his arm puckered at the cries of the shadows, and a thread ran from the mark through him, so that he dangled like a worm on a hook, binding him as he struggled to free himself.

Hands picked at him, working to tear him apart. He pushed, kicked, found flesh willing and waiting beneath his palms. Flesh marked similarly to his own.

Orn could not escape. Skin turned fractal with an etched bolt of lightning or the blade of a scythe or a crescent with wicked intent. They clamored after him tirelessly until he could hardly breathe.

Their words skittered across the surface of his brain as their bodies became a monolith against his own. Trapped. Then one familiar face appeared.

"It's time to let go, Orn. Stop fighting."

"Jord, no," Orn pleaded, tearing his gaze away and screwing his eyes shut as he threw his head back and screamed.

As a scream shattered the peace of the night, Gaulf's eyes slowly opened. He did not need to look to know where the sound came from. What dreams the man suffered, Gaulf had watched from within the obscured edges of his own dream. The farm boy felt a pull toward the old knight.

Crawling out of his bedroll, Gaulf moved with little to no noise. Not that it mattered much, with the way Orn was screaming in his sleep. Still, he did not think waking the man would do either of them any good with Orn's sword lying nearby.

Something inside of him shrunk away from the weapon. The flames of the fire reflected in the steel of the blade, moving upon its surface. Stretching his arm, careful of the now-quiet atmosphere of the camp, Gaulf reached for the sword's hilt. As his fingers wrapped around it, the world lurched.

The vast emptiness within the sword called to him. A calm quiet overtook him, left him feeling cold and bereft. Alone. In his grasp, the sword shifted the visions around him. From an impossible hallway of reflected light to a growing gloom. The cessation of being. Nothing, well and true, given physical form in his hand.

Until it seemed like he would become nothing by the sheer act of holding it. The quiet became too much to bear, but he could not let go of the sword. He forced the blade inside its scabbard and placed it across Orn's lap. He then seized the knight's hand and wrapped it around the hilt.

As Gaulf let go, a pain in his arm intensified. Had it always hurt this way? He stared at the weapon once more as he moved.

"*Go.*"

A whisper, from Gaulf's own lips, and even if the voice was not *quite* his own, he knew it was time. He collected what meager belongings he had and headed away from camp. Pausing to look back over his shoulder, half-expecting to see Orn watching him, Gaulf waited. Knew that if he took one more step, he could not stop. His chin trembled.

He turned away from Orn and headed further into the murk at the edge of the firelight.

Chapter 16

HERE AGAIN

ORN STARED AT THE figure hanging from the tree. With the ratty cloak and the garbled mess of words he heard the poor bastard whispering, he felt certain he had caught Gaulf. Again. Not even three days later, the boy was seemingly the worse for wear. Orn inched closer, hand at his sword's hilt. Careful not to get too near, he tried to catch a glimpse of the person's face as they swayed midair. A root caught their hood, drawing it back so that their ginger hair hung loosely, dragging through the dirt below, carving faint patterns in the soil. Were the spirals an accident?

He dismounted and led his horse a few paces away, tying it to a tree nearby. As far as he could tell, he was alone with whoever hung in this particular snare. Orn scrubbed a hand over his face. Sleep had been nearly impossible the last few nights, ever since Gaulf decided to run off. That he awoke in solitude the following morning bothered him more than he cared to admit, but it didn't change anything. The knight had a mission, after all.

Orn looked at the figure bound by the ankles and waited. Had they actually moved, or was his mind playing tricks on him? Was this person dead?

His gaze fell lower, to the fingers that followed the sway of the wind. He started to lose himself in those spiraling marks etched into the ground. When they moved, unfurling and wrapping around each other in the soil, Orn felt a familiar tugging in the depths of his stomach.

Tearing his gaze away, Orn ground his teeth in an effort to focus on anything except the familiar, menacing patterns. "Are you alive in there, friend?" He waited for a reply, but none came. When the silence became unbearable, Orn prodded the figure. Held his breath.

No response.

Shit.

"Hope you haven't been hanging around too long." Orn waited for a response. Still nothing. "If so, I'm sorry. I had some other business to tend to, and this snare was empty as of last night." Orn nudged the figure with his hand again. No movement. "There's been so many of you crawling around lately, I had hoped to learn something that might tell me what is happening or why," Orn groused to no one in particular, hoping that talking would keep the threatening whispers increasing in volume since he saw those spirals in the dirt at bay, especially since sleep seemed to evade him lately.

Then the man's blue gaze was fixed on him, wide and wild.

"That's a dangerous look." Orn chuckled to disguise his surprise. He could've sworn the stranger was dead.

"Let me down," the man barked, swaying erratically from the rope.

Orn let go of his sword in an attempt at a truce. "Soon enough. I figured we could sit and talk for a bit. How's that sound?"

"Like you need to shove off and let me down. I can't breathe!" The words gurgled forth and the man bucked against the rope, almost bashing his head against the tree. *Not patient, this one,* Orn thought.

"Calm down. If you promise to behave, I'll cut you free right now. Believe it or not, I'm here to help you." Orn strode over to where the rope was wound around the tree, pausing to wait for the stranger's answer.

"You're lucky I don't crack your head open with a rock," the man spat, though his words were garbled. *He's been in this position too long. Blood's gone to his head.* "Or burn you where you stand."

Orn froze while reaching for the rope and found himself eye-level with the man hanging from his snare. His anger spiked, sharp and fierce enough that his words came out in a low growl. "What was that?"

Sensing his mistake, the man quickly stammered, "Just let me down, okay? Please? I'm sorry, I only want to be out of this blasted trap."

"I understand, but I can't get you out of there until you swear you won't try to flee or fight," Orn said. That the stranger was talking clearly now was a good sign. It meant the magic hadn't overwhelmed him yet, and there was a chance he could offer more information than Orn had already gathered. The old knight knew he couldn't botch this opportunity.

The snared figure bucked again, fighting against the ropes.

"Hold still! Like I said, I just want to talk." Orn grimaced as he undid the snare from the base of the tree enough that he could brace the weight of the man and lower him slowly to the ground. Once he found himself lowered, the man scrambled about in the dirt, trying to escape. Orn sighed. With a firm yank, Orn kept him in place. "Come now, I just want to chat."

"You crazy bastard," the man snapped.

Taking advantage of the old knight's distraction, he flailed about on the ground in another attempt to flee, but Orn maintained his grip on the rope. "This is getting silly." Orn chuckled as he spoke, reeling the man in with one hearty pull. "Please, for both of our sakes, stop. At least wait until you aren't tied up anymore."

"Fine. What do you want?" The man rolled over and sat up, glaring fiery daggers right at Orn.

"To start, how about you tell me your name?"

"Why should I tell you a damn thing?" the man questioned.

Orn shook his head and kept his grip on the rope firm. Just in case. "Because I'm all that stands between you and this rope going over the tree branch again. And I don't want to do that. But since we're here and cozy, why don't we have ourselves a little talk? Starting with your name." Orn tried to not get unduly angry at the man in front of him. The sting of Gaulf's sudden disappearance in the middle of the night still soured his stomach.

"Archivald," the man muttered as he rubbed his hands over his legs, then his arms, never once letting his angry gaze waver from Orn.

"I'd like to say we're well met, Archie, but I'm not going to lie to you. Not with the rocky start that we've had, huh? I'd say we're quite poorly met, but maybe we can improve on that." Orn nodded toward the rope in his hands, then the rope still around Archivald's foot. "Mind if I call you Archie?" Silence. Orn secured the rope, then thumbed through some of the papers in his pouch. Not finding what he was looking for, Orn shrugged and turned his attention to the man. "Listen, I'm just here to ask a few questions. That's it. Nice and simple, and then we can be done."

"And then you'll untie my feet?"

"Promise to hear me out and I'll untie you right now." Orn hefted the length of rope up again.

Archie's gaze met his own. The cold glare softened before the man nodded, puffing up his chest with a deep breath. Orn reached forward and he worked the knot loose. Archie's hands shot to his ankles, rubbing at the rope-burned skin.

"What do you want?" Archie grumbled.

"Tell me about your mark. Where'd it come from?" Orn tried to force a cheerful tone in his voice, but exhaustion crept in.

"How'd you know about that?" Archie whispered.

"It's becoming a common problem lately. Your talk about burning me is a dead giveaway."

"I knew I wasn't the only one." Archie seemed more than a little excited at the prospect.

Orn furrowed his brows. "No, you are not. Whereabouts are you from?"

"Ostford," came the curt response. "The locals ran me out of town. Even though I did nothing wrong. Wake up screaming once or twice and everyone throws a fit." Archie paused, looking anywhere but at Orn. "I felt like I should go east, but I decided to head west instead."

"You did good to run. The Paladin and his cronies don't take too kindly to people who are different, do they?" Orn offered Archie a wan smile.

"No, I guess not," Archie said. "I had heard the rumors, but I never thought it would happen to me. I've heard what they say, but that's not me. I didn't hurt anyone."

Not yet.

"What do you really want to know?" Archie asked abruptly.

"When did you get a spiral mark?" Orn thought if Archie was done with pleasantries, he might as well be too.

Archivald quirked one eyebrow. "I don't have a spiral."

"No? But you *are* marked, right?" Orn narrowed his eyes, his curiosity piqued.

"Yes." Archivald fidgeted where he sat, his hand moving to his sternum. His fingers were splayed over his heart.

"Mind showing it to me?" Orn motioned to Archivald's hand.

Archie shook his head and pulled his clothing tighter around him. "I woke up one morning with a handprint on my chest. The day before, I went out for a walk along the river, what I usually do when I need some peace and quiet. I heard a rumble. The earth moved beneath my feet. Not sure if I slipped and hit my head or had fallen asleep. It's all murky, but what I remember is that I dreamed that night of someone holding me, whispering to me, their hand on my heart. I woke up, covered in mud, head to toe. Stumbled back to town with everyone staring at me. As if they *knew*."

Orn chewed on the inside of his cheek, questions burbling inside of him. The story was quite unlike Gaulf's, or even his own, and yet a piece of it tied the three together: the earth moved. Orn could not help but remember the darkness coming to life. *Oh, Jord.* Orn shoved the memory aside and scratched absently at his arm. Archivald's eyes followed his every move, as if he, too, *knew.*

As the pair studied one another, Orn's unease intensified, though the stranger appeared ordinary. Not for the first time Orn felt something *off* about the man. A discordant chord was struck between them, one that he ached to find a way to set right. Had he grown too hopeful after Gaulf?

"How long since you were marked?" Orn asked, anxious to continue his line of questioning.

"Seven days or so." Archie looked at his hands, flexing his fingers.

"Tell me about your dreams. Have they changed since the incident?"

"I..." Archivald rubbed the back of his hand over his nose. "I dream of the stars above, the darkness of the sky swallowing them one by one. I dream of faces, angry and fierce and full of fire. I dream of that too—the fire. Burning me from the inside out, rendering me nothing but tallow. A wick which might set the world ablaze." Archie bit his lip.

"Hm," Orn said thoughtfully. "What about the earth rumbling? Can we go back to that? Was there a storm?"

"A storm? No, that came a few days later. I think. Listen, I don't know what else you want. Why are you doing this? What do you hope to gain?" Archivald spat the words, his fidgeting worsening.

"There's something afoot here, marking people. You, me, others. Driving us toward something, and usually disaster follows in our wake. I'm trying to discover why, in hopes that I can stop it and save us," Orn replied, praying that he seemed comforting and not like some simpleton with grandiose notions. "Tell me, when did the dreams start?"

Archivald's expression sank. "Just a week ago, maybe a bit more. I can't be sure. The days have bled together lately." He paused, and the silence stretched between them uncomfortably until he spoke again. "What if you cannot help me?" With the way Archivald stared at him, his lips moving but saying nothing, Orn realized he could *hear* the whispers. Just not from Archie. The unintelligible scrawl of words seeped from the world around the two of them, slowly but surely growing louder.

Orn searched the forest. All was quiet.

"Did you hear it too?" Archivald asked, his lips still moving long after the question left him.

"Hear what?" Orn hated this moment. Hated pretending.

"I hear someone—something—calling. Telling me to *beware...*" Archivald trailed off, his eyes flitting rapidly from side to side.

"What are we supposed to beware of?" A spike of fear raced down the old knight's spine.

"Burn it all!" Archivald cried, holding his stomach. "It makes me feel sick. Foul. Burn it all!"

Hope tumbled like a rock into the depths of his stomach, the opportunity to ask more questions dwindling. As nonchalantly as he could, Orn let his hand fall to the hilt of his sword, not realizing how his skin crawled in the wake of the act. Archie hardly seemed to notice.

The man's eyes were wide, pupils dilated so that the black of his irises had swallowed any trace of color. "Archie, you still with me?"

"You hear it too. I know you do. I can *feel* you." The look on Archie's face sent another spike of fear through Orn. If he stopped, if he held his breath for one moment, he knew he would *feel* Archie too. A lurking presence just outside of his mind.

Orn snapped his fingers, trying to draw Archie back to the here and now. "Step away from whatever precipice you find yourself at. Shove all of that away and squash it. Follow the sound of my voice."

"What's happening?" Archie quavered. His voice cracked, then broke.

How many times had Orn heard that sound? He dared reach out to Archivald, to squeeze his shoulder. "I don't know what's happening, but that's what I aim to find out."

The words caught Archie's attention and his gaze finally focused on Orn. What he didn't expect was the man crawling toward him, his head canting to the other side as he listened to something that, initially, only he could hear.

No, *no*. Orn then heard it too, a distant whisper tuned out for so long it hardly registered. They listened to the same damn thing, but only one of them was paying attention.

"Close your eyes and think of anything other than what you hear. Please! For your sake." *And mine.*

"Please, help me." Archivald curled in on himself, wrapping his arms about his body and rocking side to side.

"That's exactly what I am trying to do." Orn sighed, leaning in. "Just breathe and hold on. Do not let go."

Archivald ground his teeth together. A tidal surge of whispers enveloped him and Orn. A flurry of sounds, flitting like bats in the darkness toward them. The words, unintelligible and screeching like metal against stone, set Orn on edge.

Let go.

Let it all go.

Give in.

"Do not listen to a damn thing, Archivald." Orn strained against the mounting pressure.

"What's happening to me? What are you doing?"

"It's not me, you blasted idiot." Orn spoke through clenched teeth, his hand on the hilt of his sword became a solid rock in the chaos of the world closing in on the two of them. He tried to draw the blade, but Archie spied the naked steel and panicked.

The whispers that echoed between them were almost in sync with the barely perceptible movements of Archie's lips. Orn dared again to draw his sword from its scabbard. Archie hardly even blinked, hardly even recognized the movement for what it was.

"Archivald?" Orn snapped his fingers in front of the man's face. "You haven't hurt anyone, so don't start now. Snap out of it."

It was the electric smell pervading the air that convinced Orn he had to act. Archie cackled and crawled further along the ground, moving that much closer to him.

"Do you hear it too? Beware. Burn," Archie practically sang the words as he swayed back and forth.

"Stop this, please. I do not want to hurt you."

Before Orn could raise his sword, Archie was there. He grasped Orn by his upper arm. Spittle flew from his mouth as the whispers became a deafening roar. Orn's eyes rolled into the back of his head, and before long, he heard a scream. A moment later, his throat hurt enough he realized he was the one making that awful racket.

Archie's hand on his arm sparked something inside of him. Between them, a searing fire flared to life, driving back the darkness, if only briefly. The shadows retreated but did not vanish, lingering at the edge of the spreading connection.

Orn planted the length of steel into the body in front of him. He swore he felt every resistance in sliding it through sinew and muscle before Archie stumbled backward, severing whatever link was there as blood burbled from his lips.

"Archivald," Orn pleaded, watching Archie trip over his own feet, his hands fumbling futilely with the sword sticking out of his chest. As he collapsed, as the grass blackened beneath him, his gaze found the sky above.

Hunkering down over the man, Orn yanked the blade from his body in one vicious motion. The length of steel came free painted red, shuddering when Archie took his final breaths. The little clearing became silent once more.

Orn steadied himself against a tree as the world lurched violently beneath his feet. He made to wipe the sword clean, but the blood seemed bonded to the metal, marring its already drab surface. The blade then radiated warmth, as if alive in his touch.

Closing his eyes against the strange sense of peace emanating from the hilt, a shiver ripped through his arm. The whisperings lurking would not be quiet nor content. His mind soon began tormenting him with the faces of those who met their deaths by his blade. Unbidden though they were, Orn refused to ignore them. That is, until the last face.

"Jord." The face scrawled across his heart.

The shadowy figure said nothing in reply.

Orn stared at the corpse briefly before kneeling to search. The mark was on the man's chest. An unfamiliar one, that of a handprint splayed across flesh. Aside from that, the knight found a small pouch of coins, a well-worn dagger, and little else.

"While you might not be able to help me answer any questions, you can help me keep a promise I made. That has to count for something, I hope." Orn turned his attention back to the mark as he unsheathed the small dagger. A dizzying sensation crept over him as he looked upon the handprint, outlined in angry flesh. Was it his imagination, or had it moved as if grasping for Orn? His stomach threatened to evict its contents right then and there, before he managed to tear his eyes away briefly from the sight.

He peeked again, but only enough to ensure he was not going to nick his own fingers with the blade as he traced the mark in the flesh. Then he tilted the dagger, separating the flap from the muscle beneath with a squelch. He hated this part.

"Glad you at least kept a sharp blade on you," Orn murmured. Once he had what he needed, he wrapped the tattooed flesh and stuffed it into a leather pouch. "Thanks for these," Orn said as he wiped the dagger clean.

His body rebelled against the notion of standing, his knees threatening to give out as his head spun. Orn thought he'd keel over and kiss the ground at any moment. That worry blessedly passed.

"Didn't have to end this way." He tucked the dagger into his belt and turned from the corpse. His horse chose that moment to peer at him with what could only be called a reproachful gaze. "Don't look at me like that." The knight busied himself with gathering what rocks he could and carved a depression in the ground. It took some time, but he was able to deepen it then drag the body over. "Hopefully, you've found some measure of peace, Archie," Orn said softly, piling the rocks onto the corpse. Once done, he returned to his horse. Packing camp would be just as quick, with the mark burning a hole in his pouch, so to speak.

He could clear Gaulf's name now, claim the bounty, and get a warm bed if he hurried.

Chapter 17

THE MEETING

THE CHILL OF THE night was welcoming now that Laela could steal some time to herself. Her mount gave a nickering snort, steam spilling from wide nostrils. The moon hung low in the sky where the clouds could not hide it. Cold stuck to her like dew. Her horse shifted beneath her, the jingling of leather and brass a familiar sound. She skimmed the frantic scratches on the piece of paper from Willaime. There was a description of their next target, as well as his last-known whereabouts.

"Have we been to Cassandira before?" she asked, and Willaime shook his head. Something about the name of the town stuck in her craw, an aching tooth jarred somewhat loose from a punch.

His tone was somber when he answered. "Not with me, you haven't. Not much up there these days. The East has been silent for some time, and The Paladin took care of The Tower. Left nothing but ruins." Laela glanced at the three conscripts they had brought with them and wondered how he'd refer to them after their hunt was concluded. She never once thought to inquire after the job was done. "We would've heard reports by now."

"Maybe." Chainmail rattling and the squeak of leather alerted her to an approach, and she tore her attention away from the missive, folding it in her hand. Dolan led Gilbert, with Alke trailing behind the pair. Behind the trio sat the inky mass of The Paladin's castle, barely discernible against the night sky. Not even a few hours had passed since Ser Gregoris had unceremoniously dispatched her on another hunt. She ground her teeth to keep from wondering why.

"When can we make camp?" Dolan turned his head and spat from atop his own horse. The man had not yet learned how to sit properly in the saddle, or even how to move with the horse, and she could only imagine how sore his legs must be. When Willaime failed to answer, he somehow convinced his horse to nudge closer to the other two men. He shot her a conspiratorial look over his shoulder, only turning away when he realized she was watching him. Whatever he said then was low enough she could not hear.

"Well, I don't like it. She'll just get in the way," Gilbert said, shooting her a sidelong glance. He seemed incapable of actually whispering. Or maybe they wanted her to know that she had become the topic of conversation. She remained silent and hoped that might be the end of it. The third man, Alke, had more to add to the discussion. Sometime through the night he had started to perk up, as if the fresh air revitalized him.

"I'm telling you two, she's a gift for us. For when we're done. Just you see." This caught Laela's attention, as this was the first time that Alke had bothered to speak. She might have thought him mute but for the oath he gave in the dungeon. His voice sported a distinct whine, setting her on edge. His proclamation was nothing new, which said much about those who ended up in the cells of The Paladin. She winced when the other two men laughed in reply.

Willaime hardly appeared to be paying attention to the prisoners, keeping his gaze fixed on her instead as he drew his horse closer with a firm yank of the reins. The frown on Laela's lips was frozen in place while she listened to the continuing chatter about her status as a prize. The knight eyed the paper in her hand, and she furrowed her brow. Nothing in the description of this particular target indicated a need for her. She did not even see the need for the bait he had "hired" to come along. As if reading her mind, he shrugged his shoulders.

"No idea. I just had my orders. Same as you," Willaime said, disinterested.

"Tell us, knight, is she a loud one? I was hoping for some screaming," Alke said smugly. This elicited another round of laughter from the prisoners. Laela was no longer certain who was the leader of the trio. Gilbert's chest was puffed, as if he were mocking the way Willaime sat, and the giggling from the other men only served to egg him on.

Before she could do or say anything, the knight edged his horse closer to her own once more. The gesture was clear enough. *Don't react.* Their time would come.

"The writ said it's a firebug," Laela said flatly to Willaime.

Willaime sighed and pinched the bridge of his nose. "Another one of *those* then."

"Haven't been many other sorts—not for some time." Laela chewed on her lip, ignoring the lingering glances of the prisoners. Something felt off, and not just the lecherous bait. Her mind recoiled when she noticed the way Alke smiled, his mouth full of wide teeth. Everything about him was strange, wrong, designed to raise her hackles. But his dim eyes brightened as she spoke. "Normal procedure is to secure a perimeter, then deal with the problem. This hardly seems like the case, however."

"I don't see how we're going to be of help. Might as well just let us go. No harm, no foul, right?" Dolan's grin wavered. He made a motion as if to leave, and the other two seemed likely to follow. Laela hoped they would.

Willaime let her deal with deserters.

"Hardly think so." Willaime let his hand fall to his sword. "You've given your oath. And The Paladin rewards those who serve him well."

"What if we brain you now and bugger off anyway?" Gilbert asked, wiping a grimy hand over his mouth.

"You're welcome to try." Willaime's face split into an unnervingly predatory smile.

The three grumbled amongst themselves. Then Dolan said, "I don't know what you expect us to do."

"You will ensure those who need help receive it. You will work with us to capture this mage," Willaime said slowly, never moving his hand from his sword.

The three prisoners then whispered amongst themselves. She could hear them, their discussion on whether they could overpower her and Willaime. Before long they fell silent, and Dolan ambled forward.

"We're willing to brain any magic users much as we might anyone else," Dolan answered.

"Glad we can see eye to eye on this. I would hate for The Paladin to be disappointed," Willaime replied.

Sometime later, she found herself sifting through a pile of ash with the toe of her boot. "How far outside of Redford are we?"

"Not far, depending on how hard we want to push the horses tonight," Willaime said.

Still sifting through the pile, she could see small chunks of leather and metal not claimed by the fire. As she rolled her fingers together, feeling the textures, her stomach roiled. Her chest tightened, her breathing erratic. Faded though it was, the ash stank of magic.

"I found our lost man. What's left of him." She stood and kicked at the pile, scattering the remnants with a grimace. "Other two are probably just a smear as well, somewhere out here. No point going to the village. The mage is on the run."

Alke rubbed his hands together and blew on them. "We should go find a warm bed."

"Not if we want any hope of catching our prey." Laela watched him bristle at her tone. He started to open his mouth, but she strode over to him and poked a finger into his chest, driving him back. "We are out here to do a job. One that you agreed to. Unless you'd rather turn tail and run? I'd be happy to bring you to justice." Hearing The Paladin's words spill from her own mouth turned her stomach. Yet they had the desired effect. Alke backed down without another word.

"Where do you suppose he got off to?" Willaime asked.

She sighed and closed her eyes against the audible grumbling of the three men when they realized Redford was out of the question. Laela listened to the wind, trying to categorize the smells it carried. Heat. Magic. A trail, one she felt more than she saw.

Laela pointed without opening her eyes. "That way."

"You heard her, men. We'll continue through the night." Willaime tugged his gloves on firmly, striding toward his mount once more. Gilbert and Dolan followed, and for a moment, it seemed like Alke might do the same before he turned away.

He faced her instead. The sneer he wore was all too familiar. He was going to be a problem. She ignored him and walked forward, until he had no choice but to stand in her way or step aside.

"We'll make camp somewhere down the road when we've gained a little ground," Laela said to Willaime after Alke moved out of her way. The knight nodded, waited for her to saddle up, then motioned for her to take the lead.

Chapter 18

THE VILLAGE

LAELA OPENED HER EYES with a start as a hand closed around her throat. Alke was above her, and the noise that tore through his throat woke the camp. The others scrambled for their weapons, assuming the group was under attack. She watched Gilbert and Dolan stumble around, but her attention was drawn to Willaime, who was propped up on one arm and gazing at the scene with indifference. Once he realized what was going on, he shook his head, rolled over, and left her to her own devices.

"What did you do, you bitch?" Alke was still screaming, his voice shriller as he clutched his hand. Blood pooled from his fingers, seeping out from between them as he tried to stem the flow. He teetered then tried to skitter away, but Laela still had a hold of him. "I'll cut you to pieces!"

Laela's fingers closed around the hilt of her knife, then slammed it into Alke's gaping jaw. There was a satisfying crack of something shattering, and she jerked herself from beneath the body above her and kicked him with one foot, rolling him over so she could pin him to the ground.

"What's that?" she spat as he groggily struggled like a fish out of water. Her knees kept his arms in place, his severed finger far from the hand it had recently been part of. "Next time, it's you choking on your own cock. Got it?" She did not shout, nor raise her voice with this threat. There was no need.

Alke gurgled and stared at her in stark disbelief.

"Do I make myself clear?" Laela snarled. Alke managed to nod, unable to speak. She shook her head and grunted, forcing open his mouth with her fingers. "Then this next lesson should hammer home my point. I know you understand already, but this is for Gilbert and Dolan. Can you hear me? Yes? Good." Alke's gaze locked onto her hand, holding his finger and dangling it in the air above his face. Her grip on him held the prisoner in place, even as he tried to wiggle free. She shoved the severed finger into his mouth and forced it to close. "Swallow." He resisted. Alke's lips worked against her glove and found nowhere to bite, no way to get release.

It was another minute at least, after his skin started to mottle beneath her that his throat was finally spurred to motion in a shuddering swallow. Laela waited to be certain the digit was indeed gone and that Alke wasn't going to retch it up anytime soon.

"Let that serve as warning to you," she barked at the others, who were slack-jawed at the sight, "to keep your hands to yourself." She glanced at Alke. "If you vomit, I am going to shove that finger back down your throat."

"Did you have to make him—" Willaime started, and Laela's glare cut him off. Apparently, the scene held more interest for him than she initially believed.

"If you bandage that hand properly it might not bleed out. I suggest you do not perish in the middle of the night," Laela said to Alke. The elf was on her feet now, wide awake as she dug through her pack. This should make them think twice before they would risk laying another finger on her. Alke might, especially since he seemed the type to try to save face. At the very least, Alke would never forget the taste of his own finger, and that made her smile.

The only sound lingering in the camp now was the scraping together of the leather and brass of her armor as she moved to her horse. She busied herself preparing her saddle and supplies. Out of the corner of her eye, she watched as Willaime gave up trying to sleep altogether. He slapped Dolan out of the way, who had been making a poor attempt at bandaging Alke's finger, and started treating the wound. She found it odd, knowing what they were about, but she was not going to argue with Willaime. Not again.

Despite only having nine fingers, Alke would not be exempt from his service.

Laela gave a shake of her head, ignoring the man's soft whining and the comforting, albeit empty, words from Willaime. He did his best to calm the three down, a familiar rote she chose to pay no mind to. There would be no sleep for her, and the prisoners could choke on any sleep they managed themselves.

The elf surveyed the area around camp. Walked the perimeter, made sure to keep an eye on the three men. Once Willaime had tended to Alke he retreated to his bedroll. She could hear his faint snoring, even over the grinding of her own teeth. When dawn pinkened the sky, Willaime then woke again to rouse the prisoners. She waited, picking at a pack of food. The three men, when handed their rations, kicked up a fuss.

"First you make us sleep out here, and now you're giving us old bread and dried meat?" Gilbert groused, shaking the meager fare in one large hand.

"This is what we have. If you do not like it, you can take that up with The Paladin," replied Willaime, effectively silencing any further complaints.

The prisoners glared at her.

"You look a little green around the gills. Something upsetting your stomach?" Laela called to Alke from where she sat, watching him and the others.

None dared answer. Willaime went about dutifully eating his own food. Laela resumed cleaning up camp, kicking dirt into the small firepit to smother the remaining flames. A sudden, if small, plume of ash and smoke crept through the air.

"The longer you dawdle the more likely it is we will find ourselves sleeping in the dirt once more," Willaime said to the prisoners after he finished eating. At the knight's urging, camp broke quickly, and the men seemed a little more apt to listen to what he had to say as he guided them through the process. Laela grabbed the reins of her mount, nudging it into motion away from the others, leaving the edge of the forest behind.

The smell then hit her, the stench of something rotting near some fresh grooves in the earth. Ignoring a shout from Willaime, she waded into the thick brush. With barely a few steps taken, she saw the congealed, sticky puddles of blood where wild animals had torn the straps holding armor together, hoping to get at whatever meat lay inside.

"If that pile of ash was our burned knight, I think I found the other two who went with him," she called over her shoulder. Prodding the bodies with the toe of her boot, she grimaced. The smell brought tears to her eyes.

"Is there something worth salvaging?" Willaime asked as he studied the piles of gore.

"No." Laela turned and pushed past Willaime. But his hand caught her before she got too far. "The armor's never going to come clean and will reek of death. Someone's picked them over already." Laela wrested free of his grip and moved away from the stench.

"What's she on about now?" asked Gilbert, his eyes narrowing at the sight of the bodies.

"I want some armor. I don't care if it's got guts on it," Dolan said.

Alke remained silent, looking at nothing in particular.

"If you perform your duties well you will be outfitted properly, and trained," Willaime replied flatly.

"What if we club you down where you stand, ser?" Gilbert chortled as he spoke, poking his club toward Willaime.

"Then I'll gut you like the cur you are and drag you back to The Paladin by your entrails," Willaime barked, making the three men retreat a few paces in fear.

Their sudden silence and the stench of the corpses followed Laela, not unlike a thick cloud. Pausing to take a drink from her waterskin before stowing it again in her saddlebag, Laela climbed onto her horse without looking back to see if Willaime would dirty his hands or set the prisoners to the task. She nudged the horse into movement once more. Whatever had beset The Paladin's men had circled back this way.

When the prints turned off of the road and headed into the forest, Laela followed. Even when she lost the trail, something pulled her along. An echo, a feeling, tugging at her. The knight's words came back to her then. *"Dotes on you... Lively hunts."* Grimacing, Laela concentrated instead on pursuing what lay before her.

It was well into the evening hours before she lost the trail. She circled a few times to see if she could discover it again but had no luck. "Where the fuck are you, Gaulf?" she grumbled at no one in particular as she snuck through the underbrush into a thicker part of the forest. "Not returning to Redford, not unless you *want* to get caught, but I doubt that. We'd have seen you on the road, since Willaime wants our presence known for The Paladin's sake. You have to be somewhere out here."

By the time Willaime and the other men caught up to Laela, she was astride her horse and looking in every direction, trying to determine the right way to go.

"The trail went cold," she admitted to Willaime as his horse sidled up next to her. She took one glove off, tucking it into her belt before she scrubbed her hand over her face.

"We're nearing Swanford. If we press on, we can sleep in warm beds tonight," Willaime said.

"I am not going to let this firebug slither right out of my grasp." Laela wrapped her hands tightly around the reins of her horse.

"I figured you might say as much." Willaime sighed, then spoke to the prisoners behind them. None had tried to run, yet. "We will be making camp out here tonight." There was no resistance from the men. Not even Alke.

Maybe Willaime convinced them to play nice. Dismounting, a sudden shooting pain through her midsection nearly sent her sprawling to the ground. Biting back a yell against the sensation of *burning* that flared over her skin, Laela held onto her horse's neck. It whinnied softly, as if to calm her. Her legs refused to steady, dared not support her full weight as the world lurched sideways.

Laela drew her head up. Willaime stood some distance away, concern etched into his features. Watching her. Waiting. He came no closer, his hand resting on the hilt of his sword.

Laela spoke around the bile that threatened to rise inside of her, against the waves of nausea that radiated through her entire body. "Do you feel that?"

"Laela?" Willaime asked hesitantly.

"I'm fine. But we're close." She paused, closing her eyes against the dying haze of sunlight. On an errant gust of wind, she caught a familiar, acrid scent. "That way." Laela pointed. "I smell smoke." She traced her finger along the horizon to where the trees blotted out the sky.

"Are you sure? That is the direction of Swanford," Willaime said. "We may yet have time."

Forcing her body to listen, her mind to still, she climbed onto the horse. Once situated, her hand dropped behind her. She loosened the quiver from its straps on the saddle and pulled it free, affixing it to her belt. Then Laela retrieved her bow.

"We ride!" Willaime shouted to the three men, who scrambled to get to their own mounts. She waited as Willaime spurred his horse with a kick. Gilbert and Dolan were hot on his tail. Alke watched the others ride off, cradling a bandaged hand to his chest. Laela studied him impassively. Whether he was about to flee, she'd never know. He caught sight of her and swallowed forcefully, his face pale. With a swift kick to his own horse, he headed after the others.

"Good choice," she muttered to herself. With a shout, she spurred her horse into motion and leaned down over the neck of the beast as it seemed to sense her own budding excitement.

The hunt was on.

The town was close, and even now she could hear the wails echoing over the small hill that separated them from Swanford. And as the horse carried her over it, she spied the fire and the heavy black smoke. Beyond the devouring flames, she saw something crawling, moving like an inky ichor along the ground.

That it was a human, Laela had no doubt. Two arms, two legs, and a flowing cloak. It always was a human. *Never an elf.* How many times had she hoped for that? If only to find someone familiar, someone who might help her. But no. Whatever crawled down there was disappointingly mortal. Yet as she watched, the shape of it, ill-defined and nebulous in the undulating shadows, she knew what it truly was. *Mage.*

She *felt* it down there, drawing her gaze wherever it traveled. People ran for safety amidst the spreading fire, some dragging along human-ish shapes behind them. None of it held her attention for long like the threads of magic, the stench of it. Putrid. That she could scent magic was one of the reasons The Paladin tolerated what little resistance she yet held against him, a gift of her elven blood.

She hated him that much more for it.

"You will be my sword, Laela. I will wield you against magic itself."

Laela rode her horse as close as she dared before she leaped out of the saddle. She whistled at her horse and leaned in, patting it as she whispered, "Wait here. I'll be back."

Trudging off at a brisk pace, adjusting her quiver and readying her bow, she ran toward the conflagration. Willaime and the others had not waited, had already ventured forward. She searched for a low building and used one of the barrels to climb to the roof of one she thought would suffice. This gave her a better vantage point and let her sprint along the thatching, closer to the heart of the village proper and the fire raging there. From her roost, the concentric circle layout of the village drew Laela's gaze. Wooden houses grew darker as the flames licked at them. Fresh wreaths smoked, adding to the building flames. Laela watched some villagers herd others toward what she guessed to be the main hall.

Surveying the scene in front of her, she saw that Willaime had ushered the prisoners into the center of the village. They headed for the slithering shape whose cloak flailed behind it as it crawled along the ground.

No clean shot.

Willaime thumbed through a weighty tome he had retrieved from his saddlebag, a book he perpetually kept close. His movements were practiced and quick for someone layered in plate and chain, the heel of his boot scratching a few rough symbols into the earth. She followed him to ensure that no one would interrupt his work. The three men watched him before realizing that, with Laela virtually gone and Willaime busy, they could disappear in the chaos. Laela thought to loose an arrow now, but she had to protect the knight first and foremost.

When he completed the circle, Willaime stood on the first symbols and hastily etched a series of crosses pointed inward toward the village. He closed his eyes and lowered his head. Something *snapped* into existence around the town, shadowing the crude line that Willaime had carved. It made Laela's stomach clench, her body growing cold.

"I *hate* it when he does that. I don't see why The Paladin tolerates it," she said to herself with a snarl, the world teetering again. She maintained her footing on the rooftop as the knight strode forward. She watched all of this going on without really seeing it. Instead, the arrow she had nocked was trained on the nine-fingered fool. She'd made a promise that he was first, and Laela planned to keep it.

Chapter 19

BACK IN TOWN

"**M**AKE SURE SHE'S FED and brushed by morning. I plan to ride before first light. Get me some fresh vegetables too." Orn flipped a silver at the stableboy, who looked like he'd just woken from a nap in a haypile. But the kid sprang to life once he saw the glint of coin in the torchlight. Orn watched to ensure the boy was not going to crawl back to sleep the moment he turned his back, and when he was certain his request would be properly attended to, Orn strode toward the village.

Redford might have been lively at one point, but now there was a pall hanging over it. Most of the small houses sat quiet, their lights dim. A few were dark. Scant decorations remained from a recent festival, forlorn and forgotten. The sparse village lacked much in the way of life and joviality. Walking through the main path past the town hall, Orn could almost picture how it was before. *Almost like home.*

A sharp pang for his own past threatened to overtake him. Abandoning Oldcliffe and the life he had led there was no choice at all. Absently, he scratched his arm, shaking away his thoughts and heading for the little inn at the end of the path. There he spotted the first signs of life: lights and congenial talk filtering out of the wooden structure. The sight eased his initial concern at the emptiness of the town.

He yanked the slightly warped door open, a bit harder than he'd intended. The knight searched the room, noticing that he had drawn the attention of every person in the inn. Farmers and workers alike, dressed in faded homespun cotton pants and tunics dyed with the stains of their labors. After they realized he was no threat, the patrons went back to talking and drinking, albeit much more subdued than what he'd heard from outside. Strangers were a rare spectacle in this corner of the world, and trusting outsiders never came easy for people in secluded villages like this one. But Orn was hardly a stranger. He'd been through this place only the previous day, but it appeared their uneasiness hadn't abated.

The knight supposed it was the nature of the job he had been hired to do. It weighed heavily on the townspeople. This close to harvest, there would usually be festivities. He had seen the decorations in the village, charred as they were, and made the connection between the scene before him and Gaulf's story. He shuddered.

The town had accepted his offer of help, the bounty barely posted but a day. Orn heard of it in passing and headed here straightaway. They had wanted the murderous mage dragged before the mayor to answer for his crimes by hanging him in the town square as a warning.

"Did you find Gaulf?" Del asked as Orn approached the rickety table where the man sat.

"I did," Orn replied quietly, glancing nervously at the other patrons. He had no idea how they'd react to the news he bore, starved as they seemed before for some public violence. "I tried to talk to him, but there was nothing left to reason with."

Del opened his mouth as if to speak, and Orn flinched at the pain he saw written in his features. Orn waited, his hand idly scratching at his left arm before realizing his error. How often had he found himself reaching for the mark lately?

"Did you bring proof?" Del asked, leaning forward as if the two were discussing something much more clandestine and not a town matter. "His parents are beside themselves. The mayor is talking about running them out of town after the mess he caused in his escape. Burned a knight to little more than ash."

"Is this proof enough?" Orn hoped the scrap of skin he'd removed from Archie's body would convince them so that the knights would abandon the hunt for Gaulf. He tossed the bloody patch of marked flesh onto the table where it landed with a sickly *plop*. Del turned away in disgust, hardly taking account of the ragged, blue shape of a hand tattooed on the flesh.

"I beg you, dispose of that," Del said, his voice muffled by the sleeve of his shirt pressed against his mouth and nose. Orn shrugged, scooped up the flap of flesh, and threw it into the hearth. There was a flare of light as the skin erupted in the intense heat that he knew better than to stare at for too long.

He hated this part, but a job was a job. They were not strict about the "alive" part of the writ, thankfully, even if they did seem saddened by the outcome. Out here, farms were a family's only means of survival, too precarious to risk with something so volatile and unpredictable as magic and its wielders. And while Orn understood their fear, cutting down innocents was not the profession he dreamed of.

"Little bastard put up a fight." Orn didn't mention the fact that the "little bastard" was, in fact, Archie and not Gaulf, but he figured he owed them a story of sorts. "Didn't want to play nice." *Didn't want to answer any questions either.* Orn grunted, mostly to himself. "Things got ugly."

"Mayor's demands are met. Should keep the knights off of our back," one of the farmers muttered as Del retrieved a bag of coins from his belt. The sullen innkeeper slid the pouch across the uneven table with a sigh. Orn picked it up and shook it, feeling the weight of the coins inside, then affixed it to his own belt. Del vacated the table, and the small crowd that had gathered while they talked dispersed. Before Del could get too far away, though, Orn surmised things were about to get a lot worse.

"Shit," Orn groused when he saw a wisp of a girl striding over to his table with grim determination. Her face was marked with a black handprint, one he recognized instantly. *Jannie.*

"Liar!" Jannie screamed, poking her finger in Orn's face.

"Listen—"

"You listen! Where is Gaulf?" Jannie asked, an edge to her tone that betrayed more than merely her anger. She was desperate. But Orn could not trust himself to not tell the truth. Not if he wanted to keep Gaulf safe and keep the coin.

"Come on, Jannie. Come away. It's not his fault." Del placed a comforting hand on her shoulder, gently tugging her back. "Leave the knight be."

"He's still out there, Del. This man is a liar and a thief!" Jannie sobbed. Del tried again to hold her back, but she wrenched out of the innkeeper's grip and practically launched herself at Orn. "You're wrong about Gaulf! Wrong!" She then spun on her heel and shouted to the room, "All of you are wrong!"

"Keep this up, and they'll be back. In force," Del said calmly. The words seemed to take the wind out of her, and she sank against the older man. He finally led her away, but Jannie's wails echoed through the room, a haunting sound to Orn's ears.

"Poor kid," he muttered to himself. The little inn never quite returned to its former mood. Orn took a sip from the mug Del offered him, trying to shake the sight of her burned face from his mind. Gaulf's story came in sharp relief then, and Orn was glad that the boy managed to escape his fate, for now. The wood of his bench creaked next to him, alerting him to the presence of another. He hoped it wasn't someone who was after more details of Gaulf's demise.

"If you're still aching for coin, ser, there's word of another mage running amok in Ostford." The farmer shied away from Orn's glare when he turned to get a better look at the person who'd sat next to him, but he did not leave the table.

"There are no sers here," Orn said flatly, in hopes the farmer would take the hint and leave.

"What's that now?" the farmer asked. He blinked light-brown eyes and looked Orn over, driving a hand through his blond hair. "How do you mean?"

"No knights here, I'm afraid."

"But your armor—"

"I am no knight." Orn scowled, accepting another mug of ale from Del. He realized quickly the farmer wouldn't yield. Orn sighed. "Fine. How much?"

"Don't rightly know, but coin isn't what knights are for. You're here to help, aren't you?" The farmer shrank in the face of Orn's glowering and pointed to a scrap of paper affixed to the wall. "Came in just this morning."

Orn muttered his thanks, then made to leave, but the farmer wasn't quite finished.

"Guess the proper knights have their hands more than full. Figured you might be one of them willing to help." The farmer huffed and crossed his arms over his chest. "See, my son's a handful, and I hoped you'd take him on. He won't ever settle down until he's had a bit of adventure."

"Is this what your son wants?" Orn asked.

"Chindler doesn't know what he wants," the farmer said, shaking his head.

"How about not shipping your son off to danger with the first not-knight you stumble upon?" He had only wanted to collect the bounty and get a drink. It was supposed to be simple enough.

"But, ser—"

"Thanks for the information about the writ. I'll make my way from here," Orn replied, hoping that he had silenced the farmer for good. The stranger shrugged then stood, abandoning Orn at last. "Never a moment's rest." He left a stack of coins next to the mug, then approached the writ on the wall. There was more here than he had bargained for. "Suspected use of magic, causing havoc, communing with darker forces." Orn sighed when he saw the name. Archivald of Ostford. *It was just a matter of time.*

There were a few other writs on the wall, and Orn skimmed them all. Five or six missing persons missives, from New Cresthill to Cassandira to Haven. Orn frowned. No mention of markings, or anything else, and yet something in the writs *spoke* to him.

"This gives me more questions, not answers." He tore the writs from the wall and meandered to the bar. "I'm going to need a room and a meal for the night and morning," Orn said to Del, already taking a mental tally of what coin he'd have remaining. "Maybe send a note for me to the shop, give the proprietor a list of supplies I need?" Orn parted with another stack of coins with no little amount of reluctance. "Another drink too."

"You hardly finished the last one, ser," Del said, but didn't hesitate to fill another mug and slap it on the bar in front of him after scooping up the coins. Before Orn could correct him, the man was gone, leaving him with a sticky mug full of the same questionable contents.

Orn took a swig, then grimaced. "Not sure if you brewed a bad batch this time, but that's a vicious bite there." Orn was mostly mumbling to himself as he stood, wobbling. The aftertaste was bitter on his tongue, and a shiver ran through him like a sword. His stomach soured, and he fought the urge to retch.

Was he tired, or was the ale that strong?

"Have my stuff ready come morning, yeah?" Orn called to Del as he started for his room. Silence enveloped the inn, all eyes on him as he departed.

Chapter 20
SHE COMES

ANY HOPE GAULF HAD of keeping count of the days had long since melted away. Orn's words chased him in and out of the cover of the forest.

Sra curak.

To avoid them, and detection by the locals, he changed course several times. This far from Redford, the only home he'd ever known, he was well and truly lost. And he didn't know how to fix it. For the first time in his life, there was no meaningful way forward. Rather, *tomorrow* had become something to fear. The scent of charred flesh lingered in his nose, an unwelcome reminder calling to him.

With his entire life somewhere on the road behind him and a bounty on his head, Gaulf could only focus on survival. Every tree and bend in the road seemed the same, every forest noise resembled that of clanking armor or Orn's voice. Heading east, into the densest part of the vegetation, Gaulf worried he would soon see the sun disappear. Ever since he was marked, he hated the nights. They were full of dreams he could not shake.

A figure stood in the middle of the path before him, head upturned. Here, the canopy was stretched thin enough that the sky bled through the branches. Gaulf was perched above the small stream that meandered close to the road, his cupped hands halfway to his mouth.

"It's night?" That observation—and not the strange figure—gave Gaulf pause as he noticed the shadows gathered around the trees, their bare trunks hardly touched by the light of the moon. Even the stars seemed shy in their celestial blanket, shielded by a spattering of ominous clouds. *Wasn't it day only a moment ago?*

A severe face, eyes creased in concern, stared at Gaulf kneeling by the stream. He recoiled, expecting momentum to carry this stranger forward and straight into him. It took Gaulf more than a few moments to realize there was no impact.

Peeking with one eye, he saw nothing but trees.

"Who's there?" Gaulf's question went unanswered as he clambered to his feet. The path he had been following was suddenly overgrown, and he fancied that it might have been a road once. He heard the creak of a wagon, the rumble of a passing caravan, and Gaulf closed his eyes. He could sense that long ago this had been a well-traveled road. Echoes of lives eddied around him, and before he could stop himself, he stretched out a hand to touch one of them.

Thick fabric, soft against his fingers. Gaulf prayed that he touched some sort of weird tree instead, a leaf like no other, or some wild animal. But no. The fabric moved with the not-so-gentle stirring of someone out of breath. Gaulf dared open one eye again.

Across the stream from him stood that figure, symbols stitched into his fine robes.

A hand.

A lightning bolt.

An archway of stone.

A burning wheel.

A scythe.

A quill.

Fear shot through him, mirroring the fear in the man's eyes as the two of them stood so close yet so far apart. Slowly, Gaulf lowered his gaze, catching the last symbol stitched into the man's clothing.

A spiral.

The pain in Gaulf's arm flared, violently twisting in his flesh.

"*Remember.*" Gaulf's mouth moved, had said the word, but it was not him.

"He's coming," said the strange man across/not across the stream. The burbling water melted away, the trees receded, and the sky cradled a full and bright moon surrounded by a sea of stars. Nary a cloud, nary a soul but the two of them, however this man was right. Someone was coming. Gaulf could feel it. "I am as good as dead out here..." the man continued as if Gaulf ceased to exist, his gaze fixed on something over the young farmhand's shoulder. "Ser Gregoris is near."

Gaulf realized then that the man carried a large staff in one hand. The same symbols from the robe were carved into the wood, forming a pattern. The sight of them was burned into his vision with searing clarity while the man became hazier, the edges of his form transforming into mist.

"Do you need help?" Gaulf asked in desperation. "Can you help me?" Silence. "Hey! Stop!" Gaulf shouted after the man turned and ran away. Alone once more, he had no choice but to follow.

The further he went, the stronger the sensation grew that something or someone stalked him. His heart thumped in his chest as his lungs struggled to work, and yet he ran.

Where had the stranger gone to? That question nagged him, the answer fleeting as a dream upon waking. The air grew thick. Gaulf ran onward.

"What—" His single word hung in the air as he tried to puzzle out the night sky. At first, he thought a storm was forming, the clouds again obscuring the stars above. But no.

Gaulf witnessed the little balls of light wink out of existence one by one. A vivid scar of darkness spread across the black. All that remained was the moon, hanging like a glaring eye trained upon the farmhand. Every thrum of his heartbeat echoed in his ears, a crashing thunder, and with each breath the moon drew closer.

Accompanying the burgeoning darkness came a series of whispers in the trees. As he turned his head, countless conversations sprang to life around him. Remembrances not his own assaulted him from every direction, too many voices to make sense of at first. From the shadows themselves the voices crept.

"The Paladin must be stopped. His war against magic is folly. He has doomed us all." More voices rose in the night, contradicting the claims of the first. *"The Paladin protects us against those who use magic. The Paladin holds firm since The Rising, shielding us from those who seek to do us harm."*

Part of him tried to hold onto the stories his parents told, that he heard repeated throughout the village. The Paladin protected them against the corrupting influence of magic and its wielders.

The spark inside of him smoldered briefly, a counterpoint burning away all he had ever known or believed with its whispers. Exhaling, Gaulf ran.

But he could not outrun the sounds following him. Inside of him, weaving through him. Not just from the darkness, but from that mark on his arm. A cyclone of power building, cresting to the point he worried he might drown in his own flesh.

A tendril of light suffused him much the same as the orb of light he chased into water the day he was marked. A calming golden warmth burrowing deeper inside his chest. Raising a hand, he expected piercing pain, but there was none. He watched while the light shifted then faded, with images of the robed man and his staff in various stages of outrunning whatever chased him. Chased *them*, Gaulf realized, as he heard a metal clanking in the distance. Spurred by the noise, Gaulf ran, following that golden thread. From its warmth came comfort, and he could only hope it would show him the way.

Time ceased to have meaning, the world around him manifesting in fits of awareness. Only when he felt a spot between his shoulder blades itch did he stumble from the sudden sensation.

The golden thread traveled so far behind him that it was impossible to determine its end.

Waiting near the edge of his vision was a knight astride a horse. He flickered in and out of reality, a specter on the dark horizon. Steam poured from his helmet in the chilly air, but to Gaulf it seemed like breaths of flame. His armor, too, boasted the sickly orange color, as if freshly forged.

Mounted next to the knight was another figure. Diminutive though she appeared beside the armored man, her presence overshadowed that of the knight. There *she* sat, the face that had plagued him at the festival, in every waking dream, in the depths of his dark cell. However, when Gaulf studied her face, he soon understood that it was not the same woman. The face staring him down did so with a sharper edge. Beneath a bramble crown, her bronze hair wild and woven with trinkets of bone and leather, she regarded him with contempt. It paled in comparison to the look she gave to the armored knight. Gaulf shook his head, taking a step away from the mounted pair. Distant, across the dream-like length of the road, he saw them clear as day.

Too late Gaulf noticed the knight's raised sword. A crack of lightning struck as the weapon lowered, pointed across the stream. Right at Gaulf's heart.

"Ser Gregoris, *please.*" The strange figure appeared next to Gaulf. "Stand down." Gaulf watched him plant the end of the staff into the ground before the man looked at him. "*Run.*"

Gaulf ran.

Gaulf dreamed of darkness binding his limbs, immobilizing him so that it might swallow him whole. But instead, he collided with someone flesh and bone who held him in a hug. Meeting a pair of concerned brown eyes set in an angular face surrounded by a halo of golden-brown hair, Gaulf thought he was hallucinating again.

"Ho there! What has you causing such a ruckus, my boy?" The man's arms squeezed his own reassuringly, and Gaulf noticed he had been screaming. His throat raw, aching, fell silent as he wrested control of his body from the living dream that claimed him.

"Let us get him warmed up by the fire, Booth. Festival's ready to start." Another figure stepped into view and briefly, Gaulf believed it was his mother.

Ma. The word died on his lips as Booth turned about, ushering Gaulf alongside him. She was nothing like his mother, but her voice, warm and caring, felt like *home.*

"Boy, can you speak? Do you have a name?" Booth searched his face.

"Gaulf." A rasp, followed by a series of coughs as he tried to clear his throat. Booth's hand swatting him on the back brought tears to his eyes. When the coughing subsided, Gaulf shied away from the pair.

"We're not going to hurt you, child," the woman said.

"Where am I?" The village might have been *home,* until he studied it a bit more closely. It was not that the architecture of the buildings was the same as those of Redford, for these were built of a darker wood, and there were decorations covering every available surface. Gaulf caught sight of the statues holding familiar arched blades in the town center, cast in the dancing light of the bonfire.

"You've come to the village of Swanford, stranger. Quite in the nick of time too, because we're in the middle of our harvest festival. We can get you something warm to fill that belly." Booth ruffled his hair and Gaulf could not help but smile.

Swanford. A village not far from home, but a world away to Gaulf. His mind spun with the things he had heard his parents say about the village and its inhabitants. They hardly knew how to plow a field, the lazy louts. Gaulf giggled and shook his head.

"You okay?" Booth asked.

"Oh, aye." Gaulf nodded, swallowing another unbidden laugh.

"What happened to you?" The lady stepped closer tentatively.

"Let's give him time to catch his breath, Geralyn," Booth said.

Something passed between the two of them before she turned to Gaulf. Her scrutiny made him want to turn and run, but instead he froze. "What brings you out tonight, screaming loud enough to shake the earth?"

There were too many words colliding in his head, lodging in his throat. "I—running—" he sobbed around the barbed words. "The Paladin."

"I see," Geralyn said grimly. She leaned forward, the hard lines of her face softening. She studied Gaulf that much closer, reaching toward him. He flinched in response, but not far enough that she couldn't brush some of his hair and wipe some dirt from his face. "I need you to be honest with me. Are you going to remain calm and let us feed you? Maybe give you a place to sleep?"

Gaulf nodded solemnly, then Booth turned him toward the village center. There were a number of people there dressed in their finest, trying their best to appear uninterested in the trio.

"Is everything okay, Geralyn?" asked one of the villagers, a balding man with ruddy cheeks accentuated by laugh lines.

A thick tension squatted in the air, but with a wave of her hand, Geralyn defused the general concern of the others. "We just found a stray out here who needs a good meal. Say, Thabe, does your barn still have a straw bed?" The flushed-faced man nodded in reply. "Then he can sleep there after we retire for the night. Let's carry on!"

Music picked up, matching the tempo of conversations resuming where they had left off. Geralyn left Gaulf in Booth's care, then headed toward the far seat of the table, which looked like where the mayor usually sat back at home.

"Let's get you some food," Booth said. There was a whirlwind of movement as people cleared space at a table for Gaulf. These were not his friends, but they offered him warmth and welcome all the same. His heart lurched in his chest, and a name fell silently from his lips. *Jannie.*

Booth introduced Gaulf to the villagers at the table, and though he tried to hang onto the information, the parade of names came and went in a blur. Especially after a plate of food appeared in front of him. Gaulf ate politely, working to soothe the gnawing hunger in his gut. Before Gaulf could swallow another mouthful, a mug of cider was set down beside his plate. Gaulf paused long enough to drain half of the mug in one fell swoop. The bite of the cider burned his tongue, and it reminded him of his father, of the sips he'd let Gaulf take when Ola and Elga distracted his mother.

"Slow down, my boy. That cider packs a fair punch." Booth chuckled as he sat next to Gaulf. Most of the others had already finished eating, yet still hovered. They watched Gaulf out of the corners of their eyes, not quite certain of the stranger in their midst.

"Thank you, sir. Again," Gaulf said between bites.

"Call me Booth, no *sir* necessary." Booth offered a smile.

Geralyn stood some distance away, a protective look on her face. For a moment, Gaulf could hardly tell if it were out of concern for him or because of him. He shuddered.

There was not a familiar face to be seen, and yet, it *almost* felt like he was home. Gaulf could almost envision having grown up here, could see himself running with those his own age, whose attention and curiosity never strayed far from him.

"Is everything all right, Gaulf?" Without his noticing, Geralyn had replaced Booth at Gaulf's side. Now that the whirlwind of activity had died down and he could look closely, Gaulf recognized her. Not in who she was, but what. She reminded him of Arthur's father.

"Yes, ma'am," he said quietly, his voice cracking with a sob he barely restrained.

"Far from home?" Geralyn probed cautiously. "Where do you hail from?"

"Redford," Gaulf answered before he understood what he had said, the danger he had put himself in. He could imagine Orn's disapproving face, disappointed in him for his blathering. Gaulf froze, hoping for a chance to bolt. Geralyn's hand on his shoulder stopped him.

"No one's going to hurt you here. Not if I can help it, and I'd like to think being the one in charge counts for something." A wry grin stretched Geralyn's face. "Stay. The festival show is starting soon." True to her word, many of the young villagers began clearing empty tables, pulling them from the center of the town to make room.

"Festival show?" Gaulf asked, confused.

"The festival spans eight nights, and tomorrow's when we give thanks to those that protect us from the evils of the world," Geralyn said, gesturing to The Harvester statues Gaulf noticed earlier.

Something made Gaulf's skin itch, and one word came unbidden to his mind. He almost choked as he bit back the word he wanted to say, half formed on his lips, but dared not give it life: *magic.*

"We can talk more later. I have some business with The Reapers that I must tend to." Her words struck a chord deep inside of Gaulf.

"Who?" Gaulf blinked as an ominous picture started to form in his mind. He could see The Harvester and Scythe, come to collect. Is that what The Paladin called his knights? Were they here for him? Those questions burbled in his throat when his stomach wrenched sharply with fear.

A series of solid *clanks* filled the area as if in answer. Gaulf's heart stopped, bile threatened to spew from his lips, and a chill ran the length of his spine. *No.* He would not let that happen. His hands then warmed, the fire alive and waiting just beneath the surface of his skin. Smoke filled his nostrils.

Across the way, a solitary knight stepped out of the darkness at the edge of the village.

"Oh, no. No. Not again, please," Gaulf muttered frantically.

"No one here is going to hurt you, Gaulf. Quite the opposite, if I have my way," Geralyn repeated, winking as she squeezed his shoulder again, then stood and strode off. Gaulf swallowed the sharp lump in his throat and tried to keep his eyes on her.

Gaulf still wanted nothing more than to crawl under one of the tables, to find somewhere to hide. Or to run. Run. *Run.*

Movement seemed impossible; his body refused to respond to his pleas. The bonfire swelled, driving back the shadows of night. The knight stood tall, his hand on the hilt of a sword buckled to his belt. The knight's armor boasted not the splendid reds and golds of The Paladin's men, but were instead etched with words, scrollwork.

The mayor approached the strange knight, her hands clasped together in front of her. Did she steal glances at Gaulf as she spoke? The roar of the fire, the commingling of so many voices, crushed any hope he had of overhearing. Every second that passed drew a sharp nail against his back, and he was certain doom lurked in the shape of that knight.

With his head swimming, Gaulf set the mug down. He left the table, stumbling after lifting his leg over the worn bench.

The knight glanced his way, pinning Gaulf where he stood. Was his sword slightly drawn from its scabbard? The dance of the fire blackened the words on the scrollwork armor, and a vigorous shake of Geralyn's head, another glance in his direction, determined his decision.

Gaulf ran, or would have, were the way clear. A solid wall of bodies and limbs prevented his escape. A bell rang.

"Don't leave yet."

"The show's just beginning."

"There's more pie."

"Get this boy another cider!"

He could not get away. The warm press of bodies pushed him further. Their jumbled words assaulted his ears, and beneath all of it lurked another scraping clank of metal that vibrated his teeth. A tornado of emotions followed by a brilliant eruption of the bonfire.

"Come, friends. Let us settle into our places for the festival show. This last night, let us remember that which drove back the darkness. Tonight, we pay homage to The Harvester." Did she turn to look at him? Gaulf's blood ran cold, though a fire raged inside of him.

Booth turned him about, wrapping a protective, comforting arm around Gaulf's shoulders. "Stay, boy. Calm yourself. Geralyn gave her word; no one's going to hurt you here."

Gaulf tried to square his shoulders and straighten his spine, to stand tall as his da had always told him to do in the face of a problem. But the stench of the fire, both the bonfire and the one inside of him, only added to the nausea. Saliva filled his mouth, and he swallowed it quickly.

The Harvester loomed in front of him. Or so he thought. A part of him saw the figure for what they were, a costumed villager carrying a well-worn scythe. Six other figures stood at the edge of the firelight, barely visible in the shadows. The rest of the village and its inhabitants ceased to exist. The world itself narrowed to the two of them: The Harvester and Gaulf. The mark on his arm pulsed in time with his heartbeat as The Harvester raised his Scythe to the sky.

Gaulf's heart lurched, and he closed his eyes, awaiting a blow that never came. His breath lodged in his throat. He slowly opened his eyes and found himself alone again out on the road. Standing in front of him was the robed man, his staff raised to the full moon. The world split where he stood, so that the images of the village and the strange man were overlaid. He tried to make sense of it. Which was real, which was not.

The mage stood in front of Gaulf at the entrance to the sleeping village behind him. Gaulf glanced down the road toward the thundering dust cloud. Even at this distance, he saw the lead horse and the figure atop it. Sword raised high, armor gleaming in the moon's light, followed by an army of similarly clad figures. Coming for blood.

Coming for him.

Neck and neck with the armored figure who loomed over the others rode a face that was passingly familiar. The visage that haunted his dreams while trapped in that cell in Redford. And yet again, somehow, Gaulf knew that it was not *her*.

She rode, hair-bound bones rattling in a cascading wave behind her as she thrust her hand forward. Toward him. Gaulf stepped back as if lanced by an arrow.

Shivering, feeling that vitriol like a slap to the face, Gaulf turned away. This brought him face to face with the man now at his side, who leaned heavily on his staff, his breathing labored.

"Ser Gregoris has gone mad, but I still harbor hope that I can make him see reason. They're coming." Frantic, the mage spoke in circles, his eyes wide. He slammed his staff into the earth. "By The Hand, by The Door, by The Spiral, I summon thee: earth and stone, flesh and bone. Protect me." The ground beneath Gaulf's feet came to life. The symbols on the man's robes and staff began to glow.

A mage. Gaulf watched the magic coalesce with the spell. A warm light moved through the man, through the staff, and then through Gaulf.

Wrapped in that web of light, Gaulf could do little more than watch. Too late he noticed the tendril inside of him bleeding through his body. His hand moved in the light's direction, mimicking the mage's movements. His mouth spoke the words as his mind was torn into a third shard, between the now and the magic.

Trapped in a body turned cage, the magic was building. He saw The Hand, The Door, and The Spiral digging deeper into his arm, consuming him from the inside out.

Magic. A burning light, a cascading, raw force not unlike a whirlwind carving at his insides as the spell was completed. Wholly different from conjuring fire, this came like a structured torrent of chaos. The earth split, and pebbled hands clawed their way out. Gaulf dragged his gaze from the stone creatures birthed from the ground and looked toward the road.

"Thank you, for the protection you're giving me," the mage said sorrowfully. Gaulf felt the man's anguish in his own heart as the stone creatures charged forward, their momentum creating a contrasting thunder to that of the horses' hooves. "That might buy me some time." Then the mage turned and took off. Straight through Gaulf, whose knees buckled at the sudden impact. The vision of the mage dissipated into smoke, revealing Booth grasping Gaulf, dragging him to his feet.

"What did you do?" Booth shouted in his face. The man's eyes were wide, full of fear.

As Gaulf opened his mouth, the stench of fire filled his nose and made him retch. Flames spread, casting the entire town in a series of dancing lights. Treated wood, homes, canvas. Gaulf recoiled, his mind slamming back to reality. Colors bled into the world as his mind tilted, scrambling for purchase.

These creatures were not made of stone alone but carried with them a burning ember. They looked like little humans born from the earth itself—grasping hands, hungry mouths—and they unleashed violence upon the village. In the fire, Gaulf saw afterimages of The Hand, The Door, and The Spiral everywhere.

The decorations burned first, a wick to the conflagration that followed. The creatures then lashed out at anyone who tried to fight. Screams filled the air, and spilled blood muddied the ground. Smoke and ash drifted skyward, floating on gusts of wind that served to only fan the flames.

The flames then spread to the statues in the town square, where the web of decorations and tents were thickest.

But in the flailing dance of villagers fighting for their very lives, something else lurked.

Something darker.

Gaulf retched again as that mote twisted inside of him, spreading as the fire did. He tried to make sense of the scene around him as he searched for escape, only to nearly run into one of the summoned creatures who chased after a person dressed as The Harvester.

Attempting to flee in a different direction, he still sensed the creatures surrounding him. Bound to him, to his life.

He wanted *more.*

Not creatures, but the power that wrought them into existence.

Magic.

A quiet laugh fled his lips, followed by a torrential outpouring as he coughed from the acrid smoke.

"*Beware.* Burn it away. Burn it all."

Chapter 21

THAT NIGHT

WHAT DREAMS CAME WERE a slithering smoke that tangled about Orn, who found himself trapped in the thin blanket. Flickering lights made it impossible to concentrate on anything other than those glimmering flashes that managed to break through the darkness. His body ached, a bone-deep pain that made him whimper as it settled. He felt the brush of heat on his face, and the scent of smoke lingered in the air, coiling in his lungs like a hissing serpent.

Orn's eyes popped open, seeing nothing but darkness blanketing the room. His hand groped for his sword, but when it came up empty, he thought his heart might burst out of his chest. Squirming, the knight fought his way out of the binding blanket, sweat-slicked and feverish. He rolled out of bed and onto his feet, noticing the hearth had gone cold. The water in the washbasin did not help matters much, but did aid in rinsing away the remnants of his strange dreams.

Orn peered out of the window, checking to see if the sun had risen. Night cradled the small village of Redford. Debating crawling back into bed and trying for some sort of rest, Orn sighed. The mark on his arm burned, ache worming through his entire body. Grimacing, Orn turned away from the window and set about preparing to leave. Weary fingers relied on muscle memory to get into his armor. He busied himself with adjusting the straps and buckles to keep his mind off the pain emanating from the mark. The familiar weight of the metal was almost enough to distract him. Almost.

What had once been a shining suit of armor was now little more than a shabby collection of steel and leather. He admired the new pieces taken from the knights chasing after Gaulf. When he had to, Orn filled in the missing pieces with chainmail. Altogether, while the armor was hardly pretty, it had saved his hide numerous times. He did not need it to be shiny or anything of the sort. Nor did he want it to be.

Once he was ready, he crept out of his room and left the inn. The fresh air cleared some of the fog from his head. He made his way to the stables.

"Good evening, Delilah. Did you miss me?" Orn dug through the saddlebags hanging in her stall, assessing the provisions. At least the stableboy did a thorough job. Fishing out a few carrots, he fed Delilah after opening the gate. "Seems like we're hardly ever in one place for long, much as both of us would like. But I feel something in the air tonight."

Delilah stomped out of the stall in reply. Orn clucked his tongue at her as he prepared her saddle before he led her out of the stables and through the sleeping village.

"We're back on the move, old girl," Orn said, earning a snort from the horse. As starlight gave way to day, he climbed into the saddle and let Delilah carry him onward. When he came to the river, the knight headed eastward, following the flow of the water. The thought of stopping and making camp crossed his mind a few times, but instead he continued riding. Orn kept an eye on the forest's edge, half expecting to see Gaulf there. Disappointment followed.

Orn shivered in the saddle, wishing he had stayed in bed, no matter how uncomfortable that blasted straw mattress had been.

"Shit." The world beneath Orn tilted. He dropped his hand to the hilt of his sword. Looking off in the distance, his mind tried to piece together what he saw. Another sun was setting, this time in the east. Or was it the sunrise? He nudged Delilah into a trot when he spied smoke through the trees some few miles away.

When Delilah seemed ready, Orn let her stretch into a swift gallop that caused his teeth to jitter in his mouth.

"Hurry, Delilah!" Orn yelled, his words whipped away with the wind as he steered her along a path barely wide enough for them. Hoping that he'd not get unseated by an errant branch, his heart raced, burning away the dregs of exhaustion.

The trees gave way and spit them out of the forest onto farmland. Flames were climbing higher and higher, devouring a little house and edging toward the town behind it. The mark on his arm thrummed. As if it felt something in the fire. *Magic.*

Chapter 22

CHAOS ENSUES

BODIES LITTERED THE NOW-UNRECOGNIZABLE village square. Fire had spread in every direction, consuming all in its path. Orn half expected a scaled dragon to poke its head around one of the crumbling structures. Instead, he spied three rough-looking men raising crude weapons against an unseen foe. Were they the cause of this havoc, or were they merely opportunistic vultures?

The old knight slid off of his horse and swatted her on the rump, sending her to the safety of the forest behind them.

The smoke wound through the narrow pathways of the town, and Orn heard the frantic yelling of the three men but could not quite make out the meaning. From what he could tell, it did not seem as if they were here to help.

"Don't tell me I've run into the only fire lately started by mundane means," Orn groused to no one in particular. But instinctively, he knew better. There was magic here.

Orn moved along the side of one of the few buildings untouched by the flames, stopping to survey the scene. Briefly, Orn debated abandoning the town to its fate until the fire cleared. With the three men lurking nearby, he feared he would end up on the wrong end of a blade before he could determine the source of the magic he sensed in the air. With the carnage spiraling through the village, any hope Orn might have entertained for answers quickly dwindled. A commotion not too far ahead stopped him short. There was a grunt, and a bit of yelling, followed by the unmistakable sound of fists making impact with flesh.

By the time he could sneak along the charred alley to get another peek at the men, one was missing from their number. The smoke obscured the ground, but the man who was unaccounted for suddenly appeared, wild-eyed as he searched for something in the growing haze. His back was to Orn, who had taken this chance to shift closer. The poor fool seemed rather out of place, what with the shaky grip on his sword's hilt. Even if he hadn't been the cause of this disaster, the bloodstains on his clothes were enough to settle the matter in Orn's perspective.

"What're you about, friend?" Orn called from where he stood. The man whirled around, his face etched with fear.

"What did you bring us into?" the stranger asked frantically. Orn raised his hand placatingly, lowering his sword in hopes the man would not attack prematurely. He needed answers first.

"I'm here to help," Orn replied with a reassuring smile. The man shook his head and resumed his search.

"If I find her, I'm going to slice that bitch from neck to nether. You get in my way, you die too. Got it?" The warning sent a shiver down Orn's spine. This man was a problem, one he knew how to solve. "Screw you, and The Paladin, and oaths. I'm getting my revenge, and then I'm leaving this damned place."

"You aren't here to help?" Orn asked cautiously.

"Not since that fucking she-elf took my finger. Made me swallow it," the man spat. Orn raised his hands defensively, taking a step backward. "That's what I thought." The man turned his attention away.

Orn closed what distance remained so that he was close enough for his arm to slip around the man's neck. He struggled in the knight's grasp, choking on a scream.

"Shh, calm down. Can't have you hurting anyone or standing around like a vulture. People are dying, and now, so are you." The man's body went rigid when Orn moved his blade into place. The tip of his sword pierced his belly clean through, the stranger's blood spilling from the wound in wide rivulets. Orn grimaced at how easily the sword had passed through the man. Whatever fight he had washed away with his life.

Orn freed his blade from the corpse, using his boot against the man's back for leverage. He tried to wipe it clean, but the blood clung to the weapon and caught the glow of the fire, giving the dull metal a shine that attracted the knight's gaze.

An eerie quiet descended on the town. Panic rose in Orn's chest, but he swallowed hard against it. There came a tremor in the ground beneath his feet. Something edged in behind him, and the world seemed to slow. Orn waited for the killing blow to land, waited for the lance of white-hot pain. When it didn't come, he turned to see whatever had come upon him but Orn only noticed a hastily carved line in the dirt around the village proper.

"Shit," Orn muttered after finding himself damn near toe to toe with a slavering jaw full of hundreds of jagged teeth. It was chewing on a hunk of something, and seemed to burn that much brighter for the consumption. A putrid tongue licked at the burnt lips, and the smell that emanated from its mouth was sour. The laugh that followed from the being—*almost* human but for how its stony flesh glowed red hot—set Orn's teeth on edge.

"PREY."

The word was thunderous despite the fact it had not been spoken. Had it? His head rang as that rumbled word bypassed his ears to instead drill straight into the meat of his brain.

The blood that stained his blade took on an unhealthy sheen. There were markings along the center of the sword that seemed to drink in the fire, the blood, the smoke. Orn brought the blade to his face, his eyes struggling to focus. A spiraling pattern, a scythe, a lightning bolt, a door. More swam against his vision, but he could tell one thing: the sigils hungered for more. The blade felt alive in his hand, and his gaze traveled the length of it until he came to the tip and spotted the tendril of smoke drawn into it from the beast in front of him. Orn's face split into a wide smile.

"What do we have here?" Orn asked, staring down whatever this thing was. None of the mages or bounties had mentioned anything like this. He realized if he turned to run, he'd be crushed beneath the sizable bulk of this *thing* should it decide to trample him, so Orn stood his ground. He settled into a warrior's stance when he sensed the creature's malice. The beast was trying to push at him with more than its stench, and whatever it was disappeared into Orn's sword.

Then the beast swiped at Orn with its claws.

Orn brought the blade to bear. The creature moved faster than he would have thought capable for something of its size. Its flesh crackled and blazed with heat, and Orn feared he'd be burned to a crisp. Orn took this chance to swing, giving what he hoped was a frightful yell as he did so. The creature shied away briefly, and Orn swung again, feeling his sword connect with its side. It vibrated in his hands so hard the ache shot straight to his shoulder as the creature regained whatever senses it had. The giant, fiery hand, freed from its host, writhed on the ground while Orn swung the heavy blade one last time. The beast let out a rumbling howl and turned to escape.

Orn stared dumbfounded, not believing his luck. "That worked much better than I anticipated," he whispered to himself. He glanced at the sword in his hand, the hilt still thrumming in his grasp. The creature loped off into the distance with its ember-spewing stump cradled to his chest. The knight understood he would have to give chase. The creature couldn't be permitted to harm anyone else.

But any hope the creature might've harbored for retreat was extinguished as it collided face-first into an invisible barrier near the edge of town. It crumpled to its haunches, emitting what Orn could only assume was a whimper. This was his chance. He could not give it time to recuperate. Orn drew his dagger, keeping his sword in his dominant hand, and launched himself upon the wide back of the creature, stabbing wherever he could find purchase. The blades sank in its flesh without much resistance, each puncture accompanied by an unnerving howl. The creature tried to shake off the knight, but Orn reached its shoulders before it could do much of anything.

At the apex of its spine, Orn plunged his sword into the creature once more, holding on tightly as it thrashed about, desperate to be rid of the knight. The beast reared, and Orn ripped the length of his blade out of its strange flesh, then forced it back in as far as he could, piercing the creature straight through.

The ground shook as it collapsed, sparks and embers flaring after Orn was tossed from its hulking form. He skittered along the ground, only coming to a halt when he thrust his dagger into the earth. Orn managed to find his feet, righting himself as best he could. Taking stock of his injuries, the knight cataloged the new aches and pains blossoming across his body.

Somewhere in the distance, someone shouted commands.

"I'm going to feel that for a few days," Orn said, choking on the thick smoke that hung in the air. He spotted his sword lodged beneath the body of the creature.

Cautiously, as if expecting the beast to reanimate, he withdrew the blade, watching in horror as the stone flesh crackled and rippled, its essence spilling from it and into his sword. After the blade drank its fill, the monstrosity became nothing but charred rock.

Whatever barrier the stone creature had collided with, Orn saw it as a shimmer separating him from the surrounding forest. "That can't be good." He swung his blade against it, meeting solid resistance and creating sparks. He then observed the line in the dirt let go of its hold on the smoke, and it bled into the night.

Orn heard more howls and cursed.

Too late he realized that there was more than one creature.

He barely had a chance to react before another coalesced out of the shadowy murk to lunge at him. Although it was smaller than the other, its form still dwarfed Orn. The knight sidestepped to avoid being crushed beneath its smoldering girth. It landed with a solid thud in front of him, hardly pausing before it lunged again. Orn struggled to find solid footing, hoping he might brace himself against the onslaught of attacks and find room to draw his weapon again. The creature howled in agony, or rage—he couldn't tell which.

The creature's attacks were sloppy, making it easy to deflect most of them so that he could draw his sword. Striking at the beast was easy enough, now that Orn knew what to expect. Each time his blade connected with the creature's flesh, it howled, a sound so loud it nearly split the world in two. It grew frenzied with the pain, fiery breath spewing from its large mouth. Orn parried as best he could, but with each attack of the creature he lost ground, his footing unsteady.

Orn circled the beast, driving it toward the center of the village. The attacks grew more and more sluggish, until the creature collapsed after tripping over its own odd feet. Orn moved forward to thrust his blade up through its jaw as it tried to bite him. The creature shuddered, and its fiery breath became little more than black mist. Orn coughed, then tugged his sword free.

A giant hand swatted at him, knocking Orn off his feet. Another creature loomed above him. Compared to the first two that lay in crumpled heaps of stone and cooled embers, this one seemed to tower over the blackened buildings.

Orn had a moment to wonder how he had missed one as big as this beast when he was sent flying by a powerful swipe. He crashed into one of the houses through what remained of the front door, only stopping thanks to a solid stone hearth that had somehow withstood the flames.

The world spun in his vision, souring his stomach. Orn tried to stand a few times, wobbling before he managed to get his bearings. He kicked debris out of the way as he trudged to the hole where the door once was, but flames sprang to life around him, quickly devouring what remained of the structure.

There, in the shadows created by the fire, he saw something move. No, not something. Some*one*.

Whoever it was hid among the flames as they spread, engulfing the house in a shimmering light and revealing a face that had seen better days. Beneath the layers of grime and black soot, Orn thought he recognized...*Gaulf?* Steeling himself against the possibility, refusing to believe that whoever stood across the blanket of fire, hidden in a cloak that seemed to smolder and yet did not burn, could be the boy. The face glared at him with eyes that glowed hotter than the fires around them, flesh waxy and stretched.

Please, no. Regardless of the bounty, Orn knew he had to do something.

"What have you done?" Orn barked, reaching for his sword before realizing he had lost it when he was thrown into the house. Instead, he groped for his dagger, but his shoulder gave. The world went white. Something was wrong, but he had no time to tend to his injury. Glancing at the mage, an idea came to Orn.

He was near enough, so Orn moved quickly, grasping the mage by the back of his head. This close, Orn could not help but clearly see the face hiding, fearful and afraid, beneath the hooded cloak. Those blue irises bored through him, and Orn paused.

"Gaulf, what have you done? Snap out of it!" Orn hesitated, thinking he spied a spark of recognition in the mage's fearful eyes.

"Burn it, burn it, burn it," Gaulf chanted, stuck in whatever magic trapped him. Orn could almost feel *something* wrapped about the young man.

"Well, here goes. Wake up!" Orn slammed his wounded shoulder forward into Gaulf, hoping to knock some sense into the farm boy. There was a sickening crunch that threatened to make the man topple. Orn managed to hold on just enough to keep his footing as the pain faded. The boy turned and sprinted away from Orn and the burning house.

Fire erupted between Orn and the retreating Gaulf, forcing him back from the sudden rush of heat. Above him, the ceiling beams began to protest their weight while the fire chewed through them. The roof collapsed seconds after Orn stepped out of the way, but the ensuing rush of embers and smoke knocked him off of his feet. Burning wood exploded from the house, and he scrambled for purchase. Most of the larger pieces missed him in their descent, but he had to shake off the burning shards that fell on him like rain. Once he was clear of the house, he slumped to the ground and closed his eyes, taking several deep breaths.

When he opened them again, Orn noticed that the few untouched houses were now alight, and there were villagers sprinting in every conceivable direction, trying to escape the growing inferno. None of them mattered. Not now anyway.

Only Gaulf mattered.

Where had he gone? He scoured the area but saw nothing. His sword lay in the churned dirt not far away. Orn crawled toward it, keeping himself underneath the thick cloud of smoke. Once there, he rolled over onto his back and tried to sit up. Something gave way, and his body tremored, refusing to listen to his command.

"Maybe this is as good a place as any to rest." Orn choked on the acrid smoke, his eyes watering. "Maybe not."

There's still work to be done.

Chapter 23

ALL HELL BREAKS LOOSE

Laela and Willaime watched the stone creatures grow as they ate. She stole a sidelong glance at her colleague each time he flinched when someone died, but he was hardly distracted from his work.

"We'll have to use the bait," Laela explained. The villagers were dying, and Willaime worked too slowly.

"Do it," he replied, his forehead beading with sweat.

Laela nocked and loosed an arrow. It hurtled through the air and sliced the muscle of Gilbert's neck—a clean shot. It would kill him, in time. But more importantly, the smell would attract the creatures. Gilbert stood there, gaping at the bleeding wound. He dropped to the ground and began crawling through the dirt, leaving a bloody trail in his wake.

Bait.

"There you go," Willaime muttered under his breath.

"Why does The Paladin let you use magic?" Laela scowled at Willaime, who appeared confused by her question. In truth, she had said it without thinking, though it was something that spurred anger within her, that Willaime should be permitted to wield magic that would earn anyone else a swift execution.

"You know very well this magic is used only to contain, to minimize the damage. It's not so much magic as it is the antithesis." Willaime sighed, shaking his head. "We can talk more about this later. Whatever this mage is up to, it's unlike anything I've seen." The scent of Gilbert's blood finally caught a stone beast's attention. It sauntered closer, licking its strange lips. "There's a second one!"

Laela scoured the roiling darkness for the creature, then watched as a flash of light sparked from Willaime's fist. Trouble was upon them. The elf nocked and loosed an arrow, and it pierced the belly of the second thug, sending him stumbling into the smoke captured by the magical boundary encircling the town.

There was no need to linger. Screams soon echoed through the area, the surest sign that another of the creatures had taken the bait. Willaime would direct his focus toward those they had ensnared while she climbed the rooftop of the nearest house free of flames. The afternoon sun cast long shadows across the thatching, her own slender in the dancing light of the fires. Her brass armor caught the firelight and reflected it, making her a beacon in the darkness.

Maybe the mage would spot her and reveal himself, saving her the trouble of this blasted search.

A house not far from where she perched burst inward, the wood protesting the sudden warping caused by the searing heat. Sweltering wind carried desperate shouts as the structure collapsed entirely, and Laela hissed in frustration.

"Bastard has to be nearby," she groused to herself. She studied the area again, but with the trembling of the flames and the thick smoke there was nothing to find. After climbing down the side of the house, she planted her feet firmly on the ground only to be nearly knocked over by someone slamming into her.

"Please, help!" Hands tore at her armor, at her hair. Laela tried to disengage without hurting the wailing woman. Her wild brown eyes were beseeching Laela just as much as her plaintive cries. The woman's ash-stained face was replaced by another, a man with rougher edges. He tore past both carrying a bucket overfull with water. Laela steadied the woman as yet another villager raced by screaming commands, directing others running about frantically. *Must be the mayor.* Laela pointed the woman toward someone who could help, keeping her moving along.

In the mass of gathered bodies she saw someone slip around a wall. They ran, weaving their way through the press of bodies and past a burning barn.

Laela took a knee, drawing a deep breath to hold it. With an arrow already nocked, she exhaled slowly and tasted the wind. This shot would be difficult, what with the fire and the smoke, but she led the target as he darted between buildings, waiting for the right opportunity.

"Has to be our mark," she whispered to herself, then bit her lip hard. The pain helped focus her mind, to blot out the chaos around her. She loosed the arrow, losing sight of it when the smoke billowed up and around her, spraying embers in her face. She coughed and threw her arm over her mouth and nose, hoping to keep the worst of it from her lungs.

Hopefully that arrow would find its mark and she'd get lucky with a trail of blood to follow. Without taking a second to check, Laela pushed forward, prepared to shove the villagers from her path. Luckily, they were little more than a nuisance, most of them jumping out of the way when they saw her coming.

Laela searched for a limping figure or someone with an arrow sticking out of them, even without the certainty that the arrow had indeed hit the target. "He couldn't have escaped so easily." Her temper rose like bile in her throat, her eyes stinging in the relentless smoke. But she ignored it, jogging forward to find the arrow in the dirt, tipped with blood and smoldering. The stench turned her stomach, but she smirked. At least she had hit him.

"What happened?" Willaime called from a distance.

There was still one boulder-like beast prowling through the haze. The circle Willaime had built was gone, the magic vanished. Laela cursed and sprinted toward the knight. This was not going according to plan.

It was his armor glinting in the sunlight that betrayed his position. And she wasn't the only one who noticed.

The twisted stone being that had been gorging itself on one of the arrow-stricken corpses lifted its head. Did it sense freedom at hand now that the binding was freed? Sniffing, it turned toward Willaime, and that grotesque face split into a hungry grin. It chittered, an eerie sound, calling to the others of its kind elsewhere in the village. Another answered its call, and soon the air was filled with their haunting song.

"Over here, Laela!" Willaime yelled over the cacophony. Laela saw the look on his face, his eyes gone wide enough she thought they might pop out of his head. He pointed behind her. "Do you see that?"

Laela looked to where he indicated. The keening of the creatures tore a hole in the center of the village, and a hand stretched forth from it. Laela made to answer Willaime, but stopped when she saw that his eyes had gone empty and his face slack.

"Willaime?" She followed his gaze to the taloned, stonework hand that reached out from the wound in the wind. It swatted at townsfolk while another hand appeared from the hole. Then there were screams, and the elf wasn't certain her own hadn't been added to the chorus. Her feet moved of their own accord, bringing her closer to the chaos, no matter how much her mind resisted. What followed was a sickening crunch—an eldritch being hoisting itself through the opening. As it climbed free, the rent in the air closed. Laela turned to look for Willaime, who backed away, shaking his head.

For a moment, Laela thought to conscript one of the villagers, send them off on a horse to Haven. But any assistance was leagues away, so she tried to make her way to Willaime, to forge a new plan, one that would end with their survival.

Unfortunately, there was nowhere to go where the creature wouldn't find them, and the addition of another gaggle of villagers only increased its efforts. It tore into them, swallowing people whole one after the other. The ones who managed to escape its jaws weren't so lucky. Their broken bodies littered the area, mute testimony to the carnage this creature had wrought. The stench of offal overpowered even the harsh, acrid smoke that permeated the town. That new odor rose from the putrid pile of stone whose skin crackled as it cooled and blistered, the pustules exploding in spurts of lava. With each body it tore into, it seemed to burn brighter.

"This is it. Fuck. At least I had a good run." The words were followed by a panicked laugh from deep within Laela's throat.

Ignoring the fetid taste at the back of her mouth, she screwed her eyes shut and shook her head. She took deep breaths to still the rapid pace of her heart, silencing her instinct to flee. None of it made sense, and her brain could not comprehend what she was witnessing. Nothing like the mages she'd recently captured, smallfolk only trying to survive, terrified of their own powers. This was old magic, something she had not seen for some time.

"What happened?" she asked when she finally found where Willaime had wandered off to, disappointed to see him frozen in place. She had never witnessed him so flustered, and it unnerved her to the marrow. "What's wrong, Willaime?"

"Something *severed* the protection. I saw some idiot out there with the new recruits. Fighting them. He killed Alke, then he destroyed the circle," he said, the tremor in his voice betraying his fear. "I do not know how. Didn't get a chance to draw it again. Not even sure I can now. Oh, fuck."

"Since when do you swear?" Laela raised an eyebrow but did not push the point. She took a moment to look at Willaime, to really see him. His face was ashen. Using the rod given to him by The Paladin, the one that made her teeth ache if she stood too near, and that blasted book to cast the bindings around these villages demanded much of his energy, but this was beyond that. It seemed like he would collapse at any moment. If he did, Laela was not certain she would ever get him back to his feet. Willaime opened his mouth to speak but made a hiccupping noise and placed a hand over his plated chest.

"I am not sure what is going on, Laela." Willaime shook his head as he made another noise of distress before his head whipped around.

"What is it?" Laela tried to see what had caught his attention. The creature was staring at a figure in the distance. It wasn't a villager. At least, Laela didn't think so. "Wait here!" she called to Willaime, not waiting for an answer. She wove around some of the corpses abandoned in the large creature's wake through the small village. Silence descended, something that settled within her deeper than her unease.

Laela found the corpse of one of the other prisoners, his body thoroughly mutilated.

Some yards away, there was an idiot swinging a sword about wildly while the large stone hand swatted at him. She took off at a run, but the larger creature sprinted away, covering more ground with its wide gait than she knew she could keep up with.

"That blasted fool," she cursed under her breath. Anger built inside of her, threatening to erupt. She would free it. All of the hate she held for The Paladin, for his knights, for magic and those who use it, and even for Willaime, pooled inside of her, directed toward this lone knight, blinding her to the ongoing threat. Whoever this newcomer was, he became the center of her world, the target of her rage.

Chapter 24

THE ELF

"**W**HAT THE FUCK WERE you thinking?"

Staring up at the form straddling him, Orn tried to remember exactly what happened. It took longer than he cared to admit for him to realize that the person pinning him down was a woman. She was wearing a dress unlike anything he had seen before, the fabric woven with an intricate latticework of leather and metal.

"How hard did that thing hit me?" he asked around the pressure of a cold blade against his neck. "Do you mind?" The dagger withdrew, permitting him room to focus his gaze on the person atop him.

The woman shifted some of her weight off him so that he could move somewhat, though not freely. The dagger remained near his throat, but it was pointed toward the village. And she was screaming. He could hardly make out the words as they tumbled from her mouth in between sobs.

"Slow down, please. Tell me what's going on," Orn urged when he was certain that she was not going to make good on her threat.

"They're dead. All of them," she whispered shakily, surveying the piles of ash and flesh. This brought him to his senses, and he blinked at her. All of them? His stomach turned. The fires refused to diminish. They weren't out of the woods yet. "What have you done?"

"Then they're lucky, even if they wouldn't agree. We'll soon share in their good fortune ourselves if we don't move," Orn replied, horrified at the sight behind the woman's shoulder. A creature was slithering in their direction, destruction in its wake. There were others nearby, claiming whatever viscera was left from the initial attack. The village proper was a bed of gore, and the scene forced bile into his mouth. "We have a few friends that we might want to take care of first. Then we can continue...whatever this is."

"You weren't supposed to be here," she barked, raising the dagger above his face.

"Look, I get it. Can we argue about this when we don't have monsters bearing down on us?" Orn snapped. The color drained from her skin as she absorbed his words, then she turned to glimpse the danger that threatened the pair. When she did so, Orn noticed the point of her ear piercing the veil of her hair. An elf?

She rolled off him and came to a stop on her knees, ready to lunge. Another dagger appeared in her free hand as if from thin air, then she stood. Orn worried she might pounce on him again, but instead, she raced past him.

Not wanting to be outdone, Orn scooped up his sword and managed to catch her, matching her pace easily. The creatures detected the two as they neared and screeched, a sound that vibrated Orn's very bones. He turned away from her and she caught the hint, pressing her back against his.

"Did you see another knight in the area? One wearing the colors of The Paladin?" she asked.

"We can have a question-and-answer session later. Let's survive first." Orn gripped his sword tighter, keeping it in front of him as the creatures rushed them.

Orn was pleasantly surprised when she mirrored his movements, and together they lashed out at the small horde while narrowly avoiding their fiery claws.

"Watch your clumsy feet, you oaf!" she shrieked, and he heard the squelch of her daggers when they slid into one of the creatures. Out of the corner of his eye, he watched her toss the being to the side and whistle. Orn was suddenly very thankful she had not cut his throat.

"*Excuse me*? You're not exactly staying out of *my* way." He hacked away with his own blade, removing pieces of the creatures each time they came too close. They seemed to fear the sword and retreated a few feet, circling like vultures, calculating their next moves.

"Shut your mouth." She pressed her back to his once more and twisted. He felt her move and followed as best he could. Somehow, they managed to not trip over one another, and whenever their attackers thought to shuffle closer, she moved again and made Orn follow. They fell into a pattern of swirling blades and quick retreats, with the woman as his defense counterpoint, nicking those who dared attack his blind spot. Orn sliced through a beast in his path, and his blade flashed while it drank the flames spurting from the fresh wound. The creature squealed, spitting sparks at Orn when he landed another blow.

"Are you doing all right back there?" Orn hardly waited for an answer before he brought the sword down on the creature's strange head, then the woman finished it off with several well-aimed dagger thrusts.

"Just keep up, you oaf!" she answered, causing him to stumble when she backed into him. One of the stone beasts sought to take advantage of that momentary lapse, but thankfully he brought the sword up in time for the blasted thing to impale itself upon it. It writhed around the length of his weapon, its slavering jaws working as it crept forward inch by inch. Shoving it away with a hearty kick, Orn looked over his shoulder at her.

"Keep calling me that and I'll give you a good stomping after we get out of here."

"Nothing would bring me greater joy than to see you try, *oaf*." Her words were punctuated by the sound of her daggers piercing flaming flesh and the ensuing wails of pain. "You've ruined this mission." Orn winced at hearing the unearthly cries, and he almost regretted his provocative attitude.

"Did your mission involve you getting stuck out here by yourself? I'd wager not, which means the knight you were looking for abandoned you." Each word landed like a blow, and the woman flinched. Something was off.

"Willaime? He would not *dare!*" she hissed, a wild look on her face.

"The way I see it, he did, or he's dead. Either way, it's just the two of us, and you need to quit squabbling with me so we can get out of this. Alive. *Please.*" The last word hardly softened her rage, but Orn had no time to add to his retort. He took a swipe hard enough to rattle his own senses from one of the more determined creatures. The searing heat of its attack lanced through his armor. The creatures formed a ring around them.

A few more times they stumbled over one another, and Orn muttered curses whenever he would trip over her feet. They tried to find a rhythm that would not leave them flailing or open to attack, and the woman remained silent and seething throughout this process. Orn waited for the press of a dagger against him that never came. Instead, he realized that they had made a dent in the population of the horde. The bodies of the creatures littered the ground, transformed into little more than piles of embers.

When it was safe, Orn spared another glance over his shoulder to see how she was doing. The woman was no longer against his back, and he expected to find her gone when he turned. But rather than perforating his internal organs with her daggers, she leaped off of one of the fallen creatures before it crumbled into ash for leverage in her next attack. The brutal intensity of her strikes caught one of the few remaining creatures off guard. With their number dwindling, they spread out, cautious of the pair. Orn paused and watched her work.

"Glad I am not on the receiving end of that." His words were followed by a low whistle at the sight of chunks of burning stone-like flesh flying through the air. She sank one dagger into a thick shoulder while repeatedly stabbing wherever she could find purchase with her other blade. Orn closed his mouth from where it had fallen open when she slid off of the rubble-strewn corpse and stomped back toward him. Covered in soot and smoke, her eyes blazed in the light of the fires and Orn swallowed. Hard.

"We're not done yet." She pointed her blades at those that remained. There were but two stone creatures left, smaller ones that lingered further away to feast upon the fallen villagers while their larger brethren fought. Perhaps the smaller ones were more opportunistic, taking what they could when it was available.

"It would seem so," Orn said, rolling his shoulders. His sword sang for *more*, his eyes stinging from the mixture of sweat and smoke. The small creatures flung themselves at the pair, and Orn leaned into the fray. At least when these beasts died there was little left of them.

Breathing became difficult, and his head became fuzzy. There was a cloth in his pack, but it would have to wait until they dispatched the newcomers. Orn only hoped they could hold out long enough.

"Ready for round two?" he asked, and she nodded curtly.

And together, they rushed the creatures.

Chapter 25

AFTER THE FIGHT

WHEN ORN REALIZED THAT both of them had survived the onslaught he took a knee and drew a shuddering breath. It demanded every ounce of effort remaining to him to not crumple to the ground. He watched the woman scour the village. For the one called Willaime, he assumed. Had the three men also come with her to this place?

It was no matter. Not for the moment, at least.

Orn closed his eyes and flattened his palm against the dirt.

"What are you doing?"

"A moment of silence for the dead." Orn glared at her. "And then I am going to bury them."

She scoffed. "Not if you plan to actually catch this bounty."

"Maybe you're right." Orn hated to admit it, but he now understood that he did not follow Gaulf's trail alone. The farm boy had caused a right mess, but Orn had witnessed the look in his eyes. Fear, pain, confusion. There might still be something of the Gaulf he knew left behind, and that was enough to get the knight to his feet. "You know, you could take the time to find this Willaime. I'll go after the bounty myself."

"If Willaime lives, he will find me. He always does." She shook her head and turned from Orn. "I shall accompany you to find the mage."

Though her determination frustrated him, he decided to be silent on the matter for the moment. Orn said a quick prayer for the collection of human carcasses strewn about the village and for the few survivors. He was not sure which was the preferred fate at this point.

Life would take time before it ever felt the same for those who had lived. They would spend many years trying to rebuild not only their homes but their resolve.

Orn spied the woman rummaging through the piles of bodies and rubble. "If I mucked something up for you, understand that's the story of my life, but I do apologize." Orn removed one of his gloves and scrubbed a hand over his face. Slick with sweat and covered in grime, he imagined he cut quite the grotesque figure. "Maybe you need to catch me up on exactly what happened here."

"Willaime and I came here by order of The Paladin to seek a mage who wrought havoc in Redford and brought destruction to this town," she replied, poking at a crumbling corpse of ash.

"And this Willaime is the one that ran off?"

"I told you already that he would not do that!" She flung a handful of ash at the ground.

"There's no one here but the two of us." Orn shrugged, then gestured at the village. "I will help you look, but I would not expect to find him."

"He would not abandon me, and if he did, it would not be willingly."

"I could hardly blame him if he did. A few minutes with you and I am ready to desert you myself," Orn muttered, much louder than he intended. He regretted the words as soon as they left his mouth. Not because they upset her, but because he had seen her daggers in action, and they were undoubtedly sharper than her glare.

"If he left me here then his life would be forfeit," she said flatly, as if that explained everything.

"Then perhaps he's dead or trapped beneath rubble. Those would be the only other options. But with the bounty on the run, we have bigger problems." Orn wasn't sure if she was listening to what he said or if she was simply wondering where to stick her daggers first. He retrieved his sword and started cleaning it. The soot had morphed to a thick mud that clung to the metal. "If you are going to stick me with those blades of yours, make it quick. I could use a nap." If he had to die, she would hardly be the worst cause.

She continued her ransacking efforts. Whatever she was searching for remained elusive, as it was not long before she moved on to another pile. And then another.

"The way I figure it, I don't believe this mage was in control of these creatures. That's not something I've seen before," Orn explained.

She let out a scream that surprised Orn, and he took an involuntary step back. "Of *course,* the creatures were out of control. They are only summoned to sow chaos and destruction! But we were prepared for it. We had a plan and bait, though it all fell apart when some oaf inserted himself into the fray."

"Bait?" *The men...* "Listen, I only murdered one of them. He was excited by the carnage, hunting for the sort of fun that would see him hanged in normal circumstances." Orn shot her a knowing look. "And someone put arrows in the other two." The quiver on her back hadn't escaped his notice. Orn had seen the corpses, dressed like the one he had slain. "I think your plan fell apart long before I got here."

The woman sighed. "We didn't get here soon enough. But we weren't the first sent out after him. We were sent to finish the job."

Orn started to say something before deciding better of it. Instead, he asked, "You sure you weren't meant as bait, same as those men?"

She chuckled darkly. "I know I am bait. One of these days, someone'll even manage to run me through. Those men? Well, I shot to wound, not to kill. These *things* seem to prefer a meal they can play with."

"My way didn't cause suffering," Orn said. "Wounding them so they'd bleed out and be consumed? That's cruel. I cannot deny that it makes a certain amount of sense. But..." Orn swallowed, blanching a little, "that does not excuse it."

"Not that I owe you any sort of explanation, but they deserved it. One thought to get handsy with me. Ended up losing a finger for his troubles. But all three were slated for execution before we conscripted them into service. If nothing else, their deaths were supposed to serve a purpose. One that you screwed up."

"Based on what I saw, the chaos came as just as much of a surprise to the one who started it. That aside, you owe me one."

"How do you figure?" she asked incredulously. "And what do you mean, *I owe you one?*"

"You are free to run back to wherever you came from, princess. This bounty's mine." Before Orn had finished speaking, she had a dagger out again, knuckles white from her tight grip.

"*Your* bounty?" She laughed, and Orn thought he saw mischief in her eyes.

"Well, I did say that you owed me, didn't I?" Orn nodded, keeping an eye on the dagger in her hand.

"Then I suppose I'll have to accompany you to ensure you manage to collect." She sheathed the dagger and retrieved her pack and bow from where she'd left them.

"That's hardly fair. And I don't need company." Orn grimaced at the thought of the woman joining him on the road.

"If I return empty-handed the next execution will be my own, then yours will follow." The grin she gave him made Orn's stomach drop.

"I have a knack for evasion." Orn tired of this conversation and did nothing to hide it.

"You said it, oaf. I owe you, and I plan to clear my debt by helping you hunt for this mage."

"I may have been too hasty. I suppose I can forgive a debt just this once." Orn paused, narrowing his eyes at her. "I have no doubt you'd turn on me in an instant."

"I should arrest you. I would have every right, and The Paladin would approve. Maybe I will, after we capture the mage. He's my top priority. For now," she said.

"You are welcome to try. I work best alone anyway," Orn answered.

"I've already told you that my life is forfeit if I return empty-handed," she spat, taking a step toward him. "I am coming with you, and there will be no arguing otherwise. If we succeed, you can keep the reward. I have no need for it."

"What's your name?" Orn asked, resigned. It seemed he was stuck with her for the time being, so they might as well introduce themselves. When she did not reply, Orn sighed. "Come on, princess, I'll need to know your name eventually."

"Laela. And stop calling me *princess*. I am no princess," she snapped, but Orn noticed something dark lurking behind her eyes.

"Do you have a mount?" Orn asked, letting his gaze sweep the town.

"Of course I do. I come from Haven, an agent of The Paladin. I'm not some backwater farm boy playing knight." The insult struck home, but Orn didn't flinch.

"Good to hear." Orn brought two fingers to his lips. His shrill whistle sundered the silent air. In the distance, he heard the answering neigh. Thankfully, Delilah had not run far, and he could try to get away from this damn elf. The one the villagers whispered stories of, the one working for The Paladin. Just his luck.

His mind circled back to some of the nights spent drinking in taverns, or days trudging through new villages. People gossiped about the *elf*, as if she lurked in the darkness. Parents cajoling their kids to behave, warning them about The Paladin's creature that would come to get them if they didn't. How long had she been doing this, to have earned such a reputation?

Delilah trotted over to him, and briefly he thought to flee. He wondered how far he'd get before she came tearing after him.

"You're not the only person who's got a trained horse." Laela mimicked his whistle, and Orn heard the neigh seconds later. He cursed beneath his breath and clambered onto his horse. She practically vaulted into her own saddle, as if she expected him to try to escape. "Consider yourself conscripted into service."

"Is that so?" Orn asked, rolling his eyes. He leaned toward Delilah's long face. "This one here thinks she's conscripting me. Fancy that. It's really the other way around." Orn clucked and kicked his horse into gear, holding on as she broke into a gallop. It was not long before Laela had caught up with him and kept pace.

There was no looking back. There was nothing left to see but embers and ash.

"It hardly matters who is conscripting who," Laela said. "But, as I am on official business for The Paladin, I believe that my authority supersedes yours, barbarian."

"If that helps you sleep at night, princess." Orn's voice was gruff, and he looked anywhere but at her. "Look, I need to know that you are going to work with me. Not against me."

"I said I'd help. What more do you want?" she asked, an edge of irritation evident in her tone.

"To start, how about keeping those daggers away from me? Still not sure I am keen on the idea of your company." Orn shook his head as he shifted in his saddle. Laela made a rude gesture with her hand, letting him know how little she cared about his acceptance or comfort. "And how do you intend to pay the bounty? Do you carry that much coin on you or am I expected to accompany you to Haven?"

She replied through clenched teeth, "I will ensure that you receive your reward, then I will take what proof I need to satisfy The Paladin. That means I am with you until we complete this hunt. Until then, you should give me a name to call you besides *oaf*."

He remained silent as she waited for his answer.

Now that they had left the village behind, night was settling upon the world. The tinge of smoke lingered at the back of his throat, an obnoxious reminder of the events of the day. But even that seemed to be gradually lessening. Tomorrow, the skies would be heavy with soot and full of scavengers. His breath misted in the frigid air, which also seeped into his bones, bringing back an all too familiar ache.

Laela turned away from him with a grunt when she gave up on getting an answer. This afforded him the chance to observe her. He fancied he could see where his words slid in the chinks of her armor. This knight she had prattled on about was a weak spot. As much as she seemed to know the man, there was an uncertainty in her proclamations about his loyalty to the cause. There was doubt in her voice, and if he decided to continue with the verbal thrusts, he thought he could shatter that armor to see what lay beneath.

The gentle rhythm of the horse plodding along the road was enough to lull him into a daze, the only thing keeping him anchored in the here and now was her presence. What she had said about The Paladin and the forfeiture of her own life if she returned empty-handed bothered him, and he wasn't sure why.

"Orn," he said, and it seemed to rouse Laela. "My name, instead of 'barbarian' or 'oaf' or whatever else you could come up with."

"Was that so difficult?" Laela smirked at him, and Orn resisted the urge to push her off her mount.

"Yes," came his curt reply. Orn debated asking her for more information about The Paladin and her service, giving voice to that thought burning at the back of his mind. In the end, he dared not open his mouth. Orn had the distinct impression that should he push too far he'd find himself with a dagger pressed against his back.

A sigh escaped him as he rubbed his eyes. He wanted to sleep, but he did not trust that he wouldn't slide right off the saddle, nor that Laela wouldn't leave him behind, snoozing in the dirt.

"I have a feeling we are both going to sleep heavily when we reach Ostford. Shaking you off my tail is going to have to wait until after that." Orn chewed the corner of his mouth thoughtfully. His hands were wrapped in the leather reins, and he suddenly felt inexplicably fidgety.

"Your ears are smoking something fierce." Laela spoke before he could. "Please do not overburden your poor brain on my account."

"Well, *excuse me*, princess," Orn groused. "I've been stuck out here on my own so long, I'm afraid I'm not used to such stimulating company. But I figured we might compare notes. Why Swanford? Why the bounty in Redford and Ostford? Why are there marks—" Orn stopped himself, worrying for a moment he had divulged too much information. "You've seen the marks, right?"

"The marks are how we identify them," she replied quietly, her features colored by unease.

She was baiting him. He wasn't interested in participating, especially if there were no answers to his questions. Orn had much more important things to concern him.

Gaulf, where are you?

Chapter 26

THE QUIET RIVER

EVENTUALLY, THE ONLY REMAINING stench of smoke was that which clung to their clothes.

The small forest by the village gave way to hills filled with crops that would likely go to ruin, and Laela heard the slow, wheezing creak of a mill in the distance. The oaf kept pace behind her, and she was just as eager to be free of him as she suspected he was of her. But she had a job to do. With Willaime gone and the firebug on the run, she had no choice.

They rode past a cottage that was shuttered against the night, and she wondered to herself if there were anyone inside. Part of her wanted to stop, to see if the firebug had visited this place.

Laela almost called for a halt before Orn paused. So, she listened. No magic.

The road widened and smoothed out beneath them, transforming into something more than merely a trail for travelers. It was well-worn, broad enough for two wagons to journey side by side. She stole a glance at Orn. He almost looked peaceful, moving with the horse, walking on the knife's edge between consciousness and sleep. Except for the gore and ash that was splattered across his mismatched armor, and that his hands twitched against the leather reins, there was something of the familiar about the old knight. Something she couldn't quite identify.

Laela busied herself by checking the map tucked inside of her book. Time had not been kind to the parchment, but she could see they were near Ostford. A few days in the saddle and making a camp with nothing but silence had made the elf restless. While Willaime was often quiet, this felt *different* somehow. She did not like the knight's silence, but neither would she be the first to break it.

She ate from her pack of supplies, and Orn did the same. They stayed out of one another's way, for the most part, over the two days of travel. Laela led them down a path that wove in and out of the forest, searching for any sign of the mage. A few times she thought she caught the tail end of something, but it vanished whenever Orn tried to catch up with her.

Ahead, there was a bridge stretching over a small creek, and just beyond that, a town huddling against the curve of a wider, lumbering river. And though it was night, there were signs of life among the wooden structures. Once they were over the bridge, they discovered a larger one leading into town and crossed it. When the hooves of their horses clattered over the stonework, she saw Orn snap awake.

Laela turned right once they crossed that bridge, unconsciously following a familiar path. It wasn't more than a block before they came upon an inn, its sign boasting a damaged wine cask. The Cracked Cask was where she had met Willaime after jobs that brought them to the area, and she felt conflicted about the possibility of seeing him inside. If he were there, it meant he had truly abandoned her. If not...well, she would need a new partner. She shook her head and slid off the horse, tossing the reins to Orn. Part of her wished she had taken the time to look for Willaime, another part of her found freedom in the fact she had not, and a third part of her hated that she cared.

"Settle up. I'll be inside." Laela did not give him a chance to argue, but out of the corner of her eye she saw Orn grousing to himself. She pushed through the side door of the inn, and was met with a welcoming blast of heat from the kitchen. The smell of bread baking at the hearth pulled a contented sigh from her lips as she sidled into the main room. The man working the bar was cleaning spilled beer off the countertop and listening with blatant disinterest to the rambling of some drunken idiot. She waved, catching his attention. Before he left the drunk, he retrieved a stained ledger from under the bar.

"Usual?" the barkeep asked, warily glancing around the room for prying customers.

"Just one—" Laela caught sight of Orn by the door. "Two. With baths." Some of the patrons shied away from her when she entered moments ago, and she could only surmise it was due to the lingering stench of smoke, road, and sweat. The elf did not recognize the faces of those closest, but that hardly meant they did not recognize her. Instinctively, she thought to pull up her hood, then decided against it, settling for tugging her braid over her shoulder. "Also, ensure our rations and waterskins are refilled. We might not be back this way for some time." She drew a leather cord from around her neck and flashed the coin attached to it. He hardly even looked up from the ledger as he started to write the receipt. "Two rooms, yes. Oh, the other one might be drinking, but not on this tab." He added another line to his ledger before it disappeared under the counter. Two keys were slid across the bar, and without another word he returned to his duties.

As Laela grasped the keys, she wondered why Orn hadn't simply ridden on, taken this opportunity to do just as he had threatened. She supposed it was no matter, waving him over after he came into the inn. When he approached, Laela tossed one of the wrought-iron keys to him.

"Let them know when you want some bathwater to ruin. Drinks are on you. Food and room are covered." Laela headed up the stairs and left him standing there.

Silence echoed, tangible, thick, and near black in the dim light of a few torches high over her head. Fire danced seductively off armored knights towering over her like giants, but was swallowed when it dared to touch the floor. Bare feet dripped tendrils from skin to floor as she took a step forward, a squelching noise accompanying her footfalls. Her once-white nightgown was now stiff and red, and it was all she could do to not look down.

Never look down.

Instead, she found herself looking up so that she could not see faces lost in the shadows cast by armor. She knew what they were going to say. She saw them speaking to one another without the movement of lips, and anyway, she knew the conversation by heart.

"I think we've gotten them all."

"The Paladin has dealt with the queen."

"Embrosi has fallen."

One turned a grizzled face toward her as he spoke her name. Another peered at her while wearing a stoic expression bordering on anger. All stared at her now, their dark eyes nothing but empty holes in skulls, the flesh peeling away from the bone.

"And who is this?"

The giant armored humans crouched, surrounding the child as she stood defiantly before them, blood inching up her body. Coating her fingers. Sticking to her hair. Swallowing her whole. One kneeled in front of her, close enough that she might lash out with the dagger she found in the pile of bodies. Her mother's blade.

"Oh, but what are you?" A familiar voice emanated from within the confines of the armored figure looming in her gaze. Ser Gregoris. The Paladin, in his fine armor and stern demeanor, glared at her, fire filling the darkness of his eyes. She lurched forward, screaming, the blade in her hand scoring a mere scratch against his armor.

She screamed. Walls began to crumble, provoking waves in the blood. Rising, rising, until she knew it would pour down her throat. His laughter echoed in the darkness.

As always, Laela woke with a start but dared not scream. She bolted upright, cold water sloshing over the edge of the tub. Her knuckles were bone-white as she grasped the edge, struggling to remember how to breathe when the dream receded. But another image remained: that of her mother, bent and broken in death as she had never been in life. Empty eyes that followed Laela wherever she ventured, even now. Especially now, in the service of The Paladin. Laela hated it, waking like this, old wounds reopening and scrubbed raw.

She laid in the tub until the tingling fright of the dreams trying to drown her abated, watching the water fall in droplets from her hair. The room around her seemed fuzzy, as if the armored giants would burst through any moment, as if she were unable to fully rip herself out of that dream.

The images spurred the same unease they usually did, and the elf tried to ignore it while climbing out of the tub. The dream was a bizarre, augmented retelling of what had actually happened that day, centuries ago. Laela dared not think about exactly how long it had been, how many years she marked on a wall of the home stolen from her before that task became oppressive.

The Paladin had renamed it: Haven.

Some days Laela managed to block out the memories entirely, relying only on the frightening dreams that chased her since she was but a child. Blood raining from the heavens, the voices of unseen gods, the crush of a crowd tearing her away from the throne room.

Piles of bodies.

Her eyes screwed shut, and she pressed her fingers against her temples, trying to banish the remnants of the dream. Taking a bucket of clean water Laela found near the tub, she poured its contents over herself, shivering against the sudden chill.

After drying off, she dressed, focusing on the present to allow nothing else to occupy her thoughts. She tugged her boots on, then checked her weapons for dull edges. Just in case.

Once she was certain each blade would easily carve through flesh, she moved her hands to the wet hair clinging to her neck and jaw before collecting her belongings and heading to her room. Briefly, she wondered again whether the old knight had abandoned her.

Oh, well. She'd find out come morning.

Chapter 27

THE RIVER RAGES

GAULF CREPT CLOSE ENOUGH to see the signpost. The smell of food cooking spurred him onward despite the echoes of screams in his ears and the acrid stench of smoke clinging to his cloak. When people clambered out of an inn ahead, Gaulf darted away from the main path, heading for a nearby riverbank.

Gaulf's gaze drifted toward the far shore of the wide river. Without some idea of its depth, he dared not entertain the thought of crossing. If the water's current did not sweep him away, the cold of the night would finish the job.

His hands itched to move, to etch those strange sigils in the air. The need burned him, clawing its way through his skin and making his stomach sour. The warmth of that light burbled inside of him, happier than the river. Unlike the current, however, the tendrils found nowhere to go. His body, like a cage, contained it for fear of the consequences of letting it loose. Gaulf feared going to sleep, feared closing his eyes.

Whenever the competing emotions in his mind became too much and Gaulf tried to center himself, another vision would creep to the forefront. Past the corpses wreathed in flames, Orn stood waiting in judgment, his strange blade in hand.

Something about that sword scared the life out of him.

Gaulf followed the river until it led him closer to the town nestled atop a set of fog-ringed hills. Ostford appeared inviting and warm, and he drew his cloak tighter around him. The lights of the village danced in the fog, and he heard the sounds of pleasant chatter carried on the wind.

Then he thought he heard someone speaking directly to him.

"Who's there?" Gaulf's voice cracked and his teeth chattered. Whispers unfurled within the fog, wavering and wobbling.

Pressing his palms against his eyes, Gaulf tried to scrub away the world, but the sounds only amplified.

"No, no, no. Stop, please. I'm tired. I'm just so tired." The ache in his bones grew worse with each step, and he stumbled over the exposed root of a tree. Gaulf forced himself to turn from the village to delve deeper into the fog, his boots squelching in the muck as he walked.

Another strike of pain brought Gaulf to his knees, splashing in the cold mud that embraced him. He opened his mouth to yell but nothing came out.

Gaulf stared at his reflection trapped in a puddle of water. The face peering at him bore no familiarity. The eyes were clouded with specters, the lives he'd taken, and grime marred the rest of his features. The face morphed into another, one far beyond his own years and grizzled. The mouth began moving without sound at first, then an eerie noise rose, building higher and higher into a crescendo, a buzzing in his head.

Gaulf thrust his hand into the puddle, splashing away the image of the man in the robes who haunted his dreams. A sickening lurch inside of him threatened to collapse him entirely as the water revealed another face: his own. But it was not his own as he knew it. Rather, the blue of his eyes burned like molten coins. His flesh became translucent in the glow when the power tested the limits of his body, seeking release.

"Leave me!" No answer came, not that he expected one. "What do you want?" Gaulf sobbed quietly. Heat flooded his cheeks as he explored his features with his fingers. Frustration built inside of him until he thrust his hands into the puddle again. They began to glow, and the water sizzled against his flesh.

He screamed.

"Burn it, burn it, burn it. Clean, cleanse, burn." Gaulf's lips formed the words, each one scraping its way out of his throat, but the voice was not his own. "Burn, burn, burn out the corruption."

Gaulf couldn't stop. But he could fight.

"Leave me be!" Gaulf shouted into the night. Smoke poured from his mouth, clogged his nostrils, suffocated his lungs as he bit back the fire. Gaulf swallowed embers, clenching his hands in the mud.

Shadows moved about, cast by his light. Shapes in the fog slipped away from his scrambling movements until he reached the river and dunked his head into the raging current. In the shallow water, Gaulf opened his mouth to scream. For all that he had, for all the air he held, until his lungs burned and his throat complained.

Whatever heat had suffused him evaporated almost as quickly as it had come. Gaulf shivered and scrubbed the mud away. As much as the cold hurt, it was a reminder that he still had some semblance of control. The pain drove out the fugue threatening to overwhelm him.

Gaulf lay there shivering as the fog within and around him started to recede further. The weight of someone's attention speared the middle of his back.

"What the fuck were you thinking?"

Gaulf rolled over as another person pinned him to the muck below. Knees pressed against the crook of his elbows, drawing a howl of pain from Gaulf's mouth. His teeth snapped shut when a dagger appeared in his sight, and the form sitting atop him came into focus. The woman from his dreams.

But she was a phantom, like the figure in the water's reflection.

When the next breeze claimed her form, Gaulf blinked and closed his eyes, finding his way to his knees. No more than a moment later, Gaulf heard the telltale sign of approaching horses.

In the faded light he could hardly make out the shapes, but anyone riding at this late hour meant trouble. Gaulf found the nearest hiding spot, crawling between one of the large bushes and a misshapen boulder. He tried to catch his breath, tried to slow the thundering of his heart, but fear shook his body while he waited. For a sword to pierce the bush, a gauntleted hand to drag him out and to the gallows.

The solid *clank* of armor echoed in the night.

The rapid pace of his heart slowed as Gaulf caught sight of the riders, now damn near close enough to reach out and touch. *Orn.* The name was on his lips before he realized his mistake. The woman from his visions sat atop the second mount, her dagger-like eyes searching. Gaulf slapped his hand over his mouth.

Orn had promised to help, but he stood with her. Gaulf regretted running, taking off in the middle of the night, and for a moment he lost himself in sorrow. Had he stayed with Orn, could the man have helped him? Could they have helped one another?

"Help," Gaulf cried, a strangled noise consumed by the nearby river. The urge to scream ripped through him, and with it, the blossoming heat within. By the time Gaulf found some degree of control, he made up his mind to cross the bridge and enter the town. Orn had disappeared, and so had the strange woman. The woods were quiet once more.

Creeping out of the bush, Gaulf started down the road toward Ostford while listening for any threats. He wanted nothing more than to curl up somewhere and sleep as his feet dragged against the rough planks of the bridge.

Standing now in Ostford proper, a village small enough he could see clear to the other side, Gaulf tried to picture his home. Where Swanford was almost the same, this place he found to be anything but. The smell of wet earth and algae from the lake were also distinctly different from the familiar scents of Redford and its lush forests. Beyond that, the houses sat squat and warped, as if cobbled together poorly, and were surrounded on three sides by water. There was no town square to speak of, and the largest building here seemed to be the inn.

Though it was quiet, shapes and silhouettes still moved through the smoke caked on the inn's windows. Any resolve he had disappeared into the pit of anxiety in his stomach. Gaulf turned toward the stables.

"What are you skulking about for?" asked a stableboy when he rounded the corner, pitchfork in hand. Gaulf thought the boy little more than a fresh-eyed babe, but no. He was not much younger than Gaulf himself. The stableboy poked the pitchfork forward.

"I'm just trying to find somewhere to sleep!" Gaulf held his hands up, retreating as the stableboy warily advanced on him. Briefly, the world twisted, leaving him imagining their positions reversed.

Gaulf could almost *feel* the rough grain of the pitchfork in his hand while he stared down some wild-haired, muddied person who came out of nowhere. He would do the same, rushing forward to protect his charge when threatened.

"Leave this place!" The stableboy waved the pitchfork frantically, and Gaulf worried this commotion would be overheard.

Swallowing the lump in his throat, Gaulf charged the stableboy, hoping to escape. He soon felt the familiar pull of *magic* in his veins.

By The Wheel, by The Door, by The Spiral, by The Scythe. Unbidden, the thought came, sparking something to life inside of him.

The words were on his lips, but Gaulf refused to surrender to the power. Not again. Never again. Not daring to look back, Gaulf ran as fast as he could. Moving silenced his mind, silenced that quavering part of him that *needed* to be released.

Chapter 28

WAKING

GRIPPING THE KEY IN his hand, Orn watched Laela retreat up the stairs. The thought crossed his mind that he might turn and stride right back out the front door, but exhaustion soundly conquered the notion before the old knight could act. Besides, knowing his luck, she'd be on his trail before he even made it out of the village.

"Must be getting soft in my old age," he said to no one in particular. The man behind the bar was watching him expectantly.

While the prospect of another drink seemed sublime, his stomach turned at the idea of anything but sleep. He plodded up the stairs to his room, locking the door behind him once inside. Then he sighed after shoving a chair under the doorknob.

"Just in case," Orn muttered to the empty room. Habit compelled his movements, and instead of sinking into bed, he set about cleaning his armor, the task just mindless enough he could pretend he were anywhere else. Gunk and char, splatters of gore and blood were scraped clear of the metal, though it would never be completely clean. He then peeled off sweat-sodden clothing and hung them out to dry near the fire in the room's small hearth and shivered. This far north and into the coming winter, there was a chill that invaded his bones.

Orn promptly collapsed onto the bed and stared at the wooden beams above his bed.

"One. Two. Three. Four. Five." The words were meaningless the more he repeated them. Lately, the cadence of this chosen mantra was the only way he could lull himself to sleep. "One, two, three, four, five," Orn whispered, his own voice oddly alien to his ears. "One." His tenuous grasp on reality snapped. "Two." The bed vanished beneath him. "Three." The slight chill of the evening air faded. "Four." All but the slight haze of existence diminished and Orn hung there, clasped between consciousness and dreams.

"Five." The peace of not-quite sleep crashed down around Orn as he tumbled the short distance upward to being fully awake. He laid there, staring without seeing, for a few more minutes. Orn relished that empty void within that felt nothing, was nothing, within his flesh. But the strain to remain there was futile, burning away the haze he had cocooned himself within. He opened his eyes and tried to remember where he was. The ceiling above him was unfamiliar, however it was the ache of a battered body that stirred his memory.

Was Laela still here? It seemed too much to hope for that the elf had woken at the crack of dawn and had left him behind. Orn had never enjoyed such luck.

He groaned, stretching. How long had it been since he had had a good night's sleep without drinking himself halfway to oblivion? At any rate, it didn't stop the nightmares that waited for him behind the darkness of his eyelids. Those visions of fire and violence were relentless, and he had yet to understand them.

Hunting mages was affecting him. It had to be.

How many more times would he fail at finding answers? How could he help those marked? Or help himself?

The dreams were stronger since he met Gaulf. Orn's control had wavered. His own mark itched, but he dared not turn his full attention over to it. He could not. *Not after Jord.* Grumbling to himself, he rolled out of bed. If Laela were still here, she was likely already waiting for him at the stables.

There wasn't enough hot water or lukewarm ale in the realm that would banish a vicious headache as it brewed at his temples. Orn tugged on his clothes and yanked the chair free of the door before departing, carrying the bags containing his valuables. He strode down the hall to the waiting tubs.

"Hot bath. And I mean *hot*." He paused, then pointed at the second tub. "Fill both. Extra soap too." The person minding the baths sprang into action, and Orn shrugged out of his soot-coated clothing.

Once the first bath was ready, he scrubbed his clothes with soap and tossed them in the tub, stirring the graying water with his hands as dirt leached from the fabric. He would need new clothes soon, but he doubted they would linger in a village long enough for him to purchase some. Once finished, he wrung the excess water from them and hung everything near the fire to dry.

"I missed this," Orn said as he sank into the water in the second tub. It had cooled a bit while he had washed his clothes, but that made little difference. Ash and grime loosened from his flesh as he scraped it with soap, and before the bathwater could turn completely black, he shuffled out of the tub.

At least he was *mostly* clean. Mercifully, his clothes had dried fairly well. As he dressed, he caught a glimpse of himself in the small mirror mounted on the wall. He combed his hand through his graying hair, intending to straighten it somewhat, but stopped suddenly.

"*Beware*," came the word from his lips, but not from him. Staring at his grinning reflection, a wave of vertigo slammed through Orn. The mark on his arm flared, burning his flesh. Closing his eyes against the spinning world, he smashed the mirror into shards.

He licked at a small cut between his knuckles, noticing the nearly imperceptible change in the reflection of the tiny shards scattered on the ground. There was something behind his eyes, something he could not categorize. Ignoring that for now, he grabbed his belongings and padded barefoot to the main room. Without his armor, the old knight was silent as he walked.

"I owe you for the mirror," Orn explained to the innkeeper, then he motioned toward Laela. "Maybe you can add that to her tab." She shook her head and Orn grimaced as he mentally tallied what coin that might leave him.

"What else can I do for you?" The innkeeper hardly looked up from the rag as he polished a mug. What was it with innkeepers? Always polishing a mug.

"Eggs. Six will do. Potatoes? Oh, and bread. Maybe some cheese... Bacon too. I can smell the fat sizzling from here," Orn said, paying little attention to the common room.

"Just cooked up a fresh batch of potatoes this morning. Should still be warm." The innkeeper made an exasperated gesture and dug around beneath the bar, retrieving a leather-bound tome, and then flipped through it. He glanced at Laela, who tugged at a corded necklace, flashing something too quick for Orn to see. Whatever that meant, it seemed to serve as an adequate answer. "Three silver for the mirror." He tapped the ledger.

"That's robbery," Orn groused. Of course, Orn knew what would happen if he tried to haggle: no breakfast. Orn fished three coins from his pouch and groaned. "The mirror was already cracked."

"Considering the state of my tubs, I'd say you're getting off cheap." There was an edge to his smile, noticeable beneath his thick, red beard.

"Fine," Orn muttered. He dropped the coins into a neat stack on the counter. The innkeeper was quick to snatch them up before Orn could change his mind, pocketing them in his apron. He closed the ledger and it disappeared beneath the bar, then departed to the kitchen. The delightful scent of the freshly cooked food filtered into the common area each time the door swung open, warring for dominance with the familiar smells Orn associated with inns. Well-worn furniture adorned the place, the tables remarkably clean and free of the usual scars from drunken patrons. The place almost felt comfortable.

But there was one thing that kept him on edge, and even though Orn kept his gaze on his table, he could not ignore the other person in the room.

"So, you didn't knife me while I slept. Fancy that," Orn said. Somewhere in his dealings with the innkeeper, Laela had wandered over with a mug full of steaming cider. Orn hoped the man was smart enough to bring one for him as well.

"The day is young yet," Laela quipped, then took a sip from her mug. Was she smirking? "You did not leave in the middle of the night."

"It would appear so. A decision I am certain to regret." Orn sank into a chair and stretched, the flat of his palm resting on the smooth surface of the table.

"I'd be disappointed if you didn't," Laela said flippantly, slapping a book on the table. She fell silent as she studied it. Orn, curious, attempted to take a peek at its contents. Within the pages there was a crudely drawn map that drew his attention.

"What do you have there?" he asked. When she failed to answer, Orn leaned back against his chair, crossing his arms over his chest.

The innkeeper emerged from the kitchen carrying an impossible amount of plates, each one boasting a veritable mountain of food. He set down an empty plate in front of Orn and proceeded to pile food onto it. The potatoes were smothered in garlic and onions, with a hint of spice from peppers. He could hardly remember the last time he had a meal quite this appetizing, or when he last had time to actually sit and enjoy it.

Orn was already digging in, each bite a little slice of perfection. He nodded his thanks at the innkeeper as he returned with a carafe of cider and filled a mug with the steaming, amber liquid. He took a drink, savoring the warmth and the flavor while Laela continued to study the book on the table. An abrupt rage swelled inside of him, and a vision of him setting her alight flashed across his mind. Even the way she sat, prim and proper, set him on edge. He came back to himself, shaking away the storm that threatened their peace. His anger was getting worse. Answers couldn't come too soon.

"Here," she said, sliding the book toward him. Orn hunched over the table to see what she was pointing at. "We're here, at the River Limnh. There are a few roads that do not turn into mere ruts in the dirt. The one we've been on, back toward ho—" Laela hesitated. "Haven. We're heading in the direction of Cassandira and The Tower of Fragments."

"Something making you uncomfortable?"

"My mother always hated The Tower of Fragments, bemoaned that it drew barbarians into our land year after year. Told me it held the key to our future. No, that it *was* a key," Laela replied, glowering. "I don't remember it fully, though. There's so much I don't recall." Laela's scowl deepened. "There were once many roads. To the south, to the desert. But no... How long ago was that?"

Orn started to speak but thought better of it. Poking at her, pushing buttons, hardly seemed the thing to do now. She was sifting through something in her head, and he was not willing to risk the relative peace of the morning.

"No, that's the wrong spell. Those creatures weren't vanishing when they died. The firebug would've needed iron for this sort of summoning. More preparation than what I witnessed in town. This doesn't make sense. At all." Laela scrubbed a hand over her face.

Orn chose his words carefully, knowing how very thin the ice beneath him was. "I am not sure what you think you're reading there, princess, but I haven't seen anything like what you're talking about. That's not like what I've, ah, experienced."

Orn could not ascertain whether she had heard him, and watched Laela as she turned several pages, her finger following the text sprawled across the page. With little else to do, Orn was more than content to continue devouring his breakfast. He was picking at the bread and cheese, wondering when Laela would arrive at the point of her research. She had set the map to the side as he looked at the various routes indicated.

"That's not what you experienced? Would you care to elaborate on that?" Laela questioned sharply. Orn took a bite of potatoes and chased it with a pull of cider.

"What you're describing? This sort of planning and summoning using specific materials? I haven't seen that. The folk I've encountered are scared out of their gourds, lost in a sea of chaos they can't understand, let alone put a name to. Oh, aye, some of them figure out that they have magic, but not one of them understood why this curse was thrust upon them." Orn remembered each of them, their deaths plotted out in his mind on the map she had displayed on the table.

He had failed each and every one of them.

"What's the matter?" Orn's gaze fell on Laela. The look on her face was almost comical. "You're staring at me as if I've grown a second head."

"That cannot be. These are simply not normal people. They are mages." An unasked question hung in the air between them, and Orn wasn't certain he would have the answer.

Orn shrugged. "If you say so. If it quacks like a duck, flies like a duck, and you don't stop to talk to it before threatening to stab it, then I suppose that's what it is. I've lost count of how many, but I'll say this again: not one of them asked for this. Not one of them was a mage, as you describe it. Quack, quack, princess." Orn swallowed the lump in his throat.

"They use magic, and so they must be dealt with," Laela snapped.

"I think the next question is: how many have *you* hunted? Were they marked?" Archivald flashed through his mind. Orn clamped his mouth shut before unwise words could surface. The image of the marks came next, clear enough to Orn's mind, but when he tried to convert their meaning into words it never seemed to work. Describing the marks was never easy. Not when it was difficult to think of without feeling a creeping sensation in his spine.

"In recent times? Two, maybe three? Beyond that, I could not begin to put a number to it. I've been sent mostly to the southern mountains over the last few months to ensure no one escapes north. I've seen markings on hands, I think. Wrists too. But that's how mages work. They taint their flesh with the sigils of magic to bind it to them, like The Spiral. The mark of magic itself," Laela explained.

Orn leaned forward again. "How do you know this?"

"My mother taught me the seven symbols of magic." Laela turned the book around so he could see. "The Lightning Bolt, The Hand, The Door, The Quill, the Scythe, and The Wheel." Each flipped page revealed another symbol, until she stopped on one detailing The Spiral.

"I've seen enough." Orn pushed the book away, his stomach queasy.

The morning was still young, that strange, quiet time when most folk were either already working or were stumbling to bed after toiling the night away. "We can continue this later. Meet me outside when you are done," Laela said, carefully studying the abrupt change in Orn's demeanor. She rose from the table and hoisted her pack over her shoulder. Without another word, she vanished into the back room of the inn.

Orn was already reaching for more food. But the thought of another bite turned his stomach, made him want to retch even though he still felt hungry. Empty. Orn dropped his fork, letting it clatter against the mostly empty plates.

"Laela must have helped me eat some," Orn grumbled. There was no way he had devoured all of it. He groaned as he left the table. Orn took a moment to bask in the silence of the main room, wondering what Laela had scampered off for, but he knew already that she hadn't abandoned him. "If she was going to leave, she'd have stuck a dagger in me last night."

The food sat both heavy and delicious in his stomach, slowing his movements as well as inhibiting his motivation. He savored it regardless. There was no way to know when they would next find a proper meal. Orn finally felt the warmth of the cider coursing through his veins perking him up.

"You have your job cut out for you," Orn muttered to himself, stretching his limbs.

When he returned to his room, Orn gathered his belongings and shrugged on his armor, preparing for the coming adventure. He made quick work of the buckles and straps, as if he'd been doing this for the whole of his life.

Once finished, Orn departed the little inn. There was a distinct chill that cut through his armor while the knight waited for his eyes to adjust to the strong glow of the sun. Squinting, he scoured the grounds, spotting Laela near the stables. He waited briefly, watching her care for her mount.

"If you could fetch my horse," Orn called as he strode over, motioning to the stable hand, who ducked into the barn. Laela's horse was nearly ready for travel, and Orn peered into the depths of the barn. The poor boy was struggling with the knight's horse, who seemed reluctant to be brought out of the comfortable stall. Eventually, his stubborn girl relented, letting herself be led out. "Thank you," Orn said as his horse's reins were handed to him. He led her out of the barn before starting his own slow and methodical process of soothing. The horse neighed and rammed her head into him, nearly driving him off his feet. He clucked his tongue at her and took a firmer hold of the reins so that they were eye to eye. "Next time I will make sure to leave you more feed to munch on while you enjoy the show." Orn laughed, his words devolving to little more than soft sounds while he arranged his bags. He paused before climbing into the saddle. There was something scratching at the back of his mind.

"What are you waiting for, oaf?" As if on cue, Laela glared at him. "In case you forgot, we have a job to do. The trail grows colder by the minute."

"Before we leave, we need to talk..." Orn straightened himself in the saddle. "How far between each 'job?' Mine were sometimes separated by many days' worth of travel, and that could break a good mount."

"As I said, I started my hunts much further to the south. They came over the mountains. There was a sea town... Vennal? No. It's not there anymore. Not since The Rising." Laela pursed her lips in thought. She turned and plucked a scroll case out from one of her packs, then retrieved a loose stack of well-worn paper and flipped through the pages. Her eyes darted across the cramped writing, her face scrunched as she mouthed a few words.

"What is it, princess?" Orn grinned as she went stiff at the sound of that nickname.

"Past writs of arrest," she answered gruffly. "One where Vennal *had* been. This one here," she held up one of the pages, "was further south. Maybe a week's difference. Another was at the foot of the mountains, which is," she paused here again, consulting another page that had a hastily scribbled map, "a week south of here, give or take. And dead. All killed. Those are just the recent ones on the run from New Cresthill."

"That explains much of why we have not run afoul of one another before this," Orn replied thoughtfully.

"What point are you trying to make, oaf?" Laela searched his face, looking for answers there. Orn shrugged his shoulders and fiddled with his pack. "Spit it out," Laela hissed.

"Only that it's getting worse. I ran into two this last week alone while you were hunting yours. The one we are already chasing, and another. And you know what? They didn't attack me, but their numbers are increasing."

"And?" Laela sighed.

"You said they mark themselves, but what if that's not always the case?" Orn leaned in the saddle to inch closer to the elf.

"It's possible but irrelevant. They have been dealt with, one and all. Until *someone* let this one get away. After burning down half of Swanford. Tell me that's not a problem." Laela's tone was terse, her words clipped.

"It doesn't matter that this could have been orchestrated by someone? Marking innocents?" Orn asked, incredulous.

"Not unless you have evidence," Laela replied curtly.

Orn shook his head. "What way were they going, princess?"

"What?" she asked.

"If you were tracking them, where were they headed? What direction?" Orn reached for the map, but she shied away from his sudden nearness, clutching the paper to her chest.

"Fine," Laela muttered after seeing his serious expression, handing him the map without further argument. Orn studied her markings, lining them up as best he could.

"Do you see anything odd?" Orn said, staring at her.

"A trail of corpses, jobs that need doing." He saw her eyes widen as she studied the map with more scrutiny.

"What do you see?"

"That doesn't make sense." Laela glared at the paper, as if she could change a fact by a simple wish. "They were heading east. Each and every one of them." Her words followed the lines on the map, the trails she had marked from the start of a hunt to the end. Her brows knit together as she chewed on her lip, and a litany of curses poured out from under her breath. "But what does that mean? There's nothing but the ruins of The Tower out there. Beyond that, not much more than swampland."

"It means we go east, princess."

Chapter 29

To The East

The conversation stalled, and Orn left her to study the map while he performed a last-minute survey of his saddle-bags, hoping he hadn't forgotten anything at the inn. Once he was satisfied his belongings were in order and that Laela had finished her own assessment of the map after secreting it away into her main pack, Orn waited until she started her horse forward before nudging his into motion.

The road was filled with gaunt villagers in threadbare clothing. Some carried baskets of fabrics and sundries on their back, but another group pulled a cart laden with wilted crops. Orn figured they were headed for Ostford, likely to trade what items they could. Laela noticeably shied away from them, driving her horse around Orn so that the knight created a barrier between herself and the villagers. She then tugged the hood of her cloak over her head, casting her face in shadow.

Orn decided to break the silence. "You doing okay over there, princess?"

"He does not learn, does he, Petunia?" Laela spoke to her horse, and pointedly not at him.

"I guess we won't listen none to her, Delilah." Orn did the same with his own mount. "I should've figured your mount would bear a flowery name."

Laela scowled at him. "Petunia here liked that name much more than Orion. And it pisses Ser Gregoris' horse master off something fierce. Before her, I had Daylily, Poppy, Lotus, Mimosa, Scorpion Grass, and, well, I think you get it."

"I actually think I do, even if not all of those are remotely princessy sounding." Orn chuckled as he stole a sidelong glance at Petunia, who snorted in reply. Laela made a noise and reached over. She patted her horse's neck, a smirk on her face.

Orn wanted to say more, felt the questions threatening to spill from his lips, but managed to stifle them handily enough. It became obvious to the knight that the elf had a reputation, one she wasn't too pleased with.

"If we go east from here it will bring us to some ruins. Cassandira," Laela said, keeping her head down. "The other two paths are easier to travel for a mage on foot. Gaulf will need somewhere to rest after expending himself so severely. And he'll perhaps need a handful of cold iron, as a focus."

Orn grimaced at hearing the boy's name in the elf's stately accent. "I don't expect him to find some iron in stone ruins, and I am not so certain he needs it."

"Unless you have a better idea, I say it's our best option. Or are we to simply head east and hope for the best?" Laela asked snidely.

Rather than reply, Orn rolled his eyes.

Laela muttered something under her breath. Orn wondered if she were mad that she had failed to see the pattern before now—she certainly gave the impression of being the perfectionistic type. But what of Willaime? Had he also failed to discern the mages' trend or had he kept the information from Laela for some unknown purpose? Whatever it might be, something was eating away at her, but Orn hardly wanted to pry. The last thing he wanted was to endure more of her ire.

As they were wont to do lately, Orn's thoughts drifted to the events of Swanford and the figure in the flames. He did not want to believe it was Gaulf in the middle of that chaos, yet it was unmistakably the boy he so desperately hoped to save once. The telltale mark on his arm was the only proof needed. But Gaulf seemed terrified amidst the fire, not elated or filled with fury, and that made Orn foolish enough to think they might find him, that he might stay Laela's blade, that he would hatch a decent plan for the kid's salvation.

Orn remarked abruptly, "Why does this keep happening?" He hadn't expected her to answer and was relieved when she didn't. "It's either the result of an agent of chaos or there's something more nefarious at work here... What if there's more out there, leaving a trail of charred corpses in their wake, like what happened in Oldcliffe?"

"Oldcliffe?" Laela asked, sporting a white-knuckle grip on her reins. "The Paladin raged for weeks about that village. We didn't make it in time."

"Don't I know it," Orn muttered bitterly. "In any case, it's not just fire that these mages wield, though that's the prevalent element lately. First few I came across were isolated somewhat, and the locals from the surrounding towns weren't aware of their presence. If no one lives, there's no one to spread the tale." Orn found it harder than he imagined to stop talking once he began. If they were going to work together, everything had to be in the open. Well, not *everything*... Orn absently scratched at his arm.

"Word travels fast, but only when there's word given to travel," Laela agreed. "I receive my orders and am dispatched quickly. There's a fair few of us on the prowl, though I tend to be assigned the worst cases, those where there is no hope of a clean end." Here, Laela paused, as if unsure whether to continue. "We carry them to The Paladin for sentencing."

Orn sighed. If the mages were being carted off to The Paladin, his opportunities for answers were dangerously reduced. "I still cannot reckon why they are headed east. Makes no sense." He shifted in the saddle, his legs already sore. "Do you think they both headed this way? The mage and the stone behemoth?"

"If it was just the mage, he is going that way to gather supplies. If he got out of the village with one of those *things*, he may be in danger before we can reach him. Those creatures often devour their summoners. They despise being dragged into the mortal world," Laela explained. "There was once a mage who thought to build an army and fled to the plains. My mother and I merely had to wait for the stone imps to turn on him before we rode in and cleaned up the mess. Easier that way." The elf seemed to enjoy Orn's discomfort—he caught the flash of a smile behind the curtain of her hair. "He did not realize the solitude he sought was his undoing. There was nothing in the wilds to sate the beasts," she added. "These blasted mages used to stick together too. None of this wandering about alone."

"I've never seen more than one at once," Orn said, chewing on the inside of his cheek. "How'd you get roped into this sort of business, princess?" The question slipped from him before he realized it.

Laela was silent as they continued down the road. There was another group of people huddled together as the pair passed. A ragged-looking crew of six boasting haunted, wild eyes, as if sleep were nothing but a distant memory. They avoided Orn and Laela, giving the duo a wide berth. Orn frowned, smelling the smoke that clung to their clothes. The refugee population would soon outnumber locals. The knight shuddered at the thought.

Orn settled into his own plodding rhythm again atop his mount as he turned over recent events in his head. There was more to this, some larger force at work that he could not identify. The puzzle and its pieces remained irritatingly out of focus, and he was uncertain how to proceed from here.

"Some of them deserved it," Laela said softly, and Orn believed he imagined it at first. "The Paladin gave me two choices: hunt or be hunted. Took them quite some time to realize I was pretty good at hunting mages. First several times, The Paladin couldn't believe I'd made it back alive..." She inhaled sharply, then added, "But more than that, I'm in his debt."

"Is that so?" Orn murmured, more to himself than to the elf. "Aren't paladins supposed to be moral, chivalrous...nice? This one doesn't sound like any paladin I've ever heard of." He could practically hear the clench in her jaw. This topic clearly struck a nerve. "So, this is what you do for The Paladin, hunt mages?"

"Yes."

"And the bait? Whose idea was that?" Orn asked. Laela squirmed in her saddle.

"The Paladin's idea, even after I told him it was flawed. But it worked, and so it became procedure. Didn't care that it put me in danger," Laela replied flatly, though the knight detected an undercurrent of malice in her tone. "He offered prisoners a chance to serve his cause, without acknowledging the cost. They were slated to be executed anyway, so why not let their death serve a noble purpose?"

Being sent out to die, with the hope of having a chance? It didn't sit well with Orn. "That still does not explain to me why *you* are the one out here doing all of the dirty work. How long have you been at this?"

"For as long as I could hold a blade or string a bow."

"You're an elf. You were born knowing how to do that," Orn joked, and Laela eyed him, incensed.

"For as long as I can remember then. I had no choice. Fight to survive, or..." Laela trailed off with a shrug of her shoulders. "I was given a job, and I did it. Perhaps it has grown worse recently, I do not know. Nor do I care. I left thinking to Willaime. I did what was asked of me." She glanced at him. "Willaime said that mages take time to manifest, and the quicker we took care of them, the safer the world would be. This, though? This is beyond our knowledge."

"How long, princess?"

"A few decades, I think. Maybe longer," Laela said. "It all tends to blend together after a while." There was a haunted expression morphing her features, similar to that worn by the trudging villagers. "If I waited until every mage became a problem there would be little more than smoldering rubble left of every village in the country."

"Laela—"

"I brought some home to be questioned. The castle bled with the sounds of their pain." Another shrug of her shoulders. "I do what I can, in hopes I outlive all of them and am left to find peace somewhere. To find home again."

"As I said, it sounds like The Paladin is hardly the nice man the name implies," Orn remarked.

"Who said paladins have to be *nice*?"

"Why don't you just turn your blades on *them*? If you tire of this, if you want a home, then go find it. No one gets away with threatening me and mine. Except, it appears, maybe a waif of a princess." That, at least, split her face into something resembling a smile.

"Keep calling me a princess and I will find a better place to turn my blade."

"Is that a threat or a promise?"

"Yes." The sharpness of her glare rivaled that of her daggers.

Orn wondered what he could do or say that would bridge this gap between them. There was a foul odor to her story that disturbed him, and the knight felt his own bile rising at the thought of The Paladin and the experiences she described. Maybe the stories of kind paladins were just that: stories.

Laela's body relaxed atop her horse when Orn failed to speak again. He was reluctant to prod any further, especially now that civilization gave way to farmland and forests, and the road had tapered off into a worn path in the ground. Deep ruts from wagon wheels marred the dirt, but even those were faded.

"I'm going to scout ahead," Laela said, kicking up a cloud of dust as she sped off, leaving Orn to himself.

Chapter 30

FALLING

ANYTIME SOMEONE APPEARED ON the road Gaulf was torn between revealing himself or keeping his mouth shut. With no idea if the traveler crossing his path hunted him, he decided it was best to remain cautious. Lying in a depression on the ground, holding his breath as the jingle-jangle of a plodding horse crept by him, the young man hoped the low spot shielded him from view.

When the rider approached where he lay, they paused, a hesitation that seemed to Gaulf an eternity. He waited for a rough hand or a sword to find purchase in his unprotected back with each ragged breath he drew. Or worse, he would realize that none of it was real.

The visions were worsening of late, the line between waking and dreaming thinning day by day. Much like his resolve, and his body. Gaulf hadn't enjoyed enough of luck beyond pilfering some carrots from a small farm, a loaf of bread left on a windowsill, or a handful of berries from a bush he swore his parents said wasn't poisonous. And he was no forager. Gaulf's stomach rumbled, and he struggled to remember his last full meal.

He passed more than a few pokeberry bushes, which he almost made the mistake of gobbling down in his hunger.

"Purple flowers, purple leaves, eat too many and you'll suffer worse than heaves," Gaulf sang, repeating the simple poem his mother would recite whenever they would gather berries together. Thinking of those memories made Gaulf's mouth water, his stomach rebelling painfully against its emptiness.

And already the faces of his family started to fade, the details bleeding into the night. Gaulf cried at the sudden loss. Echoing his sobs were those of the village of Swanford darting between the trees, as if the chaos had followed him to this dark place. The noises woke the power inside of him, beckoning him to unleash his magic once more.

"Give in, and—" Gaulf clamped his mouth shut before more words spilled forth. The sigils danced in his mind, seared in his thoughts as if he were merely parchment to hold them. Careening, spinning, commingling in ways he recognized, despite having no idea what they meant. That which lurked in his depths *knew*, and thus, he did too.

His fingers itched to move, to trace those symbols in the air. The Spiral, The Hand, The Wheel, The Quill, The Scythe, The Lightning Bolt, and The Door. Gaulf desired little more than to bring them to life, but he knew if he did that, he might be haunted by a ghostly scream. It would sound like Geralyn, or Booth, or maybe even Jannie.

At once his heart broke, and he fisted the folds of his shirt while his hatred of himself festered in his chest. Gaulf refused to surrender to the magic's whims, the burgeoning need to *let go*. It was a constant war for dominance of his body, and he felt trapped in his own skin. Steeling his nerves, Gaulf held onto himself, though it seemed to him as if he were a stone standing against the rush of a river, slowly eroded over time.

Shaking his thoughts away, Gaulf realized the forest was silent. The strange rider was gone, and he could not say for certain how long he'd sat in the dark hiding. Crawling out of the ditch, the boy moved with caution. Upon observing that the road was indeed clear, Gaulf tilted his head skyward. The sun's rays were diminished by thick clouds, and he caught the scent of an oncoming storm on the wind. Gaulf hoped that the rain might wash the world away, scour the earth clean. Scour *him* clean. But it was hardly more than wishful thinking.

The pangs of *need*, the coils of magic—he could not trust them. Gaulf could not trust himself, not after Swanford. And seeing Orn there, then again at Osftord, he was certain his path would cross the old knight's before long. That inevitability drove a spike of fear into his heart.

The tendrils of magic inside of him writhed, spiraling toward his limbs, toward his mouth, his heart. They moved with a barbed touch, hooking into him, trying to guide his hands. It bathed him in a cascading sensation as the world blurred, twisted, and reshaped itself around him. Fire lanced through his skeleton, racing ahead of chills that broke across his flesh. Gaulf's teeth chattered against the hollowness that filled him from head to toe.

"*Sra curak.*" Gaulf's mouth formed the words painfully, his tongue convulsing to wrap itself around the syllables. He shook his head, trying to take in deep gulps of air. Screwing his eyes shut, a cough wracked his body, doubling him over as air refused to fill his lungs.

Void.

Then, a spark of light, golden and serene. In front of him, inside of him, torn in two. Gaulf reached for this light and wrapped his fingers about it tightly.

The world exploded into view. But it was not the world as he knew it. Not quite. Gone was the road, the ditch, the rain. What remained were a series of stone pillars surrounding him. Gaulf's head spun as he tried to orient himself.

The pillars enticed him into motion, though he feared each step he took. Their stone was mired by moss peeking through its fissures, and Gaulf sought to understand their purpose, but nothing came to him. He teetered on his feet when he noticed the pillars moved as he did, seemingly following him as he made his way through the forest. Toward what, he did not know.

There appeared an obelisk ahead, taller than the surrounding pillars, though made of the same stone. Gaulf stared at the structure, his eyes trailing a pattern in the stone that he barely perceived.

Until that, too, snapped into focus.

"*Remember, remember.*" A voice not his own crept from his mouth, the words both familiar and alien. There was a coiled pattern to the crevices, and his gaze followed them from the widest edges to their centers. "A spiral," Gaulf murmured, leaning closer as if that might help him study the sigil.

Pain shot through his arm, nearly bringing him to his knees. Undeterred, Gaulf turned toward the next spire, and it thundered as the vision solidified around it. From a single point on the stone edifice spread a series of branching lines. From each of these, moss grew, and as understanding came, the boy shuddered despite the warmth in the air.

"Lightning Bolt," Gaulf said, turning from pillar to pillar, naming the sigils as he went. "Spiral, Lightning Bolt, Hand, Door, Wheel, Quill, Scythe." Seven pillars, one matching the mark on his own arm, the others matching the marks on the robes worn by the man he'd often seen in his visions.

An eighth pillar remained. Gaulf felt its tremendous presence behind him, dwarfing the other seven. It lurked there, just out of sight. But he caught a glimpse of it in the corner of his eye, and the shadow it cast engulfed him in the void once more. He ached to perceive the obelisk's marking, to try to make sense of what he was seeing, but where its shadow lay the ground around it disappeared into oblivion.

Nothing remained firm under his feet, and Gaulf fell.

Into the abyss he tumbled, a silent wind ripping past him, through him, until a pinpoint of light appeared below. As he fell, the pillars tumbled down with him. Trapped in their presence, in the phantom of nothing, Gaulf careened toward that light. It sparkled and flared to life, a myriad of colors pulsing with the racing of his heart.

He tried to stymie his descent, reaching for something, anything, to grasp. But with only the wind buffeting him about and the light below, Gaulf's panic grew. The pillars and their symbols flooded the void around him. No longer merely shapes in the stone, but given life.

The Spiral turning.

The Lightning Bolt spreading.

The Door beckoning.

The Wheel waiting.

The Scythe reaping.

The Quill dripping.

The Swo—

"*REMEMBER!*" Gaulf shouted, a crack of thunder from his lips tearing the world in two. The light below swelled, slamming into him as if he stood still, and he thought that perhaps death had come. Expecting pain, for bones to snap and pierce his flesh, Gaulf shielded his chest with his arms, but there was no impact. Daring to open his eyes, he caught the first drops of rain from the storm with his face.

His muscles ached. A groan escaped his lips as that last symbol danced just out of understanding, just out of reach.

Where had he seen it before?

That question plagued his mind as he lay in the rain, anticipating another wave of pain. The symbol faded like a dream, coalescing into smoke. When he realized nothing remained, that he needed to keep moving, Gaulf struggled to his knees, then to his feet. He approached a tree near the road and leaned against it, breathing heavily. Pressing his forehead against the rough bark, Gaulf cemented himself in the moment, a reminder that this was no waking dream.

Briefly, he feared he might fall through the tree, might lose grasp on what was. Frustration rose like bile, and those seven marks came with it, dancing behind his eyelids every time he closed them. The pillars, the markings, the inexplicable understanding of what he could do with them.

Replacing him, controlling him, consuming him.

With each vision, the world lost a little more of its shape. His hold on it that much more tenuous. Gaulf sighed, feeling the tree bark scrape his skin. It was real. He was real. The darkness would not swallow him whole.

Maybe, just maybe, the pain would go away.

"No." Gaulf slapped his hand against the tree, letting the pain wake him, grounding him, and he pushed himself away from the tree. Wrapping his sodden cloak about him for some semblance of warmth, Gaulf trudged down the road.

Gaulf concentrated on moving forward. The rain stopped some hours ago, though he could not remember exactly when. Between one blink of his eyes and the next, he had gone from drenched to being cold to being dry and warm again. Hunger gnawed at his stomach, the hollow ache sharpening with each passing minute. But he continued forward.

The sound of a door slamming drew his attention and he realized, too late, he had stumbled straight into another village. People vanished in front of him, ducking into their houses and other buildings, doors closing quickly behind them.

Everything was a blur, no matter how he tried to make sense of his surroundings.

The sky darkened, permitting him some sense of the passing of time. Gaulf searched the village, trying to avoid the people gawking at him from their windows. He spotted an inn at the heart of the village: a large building, its chimney expelling black smoke in great quantities. A sign hung from the front door's overhang, the words *The Whistling Fox* burned into the wooden surface.

Gaulf trudged toward it, raising a hand for the door when the loud *thunk* of a bar sliding into place stopped him in his tracks. Flinching away from the finality of the sound, Gaulf retreated and narrowed his eyes. Half tempted to kick the door in, Gaulf turned away, hearing more doors closing in the distance. His anger burned inside of him, and for the briefest of moments he thought to let go.

The thought twisted his stomach and sullied his appetite.

As he walked away, whispered words followed his steps, but not from the occupants of the houses. The voice came from within, golden tendrils drawing him eastward. Away from the center of the village and along the road.

He stopped near a signpost marking the road to Cassandira. Looking back toward the buildings, sullen with their grimy wooden walls and sloped gray roofs, Gaulf could not be certain if the village indeed appeared that somber or if his cold reception colored his judgment. Even the trees seemed to be encroaching on the town's limits, their canopies looming over the houses and casting them in shadow.

And yet, Gaulf still felt something drawing him closer. He noticed a smaller path leading away from the road not too far in the distance. Retracing his steps, he ignored the houses on either side, paying no mind to the stares he could feel boring into him. The path carried the boy toward the forest's edge at the end of the village, evaporating into the dense foliage. Forgotten.

Gaulf forced his way through the brush, disregarding the scraping brambles that scratched at his clothing. A weight settled on his shoulders, a feeling that lured him into the depths of the forest. Other than the faint whispers in his mind, the moon was his only company.

Soon, he stumbled into a clearing. With no more underbrush barring his way, he could see his surroundings more clearly. Here, the light of the moon fell heavy across the land, highlighting a tall silhouette.

A looming tower lay hidden within the trees, its walls consumed by spreading moss. Staring at it, Gaulf felt something tighten in his chest. The world was silent once more, as if abandoned by the songs of the night birds. Very little dared inch closer to the tower and the structures in various states of decay around it.

The tower stood untouched by time. Gaulf circled the clearing, and as he did so the weight on his shoulders never shifted. It led him here. To this tower. Scared, but unable to turn away, Gaulf approached tentatively.

Two images warred within his mind, an echo of the battle within his body. One part of him saw the grand tower, a spire stabbing at the sky. The other saw the decrepit stone, pock-marked and scored beneath the layers of moss. It stood straight, and yet it leaned to the side as if threatening collapse. The door in front of him was mostly the same. Thick wood bound by riveted iron, and a ring waiting for any eager hand.

Gaulf swallowed hard and wrapped shaking fingers about the handle, giving it a firm yank. The iron groaned in complaint, but the door opened to his command. As Gaulf stepped over the threshold of the doorway, the world twisted, and lights ignited around him. Half in darkness, half in light, Gaulf stood in the circular room at the base of the building.

His head spun, trying to see clearly between the two towers in his vision, one full of darkness and the other flickering with a familiar dance of flames. The torches continued burning, a spiral pattern following the stairs that wove around the inside wall.

At this vantage point, he nearly stumbled, vertigo's grip a vice. Raising a hand to cover his left eye, Gaulf shut out the second vision and focused on the one pulling at him. Here, with half of himself blinded, he could see the room with no distraction, no nausea.

Tapestries hung on either side of each of the seven hallways branching from this central room like the spoke of a wheel. The sigils adorning the tapestries drew his gaze, beckoning him closer. At the center of one tapestry was a spiral, a mirror to that on his arm. As if moved by some errant wind, the tapestry stirred. Or rather, it was the spiral itself that spun lazily. Hypnotically.

He worried he might lose himself in the image before him. Biting his lip, Gaulf retreated hesitantly to search the other tapestries, knowing already what he'd find. The marks seemed to leap off of the fabric. Spiral. Hand. Door. Wheel. Quill. Scythe. Lightning Bolt. Each called him, bade him to surrender, but Gaulf refused.

Not one of them beckoned him like the stairway.

Following that tug, Gaulf mounted the stairs, ignoring the creaking beneath his feet, the complaint of wood and stone. His mind was consumed with reaching the tower's top floor, away from the markings, from the ache of his arm.

A floor filled with tables and chairs, and shelves upon shelves of books, soon came into view. Moving closer to inspect the tomes, he earned a smudge of dust on his fingertips for his troubles.

"What?" Gaulf whispered, afraid of being heard by some lingering spirits. He moved his hand from one eye to the other. Darkness nearly swallowed him whole. The only light came from the moon as it peeked through a gaping hole in the side of the building. Gaulf stared at the empty bookshelf, at the tatters of paper that crumbled to dust at his touch.

Gaulf tried to discern the titles of the books, but the letters spun and twisted, defying any attempt. The bindings were marked with the seven symbols, their shapes clear in the leather. Frustrated, Gaulf strode over to the stairs, answering the phantom tug to keep climbing. A few more floors, bountiful in how barren they were, teased him along. Hunger for the books grew inside of him, for the knowledge they held, an ache that only increased in strength as he reached the top of the tower. It was open to the sky, and a gust of wind ripped through the stones. Its force was such that Gaulf felt certain the tower swayed beneath his feet.

Far below and some distance away, the boy spied a little town populated by houses the size of toys his sisters might have played with once. Curious, he stepped closer to the edge. Leaning cautiously against the stones, he peered at the tiny dots of light, the only sign of life in an otherwise dark landscape. The warmth in their orange glows reminded Gaulf of the stars.

"How far did I climb?" Gaulf said to himself, as if expecting an answer. To the east, he felt the phantom tug at his chest, drawing him toward some unknown place there.

Something, *someone*, waited for him. He knew that, as certainly as he knew he stood atop an abandoned tower that once housed magic and its knowledge. He longed to know what secrets had been learned here, anything that might help him understand what was churning away inside of him. Resting his head against the stone crenelation, letting its cold surface leach away some of the heat building in his face, Gaulf cried.

With a slow exhale, he released a sweet breath of air that burned fresh and cold in his lungs, blessedly free of smoke from the village's chimneys.

And as calm settled over him, as Gaulf relaxed, the muscles of his face almost curving into a smile. Then something *snapped*. A coil of magic skittered down Gaulf's spine. He jerked around, searching for something that had brushed against his skin, but there was nothing. It wasn't outside of him. No. It was deep inside of him, buried beneath the misery and pain, hidden in the furnace of his chest.

A connection to the stone creature, growing closer. Nearer. Looking down the length of the tower and into the darkness below, Gaulf sensed the remaining creature of earth and stone to which he'd given life. Most of what he had called into being had tapered off, severed and nearly forgotten, but this one link persisted.

The fiery maw opened in an echoing cry that sent a shiver through him. Drawing away from the edge, he realized he no longer stood alone.

"*They yet come.* Ser Gregoris, you tenacious fool," came a gravelly and familiar voice from just behind Gaulf. Standing opposite him, the robed man leaned against the stone and looked out at the scene below. The berobed head turned, mimicking Gaulf's own movements, until their eyes met. "I must get to The Tower of Fragments and put an end to this. Before he imperils us all."

"Why are you doing this to me?" Gaulf spat, full of the anger burning in his chest, fueled by the mark on his arm, the life he had ripped out from under him. "Thaddeus," Gaulf said the name, unsettled, as if he had known the strange figure all along. Thaddeus turned his gaze westward, and Gaulf followed it. There, in the distance, Gaulf spied a large cloud of dust. He felt more than heard the thundering hooves charging toward them.

Thaddeus ignored Gaulf and headed for the stairs. Not wanting to be alone again, Gaulf trailed silently behind him. Questions raged in his mind, and he longed to ask them, but would the specter answer?

The man's form wavered in and out of sharpness, becoming nearly completely translucent at times. It was when Thaddeus halted in his descent that Gaulf noticed the hazy outlines of others. Books snapped shut of their own accord, and he discovered the vague form of another person following Thaddeus.

A charge built in the air. His hair seemed to stand on end, and breathing became difficult, worsening the closer they came to the ground floor. Thaddeus forged onward, gaining steam even if his following ceased to grow. Gaulf could hardly make out their silhouettes against the backdrop of night, but it was their whispers that revealed their presence. Words imperceptible but for the spidery sensations flitting through the air, cascading down Gaulf's body. His blood alternated between boiling and frigid, his vision split between the emptiness in front of him and the shifting form of Thaddeus marching, staff held high.

Thaddeus stopped, and there was then a tangible force separating them. He struggled when magic slammed through him and Thaddeus. Though he could not hear the words, he saw the mage draw familiar sigils in the air, weaving them together and drawing the power in until it burned through the length of his arms, dousing his fingers in flames.

From each of his gathered congregation, Thaddeus pulled magic from their own sigils, weaving webs of light in the darkness. As their power joined the mage, the clarity of their profiles flickered, until they were nearly consumed by the glow of an undulating spiral in the air.

The stone creature stood as if in supplication, its hands raised toward Thaddeus. The sound of grinding gravel echoed through the structure as Thaddeus pressed his palm against the fist-sized rock that served as the creature's head. When he retreated from the creature, Thaddeus left behind the glowing print of The Hand.

The creature grew in size, tugging sediment and rock from the earth until it dwarfed the tower itself. Moss bound its pieces together, and with every step the thing provoked a vicious rumble in the ground. Its savage bellow pierced the night air, and then the stone behemoth and its summoners faded from sight. As if they had never been.

Power surged through Gaulf's body, a torrential flood looking for the crack in the dam of his resistance. It shot through him and toward the dimming figure of Thaddeus. Gaulf's hands moved of their own accord. The more he struggled against it, the tighter the binding of magic held onto him.

His mouth opened to repeat the words Thaddeus had used, but without knowing them, without having heard them, the spell lingered on his tongue like a molten drop of metal sizzling in a vat of water. Heat filled him until he, too, might burst. Gaulf screamed his throat raw, the power within him escaping to complete the spell. As Gaulf fought off the urge to draw yet another summoning from the earth below, he realized the magic had to go somewhere.

It slammed into the tiny creature, bolstering its form. Gaulf felt the connection slam tight in his heart like a spear driven home. He felt the creature latch onto that, pulling from that power, threatening to drain him. If he let go, the end would come.

Let the creature consume him. That would be his penance.

And yet he could not wholly surrender. Visions of Jannie danced in his mind, her lithe form moving through the gaps in his memory, calling on him to resist. Gaulf threw his head back and screamed.

Others quickly joined. Too late he spied tendrils of light stretching from the nearby village. When they met the little creature that now stood before Gaulf, it was suffused with fire, molten and misshapen. A crooked version of a handprint glowing on its head after it splayed its strange fingers.

It tossed its head back in a primal scream. Gaulf matched the noise, his body wracked with pain as flesh-turned-tallow burned. Or so it felt as such, like a candle on fire at both ends. He was coursing with *magic*. The mark on his arm shifted, sizzled, and in the sky above, the boy saw a crevice open.

Tears streamed from Gaulf's eyes as he continued to scream. The clouds split, sundered as easily as dry parchment. He thrust his hand toward the sky, covering the wound that rent it as if staunching a bleeding injury. The scream died in his throat after he collapsed to his knees.

The stone being cupped his head, and Gaulf sobbed. He hated the thing in front of him, much as he hated himself.

For letting go. *Again.*

For giving in, even if he had no choice.

The creature grumbled gravelly in consolation, but there was fury beneath its surface, a malice that radiated from it. Craggy, rock-like teeth of obsidian were bared, reflecting the molten nature of its core. Gaulf shook his head. He could feel the link with the creature, what it wanted from him. Something he would not give.

"I am sorry," Gaulf said.

With each passing moment, the binding between him and the stone creature became more tenuous. His hand remained clenched over his heart, the source of his hold on the earthen giant. He felt its pain as keenly as if it were his own. To exist in this world, to be wrought into this form?

Without purpose?

Despite that, there was something lurking there, waiting for him to release the creature. Panic set in against this darker undercurrent that tried to pry his fingers away, chipping against his already wavering will. The heat inside of him ran cold, turning sluggish.

Bile rose in his throat, and the magic grew barbs inside of him. To hold on was to feel pain. More than he could bear, more than he wanted to. Afraid and alone, Gaulf did what he must.

Once more, he let go. He could not fight the inevitable. Something darker, stronger than him, wanted release. His creation roared, and erratic light, bluish in color, filled the black glass of the creature, spreading like a bolt of lightning through the night sky.

Gaulf tried to find purchase again, tried to reconnect to the stone beast as it turned and screamed. Unable to reclaim control, he ran.

What had he done? *Again.*

Chapter 31

THE NEXT TOWN

"WHY ARE WE STOPPING?" Orn asked, shifting in his saddle.

Laela motioned for him to be quiet. His hand shot toward the sword strapped to his back, searching the area for threats. But there was nothing, other than the blasted trees and the road.

It had been at least a day or two since he had seen proper sunlight, and the thick burgundy and orange leaves blotting out the sun irritated him.

Worse, the forest was silent. Orn kept expecting the snap of a branch or the scurry of squirrels through the underbrush or even the bleating of a deer in the distance.

"What is it?" Orn hissed, the lack of reply from Laela doing very little to ease the tension. His stomach growled, and he debated trying one of the roots she swore once were edible. "Princess?"

"Stop your incessant braying for a moment," Laela spat, her voice low. Her attention was on something ahead on the road. Orn tried again, futile as it was, to discern whatever it was that caused them to halt in their journey. When his inevitable failure became obvious to him, he sighed.

"Is this your idea of torture?" The two had hardly stopped bickering in the last few days, both only too eager to prod one another. Orn had half a mind to knock her off her mount and leave her behind. Barbs bubbled and boiled within him, but he bit his tongue.

"I am going to stab you if you do not keep silent," Laela snapped.

"Bugger this straight to the depths of the nine hells." The words were out of Orn's mouth before he could stop them. Laela glared at him, the dagger in her grip a mute warning. The old knight slid off of his horse and onto the ground with nary a protest from his knees.

Orn stretched, then began to walk, one hand resting on the hilt of his blade. Laela joined him after tying her horse to a nearby tree. He looked back to his own mount and gave a low whistle. The horse might wander off to graze, but other than that she would wait for him. Orn turned his head to find Laela missing, and he frowned. Where had she gone?

"Blasted elf," he muttered, before the slight rustle of leaves directly above his head gave away her position. Whatever it was Laela had spotted, it seemed too late to avoid it.

The trees receded when he stepped cautiously around the bend in the road, the sight of Cassandira coming into view. It was no more than a large gathering of dreary hovels than a proper village. Maybe it had been something special, once.

"Something's off," Orn said, hoping Laela heard him. He sprinted for Cassandira, an ominous feeling gnawing at his belly.

When he neared the village, he surveyed the area, noting the distinct lack of stirring for the early hour of the evening. As if the entire place had been abandoned in haste.

Looking around, Orn tried to determine what had set his teeth on edge. If this was in any way a repeat of Swanford then the two of them were already too late.

Stopping in front of the inn named *The Whistling Fox,* Orn stared at the door. The windows on either side of it. The darkness within. The hearth fires were little more than embers, and there wasn't a soul in sight.

The world abruptly split itself in two as he watched light flow from the village, a strange tributary from each of the houses meeting a larger river that vanished into the trees. And yet, a part of him saw the village as it was: a dark, lifeless husk. A pressure built behind his eyes until he closed them, disrupting the distorted scene.

"There are no bodies," Orn remarked somberly as he walked the dirt pathways between buildings. He searched for Laela, thinking that she could investigate herself. Or use him as bait, like the pitiful prisoners now lying dead some leagues back. "If that's the case I'll run her through."

"Run who through?"

Laela.

"I thought I told you to keep quiet, barbarian. Your caterwaul-ing will alert our mark." Suddenly, Laela appeared next to him. Orn cursed, nearly leaping out of his skin.

"You. I will run *you* through."

"You'd have to improve your stealth skills first. The way that you clank with every step, I could shoot you in the dark." Laela smirked as she stared pointedly at his mismatched armor.

Orn rested a palm against his chest. "Helps keep a sword out of my gut, princess. And removes the need for surprise." Orn shook his head at her obvious enjoyment. "Did you find anything?"

"No thanks to your bellowing," Laela replied, motioning toward the last standing tower in the distance, somewhat obscured by trees. This spire, unlike the rest of the village, was constructed of worked stone. "There're three bodies up ahead. And one that appears to be sleeping in what remains of the tower."

"Where's the rest of them?" Orn asked.

"Sleeping?" Laela offered, though the uncertainty was obvious in her expression.

"The houses are empty. The inn is empty. Like everyone just disap-peared." Orn frowned.

"Well, whatever is ahead, it reeks. We do ourselves no favors waiting for it to come to us."

"I can feel it too." Orn glanced around the village warily. "But if anyone is still alive, they are going to need our help."

She nodded, but otherwise said nothing.

After staring at the decrepit tower for longer than he ought to, Orn soon realized he was alone. "Laela?"

A visceral fear tore through him, a dread heavy on the air. A shriek echoed through the surrounding trees, and the knight felt it in his bones. In his ears. The slice of sound against his eardrums, as if they'd shattered.

Orn feared he had gone deaf. But the screaming never ceased. It had merely risen in pitch, ringing impossibly loud in his ears. Then, as quickly as it came, it stopped. Thick silence followed, and Orn felt such relief that he collapsed to his knees, breathing heavily.

The world lost its shape, the ground seemingly hollow beneath him. He blinked away the onset of tears while struggling to make sense of what was happening.

Orn froze when that piercing cry returned. This time, it was a chorus, and the silence that followed was hardly as sharp, but the persistent buzz that vibrated in his ears made him stumble. Orn's stomach lurched, and he worked his jaw, the motion doing little to quell the nausea. Were there a tree nearby, he would bash his head into it to free himself of this agony.

The agitated keening returned, and Orn's eyes watered beneath the onslaught of the sound. He pressed his palms against his eyes, scrubbing at his face in a desperate attempt to focus his attention elsewhere. The village melted beneath his feet, and strange colors he could put no discernible name to swirled in his vision. Orn gagged, nearly retching.

Then, as quickly as the keening had begun, it ended. Orn waited in fear, certain that another wave would come any moment. But there was nothing. Only blessed silence once more, and Orn tried to re-member how to breathe. Normal color returned to the area, restoring the muted grays and greens familiar to this region.

Orn barely managed to recoil from a shambling form reaching for him. Stumbling over his feet, he clumsily sidestepped what appeared to be a hand, though not entirely. Its flesh grazed his armor, leaving an oily residue in its wake. The fat of the flesh was wicked, and the tips of the fingers were alight. Orn retreated further when the hand swiped at him again, and he noticed it was attached to an impossibly long arm.

"Nope, I don't like this," Orn muttered to himself. A part of him wanted to flee, to leave this place to its fate. But he would not.

The arm stretched toward him again, accompanied by an unsettling squelching sound. Orn managed to bring his sword up to bear before a searing pain set in. With the pain came a quick, blinding flash of light. The oily residue left on his armor caught flame, burning against the metal surface. Orn cursed and frantically patted his chest, hoping to smother the fire, but as quickly as it flared to life, it burned out. If that *thing* had laid a hand on him, Orn would be but cinders now.

He thought to yell for Laela, to call for aid, but the elf was nowhere in sight. And a chorus of keening pierced the air, indicating that the shambling mound of fleshy coals he had just encountered—that vanished—was not alone. Wherever it had retreated to, it had friends.

"Great. Just great. And me without a princess." As much as Orn loathed her presence, the lack of it was far more disturbing. He strode forward cautiously as creatures wrapped in what looked like melting wax and what might once have been clothing started to clamber out of the building. Their bodies, once presumably human, coiled around a burning energy that called to him.

Let go. Let go.

Orn shook his head, fighting off the crackling beacons of pain and heat. He shuddered at the thought, shoved it away as he approached. Their arms, impossibly long and dripping something that sizzled on the ground, were outstretched toward him. One was closer than the rest, moving fast.

Lashing out with the sword, Orn sputtered when his blade bit into flesh. Fire and blood followed in a splash of heat that crackled and hissed as it hit the ground. Nearby grass turned brown, then black, withering with every step the creature took. Orn thrusted the sword in its belly, and the creature let out a sound, but it kept coming right for him despite its wound.

If aid did not arrive, Orn might die here in this wretched village.

Chapter 32

INTO THE TREES

"I swear that oaf will be the death of me." Laela cringed as Orn prattled on in the distance. "Smelly, stupid, swaggering barbarian," she ranted, finding purchase on a tree branch high above the target of her words. The bumbling knight had hardly ceased his noise, and it demanded every ounce of her willpower to not nock an arrow. It would certainly settle most of her problems. "I do not know why I did this."

The elf's regret at joining Orn had only grown in the time they'd known each other. His thoughts on The Paladin nagged at her sensibilities, but there was an undeniable ring of truth to Orn's words.

Nevertheless, Laela could not return without her quarry.

Not without Williame either, assuming, of course, that he had not abandoned her. That he had not simply returned to The Paladin for aid or because...*she* was in fact the problem, and the problem had been handled. It fit the pattern.

But why?

She had served faithfully, done whatever was required of her. Though perhaps not without some antagonism on her part. But The Paladin was not so foolish as to order the elimination of his most effective tool. And she could not believe that Williame had indeed deserted her, but his corpse was missing from the village. Questions burned in her mind, overtaking everything like wildfire. Had he saved himself, as Orn had declared? Laela gave her head a violent shake at that thought, as if the motion could change anything.

"Shit. Now where'd he get off to?"

Laela slipped from branch to branch after noticing the knight's absence, testing each one carefully. While this did not afford her an easy path to the structure ahead, to whatever waited for them within it, it would keep her hidden.

"Let the oaf handle matters on the ground. Might end up doing me a favor." And she settled in to wait. If this went to plan, she would have her quarry and be done with this wretched place. She could part ways with Orn and return home.

Home. The word was a hollow sound in her mind, conjuring no sensation of familiarity or comfort. The Paladin was waiting for her return.

"That's no paladin I've ever heard of," Laela whispered Orn's words aloud, hating the bare truth in them. Could she do as she always had, come back to that place with another body, only to be sent forth for another?

She shuddered at the thought and stared at Orn, at his piecemeal armor, at the clumsy swinging of his sword. He was a backward sort of knight compared to what she was accustomed to, but his instincts about The Paladin unnerved her.

Hidden in a copse, she observed that though the stone of the structure refused to burn, the place was already a charred husk. Nevertheless, there was something moving inside.

Orn's frantic thrusts made her wince, and not only because they were unpracticed. Whatever he was fighting, there was also something else lurking nearby.

"Pay attention, you dolt!" The noise attracted the attention of one creature circling Orn. He was soon surrounded. "Fine," she muttered angrily, searching for a closer vantage point. "This'll have to do." She shifted further and severed some of the smaller branches in her line of sight. Drawing an arrow from her quiver and quickly nocking it, Laela held her breath. Orn had not yet noticed the creature behind him, and she tracked its movement with her arrow. The wood of the bow creaked as she tugged the string.

A shadow darted from the building to a nearby tree. She could hardly calculate its size due to its speed.

Torn between the new addition to the fray and the creature tracking Orn, Laela understood she had precious seconds to determine her next course of action. Everything was unraveling rapidly, an occurrence entirely foreign to her. The branch splintered dangerously beneath her, so she shifted her weight and withdrew just enough to remain aloft. If Laela had any hope of helping Orn, she couldn't afford to give away her position.

"Move, oaf!" Laela ordered, watching the knight's sword spark when it bit smoking flesh. A part of her recoiled from the sight of such magic. But another part of her wanted to decipher its origins, and the elf's mind sifted through all known spells, growling in irritation when nothing matched.

The wind through the leaves was no more than a whisper. All that existed in the world was the arrow and the creature behind Orn.

She loosed the arrow.

It hadn't occurred to her that Orn might be waiting for the right moment to turn about. That, perhaps, he could actually be aware of his surroundings. But Orn swiveled on his foot and lunged at the shambling molten being behind him.

Helpless, Laela watched the shaft glide through the air toward Orn, and winced when the arrow glanced off of his armor. The force shoved him back a step and well within the grasp of the other creature. She nocked another arrow and loosed. It slammed into the creature, whose arms were now wrapped around the knight.

Nock. Loose.

The arrow found purchase in Orn's shoulder as the creature tugged him backward. His shriek echoed throughout the village.

"Gods damn it!" Laela scrubbed a hand over her face. Taking a deep breath to center herself, her hands began moving of their own accord. She nocked, drew, and loosed. One after another. Laela focused her attention on the creature that held Orn in its burning grip, ignoring the other stalking beings nearby. The first arrow met its mark, sinking into the creature's strange flesh. It released Orn with a pained howl, and the following arrows skewered its body, even as the wood of the shafts caught fire. That creature fell, but it was just one of many.

The rest closed in, surrounding Orn.

"Shit." Laela jumped to a lower branch, looking for a spot to land softly. As she descended, she disregarded the cries coming from below.

It would be nothing more than a dangerous distraction to listen, one that could cost them their lives.

When her feet met solid ground, the elf grimaced at the sight of an arrow lodged in an opening in Orn's armor.

Her breath caught in her chest as she pulled the bowstring to her face, staring at the grizzly scene before her. One breath, one heartbeat, and she let another arrow fly. A second followed, and then a third. The clambering creatures staggered when the arrows found purchase, two in one and the last in the other, driving a few from the heart of the fray and away from Orn.

It was an opportunity the knight did not waste. He made wide swipes with his sword, favoring his uninjured arm. Between the two of them, they were able to defeat the creatures without further incident, but when it was over and the eldritch beings lay dead, Orn spun on his heel to face her with a face full of rage.

"You shot me!" Orn snapped, sword in hand. He pointed the blade right at her, wobbling forward. "I should skin you and hang you from the trees, you gods damned elf. You used me as bait, didn't you?"

Now that she was close, Laela could see that the creatures' bodies had been reduced to ember and ash. Ruined lungs hissed as they breathed their last, whatever served for mouths cracking and seeping with blackened blood. The dead filled the air with an unbearable stench of melted flesh, charred bone, and boiling blood that threatened to turn Laela's stomach.

"No," Laela replied flatly, checking her own body for any sign of injury. When she was satisfied, she met his steely gaze. "At any rate, we have bigger problems right now."

"You shot me, princess." His voice was low, threatening.

"Occupational hazard, I'm afraid. But I can assure you, it was not intentional." She tapped a gloved finger against his plated chest, already exhausted of his whining. "You would be dead if I meant to hit you," Laela said, coughing in the searing heat that radiated against her flesh, overwhelming her nose with smoke.

"I have one problem, elf. You. I never should have let you follow me." Orn's fingers gripped the hilt of his blade so tightly that the whites of his knuckles were visible underneath the grime from battle.

"No, that's not your problem. Not yet." Laela shook her head and pointed with her bow. "There's something else here." It was almost comical, watching Orn peer over his shoulder while trying to keep an eye on her. She felt a pang in her chest at the sight of the arrow in his flesh.

"What's that, princess?"

"Trouble." There came a sound from within the building, one that was low and deep. Against all reason, Laela felt trapped, helpless, when she heard it. Her heart lurched in her chest, and the way Orn stumbled she could only imagine it affected him too.

The silhouette of a new creature licked by flames unfurled in front of their eyes, reaching for the burned corpses that lay strewn about. Its wails soon transformed into howls of rage when it turned its anger toward the two of them. Despite the change, the sense of grief was strong, and Laela winced as if taking a blow to her stomach.

Lost. Forgotten.

Infused with emotions and memories not her own, the elf struggled to remain standing. In her mind's eye she saw a dance surrounding the twinkling fires of a festival, the taste of cider tart on her tongue, and fear. So much fear.

"I never should have let you come with me," Orn groused, withdrawing his hand from his injured arm.

"As if you could have stopped me." Laela was tempted to yank the arrow out of him, guilt be damned. She nocked an arrow and took aim toward the building. Whatever had made that cry lurked there, moving in the shadows of the threshold within the stone portal. "You are in this for the gold, remember? You get the coin, I return with the mage to the castle." Her voice faltered over the last word. She was about to say *home*, but nearly choked on it. "We aren't done."

The ground was littered with corpses of burned flesh and wicked bones that were responding to the cries of the creature. Twitching, writhing, their long arms and spindly fingers reaching upward. Hollow stares met Orn and Laela when they rose to their feet.

"I am in this for answers, not merely for coin," Orn hissed through clenched teeth as he walked between the bodies, driving his sword through each one to still their creeping movements. "If you wish to continue this tired argument, princess, we can renegotiate the terms of our *agreement*. But if you shoot me again, we're going to have a discussion of an entirely different sort."

"Fine." Laela kept the bow trained on the giant hunk of burning stone in front of them, the words sticking in her throat. "I'm sorry."

"What's that?" Disbelief colored his features, but it was brief.

"I said I'm sorry."

Orn adjusted the sword in his grip. "Can I trust you, princess?"

"Yes." The word crept from Laela's lips before she considered its effect.

"Good," he whispered softly. "We can figure the rest out later. If we survive this."

The forms on the ground were remembering how to stand.

Laela loosed her arrows, each one finding purchase in the feet of the figures, pinning them to the ground. That would keep them in place for a time. Orn used his blade to finish the job, severing waxen limbs and splattering flecks of gore that charred the grass wherever it landed. Another sharp cry emanated from the stone structure.

Laela witnessed two impossibly large hands of stone and ember materialize from the tower. They grasped at the doorframe and pulled. The building groaned in resistance, and Orn and Laela retreated several feet.

The knight lashed out against another mound of flesh that had started to rise again. The blade absorbed the ichor and steaming blood, leaving the pile of ash and embers around them silent and unmoving. Laela hoped the effect was permanent.

"Oh, by the hells." Orn's jaw dropped as he studied the large hands and arms breaking the tower. "How did it even get in there?"

"I'm not sure, but judging by the size of it, I'd say our mark came this way not too long ago," Laela guessed, nudging one of the cooling corpses at their feet. What once had been human was twisted almost beyond recognition, the condition of her arrows no better. How had Orn's blade survived?

The doorframe finally gave way and the lumbering, giant form made of stone and fire burst from inside. The smell it brought with it into the clearing was somehow even worse than the sickly-sweet scent of cooked flesh, and the ground shook as it headed toward them. Laela nocked another arrow.

"Pincer strategy?" he offered, steadying himself.

"What, you cannot handle this one all on your own?" She laughed.

"This is hardly the time to have this discussion."

"You seemed to think it was a good idea a minute ago." The large stone critter clambered closer, then threw a massive fist into the earth. The ground trembled violently and the tower tilted, causing a cloud of dust to expand from the point of impact. Laela watched Orn stumble toward the monster. Her first arrow bounced harmlessly off of the thick, stony hide.

"Not sure your little toys are going to work this time."

"Worked fine enough on you." Laela regretted the words as soon as she uttered them.

"Not funny," Orn replied.

The glare he shot her made her roll her eyes. "Fine. What do you propose we do then?"

"I can distract it while you search for a weak spot," Orn answered.

"Not sure that's going to work, but we're out of time," Laela said tersely, staring at his back when he blundered forth, his sword swiping harmlessly against the stone-like hide of the creature. Orn somehow managed to dodge a hand that railed against the ground where he had been standing. She set her bow to the side and unsheathed her own sword, edging herself closer to the melee in progress. The blade felt familiar in her hands, almost as comfortable as the bow. "Do you even know how to use that thing?" Laela called as he slashed at the creature uselessly.

"Are you well-versed in fighting creatures like this?" Orn shot back as a shower of sparks flew after another swing.

Laela analyzed the boulder-like creature, looking for any sign of weakness as well as a place to strike where she could avoid being smote by its fist or impaled by the clumsy oaf swinging a blade like a loon. "Keep him distracted!"

"And what exactly do you think I'm trying to do here?"

"I want to say prancing, but even that might be too generous a term." Laela wrapped both hands around the worn leather of her hilt. When she saw her opening, she thrust her blade forward. The length of the sword slid in between stones, deep into the glowing embers beneath. Something not quite blood spurted forth, glowing hot, riddled with a sickly blue hue.

Laela withdrew as the beast howled, whirling about. She rolled out of the way of one boulder-sized fist that swung for her. The two of them circled the creature, and she thrust forward at each opportunity. Not every blow landed, but those that did sank deep into the soft interior and enraged it that much more.

"Stop hacking at it like it's a tree, and thrust!" Laela yelled, circling the beast.

"What do you think a sword is going to do against this thing?" Orn swung wildly and connected, the blade scoring the stone. Did it move just a little slower? The sword, dark against the molten flesh of the thing, took on its light, as if consuming it.

"Never mind that—lead it toward the trees!" Whatever he muttered in reply was lost as she yanked the blade free. Laela ducked another blow and searched the edge of the forest. Climbing the nearest tree, Laela found the lowest, thickest limb. There was a yell behind her, and she had to hope that Orn was following. She paused when silence descended upon the clearing, wondering if that last smash had flattened him. But when she heard him curse, that disabused her of any such notion of ridding herself of the oaf.

Once she was on the other side of the branch she spotted Orn backing away from the oncoming creature, and she hunkered down to wait once more. This large tree had another smaller one that had fallen into it, their branches locked together. One good kick should dislodge it. *I hope.*

What was Orn waiting for?

Chapter 33

THE MOUNTAIN FALLS

"STUPID, STINKING ELF SHOT me," Orn groused to himself, withdrawing from the creature even as it followed, lashing out at him. Its movements were slow and easy to avoid, however it was relentless, and Orn worried it would outstrip his own stamina in short order.

There was a heat sweltering inside of the creature, one that threatened to burn him out of his armor. His sword was useless against its stone hide.

Orn swore with the effort of his swings when the shock of contact vibrated his muscles. The blade complained as it beat against the stone. Where was the elf?

An exposed root sent him sprawling backward, but he caught a glimpse of the creature's stony form unfurling, rising to its true height and towering over him. Behind it in the trees, he spied Laela.

He would never scramble out of the way in time. The air, pierced by the whistling sound of a heavy weight rapidly descending, became hard to breathe. The crack that followed echoed through the forest and, for a moment, all was quiet.

The first thing Orn noticed was a distinct lack of pain. Then the light filtering through the leafy canopies above. Carefully, he rose to a sitting position, taking in the scene. The creature was pinned to the ground by the trunk of a fallen tree, its furious wails silenced.

Waiting a few moments until he was satisfied the beast remained unmoving, Orn struggled to his feet and retrieved his sword.

But the thing stirred, and the knight understood the battle was not yet won.

Its stone hide was cracked in a multitude of web-like patterns, spidering from the place of impact. The dead wood of the tree smoldered as fire seeped from the fissures, the stone crumbling and falling away to dust. The creature shuddered with the effort to stand, the weight of the tree too great.

"Stay down." Orn stalked the hulking mass, ignoring its thrashing. His blade thrummed in his hand when fiery blood pooled in the beast's wound.

The air sizzled with heat and smoke. Orn covered his mouth to keep from retching, coming as close as he dared to the rent in the stone hide. He climbed the creature quickly before it could swat at him and took a branch of the charring tree in his free hand.

He thrust the sword into the molten flesh below. The hungry blade found purchase in stone flesh conjured by magic, and the knight felt the hilt warm when he withdrew the blade and slammed it home again, and again. A shudder of stone and a scream of gravel echoed in the clearing. The radiating heat slowly dissipated, and Orn leaned against the hilt of his blade.

Orn paused, held his breath, and waited. When nothing happened, when no large hand tossed him into the distance, he finally released the air from his lungs. The length of his sword shimmered with molten blood, absorbing the dark liquid through the markings etched into the steel.

The blade felt different. *Alive.*

"What are you staring at?" Laela asked from behind him.

Orn turned, nearly stumbling into the blasted elf. "Might just be the arrow sticking out of my shoulder, princess."

Laela bent forward to examine him. "Let me see it."

Orn sighed and pushed his shoulder forward.

"The sword, oaf."

"Fine," Orn barked through gritted teeth, turning his blade over to her.

"Where did you say you got this?" Laela's gaze traveled the length of it, her finger tracing the markings.

"Found it, a long time ago." Tightlipped, Orn swallowed the memories that came unbidden.

Laela scrutinized Orn. "Why are you so skittish?"

"A natural consequence of being shot with an arrow."

"Well, this sword..." Laela paused, her eyebrows drawing together as she glanced at the blade again. "This sword reminds me of a story my mother told me, of beings that walked these lands and the blades that banished them." Laela returned the weapon to Orn.

"Is that it?" Orn asked, unimpressed.

"Since you're acting this way, yes, that's it." The smug look on her face made him scowl.

Laela brushed past him to study the corpse. Sighing, Orn sheathed the blade, his head swimming from the pain of the arrow when adrenaline faded. Ignoring it as best he could, he surveyed the area. Corpses littered the clearing, and the giant simply smoldered but remained still.

"I think we're clear." *For now.*

"Let me take a look." Laela turned to face him. Orn's gaze shot to his scabbard, and Laela rolled her eyes. "Your wound." She picked at his armor, not waiting for a reply. Fussing with the straps and buckles, the elf worked diligently, taking care to not widen the wound. He winced when he realized the shaft had broken at some point, and what remained of the arrow protruded from his shoulder. "Don't act like such a child." Laela clucked her teeth at him and turned her attention to one of the pouches on her belt.

"You are a bloodthirsty, sniveling...*gah!*" Orn's anger flared, and Laela took full advantage of that opportunity to close the distance between them, taking the broken shaft in her hands and inspecting it closely. The old knight felt every movement, the agony of her touch on the broken wood. "Take your time, princess."

"Your griping will only make it worse," Laela snapped, leaning Orn against the creature's corpse. The rock of its body was solid under him, and she quickly fished one of her daggers from her belt, positioning its tip near his rent flesh.

"Watch it!" Orn yelped.

"I haven't even started yet," Laela said, the edge in her tone evident, before she began working at his shoulder. With the severe angle, Orn had trouble seeing what she was doing, though it did not stop him from trying, which earned a growl from her and a lance of pain.

Orn resigned himself to waiting. This close he could hardly see anything beyond the point of her ear practically shoved in his face as she leaned over him. Was she humming under her breath? Orn opened his mouth to say something but thought better of it. He did not want to distract her, and instead tried to focus on anything other than the sensation of her digging in his flesh with her dagger.

Laela rummaged around in the pouch at her side. "Hold this." When he failed to respond, her hand grasped his and moved it to a few folds of bandages. The fabric grew sodden beneath his hand. "This one too." She shoved more in his hand against the wound and Orn pressed it firmly. "There, all done." She stood back, tossing what remained of the shaft and arrowhead to the grass. "I will have to keep an eye on that to ensure rot does not set in. I'll need more bandages. Maybe we can find supplies in some of these empty houses."

Orn watched Laela's every movement while they walked. He could feel his anger getting the better of him, but it would hardly help matters to retaliate. Without knowing for certain whether there were more creatures in the area, harming the only other possible ally he had for retribution seemed reckless.

When she disappeared behind a burned-out structure in the village, Orn found a spot to rest in the shadow of the tower. Old moss-covered stone matched the forest around it. Weathered carvings drew Orn's gaze. He ran his hand over the relief, as if the act could help make sense of its meaning. There, his fingers found a spiraling pattern in the stone, surrounded by other symbols too worn to decipher. The years had not been kind to this place.

Curiosity got the better of him and he ventured inside the tower, where the shadows were stark against the light of the clearing. Dust motes hung in the air, but this place did not feel *empty*.

"Hello?" The word cracked in his throat. The tower's innards looked like a tornado had swept through it. "Or a very large, angry stone beast." There was rubble strewn about, not all of it from the recent kerfuffle. At the furthest point within, Orn spotted alcoves where statues might once have stood. Now they were part of the debris littering the floor. He kicked at what appeared to be the head of a stone scythe. "Laela?"

"Why is it you start wailing again the second I am gone?" Laela's voice preceded her into the tower.

"I wanted to make sure you weren't taking aim again, princess."

Laela slammed a wooden crate of supplies down on an old table that, somehow, still stood. "Remove the rest of your armor so I can bandage you up properly, or do you have some more complaining to do?"

"Turn around." He fumbled with the metal pieces of his armor, setting each one on the ground a few feet away. Blood and sweat had stained his shirt, and Orn grimaced as another wave of pain shot through him.

Once he was finished, Laela prodded his wound, peeking beneath the bandage.

"What is that?" The sharp scent of something delicious filled the air. A cork appeared in Laela's mouth, then the sight of a bottle hovering over him. The amber liquid spilled out, coating his rent flesh and stinging so that his eyes watered. "Is that whiskey?" When the pain receded to an almost tolerable level, Orn snatched the bottle from her and took a long pull. The burn of good liquor soothed the ache of his body, and an entirely different sort of warmth suffused him.

"Well, that should at least help with the pain. Not sure how much blood you lost," Laela muttered as she turned her attention back to the wound. She wielded a sewing kit, drawing the needle through the edges of his wound as if she were mending a torn shirt. Orn was about to take another swig before she stole the bottle from him. "You need to keep what little wits you have about you." Laela shook her head at him before having a drink herself. "Brace," was the only warning Orn got before she poured the rest over his shoulder. The old knight winced again as she dabbed at the wound with a clean bandage. When she was certain he was not bleeding any further, she started wrapping his shoulder tightly. Laela tested the bandages, nodding at her handiwork. "We might as well make camp here for the night."

"We might need to extend our stay."

"What for?" Laela asked.

"Whatever these bodies became, I think they were once the villagers. That's why we can't find any evidence of them."

"What about them?"

"I want to bury them," Orn replied, a grave expression on his face.

"Are you serious?"

"As serious as an arrow to the shoulder. Maybe you should start digging."

"No, I—" Laela started, but Orn's glare cut her off.

"I can't very well dig myself, can I?" He pointed to his bandaged shoulder. "I'll help where I can, but we can't leave them like this. They've suffered enough." Laela considered him briefly, then sighed in resignation. "We can find a shovel in town, and most of the bodies are ash anyway. I'll continue to scour the village back there for supplies while you work, maybe find some food too. We can camp at the inn."

Laela stalked off without further argument. Orn chuckled, then gathered his armor and set off to the inn.

Chapter 34

CAMP

AFTER A MEAGER BREAKFAST the next morning, with the dead buried and the silence of the village weighing heavily on them, Laela tended to the wound on Orn's shoulder. He tried to sit very still, and mostly succeeded. That is, until she spread a pungent salve on the wound, and he turned his head away, pulling a face.

"It's not that bad." Laela glowered at him, affixing the bandage to his shoulder. "It'll help. Meanwhile, continue to find what supplies you can in the town. I am going to scout the forest and see if I can find the mage's trail. I have no doubt we are close."

"I think you might be right. Go ahead and search, but I am not certain we have much need for an alternate path." Orn poked at the map she'd left on the table.

"The Tower of Fragments," Laela said softly, following Orn's finger. "But that place has been empty for longer than I can remember."

"Can't say for sure, but this tracks, given all that we know about their movements." A hollowness opened in Orn's belly at that. A part of him held onto hope, against all reason, that he might help Gaulf.

"Unless..." Laela said, then paused.

"Out with it, princess."

"Like I've said before, my mother always prattled on about that tower being *more*. Something about a key. That magic anchored it, maybe them, in place." Laela scrunched her face up in concentration, shaking her head. "The Paladin ignored that tower, and said it held nothing of importance."

"I'm inclined to think the opposite of The Paladin on principle alone and will now assume this tower is of the utmost importance. Question is, anchored *them*?" Orn leaned in conspiratorially.

"I do not know. Mother refused to say more, other than repeating the same word, over and over: *She*. But Mother often lamented men and their unquenchable thirst for magic, always claiming more of our lands and making pilgrimages to The Tower without our consent." Laela shook her head. "Much of it is still a blur whenever I try to remember, though."

"All the more reason we get to this place quickly, before someone does something they shouldn't."

"I concur." Laela glanced toward the window, a concerned look on her face.

"What is it?"

"None of this matches what I know. What I saw, as a youth. What my mother tried to teach me," Laela answered somberly.

"Then that's what we need to discover," Orn replied. "I'll add that to the never-ending list of things to do. I'll see to the horses after searching for supplies."

With that settled, Laela left the inn. Orn did his best to clean up from breakfast, though carefully, given the stiff ache in his shoulder.

Orn rummaged through the inn's pantry, pilfering what he could, then he refilled their waterskins and made his way to the stables. Delilah greeted him, huffing for food that he happily provided. Petunia took a little coaxing, and Orn half expected to lose a hand for his efforts.

"Come now, girl. We need to get you ready to ride." Orn clucked his tongue at her, his voice low and calming. With time, he managed to convince Laela's mount to allow him to tend to her. With the two horses accounted for, he packed the food away and tied the horses to a hitching post to wait for Laela.

Orn made a quick circuit of the nearby houses, freeing any unharmed livestock from what remained of their pens. At least they would fare well in the surrounding forest. What paltry supplies could be found in the crumbling structures, the knight shoved into his pack.

Laela was mounting Petunia when he returned to the stables. He followed suit in silence, and the two departed the empty village, leaving nothing behind but corpses. The forest on either side of the road threatened to consume it, looming over the pair as they traveled. Even the sun became an infrequent visitor, the light cold and gray as the day progressed well toward evening.

Half asleep in the saddle and slow to react, Orn jolted awake at the sound of Laela's voice. "Someone's come this way. Recently." The elf slid off her horse before Orn realized what was happening.

He replied with little more than a grumbling curse under his breath as he joined her on the ground, albeit on wobbly legs. Steadying himself against Delilah with a few clicks of his tongue after she snorted at him, the knight chuckled.

"At least *you* get a chance to rest, Delilah." Orn led the mount by the reins, scooping up Petunia's as well. "What did you find, princess?" Laela squatted in the dirt, an intent expression plastered on her face. She hunched over as he spoke, barely pausing her study of whatever it was that gave her reason to stop in the first place.

Her hand ran along the leaves of a bush, fingers trailing along the soft green with the barest hint of a rustle. Orn fussed with the horses, Petunia snorting at him whenever he got too close.

"Most times I've followed a trail, it's been a simple path of destruction. What do you see?" Orn asked, closing his mouth before he gave voice to his own fears about what this development might mean. Loath as he was to admit it, he was lucky to have Laela with him. Maybe she would be more useful than he initially believed if she could pick up the mark's trail quickly enough to prevent further disaster.

"Stay with the horses for a moment. Be quiet," Laela hissed, moving past the brush to a deer trail that disappeared into the trees.

Orn rolled his shoulder with a wince of expected pain. The stitches had started to itch in a maddening way, and there was no relief in sight.

"Oh, I'll be quiet all right," Orn said to no one in particular. The pain at least helped clear his head. He continued to grumble as he towed the horses further along the road. "She'll catch up when she's done frolicking. I'll find us somewhere to camp."

Not too far from the edge of the forest, Orn spotted a clearing. He led the horses through the underbrush, feeling the snap of every branch and rustle of leaves as a threat. Somewhere, lurking in the dim light, a shadow moved. Orn reached for his sword.

"Just a deer." Orn chuckled when the antlered form bounded away from him, but his heart refused to cease its hammering in his chest. Nearing the clearing, he noticed signs of recent activity. *There was a camp here.* Tying off the horses to a tree, Orn hunkered down in front of the abandoned firepit. It was still warm. A tingle shot through the mark on his arm, and Orn gritted his teeth against the sensation.

Gaulf. He could almost picture the boy here, tossing and turning in the fight against sleep.

Orn cursed. He turned to the horses and set about caring for them, losing himself in the ritual of the act of brushing their coats. He moved carefully, thinking of his shoulder. It wouldn't do to worsen the injury, especially when he considered what lay ahead of him.

Petunia showed as much disdain for him as Laela did, but the dangling carrot eventually won the beast over. "I suspect we'll be friends soon enough," Orn cooed. The mare was a lean breed, made for riding great distances. "You'd be a problem if I decided to leave." The words didn't match his tone, but the horse's nostrils flared in warning regardless. "If I wanted to run, I would have done so long ago."

He switched his attention to Delilah, who ate the offered food without hesitation. Once they were fed and brushed, Orn studied the small camp.

Laela had yet to return, so the knight busied himself with removing the fallen branches that littered the campsite, keeping those that were good candidates for kindling. Next, Orn sought out the least rocky part of the ground and he set their bedrolls there. Beside his own bedroll, he left his sword, followed by his armor.

It was difficult to ease his wariness. Every sound drew his attention, setting his teeth on edge.

He then dug a new firepit over the old one, scooping out the excess ash and charred limbs. Orn stacked the kindling at its center in such a way that would ensure airflow, stuffing a handful of crackling leaves through each little branch. As the sun's light began to vanish beyond the horizon, Orn sighed.

"Where'd you get to now, princess?"

With no answer, Orn settled down in front of the firepit and readied his flint and steel. A spark fizzled to life, and Orn hissed at the sudden burst of heat accompanied by the scent of smoke. His stomach threatened to turn sideways, as if his body anticipated the smell of seared flesh to follow, for lately, fire had only death to join it. Absently, Orn scratched at the mark on his arm. When he realized, he reached for one of the larger branches in the kindling pile that was still somewhat green and fed it to the pit.

The way the rising flames danced across the wood drew his gaze, and he watched as curling threads of fiber transformed into blackened coals emblazoned with the red of the heat, the sight threatening to swallow him whole.

"No more of that." Orn's voice was alien to his ears, and he slapped himself across the face before he withdrew from the fire's edge. His skin felt partially singed, and the knight pushed his fingers across his forehead to make sure he still had eyebrows. "Where did the damn elf get off to?"

As if in answer, something moved just outside of the camp. Orn scrambled to his feet again, one hand tugging the sleeve of his shirt down before brandishing his dagger. His sword lay several feet from him. If it were a wild animal, he could only hope he had time to reach the weapon. On the breeze came an undercurrent of blood, coppery and thick.

Laela stepped out of the brush with two hares trussed up on a branch. She stared in obvious confusion at the scene before her, choosing to give him a wide berth, then laid the hares on the fire.

It took Orn a few moments to calm himself, adrenaline coursing through his body for the hundredth time this day. When he was certain his heart was not going to burst out of his chest, Orn took a seat by the firepit. His stomach growled when the hares began roasting in earnest.

"Not yet, oaf," Laela said, as if sensing his designs to snatch a piece of their supper before it was ready.

"Fine, princess," Orn snapped. Perhaps a little harsher than he intended, with the way she seemed to recoil. "What?"

"Stop calling me princess." Her voice was low, little more than a growl. "I will not ask again."

"Then stop calling me an oaf."

"Problem is, *oaf*, I only got to be a princess until, well..." Laela paused there, her gaze as sharp as her dagger as she watched him. "Maybe the same as a human child's tenth year. I never did the math or paid attention, but after that?" She shrugged and folded inward. "Haven't been a princess since. Especially not as long as I've been hunting wizards. That part of me is long since dead. The Paladin made damn sure of that."

"Wait, so you *are* a princess?" Orn furrowed his brow as he studied her.

"*Was*. Right up until he took my home from me and murdered my entire family," Laela explained, a hint of malice in her tone.

"I've heard the stories, that these were once elven lands, but I don't know if I truly believed them." Orn scratched at his beard for a moment, studying her. Then he leaned toward her, narrowing his eyes. "The Paladin deserves what he has coming."

"And what, exactly, is that?" Laela glared at him.

"Turnabout is fair play." Orn shrugged. "Give him as good as he gave, princess." His words had been barbed enough to lance into her, and Orn could see that they remained, painful and deep.

"Hardly matters. He's not your problem to worry about anyway. Once we're done, you can forget about the both of us."

"That's just it, though. Maybe I don't want to, and I don't think you want to crawl back to him either, do you, princess?" Orn knew he tested uncertain waters.

"Shut it, oaf, and stop calling me princess."

"If you keep calling me that, you know I am going to keep calling you princess, right?" Orn held his hands up, a laugh bubbling up in his throat, but he dared not let it out.

"I guess we're at an impasse then, *oaf*." For the briefest of moments, he thought he saw the corner of her lips lift.

After supper and some time spent stewing in silence, Orn abruptly said, "I guess maybe I knew you were a princess, even if it has been some time." He picked the hare clean before tossing its remnants into a small hole. "Why do you serve him? The Paladin, I mean."

Laela picked at the bones of her own meal, and Orn felt his stomach growl. She did not answer, did not meet his gaze, and pushed her food around as if to divine the answer from gristle and sinew.

"This is all I have ever known," she answered distantly.

"I can understand why you loathe that title."

"I just want you to stop saying it," Laela said. "Doubt anyone would believe me if I tried to use it as a title, though." Her shoulders drooped as she tore off a chunk of meat. "I am sure the world thinks me dead, right along with the rest of them." She held her leftovers out toward him.

Orn took the hare from her as he chewed on her words. "Your family?" She nodded. "You're alive and kicking. I know it's not much, but it's something. I give thanks every day I'm alive, aching or otherwise, because it's one more day to search for answers."

"What answers are you seeking?" Laela asked.

"Why mages are suddenly appearing in larger numbers than ever before. Why their powers are amplified."

"What more is there to know, except that mages are a stain upon this world to be dealt with? They are driven to seek chaos and destruction, to darken the skies with their magic. I am driven to end them," Laela remarked, but doubt crept in her features.

"If we don't figure out what's causing them to appear, we may have a bigger problem on our hands." Orn paused and, staring at what remained of the hare in his hands, tossed it into the fire. His appetite, fading quick, left him unable to stomach another bite.

"I do what I have to, so I can safeguard my own life."

"But using men as bait? I have not yet begun to defile myself by dragging unknowing and potentially unwilling men, dirty bastards or not, into a fight they have no chance of winning. Pitting them against forces they have no hope of surviving. I would rather see them hang for their crimes than to give them a false sense of hope," Orn snapped.

"Then we are not the same," Laela answered flatly.

"You're hiding in a straw house, princess. Eradicating mages, hunting innocent people, and for what? Think. Something doesn't smell right here, and it isn't any fault of yours. You're just a pretty little forgotten princess who's clearly been lied to." Orn poked at the fire, then added a few more limbs to keep it from extinguishing. Laela was staring at him, eyes hard, vicious glints of light reflecting the flames.

Orn watched emotions march across her face: anger, frustration, denial, fear. "I am *not pretty,* nor little."

"No, you're not. You're a damn lion, princess."

Laela froze, seemingly uncertain as to how to respond to Orn's unusual sincerity. Silence hovered over the pair of them, the crackling fire the only sound in the empty expanse of the forest.

"What am I supposed to do?" Laela asked softly. "Not kill this mage after he decimated *another* town? Let's say I don't return with proof, or don't bother to return at all. It wouldn't be long before The Paladin orders his knights after this mage, then after me."

"Much as I might wish to, I won't argue to save this mage. He signed his own death warrant with the blood of that last village. I expect he wouldn't be in any state fit for answering questions either." The knight's stomach soured when he thought of Gaulf. "We are on his path—there is no point in turning against the tide now. The better question is, what are you going to do next?"

"I don't know," Laela said. "Wait, what questions?"

"What do you mean?" Orn winced, fighting the urge to scratch the mark on his arm.

"You said he wouldn't be in a state fit for questioning. What questions did you want to ask him?"

Orn swallowed, waving a hand at her dismissively. "I guess I did." He sighed. "I want to discover why magic is returning to the world, and at such speed. If we could figure out why it's happening, we might be able to stop it. Maybe even get rewarded for the effort. Coin enough to carry out the rest of my days with nary a worry."

"You are hiding something."

"I think our energy is better spent figuring out our next moves," Orn replied quickly.

Laela fixed him with a glare, unmoving. "Do not seek to evade me, oaf. Or I promise I will follow through on my first threats to you."

Orn calculated the risk of not listening, his eyes darting to where his sword lay next to his bedroll. He'd never make it in time. "Fine," Orn grumbled. "But only with the understanding that once I show you what I need to, you'll give me time to explain before you start stabbing."

"Get on it with it," Laela said, crossing her arms over her chest.

Orn rose, grunting as he stretched. Once he was on his feet, his hands found the hem of his tunic, and he felt the weight of Laela's gaze. With a sharp intake of breath, he yanked the cloth over his head, and he stood there, bare-chested in the sudden chill of the night air.

"What questions require you to be shirtless, oaf? Do I really need to see your scar collection just after dinner?"

"Remember when I asked you how many of those mages were marked?" Orn asked, hoping she would come to the conclusion on her own.

"What of it?" Laela asked, unamused.

"Are you sure you're ready?"

"Stop stalling, Orn."

He turned toward the pit so that his left arm was bathed in firelight. He watched her eyes widen as they found the mark on his left arm. The blue spiral was alive in the dancing light of the fire, seemingly twisting and boring deeper into his bicep. Rough edges tore at skin that did not bleed, and there was no hiding it, the look on her face.

"I am not sure all of them had a choice, princess. In fact, I'd wager none of them did. But I haven't let it stop me from investigating. We need answers…" Orn fell silent.

He could practically feel her gaze follow the spiraling design. He waited. Whether for her to launch at him with her daggers, or to yell at him. Orn shuffled away from the firelight as if he might hide.

She stood, then circled him with a wide berth toward her horse, keeping it between them as she rummaged through her saddlebag. Laela withdrew her book and started thumbing through it, showing him the sprawling spiral inked onto the aged parchment. "That's The Spiral, the mark of magic itself. Which begs the question: how did *you* get it?"

"It's been quite a long time. Decidedly less gray in my beard when it happened."

"What came first, the magic or the mark? You said it yourself: it takes time and study to amass power on this scale. And here we are with them crawling out of the woodwork," Laela said while Orn shrugged into his tunic, hissing when his shoulder stung from the movement.

"I don't know which usually comes first, but I'm hardly wielding flames yet. Though since the mark came first for me, it would only be natural to assume it might be the case for the others," Orn explained. "Have you, or *The Paladin,* stopped to ask why this is happening?"

"I learned not to ask questions long ago." Laela shook her head. "Those who have spoken against The Paladin are often determined to be in league with those marked. I watched a knight I had known for several years hang for asking the very same questions you are now." As she spoke, Orn watched the war waging within her written plainly on her face. "You are not wrong. There's something bigger here."

"For what it is worth, I am sorry. I think I understand, much as I am able to. It's not a pretty thing to be bound to something you're powerless against," Orn said, rubbing at the mark on his arm.

"I—" Laela paled.

"I need to know that if the time comes, you'll do what's right, and not because you are following some corrupt fucking orders to drag me back to Haven," Orn cursed, spitting straight into the dirt. "If I break, princess, I'll need you to kill me, but the others will need you to continue the investigation. Figure out why this is happening, and stop it. Before more lives are lost."

Laela searched his face then, and Orn surmised she was trying to determine whether he was serious. When she seemed satisfied, she said softly, "I will."

"Good." Orn felt some relief at having laid himself bare, though there was little to be had at the prospect of death. He hardly doubted her willingness to follow through on her promise, but it seemed unfair to corner her into making such a deal.

As if sensing his thoughts, she said, "I need little motivation to flay you like a deer, oaf."

"Okay, so maybe don't be so quick about admitting it either, princess." Orn chuckled lightly. "Do it for protecting yourself, and keeping me from hurting anyone, not for The Paladin. But until then, I'll need to live long enough to stop this mage before he destroys another village." He drove his hands through his grimy hair. "Conjures more of those strange creatures."

"These are his lands, and if they are running amok, he must know something," Laela said distantly, drumming her fingers against the book she still cradled. "Maybe he has figured it out, and that's why he's shifted focus from—hey, stop that."

Orn was scratching at the mark through his tunic. There was a small vibration in the flesh, and he realized that touching it awakened a part of him that he hardly recognized. The part drawn to the flames, the smoke, the ash. He nodded and dragged his hand away, focusing his attention on Laela.

"We have to figure out what is going on, and how much The Paladin knows. I reckon he has more information than he's letting on," Orn said.

"It has not always been like this. Ser Gre—*The Paladin*, I mean," she began, nearly choking on his name. "I wish I could just slit his damn throat."

"Well, why can't you?" Orn drew a finger over his throat. "Never thought you had so much restraint."

"Believe me, I tried...when he first took my home. His armor..."

"Well, what are we to do then? We will need to discover some weakness of his, some way to get answers." Orn returned to his place on the other side of the pit as shadows gathered in the relentless march of night.

"I don't know, but when we arrive in Haven, let me take the lead," Laela said.

This close to his bedroll, Orn grabbed his sword, pulling it free of its scabbard. "I know the steps to the dance at this point, but fine, princess, you take the lead."

"One day, you'll have to tell me the story of that sword." Laela watched him with interest, and the knight felt a warning gnawing at his gut.

"I'll say this for now: it staves off the madness somehow. Haven't really figured it out yet." Orn studied the blade. It appeared normal in the moonlight, but Orn knew better.

Laela narrowed her eyes. "That confirms my suspicions, at least."

"Do go on, princess." Orn leaned in, his attention caught.

"Mother often told me stories, as I said earlier. This sword, the markings on it, are the symbols of magic. Seven of them. But that sword?" Laela motioned toward it. "This is the eighth, or a representation of it. *'And The Sword, to banish it all, and cut to the bone.'*"

"What's that mean?"

"It means that blade is a weapon built to fight against magic, against its very source. To protect the one who wields it," Laela explained. "Mother would tell me of *She*, the god locked away, bound and forgotten. If the story is to be believed, your sword was part of that binding."

"Gaulf named it Nothing. I wonder what it is he saw." Orn chewed on his lip. "This sword saved my life once. A story for another day, though."

"I'll take first watch," Laela offered, adding more kindling to the fire. "Get some sleep, old man." She rose to her feet, dusting off her dress before walking over to a tree at the edge of camp.

Chapter 35

THE WATCH

LAELA CLIMBED THE TREE and hid herself within its thick branches until she was certain that Orn had drifted off. The shimmering light of the fire settled into a dull warmth as it dwindled, so she had to rely on the moon's dim glow to search the surrounding area for the threat she knew was coming.

Orn might disagree with being used as bait were he awake, but this was too good of an opportunity to let slip through her fingers. And this time, there would be no need for sacrifice.

At least, she hoped as much.

She first noticed someone following them shortly after departing the decimated village. The stranger managed to keep pace to their camp, an impressive feat. Even during Laela and Orn's conversation around the fire, she'd heard someone moving softly through the brush several yards from the camp's edge.

Laela remained alert as the newcomer meandered through the forest, seemingly at random. But she knew better. Part of her attention was fixed on tracking those footfalls, the other on Orn while she slid out of the tree and circled the clearing before ducking into the foliage in pursuit. The elf hardly made a sound as she moved, having spent lifetimes improving her stealth. A castle could be as loud as the forest. If it were old enough.

Memories of her mother and her advisors hustling to attend to some business or another came unbidden to her mind. *Cassandira.* She remembered that dark place well. She only ever wanted to disappear into the trees, to find something other than boring, gray stone.

To learn of magic and its symbols so she could forget her mother's disappointment in her.

"Some of our kind grew up with walls and politics, not rough bark and talking to the birds." The queen's voice echoed loudly enough in Laela's head she thought her mother might have stood right next to her. *"And they're all gone now."*

Behind her she could hear the faint grunts Orn made in his sleep. How long had it been since he had sworn that he was going to leave her behind as he hunted their prey? A week? And yet, here they were.

He had fallen asleep promising to help her storm The Paladin's castle, but she couldn't stop thinking about the knight's revelation. Orn was marked. And while he seemed determined, Laela's certainty about his condition or that of the other mages failed to match his own. Maybe he truly believed he would find the answers necessary to solve the larger mystery at play. She didn't have the heart to tell him that belief was a dangerous illusion.

The presence in the distance retreated, but Laela watched the dark shadows. She absently pictured herself ending the marked man asleep in his bedroll, or knocking him senseless and dragging him back to Haven.

The knight could be useful as bait to capture Gaulf, then she might return to the capital with both mages. Maybe even keep the sword for herself. That part of her fought to act the hunter The Paladin expected her to be, but still Laela found herself unable to betray Orn.

None of this made any sense.

What Orn said did, though.

Continuing to turn Orn's words over in her head, Laela questioned the circumstances that brought her into The Paladin's service. It was simple before she met the knight, hunting wizards and other fallen men, keeping towns from collapsing under the weight of hatred and evil. Their purpose was clearly defined, allowing complacency to settle over her. She dove headfirst into her work for The Paladin, never needing a moment to breathe, to bother with investigating more thoroughly.

The elf had never questioned her role in his plans. Not anymore, at least. Whenever she had tried, he would prohibit her from leaving Haven or lock her in the dungeons.

With the screams.

She shuddered and shook her head, her heart racing with the onslaught of the unbidden memory.

Laela then thought on the last few decades of her life as she kept watch, trying to piece everything together. Another rustling drew her attention, and carefully, she nocked an arrow. Stepping quietly, the elf left Orn's sleeping form and the firelight behind. The sound of branches snapping, of leaves crunching underfoot, became much louder, until Laela saw a slip of a girl outlined by silver moonlight.

Laela paused for a moment, her heart skipping a beat when she caught sight of a blackened handprint on the strange girl's face.

Chapter 36

A Familiar Face

Laela nudged Orn in the ribs with her boot. "Wake up." When the words failed to elicit a response, she did so again. The shocked look on his face when he abruptly woke brought a smirk to her own, and she stepped on the blade of his sword before he could grab it, waiting for him to realize that they weren't in danger.

"By whatever dark hole you crawled out of, princess," Orn grumbled, bleary eyes shaded against what little dim light filtered through the trees. "What time is it?"

"Must you incessantly bray? It's time for us to have a talk." When he failed to move, Laela prodded him with the toe of her boot again.

"Five more minutes," Orn replied groggily.

"No. Someone's out there, someone who's been following us since we left the last village," Laela snapped through clenched teeth.

"I'd have expected you to kick a lot harder then." Orn bolted upright, his hands rubbing at his eyes. The knight's bones made audible noises as he struggled to his feet, stretching and popping. "How can you be certain there's no danger?"

"Because I've seen her. A marked girl, who seems determined to speak with you. No magic that I can sense, though, despite a blackened handprint on her face. She's in the forest just there." Laela pointed toward a dark expanse of trees. "Scream if you need help." The elf disappeared into the underbrush several feet away.

After a moment of straining, Orn heard the noises. Someone was indeed traipsing through the forest cautiously. He held his sheathed sword in front of him and waited. The silhouette of a young woman crouched in the grass froze as Orn met her eyes in the darkness.

"You can come out, Jannie. We already know you're there. Let's have a little talk, yes?" Orn waved a hand toward the figure hiding in the shadows.

With no Jannie in sight, the knight sighed, then made a show of setting his sword on the ground. Laela was nearby, and he hoped she would keep an eye on the situation. He placed his trust in that, and in her, as he waited for some sign that Jannie would reveal herself.

The figure in the brush stalked toward the campsite. The slight flare of flames in the firepit cast her in stark relief. The handprint on her face, the hatred in her eyes, and the dagger in her hands told Orn all he needed to know.

"Good evening, Jannie." Orn hoped he had remembered the girl's name well enough. And while he was thankful that Laela had not taken matters into her own hands, he found himself wishing he had not abandoned his sword.

"Don't you dare think to greet me in such a friendly manner!" The young lass pointed her dagger at Orn as she spoke, standing a few steps away.

Jannie's face twisted first in rage, and then in confusion when he held his hands up placatingly. She opened her mouth, then closed it, squeezing her dagger's hilt tightly.

"Talk to me, Jannie. I can see the words chewing a hole in you," Orn said softly, not daring to take a step closer in case she planned to start stabbing.

"Where is he?" Jannie asked angrily. "I know he's out here somewhere. What did you do to him? Where's my Gaulf?"

Orn's shoulders sagged. "I-I did not hurt him. I am the liar you named me, but I know not where he is."

"Why? Why take our hard-earned money? Why make us think him dead?" Her body shivered violently, as if refusing to absorb the information.

"The coin was nothing more than a bonus—" Orn started, but her growl cut him off.

"A bonus to you, but a bounty we *had* to offer, lest The Paladin's knights come back looking for more trouble. One that ate into our village's already depleting stores."

Orn scrubbed a hand over his face. This wasn't going as well as he hoped. "When I turned in proof of bounty for Gaulf, that cleared his name. I gave him a chance to escape and to be free, without fear of being hunted. To find a life somewhere else. Another died for his freedom." Orn grit his teeth, shaking his head. "I am not the one you hate, am I?"

Jannie paused, her eyes widening as she stared over his shoulder. He did not have to look behind him to guess what had happened.

"Princess, put it away. I have this under control."

"She's trying to stab you, oaf. That's my privilege," Laela warned.

"No one's getting stabbed tonight, got it?" Orn grimaced, hoping to pacify Laela and keep the tenuous peace.

"I just want to find Gaulf. I know he's out there. I know he needs me." Jannie sheathed the dagger at her side, then fidgeted with her tunic.

"Listen and listen well. I'm afraid that he might not quite be the Gaulf you remember," Orn said, praying that the tremor in his voice wasn't too noticeable. He felt her pain keenly in the hollow part of his chest, and wanted nothing more than to reassure her. But the knight didn't trust himself to tell her what he feared had become of the genial boy he'd briefly known.

"What makes you so damn sure?" Jannie demanded, her eyes welling with tears.

"This is not my first experience with those marked, and I'm not hunting them merely for the coin, nor for sport." He sensed Laela bristle behind him.

"Then...why?" The question surprised him, because it did not come from Jannie, but from the elf.

Jannie's gaze traced his face appraisingly, as if waiting for Orn to attempt to wriggle out of their joint interrogation. Orn wished he could melt into the ground, disappear entirely. Anything other than giving a true answer to that question. *Why him?* That thought plagued him for longer than he cared to admit. His arm burned where his own mark lay heavy upon his flesh.

The knight decided to gamble. "I'm marked. For some time now." Orn paused, still surprised by the admission even after choosing to divulge his secret to Laela. "I wasn't alone. My closest friend—the other half of my heart, really—was marked too." A weight that had long pressed against Orn's chest suddenly lifted, and his body felt light for the first time since Jord's death. "Took him quick. But I was spared. I tried to help him resist whatever was happening to him. The visions, the darkness calling. In the end, the magic claimed him, same as all the rest. Everyone but me. I did what I had to, so I could save my village. I killed him, before he could hurt anyone else."

The information seemed to settle over them while the fire crackled and hissed in its pit.

"That's why I've spent my time since searching for answers, to understand why this is happening and stop it," Orn added, turning on his heel and marching toward the center of camp. He had spoken his piece. If Jannie or Laela wanted to stab him, so be it. "I'm sorry that I cannot tell you where Gaulf is, but we're trying to find him. And this trail leads to nothing except death."

"I'm not leaving, not until I see him," Jannie said firmly.

Laela looked ready to argue, but instead, she said, "We won't be responsible for you. If you get in the way, you're on your own. Got it?" Laela approached Jannie cautiously. "Get your dagger out. Holding it like you were, you're liable to cut your own damn thumb off. Here, let me show you."

"You never cease to amaze me, princess," Orn whispered so as not to be overheard while he watched the scene before him.

A wave of vertigo then slammed into him. Orn opened his mouth to speak, to say anything, but found the ground rushing up to meet him instead.

In the depths of the cavern, darkness swallowed Orn whole. Jord screamed somewhere out of sight, the sound emanating from everywhere

and nowhere all at once. He tried to find his friend, tried to find purchase in the darkness, yet it moved as a wind, buffeting him about in the black. The mark on his arm twisted, rubbed raw against his flesh while it sank into the muscle.

Orn fought against the whispers in the void, refusing to let it overwhelm him. Onward Orn trudged, with no idea of his direction. To stand still was to sink, and so he moved. Reaching his hand toward what he hoped was the scream's origin, Orn found something solid to grasp onto.

He wrapped his fingers around warm leather, grooves already made for his grip as if the blade were his own. Tugging free the sword, Orn swung it with all the strength he had. The dark solidified about him, but every frantic swing forced a temporary retreat. The blade tore at the thick, billowing void, which parted, fading under the furious onslaught of attacks. The scream building came not from the lack of light, but from the man wielding a weapon against it.

The inky darkness soon parted to reveal Jord's broken form.

But Orn recognized the trick. It was not his Jord. Words, spidery and sharp, were flung at Orn, who only had his sword to hide behind. The darkness swelled with Jord's screams, lashing out at Orn.

Orn defended himself, fighting against the black's tentacles to find the true Jord. And when he did, when his friend screamed, his flesh squeezed by veins of blue and black, Orn took one last step forward.

"Help me," Jord croaked, then shrieked. The earth quaked beneath their feet. "BY THE SPIRAL, OPEN THE DOOR, DRAW DOWN THE LIGHTNING—"

But he never finished.

Orn forced the blade through Jord's belly. His friend's pleading eyes stared at Orn as Jord's mouth worked silently to form words. Even if he could not hear them, Orn knew what they were.

Help me.

Orn yanked the sword free and left, launching himself into the darkness. More faces waited there, some he could hardly remember, but he knew them all the same. They were written on the surface of his heart, even if he had drunk away their names with the money he earned. Each one spoke.

Help us.

The voices changed. The words shifted. No longer begging for help.
Come with us.
Join us in the dark.
Sra curak.
Archivald's face, bleeding, split wide in a grin, was festering and burbling with rot. The darkness followed, hammering Orn to the ground. The void crackled with a faint blue light, radiating from a single point at an unknowable distance.
Another spiral marked onto flesh.
A young farmhand, forging ahead.
Alone.
"Gaulf!" Orn shouted, twisting beneath the tendrils of shadow, trying to wrest his way free. "Stop! Let me help!" Hopelessness gnawed at his insides, conquering everything else. Despair. Failure. How could he help Gaulf when he had failed so many others? "Please."
The gloom engulfed him.

Orn expected to see Laela and Jannie ready to make a pincushion out of him when he woke. Sweat soaked his tunic and brow, and his stomach roiled. Briefly, he thought the darkness followed him out of the dream. Wiping the sleep from his eyes, Orn struggled to a sitting position. His arm burned, and his hand went reflexively to the mark there.

His flesh felt hot, and his throat cracked as he tried to speak. Something thrummed through the air, coursing like a lightning bolt aimed right at his heart.

Magic.

"What's that?" Jannie whispered, and Laela hissed at her.

"You're as loud as the stinking barbarian, girl. Shh, it's just a deer," Laela answered, but her body was rigid.

"Are you sure about that, princess?" Orn clambered over to where the two of them sat peering out into the trees. "If it is but a deer, what is wrong with it?"

"Shut your mouth. I wasn't going to scare the girl." With the moonlight coming from behind the clouds, the deer was cast in a light that was a sickly hue, similar to the one in Orn's dream.

The deer, in turn, stared at the three of them, blinking its eyes languidly. Multiple sets, moving in an almost wavelike pattern as they closed and opened independent of one another.

"What *is* that?" Jannie paled. Orn shifted closer, the deer's eyes following his movement.

As he approached Laela and Jannie, the knight spied the explosion of antlers atop the beast's head, a fractal outpouring of bone from the deer's skull that seemed too heavy to bear. They rose upward, breaking into little grasping fingertips that speared the air as the deer snorted and snuffed, its head swaying in the silver light.

"I don't think we want to scare this one," Laela warned, and Orn spared a glance to watch her fingers reaching for the hilt of her dagger.

The deer lifted its head and let out a noise that could be mistaken for a laugh.

"Are you seeing this, princess?" Orn whispered rhetorically.

"Yes. What this *is*, though, I have no idea," Laela replied.

"Do you two hear that? It's Gaulf!" Jannie sprang to her feet, but Laela yanked her down by her tunic and held her in place.

Laela was looking a bit green around the gills. "My skin feels like it's on fire."

"He's out there! I *feel* him!" Jannie screamed before Laela clamped a hand over the girl's mouth.

"Something's not right." Orn remembered his dream, and his head swam.

Jannie went wild in Laela's grip, biting the elf's fingers. When Laela released her to cradle her hand, Jannie sprinted toward the deer.

"Get back here!" Orn tried to catch her, but she disappeared into the night. Gone, too, were the light and the deer. The sour stench in the air, the curdled feeling in his stomach. "Come on, princess. We've got work to do. Jannie is out there somewhere, and we'll need to find her before she gets herself killed for her troubles."

Chapter 37

THE END

GAULF'S FEET REBELLED AGAINST his mind, leading him further from villages, from comfort, from anyone who might be unfortunate enough to cross his path. With each heavy thud of his weary heart came a lance of electric pain and a heightened sense of awareness that his body was hardly his own. Whatever magic lurked within the young man had wrested control for itself, and even in the brief moments when Gaulf's mind cleared, the insistent tug of its influence never dimmed.

There was nothing to be found in the forest but overwhelming solitude. Between the dreams that overtook his sleep and the whispers that echoed in the margins of his hearing, he wasn't altogether certain of his grip on reality. The power contained by his fleshy prison had caused devastation. The thought of what he'd done sickened him, but despite that, the magic shaped his desire for much worse.

Time had no meaning. The celestial bodies glided across the sky in their usual custom, though he could not determine whether their movements were evidence of truth or some repetitive fever dream. Even so, Gaulf's feet dragged him eastward toward some unknown future.

Quick flashes of the robed man's silhouette flitted through the trees in the boundaries of the forest, the sound of hoofbeats and clanks of armor chasing his every step.

The thin soles of his boots met a surface decidedly different from the soft soil of the damp earth. A forgotten structure lay in ruins before him, its stone broken and marred by an invading army of thick moss. A separate view of the building revealed in Gaulf's left eye displayed the place as it had been in a bygone era. Tall and towering, shining through the fog in his mind.

From within its windows shone beacons of blue light, bold and bright against the night sky. In the ruins, the light still flickered but was a pale, unearthly color that scorched to gaze upon.

Gaulf's feet drew him onward, into the building beneath the looming tower. He passed through the threshold framed by once-grand doors thrown wide open, one hanging off of its hinges. Inside, the stones were marked with familiar symbols.

The narrow hallway opened into a room, and again Gaulf struggled between split visions of the past and present. The seven symbols hung in tapestries miraculously untouched by time alongside other fantastical scenes woven in colorful threads.

One featured eight pillars rimmed by water and mountains, the symbols etched into their marble. However, the eighth pillar sported no such symbol, but instead was shaped to resemble the hilt of a sword protruding from a mound of rocks. At its base was one word.

"Osivesi," Gaulf said softly, the muffled echo of his voice bleeding into the stone.

A scraping sound drew his attention, and too late Gaulf realized he had not ventured into the ruins alone. Others stood apart from him in the room. At first, he thought them mere specters, much like the robed man who haunted his steps, but he could *see* them, and more importantly, they could see him.

"Are you real?" Gaulf croaked.

Six figures with shining eyes beneath ratty hoods moved to encircle Gaulf.

"Who are you?" Gaulf's heart hammered in his chest. His outstretched hand, meant to defend, nevertheless found purchase on the chest of the lead figure. Warm flesh. In quick succession, each removed their hoods, revealing men and women both young and old.

"We've been waiting for you," said six voices, not quite in sync. In concert they approached, and as they did, he could *feel* them. Or rather, not them, but the marks on their flesh. A woven web of power, enough to squeeze Gaulf's innards painfully.

"Who are you?" Gaulf repeated, his words vanishing in the wind. He thought to flee, but the small measure of control he'd enjoyed while in this strange place bent to the magic's persuasion.

The figures followed the path he charted deeper into the dark ruins.

This time Gaulf felt the tactile threading of another scene. Those same eight pillars, a complex web threaded between them, containing two giant, humanish shapes obscured by a dark cage, their likenesses radiating malice. Beneath this scene, the words: *Odyghngir no more.*

"What is this?" Gaulf tried to look away from the tapestry, but the sigils demanded his attention. The mark on his arm felt *alive,* The Spiral turning in a drilling gyre as if to delve deeper into him.

"We are called home. I bear The Hand," said one of the men, baring his chest to show the blackened handprint over his heart.

"The Wheel." An old crone, her ankle marked with a barbed wagon wheel.

"The Door." A woman, her stomach marked with a stone archway, the skin inside black and shining with an eerie light.

"The Quill." A boy about Gaulf's age, his hand marked with a quill spilling black ink along his veins.

"The Scythe." Another woman, her forearm marked with the curving blade, the sigil splitting her arm.

"The Lightning Bolt." An older man, the mark stretching from his temple and arcing across his cheek in a fractal pattern.

"The Spiral." Gaulf, or rather, the magic inside of him, spoke the words, even as he struggled within the prison of his body.

"We must *remember.*" All of the voices were as one, and through the seven of them, magic *remembered.* The world disappeared from beneath Gaulf's feet, and he began to fall, the air rushing around him. He saw the robed man approaching, until Gaulf fell *into* him. This time, he did not do so alone.

"Your incessant running has come to an end, Thaddeus. The Tower cannot help you," came a dangerous voice from behind Gaulf. He shifted, turned in flesh not his own. *Thaddeus.* The name settled over him like a mantle, and the body became his own.

Thaddeus turned toward the voice, recoiling from the tall, imposing figure encased in armor from head to toe. He held his staff in front of him, his fingers tight against the sharp edges of the symbols.

"Ser Gregoris, my friend, please. This has gone too far. You have to listen," Thaddeus pleaded, his heart hammering seven times in his chest.

"That is no longer my name, *friend*. You may call me The Paladin, protector of these lands." The voice came from within the armored figure looming in front of him, growling and full of menace.

"Please, Nichor. You have to put an end to this." It was a futile attempt, but Thaddeus tried.

"Pray tell, Thaddeus Maji, what worth do your words have? You have lied to me numerous times. Heinous, vile lies." Ser Gregoris moved closer, an armored helm concealing his face, but Thaddeus could sense his hatred. "Have I not listened? You claim magic is not the problem, that the fault lies with *me*. And yet, I can feel the corruption in it, and it rattles me to my core. Allow me to protect you and these lands. Osivesi cannot shoulder this foul, pervading force."

"I implore you to practice patience." Thaddeus flinched when The Paladin growled. "No other soul has detected the corruption you claim exists, and so this has become one man's vendetta against a force he cannot control. Dispense with this foolish crusade, I beg you. Magic is no more harmful than its wielder." Thaddeus retreated, struggling to find room that he might leverage some of the symbols on the tapestry. His mind scrambled for a spell. Desperation curdled in his stomach. "Please, friend. You can pass judgment on my apparent crimes. But let it end here, between us." Thaddeus frantically searched the room, the tapestries and statues, hoping that someone might hear him.

But the mage knew he stood alone.

"Are you looking for your friends, Thaddeus? They're here, though I am unsure how much use they'll be to you since I've already dealt with them," The Paladin explained, a wicked chuckle echoing from within his armor.

"What have you done?" Bile rose in Thaddeus' throat, threatening to spill from his mouth.

"I have claimed what I needed to end this farce. The people of Embrosi have turned to worshiping magic, this foul, perverse mockery of the natural order. You bear the last remaining symbol, that of The Spiral." The mirth in Ser Gregoris' tone turned Thaddeus' stomach, driving that spike of fear that much deeper into his chest.

Thaddeus grasped his staff, his knuckles white. The mage drew away from Ser Gregoris, ignoring the sound of a blade scraping against its scabbard. Here, in The Tower of Fragments, where magic came to humans and elves alike, Thaddeus knew he had to stop him.

"By The Scythe's curve, by The Lightning Bolt's inspiration, I call upon The Hand to grasp and to hold." Magic sprung forth at Thaddeus' call, its tendrils wisps of blue light that wrapped around Ser Gregoris.

"How *dare* you!" Ser Gregoris snarled, thrashing against the magic as if he could escape its power.

"I am sorry that it has come to this, my friend. I tried to help you see reason." Thaddeus' heart pumped as magic continued to permeate the air. "There are others out here who will act, even if you have murdered my brethren. This is damage I can repair. You are a damn fool!"

"That I may be, but I am not alone," Ser Gregoris said darkly.

Too late Thaddeus realized he had failed to notice someone lurking in the shadows.

"Queen Alizandra?" Thaddeus asked, surprised. "What is the meaning of this?"

"How dare you, Thaddeus. Traipsing through Embrosi, to this place, dragging your problems into my lands?" The bones in the queen's hair rattled as she advanced. Even though she was far shorter than him, he cowered in her presence, thinking he might wilt beneath that golden gaze.

"I-I never meant any disrespect. I only came here for my pilgrimage. But why? Why are you helping him? He is a danger to us all!" Thaddeus shrieked, readying another incantation. Magic surged inside of him, wild and torrential.

"By The Door—"

Queen Alizandra slammed a curved blade into his stomach. He gurgled in disbelief as she twisted the steel and yanked it from his flesh.

"Silly human. I've no intention of fighting you. There are more pressing matters to attend to." She cleaned the blade on Thaddeus' robes then dragged him behind her, whispering an incantation of her own that tore through his spell as if it were wet parchment.

"What are you doing?" Thaddeus spluttered, clutching his bleeding wound. His staff lay forgotten, his magic had abandoned him.

Queen Alizandra leaned closer, whispering, "I am going to give this fool exactly what he wants. Magic will be locked away. Forever. Or, at least, the rest of his life." She smirked, tugging Thaddeus into the next room. Seven tables were laid out, each hosting a shrouded form splattered with blood. With no grace to speak of, she laid him on an empty table. Her sharp face, that wicked smile, hovered over him as she cut away his robes.

"Please," Thaddeus begged.

"You'll bleed out soon, and I do not want you dead. Not yet." The queen cut the robes from his chest, the bite of the dagger against his mark somehow worse than the molten fire lancing through his innards. He cried out, his back arching, when Queen Alizandra stole the mark of magic from him. Silence descended in the aftermath, and Thaddeus felt the lack of connection to his power suffocating.

"By these sigils, foolish Paladin, I can seal magic away, but it will come with a price," Queen Alizandra explained while Thaddeus fought to remain conscious.

"Do it. I have no care for the cost." Ser Gregoris loomed over Thaddeus now, replacing the queen in his field of vision. He withdrew his helmet, revealing stringy black hair and a scowling face. Briefly, the mage thought he spied his old friend peering through the figure's cold features before Nichor became unrecognizable once more.

If Thaddeus could only *remember*.

Seven voices, chanting that word ad nauseam, were surrounded by stone ruins. A living memory.

"*We remember*," Gaulf said, his eyes opening to glimpse the six others and their markings, as well as the one on his own arm. Each was a key to a locked door. Someone pressed a dagger into his hand, and he nodded.

He knew what needed to be done.

Chapter 38

THE RUINS

ORN HOPED THE PRINCESS would stay her hand. "Don't hurt her, Laela!" From the screech and thud that emanated from deeper in the trees as he shrugged into his armor frantically, that optimism dwindled. Cursing to himself, the knight stumbled over his own feet in pursuit, but before he could make it to the trees, Laela hauled Jannie to the small campsite. "Neither of you look bloodied, so I am thankful for that, at least," Orn groused as he shot a look toward the girl. She seethed almost as much as the princess, and he stepped between the two of them. "You are right, Gaulf *is* out there. I promise you this: I am going to help him."

"Do not make promises you cannot keep, barbarian," Laela said from behind him. Orn's shoulders itched, and not for the first time. He hated when she stood behind him, but still, trust had to start somewhere.

"Someone has to try! Might as well be me." Orn's words burned in his throat, his eyes watering as he focused his gaze on the skittish girl in front of him. "Stay here, please. Tend to the horses. Give us a chance to help him."

Jannie drew a deep breath as her gaze drilled into Orn, and silence stretched on seemingly endlessly before she spoke again. "All right."

Orn nodded. "Wait here." He turned to Laela, who grunted in frustration then stalked off ahead of him. He did his best to keep pace without clanking the entire way.

Only when they were some distance from the campsite did the elf whirl on him, her dagger pressed into an opening in his armor. One false move and he'd feel the intimate kiss of that blade.

Before he found his voice, before Orn could question her, the world lurched under his feet. His stomach roiled as another tangible wave of nothing spread not just through him, but Laela as well. The color drained from her face. The knight's knees threatened to collapse beneath him. Swaying on his feet, Laela mimicked his movements, her eyes fluttering as she grimaced.

The world opened up beneath Orn and he fell. Or, that's what it felt like, as everything shifted and he found himself mired in the space between two heartbeats. Orn's heart ripped in his chest, a pain sharp and fierce, and he was tugged forward. *Something* lurked nearby, and he knew its name. *Gaulf.* How he knew, he could not say, but in the sudden, dreamlike darkness, he could sense the young farm boy.

Trapped where he stood, searching tendrils appeared from the abyss to claim his wrists, mark his body as its own. He knew if he but opened his mouth to scream, they would spiral inside and fill him until he burst.

He was fractured, broken, surrendering to the whispers in the dark. *Succumb.* The sounds reverberated within the base of his skull and etched into his eyelids. Orn tried to piece together the words scrawled in the mist formed by his cold breath, but the longer he stared so, too, did the itch inside of his mind intensify, threatening to overwhelm him.

Retching words, spidery and thick, Orn gasped when he spotted them scrawled across the very air in the black. His eyes ached, nearly bursting with a need not quite his own. And yet a part of him wanted to *let go.*

That scared him more than anything, that small desire to accept this.

But he had to fight it, had to find *her. Find Laela.* Images flashed in his head, visions of pain and ichor, of Laela in the middle of it all.

A spiraling pattern of blood and viscera with her splayed out above it.

Terrified, Orn fought against the barbed whispers of the tendrils wrapped solidly around him. He flailed, scrambling for purchase until he felt the hilt of the sword in his hand. Withdrawing the blade from its scabbard, the knight hissed when it made a sharp scraping noise. And yet, when it came free, everything washed away. Warmth flooded his limbs, his breath hitched in his throat, and his heart began to beat once more.

"Princess?" The ground was whole, the slithering tendrils gone. Inhaling deeply, he tried to calm himself in the hurricane of emotions ripping through his mind. Laela was nowhere to be seen, the pressure of the dagger missing. When he moved, Orn noticed a pinpoint of metal tracking him in the forest. Behind it stood Laela, her face devoid of emotion, ready to loose a nocked arrow. "Laela?"

"Are you...*you*?" Laela retreated a step, the arrow still taut in the bowstring. For half a moment, Orn thought to say no, wanting to answer as truthfully as he could. Instead, he waited, hoping she would hold tightly to that string.

"I'm *me*, princess. Not sure for how much longer." Orn sighed, knowing he could not lie to her. "Stubborn as a mule, I am." *For now.*

"And you smell like one too, oaf." Laela somehow managed to chuckle as she kept the arrow trained on him, even if she let the tip waver when she stepped forward into what dim light remained. She searched for something in his face, her brows knitted together. "Next time, I won't hesitate."

"That might be smart." Orn's wrung his hands, cold from the rush of adrenaline coursing through him. "Whatever's happening out there, I can feel it."

"I can too." Laela looked just as surprised as Orn felt at hearing those words.

"How do you mean?"

"I can *feel* it, like a storm is brewing." Laela shook her head.

"Not unlike what I feel. I think it means the fun has started." Orn scanned some strange ruins in the distance, as if expecting the quiet night to explode at any moment.

"From what I can tell, *he* is in the ruins. We should hurry, before Jannie grows restless." Laela slung the bow over her shoulder. "I'll head in from the left. Don't get in my way this time." Orn tensed until he spotted the ghost of a smile that played on her lips.

The knight rolled his eyes, then fidgeted with his armor.

"You're making too much noise." Laela batted his hands away so that she could adjust his cinch. Orn opened his mouth to make some biting remark, and Laela said, "Shut your mouth, or I will stab you." The comment died on his tongue.

"That is, if I live long enough," Orn said aloud before he realized what happened. She leaned back a little to review her work. The silence grew palpable. An energy built in the air, one that had nothing to do with either of them.

"Stop your prattling, barbarian. We have a job to do." She checked her quiver, looking anywhere but directly at him.

Orn was serious then. "I need you to promise me again. Promise me that if I start to lose myself, you'll put me down." He paused, then added, "Don't hesitate." Cautiously, he tilted her chin upward so she had to look at him.

Her gaze pierced him, in a way that her blades and arrows never had. "I promise."

"You want to go first?" Orn asked just as he noticed the elf's diminishing form dart ahead into the underbrush with nary a sound. Muttering to himself, Orn patted his chest with a gauntleted hand. "Here we go again."

Orn drew the sword from its scabbard. As the blade caught the moon's glow, a calm descended over him. The path to the ruins was clear, lit by the conflagration in its belly. The flames grew before his eyes, casting parts of the stone edifice in shadows. His hand never strayed far from the hilt of his blade as he started forward, thinking of the days to come. For the first time in as long as he could remember, tomorrow remained an unknown quantity. Whether he'd be alive when the sun rose felt like a question with no answer.

With the air thick enough it dripped a chilly, clammy echo of the dreams that plagued Orn, he took off. Laela's words returned to him, and against all reason, against all doubts that anyone would even listen, Orn whispered to the winds, "If any gods are listening, please, this once, let me get it right. Let me help *someone*." With that said, and with his heart heavy, his feet carried him onward. The stone walls, defined in the darkness by the fires they barely contained within, shined where they crumbled and let the light flicker out.

Having never been this far northeast, the familiarity of the ruins baffled Orn. Everything felt like a dream—a bad, fever-ridden, sweat-soaked dream. The closer he ventured to the ruins, the louder the whispers became. A part of him felt *home* in this eerie place.

So long had he fought against the call that only in its absence did he realize what that meant.

The mark on his arm burned.

His gaze trailed movement on the ramparts, and he saw Laela creeping along. *Aggravating, nimble elf.* An aching maw of a doorway yawned before him, the doors thrown wide open to flames.

Orn brought the sword to bear in defense, but his plan fell apart when a scrambling horde of stone and fire emerged, their mouths open in screams.

He thought to bellow for Laela but stayed his call, worried that he would reveal her position. One of the little creatures darted out from the underbrush, and more joined, their chattering noises carried on the wind.

Kicking one aside with his boot, Orn chuckled at the odd sound it made. But he barely found a moment to enjoy its flailing sail through the air before another leaped toward him. Bracing, Orn turned the blade sideways and thrust with as much force as he could muster. Even with the flat of the sword connecting, he felt a crackle rip through the blade when it collided with the creature.

The sword hungered, Orn could sense it. The creature flew at a tree, shortly replaced by another form with numberless limbs sprinting for his still form.

The blade sprang to life in his grip, tearing at whatever bound the creature together. Life faded from the remnants in its plummet to the ground, a quivering, crying mass of pebbles and ash.

A cacophony of hoots and shrieks broke the night's calm. The creatures beset Orn from all sides. *The little shits are everywhere*, Orn thought. The sound of stone grating drew his attention. The creatures climbed one another in an offensive effort. A few more took advantage of his momentary distraction to drop from the trees and onto his back, and it was all he could do to swat them away. Growling in frustration, Orn yanked at twisting, spidery arms, tearing them off his body one by one. Puffs of soot and smoke clogged his lungs as another pulse radiated from the ruins.

The creatures took on an unearthly glow, their cores growing hotter and hotter until they burned with a hellfire unseen in this world. Little hands reached for him, scrabbling to find purchase against his armor. Orn kept moving, swinging, thrusting. The scrape of metal on stone made his teeth ache, but he battered dozens of them before exhaustion began to creep in. Behind him, squirming piles were left in his wake, the blade effectively holding them at bay.

But when he came closer to the ruins, he realized the little shits had fallen back. As if they dared go no further.

Even if he wanted to stop, he was not sure that he could. There was a seed inside of him and his blade seemed drawn toward that eerie force within the ruins. Orn started forward while the creatures chanted behind him.

Where was Laela? Why were the creatures not following him, tearing him apart? The answer came as a dying shriek, entirely too human in origin, spilled out of the ruins. Orn dashed across the waiting threshold, the sound ceasing when he made it inside the crumbled walls of moss and stone.

"Hold on!" Orn called, unsure if that had been Laela or some other poor soul. *Magic* sat heavy in this place, causing the mark on his arm to practically dance against his flesh.

A thin corridor pockmarked with starlight and overgrown with moss led the way past the large doors. Flickering flames cast everything in haze and smoke, overwhelming his senses in his advance. Old furniture threatened to clog his path, but Orn kicked his way through. For a moment, he swore the walls swelled, that the hall elongated, that he might never reach the end.

Orn growled, determined. Kneading his knuckles against his forehead, he closed his eyes and tried to tamp down the surging bile, the fear threatening to split him in two.

Let go.

"I will not."

With no resistance in his path, he stumbled forward. Struggling to the other end of the hallway, he burst through the door into a large central chamber. Remnants of stairs lined the walls, climbing along the room. The walls, bare but for the moss, glistened in the firelight. Embers smoldered within piles of rotten furniture, and smoke coiled about the room. Briefly, Orn thought he saw the room as it once was: rich tapestries adorning the wall, rippling with an unfelt breeze.

A spiral design was threaded through the tapestry, vanishing when smoke coiled around the image. Orn then found a large slab hiding in the darkness, where even the fire dared not burn. Its edge was engraved with symbols, and he turned from them, terrified of their meaning.

Was this an altar?

The more he examined the stone, the less his brain seemed capable of processing the form sprawled upon it. A bloodied, broken mess. What he initially mistook for a corpse arched its back, releasing another inhuman, guttural scream. An arrow whistled through the air and drove into the writhing form. He did not need to look at the arrow to know who had shot it, but he winced at the solid *thunk* it made.

Even knowing the body on the slab was more unrecognizable gore than anything else, a part of him suffered a familiar ache. It was another life lost, one that added to the weight Orn carried since Jord's death.

Through ripped clothing, the knight spied a place where flesh had been removed with precision, reverence. Worse yet, the longer he stared, he realized the table contained more than one body, accounting for the sheer volume of viscera.

His mind rebelled at the sight, and Orn swallowed hard as he withdrew. Between the scene before him, the smoke clogging the room, and the heavy presence permeating the air, Orn felt like he might lose the already questionable contents of his stomach.

Orn caught movement out of the corner of his eyes. Crawling through the pile of bodies, digging its way out of the stone table, was one of the little stone creatures he thought feared this place as much as he did.

Tiny stone-and-dagger fingers pulled it free, a flicker of flame following as it sprang right into the point of Orn's sword, skewering the thing straight through. Before he could shake it off the blade, it collapsed into stone chips and rubble.

"That's enough of that," Orn muttered, lifting the blade overhead and reversing his hold on the hilt with both hands, slamming it into the corpse with a resounding snap that echoed through the ruins.

Whether it was responsible for the creation of these creatures, he did not know. It hardly mattered at any rate.

Peering up into the darkness of the partial tower, its crumbling walls failing to blot out the night sky, he listened for the sound of Laela's arrows sailing on the wind. There was nothing but the crackle and spitting of flames, the thickness of smoke. Absently, he stretched his hand toward the fire until it threatened to blister his flesh.

"Where are you, Gaulf?" Orn murmured between clenched teeth.

In the next room, the grisly scene was repeated. Another table, this one already sundered, spilling its contents everywhere. He crept closer, keeping a careful eye on this gore pile in case it decided to spit forth another stone creature. When no such event occurred, he started toward the next room, stalking deeper into the ruins.

Laela's scream cut the air and Orn whirled about, unsure of its origin. He waited for a second scream, but there was only silence. *Where is she?*

Orn stumbled, and he struggled to right himself. When that proved impossible, he tried to right the world by tilting his own body. That did not help either. Orn wobbled on shaky legs through another corridor, the pressure in his head threatening to devour his sight.

Starlight and clean air greeted him in this place yet untouched by fire, and the knight inhaled deeply, enjoying the temporary reprieve. In other rooms, the elf was absent, each space equally bereft of life. Worn tapestries, empty leather bindings, and piles of furniture in various states of disrepair.

Instead of the princess, what he found were two bodies lying atop another table. Not quite a grotesque mess, but bent and twisted nevertheless, with patches of skin peeled away. Since there was no obvious threat, he continued into the next room.

Another large table in the middle of a wide-open room, a single form bound and writhing beneath the stars with no barrier to the chill of the evening. Like a sudden fever breaking, Orn's body shivered. When an audible gasp escaped the form on the table, her eyes sprang open.

Orn retreated until his back was pressed against a nearby wall. The form rose to a sitting position then promptly fell backward, where her head and her feet touched the thick stone. Muscles strained when her limbs contorted, her back arching until Orn suspected the spine might snap. Too late the knight noticed the thin slice along her body as clothing shifted, then fell away.

She has to be dead, right?

Nothing could have survived being opened neck to navel. Orn recoiled, his next breath caught in his throat. Whatever life she clung to was gone as she shuddered against the stone with a sigh. Her body trembled, and blood poured freely from unseen wounds.

Something snapped thunderously, and whatever propelled her body slithered free. With the pulpy tentacles came the darkness, and with the darkness came the words. They called to him, enticing and menacing.

Those thorn-barbed words whispered to him of grim things. If he would just *let go* those things would become reality. The flames flared, the shadows dimmed, and then the world went gray. Orn thrust his wounded shoulder against a wall. The pain lanced the bubble, clearing his head.

The knight watched the tentacles withdraw, but his body failed to respond to the scene. What came next were hands that simply defied any reality he had ever known. Impossibly large and bloodied, reaching out of the body, as if they emerged from a door that separated this realm from another.

His sword forgotten in his hand, Orn retched watching the fingers spread, revealing a light that burned brighter than the fires raging around him. Colorless, or beyond any hue he had ever seen, yet Orn could not tear his gaze away.

The knight's mind tried to make sense of the large hands stuck within the altogether too-small corpse, the otherworldly light which carried with it a shattered music. The walls seemed to shake, and Orn wanted nothing more than to draw his sword and rid the ruins of this darkness.

Then he heard Laela scream again.

Orn turned to see the elf there, on the second floor of the ruins. She was cornered, her back against an altar of white marble. Sword in hand, he leaped at the wall, climbing to her even as the stone protested under his weight.

A cloaked figure held Laela in place.

"Gaulf, what have you done?" Orn shrieked.

Chapter 39

THE HUNT IS ON

MAGIC FILLED THE AIR.

"Where are you?" Laela swung her legs onto the ledge on the other side of the wall, scanning the ruins for any hint of movement. Rising smoke stung her eyes, making it difficult to see, but the elf managed to spot seven figures in one of the rooms laid bare to the sky.

Laela nocked an arrow. There was no Willaime, no reinforcements.

There was only her. The oaf.

And the mark in her sights.

Laela held her breath, studying the swaying of the figures as they surrounded tables boasting bodies and blood, identifying Gaulf among them.

Worse yet, she swore her mother loomed in the darkness of that room. Laela locked eyes with that haunting face framing golden eyes, but it was fleeting. She recoiled from the interaction. It simply wasn't possible. Her mother died many years ago. *All of them did.* Shoving the surge of emotions down, Laela shook unbidden memories away.

Too late she noticed the group had dispersed. In a room with crumbling walls, one of the figures climbed onto a table, another towering over the first with a dagger. In horror, the elf observed the macabre blade flay flesh as easily as if it were sliding through warm butter. The figure on the table screamed, but they were not cries of pain. They were something else entirely. Laela gagged, barely keeping herself from retching onto the stone.

The first figure then twisted, broke, became nothing but a host for spawning several little creatures of stone. A second wave of *magic* curdled her stomach, and Laela loosed her arrow. It pierced the corpse, burying itself into the cracked surface beneath.

Orn stood nearby, staring at the scene in disbelief. Scurrying along the top, trying to keep pace with the figures moving through the ruins, Laela loosed more arrows. Whether due to smoke or the tremble in her fingers, the elf could not manage a clean shot.

Though from her vantage point, she spotted Orn flailing about. "He's really lucky he hasn't lopped his own head off." Laela grimaced, watching the knight cut a path through a group of creatures. With one swift motion, she drew three arrows from her quiver and planted two in the rotted wood next to her. The last arrow she nocked, holding the familiar, well-worn leather grip in her hand. The wood sang to her, but something else arrested her gaze.

A body on a table in the middle of the ruins. There, it danced, as if it were a marionette performance.

"What the fuck is he doing?" Laela let the arrow fly, ending the eerie corpse dance before more creatures could spill from its body.

Chanting emanated from within the ruins. The words spidered visibly along the walls, making it difficult to pinpoint the origin. A wave of magic barreled into her, and she nearly stumbled from the roof. Laela scrambled for purchase, desperately hugging what remained of the wall.

She caught the glint of a bloodied blade poised to strike. "There he is." Once she regained her footing, Laela took aim. Symbols threaded the flames, casting shadows against the stone. She shut her eyes tightly, forcing acrid breath into her lungs with each inhale, and released the arrow.

Shouldering her bow, she drew her sword from its scabbard and followed the sounds of pain echoing throughout the ruins.

"Here goes." She braced herself against the wall and gave the remnants of the stone a shove. It gave way despite protest, crushing the little creatures below. Howls of pain erupted while she climbed down to where she had seen Gaulf and Orn.

When she neared the bottom, something grabbed her leg. Something cold. With a vicious motion, she jerked a dagger free and slashed without looking.

"Let go!" she screamed, cutting through whatever had coiled around her calf. It oozed, stuck to her skin. It was darkness turned solid. But Laela continued to slice at it until she felt it recede. Dangling like a worm on a hook, Laela dropped to the floor and searched the room for threats.

There, on the ground, the coil of darkness retreated into the shadows cast by the dancing flames.

She barely had a moment to enjoy her relief before something grabbed her elbow and threw her. The world lurched, the stars above grew brighter, and her grip on the dagger faltered. Laela cursed when the hazy figure kicked the blade out of her reach.

"I know you. I've *seen* you." The words spilled from the void created by a low, large hood while gold-and-blue energy circled the figure. The only visible part of the face were its eyes, which burned bright in the firelight. The figure's fingers were outstretched toward her, trailing that otherworldly energy. The smell of it made her stomach turn. *Rot. Corruption. Darkness. Pain.* "I have searched for you for so very long."

Laela tried to find her voice, but a lump formed in her throat, hampering any attempt to speak. Her hands and feet scrambled to find purchase on the cracked stone, the rotten planks of wood, but to no avail.

"They were only the key, but *you*..." His head cocked to the side as he looked at her. *Through* her. "We need you to remember."

Laela finally convinced her lungs to breathe, and she tried to kick her way across the floor. "*ORN! He's over here!*"

"Needed to remember." The mage paused. "I need you to remember. We need you to remember." He searched her face while some of the small stone creatures clambered toward the two of them. The mage lashed out, sending a creature sailing over the ruins with a swift kick. "She is mine."

The mage dragged Laela to her feet. This close, unable to help but smell the smoke and fire from below, Laela's mind dizzied as she struggled in his grip.

Where is that blasted oaf?

"I hear the call. It's almost as if *She* knew I needed to be here. Magic is bound, I saw that, but I saw so much more out there. So many doors remain locked. I needed to be here, to find *you*. *She* has been waiting so long to be free." His face twisted in exaltation, his eyes rolling into the back of his head. "Beware the Ibe Nire." A sob broke his words, and beneath the filth, beneath the stench, Laela noticed how very young he was. "Oh, by The Harvester's Scythe, I am so sorry. It was not supposed to be this way. *She* is coming home. Once we open the door. There might be one more, a broken key for a jammed lock," he added. "We must remember, remember, remember. Ser Gregoris' folly shall set us free."

"What?" Laela asked, stunned at hearing The Paladin's name. The other name, the Ibe Nire, spiraled through her mind as it reeled with a memory of her mother. *"She and the Ibe Nire shall set us free. Locked away, locked away, waiting for you and me. The Old Gods shall return, and The Tower, merely a door to burn."* The singsong voice echoed in the space around her, as if her mother waited just around the corner.

"*She* is coming home, bringing along eldritch creations. To cleanse Odyghngir," the mage chanted, tugging Laela along behind him through the ruins toward a table already stained with fresh blood.

"*She* is nothing more than a bedtime story! Stop this!" Laela shrieked desperately, thrashing against his grasp. With one well-aimed hit, the elf managed to shove the mage from her, and he crashed against the wall with an ominous sound. Given a momentary respite she didn't intend to waste, Laela retrieved a dagger from her boot.

But then the world went sideways.

A vicious slap jolted her, and stars burned black in Laela's vision.

"I am going to gut you like a fish," Laela warned, rubbing her head. She rolled off the altar and away from the mage. Spitting blood from her split lip, she kicked at the mage when he tried to restrain her.

Was this how it ended?

A shape loomed in the shadows of the fire, and she closed her eyes. *So be it.*

"Orn?" the mage spluttered, and Laela's eyes shot open. As if summoned by his name, a large shape stepped forward into the light of the fires.

"I'm here, Gaulf. Let's stop this nonsense now, yes?"

"I think it's already too late," Gaulf replied, swaying on his feet. "I can feel the marks, even now. The power *in* them. Calling to me. There, The Door awaits." Gaulf pointed further into the ruins.

The bloody scene made little sense to Laela at first glance. However, it soon pieced itself together like a puzzle, revealing a series of marks removed from flesh and stitched onto another body. A collection of symbols, six in total. They glowed with that gold-and-blue light, sparking to life against the dead flesh they had become part of.

"Why did you run?" Orn asked, out of breath, his face a stone mask. Laela looked at Gaulf, trying to imagine the young boy as the monster who had done this, who had burned Swanford. The boy Orn and Jannie set out to save, each in their own way.

A maelstrom of emotions swirled between them, fueled by the radiating waves bursting out of the depths of the ruins. Every time she shuddered, her stomach tensed and bile rose in her throat. From the looks of it, Orn and Gaulf fared no better.

Ser Gregoris' folly.

Something broke inside of her—sharp edges of hatred honed over the years. Decades beneath The Paladin's boot. And here, a mage in this tower, about to do...something... Turn the key?

What had Ser Gregoris done to cause all of this?

A part of her blanched at that thought. *The Paladin. Ser Gregoris.* The one who took everything from her. All that she had discussed with Orn came unbidden to her mind, crashing into her like a solid force. Breathing heavily, Laela closed her eyes and tried to find some semblance of calm in the turmoil, ignoring the knowing expression on Orn's face.

Laela drew her daggers and sneered. "I'll take your heart myself, mage." She spat at the ground and lunged at Gaulf.

Quicker than she anticipated, Orn stepped in front of her, blocking her path. But in her mind's eye, he was no longer the knight. Ser Gregoris stood there, drawing her leash ever tighter. *The Paladin* refused to let her go.

Channeling all her rage into the daggers, Laela charged forward, fury filling every inch of her body. Orn and that blasted sword met her every thrust and thwarted any attempt to circle him. The babbling mage held his head in his hands and screeched.

"Princess, please! Stand down," Orn managed through pants, his armor clanking as he dodged another well-aimed slash. "Let me try to help him."

"He is gone, Orn! There is nothing left of the boy, and you know this." Laela's words hung in the air, sharper than any dagger she ever wielded. Orn's face fell, but he remained between them.

"There's something different here, princess. You sense it, don't you?" Laela paused, but his respite soon ended when she made to dart around him. He thrust outward with his blade, effectively preventing her access to Gaulf. "We are closer to answers than we've ever been. If I don't help him, if we can't figure this out here and now, then you might as well end me too."

Laela stilled. "Why are you so determined to help them? After all you have witnessed, how have you not realized the danger these mages present for Embrosi?" Laela questioned sharply. "What makes you think you can be a hero after so many failures?"

"Because someone has to, Laela. If not me, then who?" Orn asked. "I can *feel* it. Crawling in my head, binding us together—my mark to his. He's taken marks from each of the bodies in the ruins. I don't know why, but we have to figure it out."

"Listen, barbarian. You have one chance here, or we are going to have big problems on our hands." Laela shook her head, the ache of remembering growing almost too much to bear. "My mother, she always told me stories of *She* and The Ibe Nire. They were locked away, but I think Gaulf cracked something open. This tower is a key." Everything her mind jumbled together started to click into place.

"The Door is opening. *She* and her children are near," Gaulf said, his voice hollow. He rose from the floor, his toes barely kissing the wooden surface. "*Sra curak. Sra curak.*"

"He's all yours." Laela gestured to Gaulf, noticing that Orn had fallen silent. She could feel the conduit that built between them, wrapping around her with such force that she struggled to resist.

A golden light borne from her sternum unfurled, tendril-like and stretching toward Gaulf and Orn. She glanced at the boy, the one Jannie had come for, the one standing in front of her. He was a mage now, using dark magics The Paladin warned her against, like every other mage she had ever hunted.

And yet, she could not reconcile that with the broken, scared figure in front of her being pulled by the same golden light.

But his light was warped, full of darkened barbs bleeding a blue light that sank into his flesh. Her heart fell when she spotted the struggle written on Orn's face. His hand on his arm, covering the mark, scratching at it as if he might tear his own flesh away. The knight's mouth moved, whispering words. The rubble around them quaked with another pulsing wave of magic.

"Orn, wake up!" Laela hated the desperation in her voice. She stood on shaky legs, the two staring at one another. Orn and Gaulf, both marked with a spiral.

"You cannot stop us!" Gaulf screeched. Gone was the scared boy, replaced by hatred and fire, his hands erupting into flames as he launched himself at Orn. Driving punches into armor with hardly an effort, leaving smoking trails of magic across the metal plate. Orn cried out in pain, trying to fight. He tempered his own swings with that blasted sword, keeping himself from hurting the boy.

And in his hesitation, Gaulf drove the knight backward until he was trapped against a far wall.

Laela muttered curses under her breath, wincing as Gaulf grasped Orn's armored arm right above where the mark lay.

In that moment, everything was still. Gaulf ceased moving, Orn froze mid-scream. Laela's heart hammered in her chest, and in that space between one heartbeat and the next, the world *broke*. The mark binding both of them reeled out of control, transforming into a swirling whirlpool that squatted over the center of the ruins, bleeding into the sky.

"Wake up, you blasted idiot, before I do stab you!" Laela shouted, stalking toward Orn. The path to the knight became difficult, akin to striding into the gales of a storm at sea. The elf searched the ruins, to the sky. Illuminated by the fires below, the clouds shifted, curling inward like the gold-and-blue light. She hesitated.

Instead of moving to attack, she forced herself between Gaulf and Orn. The cheek of the knight's flesh was hot and clammy beneath her palm.

"Wake up, you stupid oaf! I promise I won't stab you if you wake up right now and be a fucking hero. *Help me.*" Laela watched Orn's eyes focus on her face, his mouth sliding into that infuriating smile, and whatever had entered the world simply vanished.

"Princess?" Orn asked softly.

"This is your chance, Orn. To right all those wrongs. To get the answers you want," Laela said, staring at Gaulf while the boy held his head between his hands, arguing with the shadows.

Orn approached the boy cautiously, sword at his side. He wrapped his hand about the nape of Gaulf's neck, which seemed to calm him. Bringing their foreheads together, the knight whispered something indecipherable to Gaulf, and Laela's breath caught in her throat when Orn brought the sword to bear between them.

"Do it." Gaulf's words echoed in the ruins, a sense of finality about them. The knight used one hand to push the boy's robes aside to reveal the mark.

Then something snapped in Gaulf, something fierce and loud and guttural. Before Laela could intervene, Gaulf flailed and Orn forced his retreat. The boy's screaming increased, his words cleaving the air, driving sharp, painful spikes into Laela's ears.

She fell to her knees.

Orn attempted to push the blade through Gaulf, but his thrust was far too wide and the knight stumbled, as if drunk, taking the boy to the floor with him. The two became a blurred tangle of limbs while the fires spread below, casting the pair in an eerie glow. Though the smoke stung her eyes, Laela could not look away.

In his second attempt, Orn rose to his feet and slashed wildly with his sword. It sliced through the robes, finding purchase in Gaulf's arm.

Gaulf stopped screaming, and the elf feared to breathe, worried that her own lungs might burst beneath the heaviness quickly fading from the air. Blood welled around the wound, and Orn withdrew the sword, leaving the mark bisected in an angry flare of flesh that leaked blue light. A sickening squelch followed when Gaulf grabbed at his arm then dropped like a sack of horseshoes.

Silence.

Gaulf's face contorted, then calmed. "It's...quiet?"

An explosion thundered through the ruins, shaking the ground beneath their feet. Stone walls and old lumber groaned, but somehow, did not topple. Laela hurried to wrap Gaulf's wound with a bandage, barely able to process what had happened before she heard Orn curse.

"What the fuck was that?"

"We can figure that out later. We have a bigger problem, princess."

"Orn?" Laela asked, feeling panic rise in her body.

"We're too late. *Sra curak.*" Orn's mouth moved around the eldritch words as they crawled out of his mouth, his gaze growing distant though they blazed with the fire's reflection.

Chapter 40

THE OLD ONE

H IS HAND REFUSED TO listen to him. Whatever burst like a dam in Gaulf when he cut the mark flooded into Orn through the conduit that was the sword.

It was too late.

"You have to go now, Laela!" Orn shook his head, as if that might clear the thick smoke from the air. His eyes darted toward the golden light, a counterpoint to the darker blue threaded through it. Gazing upon the latter hurt, wrenching something unknown inside of him. Merely looking at it made him feverish, and his forehead broke into a sweat. His teeth clamped down hard against the words that wanted desperately to escape. "Please, go." Then, despite his efforts, the strange syllables continued to clot around his tongue. "*Sra curak.*"

The words echoed in the ruins, stoking the dwindling fires. Laela withdrew from Orn and Gaulf, grasping her daggers tightly. Orn glanced over his shoulder toward the sickening brush of light, its thrumming keeping pace with his erratic heartbeat.

"I am not going anywhere, you blasted idiot. We have to fix this."

"Whatever he did, I can feel it. He opened something. A door." Orn wrestled with the magic inside of him. The knight's hands moved to the hilt of his sword, his eyes narrowing in menace. Laela visibly shivered, readying to attack. "You...here...now," Orn repeated.

He fought against the words, trying to shut his mouth. The low hum pervading in the ruins grew louder and as it did, Orn twitched violently. The knight took halting steps forward while the walls around them cracked, juddering with whatever force moved the earth beneath them. Stone and dust rained on their heads from above. The fires continued to rage.

Orn turned his head, listening to something in the wind. Laela heard it too, a sibilant, unintelligible vibration that shot through her. The elf found herself helpless, unable to act. The whispering lured the duo toward the stone slab where one last form remained.

The marks split the body in such a way that they became the barrier to a seam of untouched flesh where something was forcing a path out. A handprint pressed against the stomach, larger than any of the stone creatures.

"*Sra curak.*" Orn bared his teeth, a wide, hungry grin on his face.

"*She* comes. The Mother of Magic," Gaulf whispered when Orn advanced on Laela. "What have I done?"

"I suggest you get going, boy, before I change my mind. Jannie's out there, with our horses." *Or she better be, at least.* "Go. I am sure she's looking for you," Laela snapped, changing positions so that Gaulf had a chance to flee from Orn as he prepared an offense. Without thinking, she spun on her heel and dashed further into the ruins.

"Orn," Gaulf said, drawing the knight's attention.

Briefly, the whispers ceased. Gaulf smiled, his cheeks streaked with tears. The mark on Orn's arm burned him with an unbearable heat. Then the whispers returned, their efforts to overcome him renewed.

"Run, kid!" Laela snarled. "I'm up here, you stupid barbarian." She kept the knight's attention so Gaulf might escape, moving the trio far from the distended stomach of the corpse in hopes that the magic's hold on Orn might lessen with distance.

Orn followed her to the next floor, where the hallway opened up to the gory scene below. The sickening squelch of flesh rending soured her stomach, and she fought not to retch.

"Princess?" Orn said, his voice quavering as he approached.

He turned slowly, following the path of her gaze. Orn's grip on his blade loosened.

Murderous thoughts cycled through his mind when he studied the mutilated corpse. It defied reason, the eldritch hand ripping it apart from the inside. Glowing with that odd gold-and-blue light, the overlarge hand provoked once more those whispers, urging the knight to step right off the ledge of the crumbling tower.

Let go.

He almost listened to its instruction, until he saw the tear in the corpse widen. Peeking through the rift, impossibly large and with a piercing stare, was a golden iris. A surge of lovely, breathtakingly sharp color swirled around the knight, preventing his movements.

Then came the budding urge building in his heart, the overwhelming need to *burn*. To press against the coils of the gaze binding him. The ruins seemed larger now, as if stretched to its limits. Orn's head swam, trying to remember his purpose.

A doorway *opened*.

Where it led, he did not know, though the knight yearned to discover what secrets lay beyond that rift. Absently, he leaned forward. A hand brushed the nape of his neck, yanking him from the precipice by his hair.

"Princess?" Orn's thoughts were cloudy, his breathing labored. Laela forced him to face her.

"Don't you dare, you stupid oaf. We won't get answers if you're dead," Laela said in a clipped tone. But he was tired of the fight. He lowered the tip of his sword and cupped her cheek with his free hand.

"You have to go. Please. *Sra curak.*" The words were thick in his mouth, bitter honey coating his tongue. Toe-curling pleasure slithered through his muscles while Orn thrashed against the fog in his brain.

She comes.

He teetered on some strange abyss, the mark roosting deep inside the cage of his body. If he would just surrender, knowledge awaited.

Nothing else mattered. Only...*Sra curak.*

Orn found Laela amidst the murk of his thoughts, his hand gripping the front of her dress and dragging her toward him.

"Let go of me, Orn." The warning was clear. Laela warred against him, trying to free herself. The knight watched her through his tenuous hold on reality, though it fragmented around him. They were almost nose to nose. She froze in his grasp. He did too, no more than a whisper away from her lips.

"Go. Run. Get out of here. Far away. **Sra curak.**" Again, those blasted words came unbidden despite Orn's attempts to swallow them. He was close to breaking.

She comes. She comes. She comes.

Let go.

She waited on the other side of that corpse rift.

"Please, princess." Orn's face drained of blood when more dark words crowded his mind. Shapes and sigils flashed in his field of vision, the same that adorned his arm and the body below, cutting into the very essence of him.

Instead of fleeing, the flat of Laela's palm rushed across his face in a vicious slap. Orn delighted in the pain, tasting blood at the corner of his lips. A reminder that he wasn't yet wholly lost to the magic.

Until fury rose from whatever depths his mind sank to, and Orn's mouth split into a bloodied smile. Laela recoiled at the sight.

The part of him influenced by the magic drank in the pain greedily. What lingered that was human hung on by a fraying thread while Laela continued her attacks. In the moments of clarity between slaps, Orn sensed the sword in his hand was burning. He knew what he had to do.

Orn undid the binding of the scabbard. The leather-wrapped pommel felt like home. The vile force slithering through him flinched from the motion, leaving him to himself once more. The whispers, now muted, were a dull roar compared to the searing heat on his face and the chaos around them.

"I swear I'll fucking stab you if you don't let go of me," Laela barked. Somewhere in the tussle, she had lost her blades, and so she stole a dagger from his belt. Orn released his grip on her dress, catching her wrist before she could make good on her threat.

"Run." The surprise on her face was almost comical when he gave her a shove. Orn savored that look, then turned from her. The elf's reply was lost in another rumble that shook the ruins, and he fled clumsily.

When he reached the edge that overlooked the widening corpse rift, Orn had but a moment to survey the scene. The giant, golden eye that once peered through the body, appraising its surroundings, was no more. Replaced by two enormous hands marked by streaks of black responsible for the broadening rift, the eye must have vanished into that other place beyond this world.

Ignoring his better judgment, Orn leaped from the edge.

Laela could only watch him. A thunderous crack echoed from below. One of the otherworldly hands stretched from the corpse, stretching toward the stars. She tried to rationalize the impossibly large hand blotting out the world behind it, but it seemed an impossible task.

She wanted out.

"ORN!" Laela shouted, dashing toward the fray brandishing his stolen dagger. "That stupid oaf." She cursed under her breath, skittering to a stop when the golden eye returned.

The idiot of a knight sailed straight for the taller hand, sword first. The blade sparked with his thrust and against all reason, found purchase in the meatier part of the palm. It caught Orn mid-attack, squeezing the plate of his armor. The knight withdrew his blade, then thrust again. Again. Again. His screams pierced the din.

An alien howl emanated from the rift. The hand moved, working to dislodge the knight who wounded it. Laela cradled her head in her hands, felt blood trickling from her ears when she heard a *snap*. Something broke, a flare of light followed, and silence descended upon The Tower. When the light finally dissipated, Laela could not see Orn anywhere.

The elf watched as the frantic hand tried to retreat, leaking ichorous blood and light from its damaged palm. The dense blood curdled, morphing into threads of dark smoke laced with that sickening blue glow before the hand disappeared into the corpse rift. The ruins trembled once more, and the wall opposite the stone slab tumbled, crushing everything beneath its weight.

Then the ruins themselves threatened collapse. Laela clambered across falling debris in a mad dash to find Orn and escape. Jumping through a window, she collided with a branch on a nearby tree. Content to hang there safely for half a heartbeat, she caught her breath and closed her mouth against a plume of smoke and dust exploding from the stone when the ruins finally gave way.

The branch splintered beneath her weight, and Laela dropped to the ground before it could sever fully. Exhaling, she rolled across the ground to ease the impact of the jarring descent. Every part of her body protested the rough tumble. The elf hissed at the onset of pain, checking herself for broken bones. Blessedly, she was unscathed.

Leveraging herself onto her elbows, she examined the ruins, noting the pockmark scar left against the landscape in the wake of the collapse.

"May the forest consume you," she whispered. *The forest reclaims everything, in the end.* Laela lay there in the charred grass, tempted to let the trees claim her too. But she had to find Orn, if he yet lived.

There were too many questions left to answer, too many things she'd witnessed to ever hope she could return to the life she'd grown accustomed to. And Laela understood she wouldn't procure those answers or chart a new path without that bumbling oaf.

Like fragments of a dream lost to waking, the details became hazy when she tried to grasp them. A large hand, the corpse rift, a knight charging forward. The world around her seduced her with its silence, and she rubbed her eyes in the soft glow of dawn.

If Gaulf managed to outpace the destruction of the tower, Laela hoped he had met Jannie where she waited in the forest. There was a wrenching in her stomach at the thought of permitting the mage to walk free, but there was little the elf could do at the moment. With a grunt, she struggled to a sitting position.

There lingered the stench of smoke and charred bodies, a fetid assault upon her senses. Had Orn actually done it? Had the knight prevented the completion of Gaulf's work?

In that moment, Laela felt well and truly alone. Without Orn, without Willaime, or any other handler, there was only the silence that squatted like a toad over the area.

She stood and warily circled the rubble, a spiraling pattern of stone and carnage. Picking through the debris, Laela retraced her steps, soon discovering her lost weapons.

There were piles of gore flattened beneath fallen walls and upended furniture, but no sign of life. *He's not here.* The terrain and detritus became more difficult to navigate the further she ventured toward what she believed was the center of the ruins, but she could not abandon the knight.

Among the remnants were small stacks of stone and ash, and the elf was relieved the little creatures had expired with the tower. Struggling fires still smoldered here and there, their muted crackles evidence of their death throes. Laela listened for any sound that might be Orn calling for help while she searched, fearing what she might find at the end of this enterprise.

Just when she felt exhaustion tugging at her limbs, a rubble mound ahead shifted. Laela waited, watching, until she heard the unmistakable sound of Orn groaning.

"I'm coming!" Laela dug feverishly into the pile, using a piece of timber as leverage and sending rocks flying in every direction. When that no longer sufficed, she knelt and tore at the rock with her bare hands. Beneath the rubble, Laela heard familiar, albeit muffled, curses. The sharp edges of the rocks sliced her fingers when she said, "There you are."

A bloodied hand shot out and grasped her, pulling her toward the mound. Briefly, she panicked, remembering the way Orn held the front of her dress, the crazed look in his eyes, and the spidery words that crawled out of his mouth.

What if he's still affected? The thought bothered her, and she wrested out of his grip, her muscles protesting the strained motions. Once free, the elf went to work, uncovering the knight piece by piece. Stones gave way to scorched beams, and Laela lifted each one out of the way.

"Don't move." Laela's dagger caught the sunlight as she held it against his throat.

"Laela?" Orn croaked weakly, drawing a deep, shuddering breath beneath her. Laela searched his face, his *eyes*, for a sign of magic's influence. Anything to justify piercing his neck with her blade.

"Are you...*you?*" Laela asked sharply. When he did not answer except for a grumpy glare, the elf withdrew her dagger just enough to let Orn breathe.

"What did I tell you about putting a dagger to my throat, princess?" Orn groused, his gaze never leaving hers. There was nothing left of the guttural, unnerving voice. Instead, exhaustion laced his tone, revealing every ache and pain he must've felt. After a few moments, Laela stood and retreated from the knight. Orn rolled over, coughing and wheezing as he rubbed his throat. Wobbling to his feet, he glared at Laela. "I told you to run."

"I considered it," Laela said, keeping her dagger ready. "But there's nowhere left for me. I cannot return to Haven, not after all of this. The Paladin could still come after you, after Gaulf. After me..."

"I might have gone completely berserk and ripped your spine out through your mouth," Orn snapped, shaking dust from his hair.

"Even that, I fear, is preferable to the fate that would befall me were The Paladin to find me now. He's made such threats before." Laela stared at the ground then, counting the number of tiny rocks in the dirt.

"Guess we have a new charge to add to our list. Save the princess," Orn replied, the humor in his tone evident. She suppressed the urge to punch him.

"Hardly the priority. We have to figure out what's happening, and how to stop it. Before—"

"Before you have to take the sword to me, I know. Should've done it last night." Orn wavered as he spoke, leaning against a mound of rock for support. Orn ran a hand over his armor. Charred, scratched leather peeled away from the metal plate, which was brittle to the touch. In the space of a heartbeat, the plate fractured and fell from his chest. "Better than my flesh, but damn. This was my favorite piece." A hollow laugh followed the sentiment, and he smeared the ash around in a poor attempt to clean himself, wincing when his fingers met singed flesh.

Laela rooted around in her pouch, then tossed a wrapped bundle to Orn. "Here." She rolled her eyes as Orn unwrapped the bundle and brought it to his nose, gagging at the smell. "You are an idiot, I swear," she muttered, trying to hide the smile threatening to crack the severe expression plastered on her face. "The smell may be atrocious, but it should soothe the burns and stave off infection."

"Thank you, Laela," Orn said. The elf narrowed her eyes at the mention of her name, but otherwise remained silent. "Do you mind?" Orn gestured for her to give him privacy.

"Fine," she huffed, turning from him. When she heard Orn remove the rest of his armor, she added, "I'll have to find the horses. My pack has bandages."

"That's new. Shit."

Laela stilled. "What is it?"

"This." Laela glanced over her shoulder, watching his palm slide from his chest. There, a scorched hole in his clothing, its charred edges peeled away to reveal the flesh beneath.

A black handprint, an exact replica of the one Jannie sported on her face.

Just where the hand had cradled the knight before he pierced it with his sword.

Her eyes locked onto that mark, then flitted to the one on his arm. Instinctively, Laela's fingers reached for the hilt of her dagger.

"Maybe it's just some soot, you know? From the fires?" Orn said, hardly convincing Laela.

"Stop that, you dolt," Laela snapped when she noticed his fidgeting, stalking forward and taking hold of both his hands so she could study the mark upon his chest. Its shape was perfect, a complete black void against his skin. The edges appeared to be a fractal pattern, but the mark defied logic.

This was a mark given by a feminine hand, one with tapered nails and now a grasp on the knight.

"I don't like this." Orn tried to step away from her, but Laela did not release her grip.

The elf ignored the look he shot her, focusing instead on that hand-print. It was like a brand, a blistered patch of skin from the fires that had consumed the knight from within. Grimacing as she retrieved the leather pouch from Orn, Laela ignored his protests when she treated his wounds. *Serves him right*, she thought, making quick work of the various burns, cuts, and scrapes.

"There," she said when she finished, returning the leather pouch to her belt. "We should find our horses. Think you're fit to ride?"

"Fit as a fiddle." The tremor in Orn's voice betrayed him. He leaned over and she thought he might faint. "We'll need to find Jannie and Gaulf."

"Are you sure?" Laela busied herself checking her gear, tightening her bow on her shoulder. Orn doubled over, and she cursed. With a grunt, he rooted around in the rubble before he withdrew his blade.

"As sure as I'll ever be." Orn studied the sword, or rather, what was left of it. Laela whistled upon witnessing the shattered edge, half of the blade missing. "For what it's worth, I am sorry, princess. But I think we still have a long road ahead of us."

Laela nodded, thinking about what dangers the path before them promised.

Orn made to depart, the broken blade in his grasp.

"Where are you going?" Laela asked, sprinting to catch up to the knight.

"Onward, princess. The day's hardly begun, and we have a long road ahead of us," Orn called over his shoulder.

"And do you have a plan in mind, or were you just going to walk off into the sunrise?"

"Would that be so bad?" Orn asked, the hint of a smile at the corners of his lips.

"There's a library," Laela said suddenly. Memories surfaced, of when her mother had visited such a place when she was but a child. Before Ser Gregoris, before mages rent the world. The library was not quite home, but her mother had gone there to study, to find answers to impossible questions.

Maybe they could do the same.

"Lead on then, princess. That is, *after* we find the two young love-birds. Hopefully they didn't make off with our horses after all the fireworks last night." The handprint on his bare chest caught the sun's light, and Laela felt a strange sense of hope at the sight.

Maybe they could get answers.

Maybe they could actually fix what was broken in this world.

"You are entirely too sappy, oaf. Come on, let's find our horses."

About the Author

Hailing from the St. Louis area, Matthew lives a life defined by logic and creativity. After the DayJob™ is done, he finds himself writing for his novels, planning future ideas with his wife, or making up stories with his daughter. Whichever the case, he loves spinning tales to entertain. On the other side of the story, he loves to tinker and learn new things. When he finds time to sit and relax, he usually does so by playing video games, watching podcasts. Or finding something else to write.

Find him on most socials (Facebook, Threads, TikTok, Instagram, BlueSky) as backwardsknight, or at backwardsknight.com

Author Matthew Siadak

ACKNOWLEDGEMENTS

Second verse, not quite the same as the first. We have been here before, but not quite like this. Here, as I sit and write this, I am looking back over the last nine years and what trials, tribulations, wins, and losses brought me to this moment. The Backwards Knight is done; you are holding it in your hands one way or another and might even be reading these words. If you aren't, then carry on. If you are, though? Let's go.

First and foremost, comes more thanks than I could ever give to my wife, Laura. Over the last twenty-some odd years, ever has she pushed me to do, and be, better. Without her, quite simply, The Backwards Knight would not exist. To her, I owe the world, and another batch of the most epic of epic cookies. Between her unyielding support, of helping plant the seed that became this book, of helping me flesh out the ideas and the initial story that became The Backwards Knight, and that she gave me the time, patience, and love needed to see it through, we have a novel. Add in our daughter, the both of them who let me escape to my office, or blather on, when there was work that needed to be done.

Next up would be E, my sage, the light in the darkness showing the way. She read the slop of the first draft and let me know that, yes, it was slop, but it had potential. She saw it, and believed in me, and helped me further work through and refine this novel into something worth half a damn.

And then came Ashley, who took what I had and worked literal magic on the words, helping me build the story up to everything it needed to be, and more, so we could whittle it back down. With her skill and expertise, The Backwards Knight truly came to life and became everything I wanted it to be and more. I learned more than

I ever could have hoped and shall endeavor to put it all into practice going forward.

I also want to give thanks to Rich, and Michele, to whom this book would not exist either. Rich, my best friend, helped me take a step I never would've taken before, and Michele took a chance on me and gave me a chance to grow and shine, and only for that was I able to make this novel happen.

And my parents, my brothers, who have always been there for me, no matter what. Without them, all of them, I would not be who I am today. All of my family, for their continued love and support.

And, of course, there are so many more who have touched my life, and this story, over the last nine years. Jeremy and Holl, who read an early draft and provided priceless feedback. The rest of the Buffalo crew, whose hive-mind was always at the ready if I needed help with world building, or even to just ooh-and-aah over snippets.

The DMIW crew who welcomed me in for sprints and slipped snipplets aplenty, and even helped me define my magic system such as it is. Much love to all of them, and sink pickle be praised!

Last, and by all means certainly not least, you. You are here, even if you aren't reading this part of the book, and that is helping my dreams come true. You have brought my creation to life within your own mind, and I can only hope that you enjoyed the journey with Orn, Laela, and the rest. I hope you'll come back for more. Hopefully we'll cross paths in another story somewhere down the road. May it be long and winding.

Also By

You can find more Matthew words in:

Novels:
The Dark Side of Super

Shorts:
In Pyxis in Heroes, Lost Boys Press
The Silent Sonata in Tales from Brackish Harbor, Quill & Crow
Have Sword, Will Travel in Zehlreg Augustus Grindstone's Spectac-
ular Western Oddity Emporium, End of the World Productions
Arkadia, available at fallenlights.net

Coming soon:
The Forgotten Princess
The Broken Sword
The Light Side of Villainy
and more...